BURN
IT
ALL

BURN IT ALL

A NOVEL

MAGGIE AUFFARTH

CROOKED LANE

NEW YORK

"Animals," from *Poetry* 77, no. 4, copyright © 1951 by Poetry Foundation. Used by permission of Jeffers Literary Properties. All rights reserved.

Published in the United States by Crooked Lane Books, an imprint of The Quick Brown Fox & Company LLC.

Crooked Lane Books and its logo are trademarks of The Quick Brown Fox & Company LLC.

Library of Congress Catalog-in-Publication data available upon request.

ISBN (hardcover): 978-1-63910-752-0
ISBN (ebook): 978-1-63910-757-5

Cover design by Heather VenHuizen

Printed in the United States.

www.crookedlanebooks.com

Crooked Lane Books
34 West 27th St., 10th Floor
New York, NY 10001

First Edition: June 2024

10 9 8 7 6 5 4 3 2 1

For my family, who have always been
my safe place to land.

TRIGGER WARNING

This book explores themes of depression and suicide, as well as substance abuse and sexual assault. If these themes may be triggering for you, please proceed with care. If you need help, please call the Suicide and Crisis Lifeline at 988.

they would look
monstrous
If we could see them: the beautiful passionate bodies of
living flame, batlike flapping and screaming,
Tortured with burning lust and acute awareness, that ride
the storm-tides
Of the great fire-globe. They are animals, as we are.
—"Animals" by Robinson Jeffers

PROLOGUE

Thea

I DON'T HAVE A first memory of Marley. We never really met, is the thing. She has always just been *there*. Her hair on my pillowcase, her laugh in my ear as we squished together, cheek-to-cheek, for a photograph—our mothers gushing about how much we looked like them at that age. Glittery butterfly stickers on her notebook, half scratched off and painted over in my black nail polish. The shimmering impressions of her lip gloss around the neck of a liquor bottle.

Sometimes I think about the way we must've looked to everyone around us once. About the doorframe in my mom's kitchen with Marley's growth chart on one side and mine on the other, always lagging several inches behind. The groove we ran into the earth between our houses.

I can see us as children, racing each other down the street on the cheap, matching scooters we begged our mothers for. Wild laughter and tongues dyed bright pink from raspberry lemonade. Can see Marley with one lanky arm slung around my shoulder, dragging me close to her side. Old movie nights and matching jewelry and shared secrets and *us*.

We must've looked idyllic once, from a certain light.

Marley and Thea, Thea and Marley. Best friends. Practically sisters.

It seems obvious now, of course. So painfully, paralyzingly clear.

We never even had a chance.

1

Marley

I T'S THE TENTH day of the heat wave. I can feel it the second I wake
up, punching right through the pitiful, wheezing AC, managing to
wilt even the plastic plants on my windowsill. Wet, humid heat bearing
down like a punishment.

It's already done its damage, the heat. My hair clings to the back
of my neck in sweat-soaked ropes and there's a thick, salty sheen of it
across my forehead. I can feel the drops crawling down the slope of my
face, toward my temples, so I push myself up and a wave of dizziness
and disorientation rolls over me. Suddenly, I'm not even sure if I slept
last night. With the amount I've been sleeping lately, it feels possible I
could've spent the whole night in a semiconscious state.

I force myself to stand up and keep steady as the blood rushes to
my feet. If things were normal, I'd slip on my favorite robe—the pale
purple one from the Southern Moon spring collection—and pad my
way to the kitchen for breakfast. Austen would be standing at the stove,
spatula in hand, looking rumpled and adorable in the morning light.
Eggs popping in the pan and the burble of the old Mr. Coffee on the
counter.

The thought of it is so real that I almost reach for my robe before I
remember, with a stab, that I destroyed it. That the apartment Austen
and I shared will be empty soon—the coffee machine packed away in

a box and the artsy print above the sofa donated to Goodwill. All the evidence of our shared life, gone. Right down to the ring on my finger.

Instead, I'm back in my mom's house, in the bedroom I tried so hard to escape. I took everything I liked from this room with me when Austen and I moved in together, then brought it back when I moved myself out. It all sits now in an open cardboard box near the closet, like it has since May, three months ago. Somehow I can't quite bring myself to put the pictures back on the desk, or the stuffed animal Dahlia got me when I was three back under the bed. Unpacking that last box feels too much like admitting defeat.

I blink at the light streaming in through the window—trying, for the hundredth time this summer, to make sense of finding myself back here, ten steps behind where I started. No real career. No friends. No fiancé.

No you.

I swallow hard, fighting back the urge to call, or even to run across the adjoining yards and lay eyes on you. I want to, desperately. But I hold myself back. You've made it clear that you don't want anything to do with me anymore. So instead of doing anything, I just stand here.

Mom is already up, which is unusual, especially given how late she stumbled in last night, the heavy *clomp* of her shoes unsteady on the linoleum, keys tossed in the vague direction of the kitchen table.

I can hear her shuffling around the kitchen. The faucet turning on, then off again. She's talking to someone on the phone, mumbling too low for me to hear. It probably means your mom is on the other end of the call. After our fight—after I moved back in—their conversations got quieter, like they didn't feel right about being best friends anymore now that their daughters weren't.

I stay in my room until the mumbling stops, and then for a few minutes after, not quite ready to face the awkwardness—the stilted air that's existed between Mom and me for the last three months. The weight of questions I can't bring myself to answer.

She knows what happened, of course. In a town like Riverside, the story of what I did spread far too quickly to intercept. She's had the good sense not to bring it up, but I can still feel her eyes on me, all the same. Can almost feel her catching the questions as they're about to trip off her tongue.

Why did you do it? Why did you ruin everything?

On the bedside table, my phone vibrates with a text. I ignore it too, but only for a few seconds. I can feel my eyes sliding toward the screen like a magnet. There was a time when it almost never stopped buzzing. Between Instagram notifications and a near constant stream of messages from you, Skylar, Austen, and the girls at work, I used to relish what little quiet time I could get. But no one texts me anymore. Not really. Just girls asking me for shift changes at Southern Moon, or Mom letting me know she won't be home.

I grab the phone and look at the screen.

Skylar Weller: 1 new message

I swallow hard at the sight of her name. There used to be a little pink bow emoji next to it that she entered herself when she put the number in my phone almost six years ago, but I deleted it last month, so now it's just *Skylar Weller*. Curt and businesslike.

Skylar used to call me three times a day, but she doesn't communicate with me anymore unless she absolutely has to, so I know it must be important. Reluctantly, I open the text and stare for a second too long.

Did y'all hear?? Another fire last night!! Dead body this time!

I frown at the screen and study the text more closely, rereading like it will say something different the second time. She's sent it to the Southern Moon manager group chat, I realize, as the replies start rolling in and names I've barely seen all summer flash across my screen. I'd assumed that they'd created a separate group chat that didn't include me for swapping gossip, and that they were only using this thread to exchange professional info, but maybe I was wrong. That, or Sky was too eager to send the message and selected the wrong chat by mistake.

Britt: I haven't heard anything. Are you sure?
Melanie: 😱
Sky: ∧ *I think you mean* 😵

The arsons are the only thing anyone in town has been able to talk about since they started, and it seems like there's a new rumor spreading about them every day. Last week at the store I heard someone say they were a government conspiracy, set to drive everyone out of their homes so the land could be sold to a developer.

The truth, which no one will admit, is that the fires are the first interesting thing to happen here in years. Decades, probably. Three weeks ago, a news crew even came from CNN to get footage of the burned-out husks where houses used to stand. There's a buzz in the air, passing through Riverside and out to the neighboring town, Sherman Hill, like an electrical current. Whispered conversations rippling as far out as Atlanta, sixty miles away—under-the-table bets being placed at the hardware store about who *they* are, and whispered gossip at the hair salon. The word *arsonist* all but rising up from the ground itself.

"Marley," Mom calls out from the kitchen. Her voice sounds hoarse. Maybe the heat got to her, too. That, or it's just another hangover. I take one deep breath and pad out of my room and into the kitchen, where she's perched by the counter, a half-empty glass of Pedialyte beside her with a smudge of faded, coral pink lipstick on the rim.

"What's up?" I say, taking in the sight of her. When I was younger, people would sometimes confuse us for sisters, and I used to love imagining that it was true. That somewhere out there was a steady, responsible, loving mother for the both of us. At some point, though, the magic ran out, and the alcohol began to take its toll on her, carving lines around her mouth and between her eyebrows. Dragging down the once taught skin underneath her eyes so she always looks a little tired. A hard-lived thirty-eight.

She's in her sleeping T-shirt, her hair pulled into a blonde bun at the nape of her neck. She still has last night's makeup on, smeared eyeliner and mascara that's melted beneath red-rimmed, tear-filled eyes.

The sight sends a prickling chill up the back of my neck. I can feel the small hairs stand up as I notice the slight quiver in her jaw, like the bottom might fall out on her control at any second. It's a surreal sight, one I haven't seen in years, and it makes me stop dead.

Relapse, I think immediately. I can't help it—the response is Pavlovian at this point. But when Mom relapses on the hard stuff, she doesn't stick around to tell me about it. Instead, she just stops answering my calls or texts, and then I don't hear from her again for days or weeks, once even a full month, before she shows back up, tail between her legs.

"Sit down," she says quietly, nodding at the kitchen table.

"What's wrong?" I ask. Suddenly, I wish I had something to grab onto. I wish I had Austen's arms around me, or you sitting next to me, ready with a joke or a sly comment to steady the erratic beating of my heart.

Mom takes a seat across the table, its old, creaking joints letting out a desperate cry.

"I'm not sure how to tell you this," she says, steepling her fingers underneath her chin. She looks deadly serious—more like a real authority figure than she ever has—and suddenly I feel so, so much younger than twenty-two.

I purse my lips, bristling in my chair. "Tell me what?" I ask.

Mom takes a breath and rolls her shoulders back, like she's putting on a kind of invisible armor. "There was a fire last night, a couple miles from here. *Another* fire, I guess."

I know she sees the confusion flashing across my face, but she finishes before I can say anything.

"Sweetheart," she says, reaching across the table to place her hand on top of mine. Her skin is clammy, and I can feel the sweat slicking her palms. There's an almost eternal second of silence and I recognize it instantly—know, somehow, deep in my gut that this is the moment before everything changes. I felt it the night Austen and I ended, too. Even before the fight, like a roll of thunder tumbling across the sky before a storm. An electric current passing through the air. Bad energy.

"This fire was different than the others. There was someone inside the house. Someone trapped. They found the—um—the remains this morning."

I raise one eyebrow, an irrational wave of anger slicing through me. She's dragging this out, looking at me like there's something obvious that I'm not picking up on.

"What are you trying to tell me?"

"It was Thea," she says, but the words come out choked, and for a long, horrible second, I think I must have heard her wrong. But then she repeats herself. "The remains they found, they were Thea's."

There's a moment of silence that crystallizes around me like amber—the dull buzz of a fly smacking against the kitchen window, the vague smell of rotting citrus, and the heat, crushing itself up against my skin and down my throat. The moment between the *before* part of my life and the *after*. Then the bottom really does drop out and Mom's crying again, wailing actually.

"I'm so sorry," she's telling me over and over between her sobs. I just stare at her as the words play on repeat in my head.

Thea's remains. Your *remains*.

"That's not possible." I can hear the words coming out of my mouth, but it doesn't feel like me saying them. I press my back into the chair hard, as if recoiling in slow motion, suddenly unsure of what to do. How to move at all when the world has tilted off its axis.

Mom squeezes my hand in hers and I almost snatch it away from her, but she's holding me too tightly, so instead I shut my eyes.

"They've got the wrong person—they have to. If the body was burned, it could be someone else. It could be anyone else," I say, when Mom's crying becomes too much.

"She had her ID with her. And Dahlia identified her this morning."

"This is *bullshit*," I say, the words coming out low and sharp, like a growl. "None of this even makes sense. Thea's *fine*. She can't be dead."

Mom stares at me with big, round puppy-dog eyes, welling with pity. "Marley," she says softly. "I'm so sorry. I don't know what to say. Thea was like a second daughter to me. I loved her too."

Now I do push away from the table, pacing back and forth across the small kitchen. I can't stand to look at her anymore. Can't bear to acknowledge the words *I loved her too* when they mean so little. My mom loved you because she had to. Because she couldn't *not* love the daughter of her best friend, or the best friend of her daughter. She didn't love you like I loved you. No one did.

No one could.

When I stop pacing, I feel my mother's presence coming up behind me. She wraps her long, skinny arms around my waist and presses her forehead between my shoulder blades, and even though I was longing to be held like this just a few moments ago, I stiffen now. The only person I've ever really wanted to touch me like this was Austen. Contact from anyone else feels smothering.

I roll my shoulders back and step away. Picture your skin—the smooth plane between your own shoulder blades, charred and blackened. Bubbling beneath a vicious, hungry flame. The thought makes bile rise up in the back of my throat. I try to swallow it down, the back of my hand pressed firmly against my lips, cold sweat beading down the bridge of my nose, but it's no use. I barely make it to the sink.

"It's going to be okay," my mother is saying over and over again as I vomit. "It's going to be okay."

But, as usual, she's lying. It'll never be okay again.

CHAPTER

2

Thea

"QUIET—HER DOG BARKS like crazy," Marley whispers. "If it wakes up, we bolt. Okay?" She pulls the hoodie up over her head and tucks her hands into the pockets. It's too big on her, something she took from Austen, probably, and I almost want to laugh at how un-Marley she looks with her long, red hair pulled into a tight bun behind her head. Her face pale without the layers of makeup she usually wears, blue eyes piercing. Right now, she's got her mouth twisted into a frown of concentration, a small line forming between her meticulously manicured eyebrows. She looks pared down and no-nonsense—completely devoid of the highly curated Bohemian-chic style that's always defined her.

"Got it," I say, gripping the handle of the knife tighter, my fingers going slick with sweat. I lick my lips and bounce forward on the balls of my feet, the outlines of houses taking shape in the moonlight. The neighborhood is only a few miles away from Riverside, just over the Sherman Hill town line, but it might as well be on another planet with the way the houses loom around us, each one a different, meticulously detailed façade, like a row of dollhouses. There's a small part of me that wants to put the knife down and wander slowly down the street. To take in the wraparound porches and Corinthian columns. Climb one of the sprawling live oaks and watch the sun come up on this place.

Instead, though, we're here to wreak havoc.

There are no streetlights on this late, but it's still bright enough tonight that someone might be able to recognize us, so I pull my own hood over my head and tighten the strings to mask my face.

Marley looks at me, her eyes shining with barely contained mania. "On my signal," she says, shaking the can of spray paint one last time. I feel a rush of adrenaline flooding through me and take a deep, steadying breath, trying to center myself in what's about to happen. In what we're about to do. Marley reaches back to me and circles her hand around my wrist, squeezing just for a second. She doesn't have to say it's the signal for me to know.

The world feels like it's erupted in noise as we spring out of the bushes and run down the street to the end of the cul-de-sac. The blood is screaming in my ears, heart pounding. Even the crickets seem louder somehow.

Suddenly, we're there, in the driveway of the little Victorian bungalow with the lavender front door. The car is right where Marley promised it would be. A VW Bug the color of polished pearl with a convertible top, and the sight of it fills me with unexpected resentment for its owner.

I drop to my knees and put the knife on the ground so that I can wipe my hand along the leg of my jeans. It's muggy tonight, and I can feel the sweat pooling along the waistband, gathering along the edge of my hairline.

I take another breath. Try to slow my heart rate. *Center*, I tell myself over and over, but it's useless. There's no centering now.

Marley has already started her part. I can hear the spray paint hissing, can smell the fumes in the air, sharp and astringent as she tags the car in ugly, orange capital letters.

"What are you doing?" she whispers. "We have to hurry." Adrenaline is coming off her in a wave. Her profile cutting like a pale shard of glass in the moonlight as she looks down on me.

Center.

Slowly, I nod. Pick the knife up off the ground and reel it back. I've never done this before—never handled a knife for anything besides cooking—but it feels good. Powerful, somehow.

I plunge the knife into the car's tire, feel the shock and the bounce of the rubber underneath the blade. There's a swell of air on my face and a sharp hissing.

"Fuck," I say, feeling the rush of it. Marley laughs. The sound bursts out of her, bubbling up from the core of her and spilling out, too high and frantic in the quiet night.

She stops abruptly, slapping her hand over her mouth, but it's too late. Inside the house, a dog begins to bark.

"Dammit," she says as we both scramble. I grab the knife just as the house lights come on and we're running. Marley darts in front of me, going for the nearest bit of tree cover, to the woods bordering the subdivision. She's faster than me, as always, and I lose sight of her slim body as she slides past the tree line. Behind me, I hear the slam of a door.

"What the hell?" says a voice. And then, "Hey! *Hey, you!*"

Footsteps are pounding the earth behind me, getting closer, and I just know I'm going to be caught before I reach the woods. Part of me wants to turn around right there—throw my hands up and surrender. To admit to everything I've done.

But I keep pushing. If I get caught, so does Marley. If I get caught, this is all over.

"Get back here," the voice is yelling, the footsteps growing so close I can practically feel the fingers closing around the loose end of my jacket. Throwing me down on the asphalt. She's faster than I assumed she'd be, her short legs pumping ferociously, bare feet slapping the ground.

And then, just as I can sense her at my back, there's a guttural howl. It sounds panicked, like a wounded animal. A death cry coming from somewhere in the nearby woods.

My blood runs cold—it's almost enough to make me pause, but instead I surge forward, taking advantage of the momentary distraction to run as hard as I can, until the sound of footsteps recedes behind me, and I slip into the woods. Darkness closes over me, but I keep running, even though I know I could hit a tree; even though I know I could stumble over whatever thing is dying horribly. The adrenaline is too strong, I can't bring myself back down from it.

"Hey!" it's Marley's voice, coming from somewhere in the tree cover. I skid to a stop and a hand reaches out and grabs me. "That was close. Let's go," she says, pulling me further into the darkness.

"Oh my God," I whisper back. "Did you hear that thing? That animal?"

Marley turns back to look at me. I can't see her well, but I can still make out the shape of her lips, the slight upward curve of them, and it hits me—it was no dying animal. It was her.

"Oh," I say. "I—thank you."

She doesn't say anything else, just squeezes my hand in hers. I let myself be led through the darkness as Marley winds her own path through the trees, slivers of moonlight catching us as they filter between the leaves. At some point, I see a flash of red and blue lights that means the police are there, and I wonder if it's Scott Martin or one of his buddies over at the station, running to the rescue as soon as they heard the call come in from this address. The thought sends my muscles into a defensive clench, and I try to push away the memory of the last time I spoke to Scott. His big, meaty hands on my hips, dragging me toward him. If he knew I was behind this, what would he do?

"We're almost there," Marley whispers, her voice snapping me back to the moment. The police lights have faded behind us now, and I can't recognize anything from this deep in the woods. Marley's hand is the only tether I've got.

The thing is, though, I don't care. I could follow her like this forever.

Eventually, we find ourselves out the other side. We pull the hoods over our heads and dart again to the car, which Marley throws into gear and guides smoothly onto the road. As if nothing happened at all and we're just two River Rats out for a late-night drive across the town line. Two women staring wistfully at houses they'll never be able to afford.

For a moment, all of my shadows are gone, blown away like cobwebs in a tornado. And then it hits me.

"The knife," I say, freezing up. "I dropped the knife. Oh God."

Marley stops breathing and the air shifts, practically goes cold. "Where?"

"I—I don't know. I had it when I started running and then I'm not sure."

"Was it in the woods or on the street?" She doesn't sound panicked, but she is. I know her feelings like I know my own, even now after all the distance this past year has created between us.

I shut my eyes and try to remember. I was running, sure I was about to be caught, and then, "On the street. When you made that noise to distract her. I dropped it then."

Marley makes a sharp right turn and curses under her breath.

"I'm sorry, I—"

"Forget it," she says. "There's nothing we can do now. Besides, all you did was slash a tire. It's not a big enough crime to justify running the fingerprints."

More silence. I pick at a piece of lint on my jeans as Marley takes the main road back. She parks and shuts the headlights off and we sit for a few seconds longer. For a moment, I feel like we're in high school again. Like we've just gotten back from the twenty-four-hour McDonald's off the highway that we used to frequent before Marley moved from Riverside to Sherman Hill. Before Mom got pregnant and David left her and my role in this world shifted irrevocably. Before we became the people we are now.

But the illusion only lasts a moment before it blinks out like a light, and I feel again the weight of the years sitting on top of us. All the lines we can't uncross. All the mistakes we're too late to undo.

"I really am sorry," I say again.

Marley glances at me. Without makeup she looks stripped. Tired. "Thea, we can't—"

"Get caught," I say, stomach flipping. "I know. Really, I do."

She nods and smooths the hair back on her head, even though it's meticulously pinned at the nape of her neck, not a flyaway in sight.

"We won't," I tell her. "And even if *I* do, I'd never say a word. You know that."

She smiles at me weakly. "I love you," she says.

I press my lips together and nod, pretending I don't feel the flip of those words in my gut—for all the times we've called each other sister, these words somehow still feel taboo.

I love you means *You could hurt me, if you wanted.*

It means *I'll protect you, if you let me.*

It means *I see you. All of you.*

For a long time, none of those things have felt true in the way they used to. But here in the dark, with our secrets nested between us, I can feel it moving through me like a wave. Too powerful to ignore.

"I love you too," I say, and I mean it. All of it.

CHAPTER

3

Marley

THE HOURS SLIP by quickly. At least, I think they're hours. I'm not really looking at the clock. Not doing anything really, except lying in bed and staring at the ceiling. Absurdly, I have to stop myself from texting you, or tearing across the yard separating your house from mine and demanding to see you.

At some point, Mom lets herself in. "Are you okay?" she asks.

I turn my head and look at her. No answer necessary, right?

"Look," she says, leaning her shoulder against the doorframe and crossing her arms. "I'm going over to be with Dahlia. Why don't you come with me? Austen will be there. I'm sure he wants to see you."

I turn back to the ceiling. "He doesn't," I say quietly. It's the only thing I'm sure about in all of this.

"His stepsister is gone, Mar. I know the break-up was hard on you both, but you need each other now."

"I'm not going," I snap. "And stop calling it a *break-up*. We were engaged, for Christ's sake."

She lets out a frustrated huff and closes the door behind her, though it's more of a slam. I imagine for a second what it must be like at your house right now. Dahlia's watery smile. The way she'll tuck into my mom's arms and cry. The twins, Milo and Finn, playing in their room—too young to know exactly what's happened but too old not to sense that it's something bad.

Austen will be there, I'm sure. He'll have called the gym to cancel his clients for the day, then sped the ten miles that separate Sherman Hill from Riverside. I can see him now, buzzing around the house, feeding the boys and putting them down for a nap to keep them out of everyone's way. Cleaning Dahlia's kitchen to a spit-polished shine as police track in and out. Trying, the way he always does, to make everything better.

If I listen, I can hear the commotion next door. The cars coming and going. The lilt of voices. The clip of footsteps up and down the front stairs. So I'm trying not to listen.

I blink at the ceiling and take a deep breath. Instead of fighting the heat, I've decided to let it in. To let it drown me. After all, what's the point? What's to stop me now that you're gone?

There's a knock at the front door, tentative at first, then more insistent. I'm planning to ignore it, but then I hear my name.

"Marley. Marley, *please*."

I sit up straight, startled by the sound of his voice. It's the last thing I expected to hear and, for a second, I think about not letting him in, but I can't do that. As much as I want to, I've never once kept Austen out, and I have a terrible feeling that if I did it now, he'd slip away from me forever.

I cross the house and open the door. "Austen," I say, taking in the sight of him. He looks awful, his black hair sticking up at odd angles, his deep-set brown eyes sunken back into his skull, like he's been living in this new you-less world for days, instead of hours.

It's only been three months since we were last in the same room— three months after eight years together—but he feels so much bigger than I remember. Even more muscled and solid than he was before. I shouldn't be surprised. Austen's always used extra hours at the gym as a coping mechanism, and with the way things ended between us, he's probably all but living there. Still, it seems like he's packed on ten pounds of pure muscle since May. "I'm sorry," he says, stepping across the threshold. "I had to see you."

Those words—*I had to see you*—I would've killed to hear them once. This morning, even. But now I can barely process them.

"What the hell is going on?" I ask him. I can't help it.

"I wish I knew. Dahlia called me this morning to tell me before the news got out. Apparently, she didn't even realize Thea was gone. She thought she was in her room asleep when the police rang the doorbell. They found her ID, apparently. At the scene."

"An ID isn't a body," I say, resisting the urge to kick at the wall in the entryway. "An ID doesn't mean she's *dead*."

"Her ID wasn't all they found," he says, his deep voice breaking, so I know he's picturing it, like I am. A charred corpse. A husk in the shape of you. "I don't know all the details, but according to Dahlia there were some other . . . identifiable remains. They asked her to take a look and confirm."

I press my lips together and manage a tight nod, the last of the hope draining out of me as everything reduces down to those two words. *Identifiable remains.* I force myself to picture you—the deep brown curls that hung unruly by your face and the sharp slope of your nose, offset by the pink flush of rounded cheeks. But as soon as I conjure the image, it's replaced with another. White skin bubbled to charcoal black. Hair melted and matted to exposed sinew. I have to swallow back the bile collecting in my throat.

Austen walks tentatively to the couch and takes a seat on the edge, pressing the heels of his hands into his eyes, like he can see it too, and I hover by the doorframe, eyes on him for a moment before I go to the kitchen and get a bottle of whiskey from the stocked cabinet above the sink.

Finally, I sit down next to him, feeling the sofa dip underneath our combined weight. I don't realize I'm holding my breath until I'm settled next to him—don't realize I was waiting for him to dart away from me like a spooked animal.

I take a long swig from the bottle and hand it over to Austen, who does the same. Somehow, I find myself wondering what will happen to us now that you're gone. Even when Austen was my fiancé, you were still important. A vital thread in the web of our lives. When the three of us were together, we still operated as a trio—Thea and Marley and Austen, like when we were children. That's why, when I blew it all up, the fallout destroyed all three of us. Why it left me alone, careening out of my orbit, untethered from the only gravitational pull I'd ever known.

Murder. You could've been murdered.

"I—Austen, you're not making sense," I say. "How are you going to show them it wasn't her? We have no idea what happened."

He opens his mouth, then closes it again, his shoulders slumping, face hardening. He's drunk, I realize. We're both lightweights. Neither of us drank very much when we were together. Austen avoided it because he hated the way it affected him in the gym, and I was uncomfortable with how much I enjoyed the feeling, like being lifted away from my problems in a hot air balloon—but suddenly I realize that I have no idea how long he's been here, or how long we've spent sipping from the bottle at my feet.

Drunk Austen has an edge that sober Austen doesn't. The alcohol wears away his affable outer layer, leaving a sharper, more serious version in its wake. "Why are you grilling me, Marley? I'll figure something out; I'm not stupid."

I press my lips together and stare at him flatly. "I know that," I say, and then I watch the change come over him, like he's coming back to himself. Like he'd forgotten who he was for a second.

"I'm sorry. I didn't mean to snap . . . I'm just upset."

"We're all *upset*," I say tersely. It feels like such a pathetic word. *Upset* is what I am when a shipment of merchandise is late, or when I have to spend half a day nursing my mother's hangover for her. This is so much more than upset. "Don't take it out on me."

"You're right. I'm sorry."

I stand up, but I'm caught off guard by the way the movement makes my head spin, the alcohol rushing down through my limbs. I sway on my feet and Austen reaches out to steady me, his big hands resting on my upper arms, warm and solid.

We haven't been this close since before our fight. Since before I fucked someone else—and, by extension, every other part of my life. It only takes a second for it all to come back.

Until yesterday, that night felt like the biggest thing in the world. The moment that defined everything that came after. Now, I could scream with how small it feels. How pointless. "Austen," I say, digging my toe into the carpet. "What happened back in May, it was the biggest mistake of my life. What I did. How we ended things. If I could take it back . . ."

Before I can even finish my sentence, he's wrapped me up in a hug. I bury my face into his shoulder and breathe in the scent of him—Old Spice deodorant and sweat and something I can't quite place. Something new.

"I'm sorry," I say, my voice muffled by the fabric of his T-shirt.

Austen strokes gently at the ends of my hair, the way he used to. "It doesn't matter now, Mar."

I tilt my head up to him and find kind eyes looking down at me. No one has ever looked at me like that but him, and it makes me ache for a time before, when I still knew my place in everyone's world—when I knew exactly what it meant to be Marley Henderson.

Without thinking, I push myself up on my toes and press my lips to his.

"Marley," he says, taking a step back. He looks almost like he wants to wipe his lips with the back of his hand, and I feel a painful scrape of embarrassment.

I look down at the floor to hide the blush spreading all the way up to my hairline. "I'm sorry," I mumble. "I don't know what came over me, I just—"

"I get it," he says, "Really I do." I have to push back a stab of resentment at his tone, placating and gentle, like it's been *him* trying to talk *me* down since he came through my door, not the other way around. "If things were different—"

I look up at him sharply, willing him not to finish the sentence and he trails off. Playing the "if-things-were-different" game is dangerous, and we both know it.

"I should go," he says instead, after a pause. "Milo and Finn will be waking up from their nap soon. I don't want Dahlia to have to worry about them today."

I nod and press myself against the wall as I watch him leave, arms pulled tight across my torso, like I'm my own straitjacket. I'm not sure what I'm trying to do—hold myself back, I guess, because that gut feeling I got at ten years old is still in my gut. No matter what happens between us, no matter how broken things are, there will always be part of me that wants him for myself.

CHAPTER

4

Thea

I REMEMBER THE DAY Marley's mom came back. We were five. A few weeks from starting kindergarten, and we'd sunk into the late summer haze together. Endless days running through the cheap sprinkler Mom had set up in the backyard or watching *I Love Lucy* DVDs on the old couch, each of us sprawled across separate ends, trying to keep our body heat from concentrating.

I thought she was my sister then. Not biologically, but in all the ways that mattered.

Sometimes I run it back in my head—that day. I wonder now how much of it really happened and how much I've spun from nothing. I remember that the TV was on when the doorbell rang. Marley was sitting on the floor gripping a melting popsicle, her fingers sticky and red with the stray drips. I'd finished mine already, and I was watching her from my spot on the couch, wondering how she managed to eat it so slowly.

Mom was with us too, in the rocking chair by the window. She was stitching something—mending a sock or sewing a button onto a shirt. She was always bringing a chore with her to the living room—onions that needed chopping, or a pair of shoes that needed scrubbing, or a pile of shirts that needed ironing. Sometimes I wanted to shake her. To beg her to sit still, just for a minute, but I never could. I knew it was because of me—because of us—that she could never sit still. And I knew that on the rare occasions she did let herself relax, it involved lots, and lots, and lots of wine, then a long stretch of time where Marley and I mostly took care of ourselves.

We all jumped when the doorbell rang. No one came to visit us back then, not really. Just Miss Lilah from the Baptist church who came by sometimes with a Bible under her arm and a plate of fresh baked muffins. But it wasn't Sunday, and Miss Lilah usually called first.

Mom put down her needle and thread and stood up carefully, like there might be something wild waiting for her on the other side of the door.

"Don't pause it," she said, looking at me. "I'll be right back."

I watched her disappear into the hall and heard the door opening. Marley laughed at something Ethel said, but I wasn't really watching anymore. I could barely make out the sound of the door opening, and a gasp. Then, strained voices coming from around the corner. My mom whispering, the tenor of her voice low and pleading. And then, a voice I'd never heard before. Higher than Mom's, and sharper somehow.

"I know it's hard to believe, Dahl, but I'm doing better. Really. I've been clean for a month."

"I'm so happy to hear that," Mom said, but she didn't sound happy. She sounded scared. I remember being jarred by it—I'd never heard her sound that way before. "But Marley's settled here. She has a routine. A schedule. She's doing so good."

"You knew I was always planning to come back for her. Now you're telling me I can't take my daughter back because she has a schedule?"

"You know I'm not, June. But it's not that simple. It's been years. I haven't even heard from you since March. You can't just come and scoop her up like you never left. She doesn't know you anymore, and no one's been inside your house in two years. You can't just come back like you never left."

"She's *my* daughter. I can do what I want with her, can't I? Besides, I'm staying with a friend until I can get the house back into shape."

"Please, June. I'm not saying no. Let's just take this a little slower. Get the house in order first. Then we can start to transition her back."

At this point, their voices were loud enough that we were both listening, Marley's popsicle forgotten, electric red drips going down the side of her wrist.

"You can't tell me how to do this, Dahlia. Not while you live here in a house *I* bought for you. I missed my daughter. I want her back with me."

"*You* left her here. For years. And now I've had her for longer than you ever did. Just—"

A blonde woman pushed her way past my mom and stood for a long second in the doorway. I remember feeling a chill off the shadow she cast, but that part is probably made up.

What isn't made up is the wave of confusion and hurt that rolled over me at the sight of her. She was thinner then than she is now, with sunken cheeks and eyes rimmed in dark circles of eyeliner. Hair so light blonde it looked barely tinted. Even in that state, there was something arresting about her, though. Something you couldn't take your eyes off of. Marley had it too—that kind of inherent magnetism, a face you didn't want to stop looking at—and it made me angry. Angry that this woman could show up and take her away just because they had the same face. I didn't really know what was happening, but I knew that.

"Baby," she said, her voice suddenly soft. She knelt down, trying to catch Marley's eyes, but Marley wasn't looking at her. She was looking at Mom. I could read the panic in her posture. One hand laid flat on the floor, shoulders tense, like she was ready to push herself up and run.

"Baby, you remember me, don't you?" June went down on her knees and crawled a few paces closer. Marley blinked and said nothing. "I was on a long trip, but I'm back now."

Mom scoffed at that, and June shot her a look so quick I almost missed it.

I could see Marley gripping the popsicle stick with white knuckles. She looked paralyzed. Terrified.

"No," I said. My voice didn't feel like mine. My body didn't either as I stood up. "You can't take her. She lives here."

"Thea," Mom said sharply, but she didn't say anything else. June looked at me for a moment, then back to Marley, like I was barely there. Not worth noticing.

"Let's go, sweetheart," she said, reaching her hand out to Marley, whose mouth was hanging open.

"I can't . . . ," she said finally, her head swiveling to Mom, then to me. "I—have my dolls here." I thought about the Barbies she kept in our room. Three of them that she'd collected over the last three years at Christmas. The painstaking, meticulous care she took in brushing their hair and dressing them in shiny outfits. The way she tucked each of them into bed with her every night.

"We can bring them with us," June said. "And come back for the rest of your things later. But right now, we have to go to Mommy's friend's house."

"June," Mom said. "Please, let's talk about this. You can stay here. Don't take her."

"You can't," I said, a little louder this time, balling my fingers into a fist. "And you can't have her. She's ours."

June rolled her eyes. "Let's go," she said again, harsher this time. "Go get your dolls. Mommy's friend is waiting outside for us now."

Marley looked helpless as she stood up.

"Let's get you cleaned up first," Mom said, taking the popsicle delicately from her clutched fist. I followed them all to the kitchen, where Mom wiped a wet rag over Marley's skin to clean the sticky streams of melted popsicle. Watched, dumbfounded, as Marley went back to the room and emerged with her dolls in her arms. Usually, she carried them delicately, like babies, but that day she held them tightly to her chest, like someone might reach out and try to take them.

I looked at Mom. She was crying, and I wanted to scream. Why wasn't she stopping it? Why wasn't she doing anything?

Finally, she unglued herself from where she'd been standing by the wall and got on her knees in front of Marley. "Don't worry, okay?" she said, then eyed June. "Your mother is going to bring you back here tomorrow morning and we're going to figure something out. Just one sleep. Can you do one sleep?"

Marley frowned. Shook her head no, then started to cry. My mom pulled her into a hug. "It's okay," she said, stroking her pin straight hair. For a second, I thought that was the end of it. Marley said no. Surely, now it couldn't happen. It had to stop.

But then June put her hand on Marley's back and pushed her gently toward the door. "We need to go," she said, and my mom let her.

"No!" I said again. "No, she's not going with you! She said so."

I charged then. Didn't even really think about it. One second I was planted, and the next I was full speed ahead. I threw my hands out and hit June with all the strength I had before Mom pulled me off and held me back, pinning my arms down.

"NO NO NO!" I was shouting as June picked up Marley, still crying, and carried her out the front door.

Once she was gone, Mom let me wiggle out of her grasp and I screamed. I charged again for the front door, but they were already gone. I caught a glance of the car zooming down the street and around the corner.

I was sobbing, the tears flowing hot and fast down my cheeks. I could taste the salt in my mouth as I screamed. Eventually, Mom picked me up again and carried me from one end of the house to the other, then back again, her arms firm around me, one hand stroking my hair until the crying stopped and I could feel sleep coming for me like a big, swooping bird.

That's what I remember, anyway. The story I've told myself a hundred times over. It's the one I want to be true.

But now—if I'm really honest—I'm not sure. Because sometimes I remember standing there, dumbstruck, watching her go. Sometimes I think I've written a story I can live with because the truth is too much to bear.

When she needed me, I did nothing.

CHAPTER

5

Marley

I T TAKES THE police a whole day to show up for me. They ring the doorbell around noon—two of them in black pants and button-down shirts. Starched collars drooping in the heat. Detectives, not beat cops. Probably down from Atlanta.

"Are you Marley Henderson?" the first one says. The man. He's older than his colleague, with a shock of thinning white hair combed back elaborately to make it look as full as possible, a bulbous nose and ruddy skin. I've only seen detectives on TV, and the sight of him is disheartening, somehow—like seeing the real person that a movie character is based on.

"Yes," I say, leaning on the doorframe.

"I'm Detective Henley and this is Detective Romero," he says, inclining his head to the woman standing beside him. She's young—late twenties, maybe—with a notebook gripped in one hand and a pen tucked behind her ear.

Standing next to each other like this, they look mismatched. Unsure of each other.

"We're with the GBI—the Georgia Bureau of Investigation—and we'd like to ask you a couple of questions about Thea Wright. Could we come in?"

Slowly, I nod and step out of the way. When I got up this morning, Mom was asleep on the couch, a tear-stained tissue clutched in her fist.

But she's gone now, I'm not sure where, the couch still sunken with the imprint of her body.

"Can I get y'all something to drink?" I ask, unsure what the protocol is for something like this. "I think there's some sweet tea in the fridge."

Henley tips his head toward me, and then I see it—the quick dart of his eyes up and down the length of my body. I'm used to the eyes that occasionally follow me across a room. The weight of a man's stare. It comes with the territory, and before this summer I always regarded it as benign, even flattering. I liked the space I took up in other people's eyelines. Liked the desire I could feel them projecting onto me. It seemed harmless. After all, I was taken. Austen and I were together for so long that no one would even think to question it.

It's different now, though. After what happened, the looks have taken on a new tenor. Harsher and less discreet. Like wolves evaluating prey. Even Henley's quick glance unnerves me.

"That sounds delicious," he says, already following me into the kitchen, where I pull two glasses from the cabinet and fill them with ice and tea.

The little one, Detective Romero, has her thumb hooked into a belt loop and one knee slightly bent. If you weren't looking closely, she'd seem causal, but I've spent six years working retail, which means I'm an expert at sizing people up in just a few seconds, and that's all it takes to notice the sharp jut of her hips and her eyes, which are darting around the room, no doubt collecting and cataloguing every inch of it while Henley stares at the tea in my hand.

"Honestly, I'm not sure how much help I can be," I say, handing a glass to each of them and leading them to the kitchen table. "Thea and I—we had a fight in May. We haven't spoken all summer."

"Do you mind if we record?" says Romero, producing a small recording device from her back pocket and placing it on the table as she takes a seat, her finger hovering over the red button. "Just a precaution, obviously. We want to make sure we're getting everything word for word."

I nod and the recording device goes on. Romero places her notebook on the table and uncaps a pen. Henley looks at me, like he's waiting for me to elaborate, but I don't.

Silence is a tactic police use to get you to talk. I heard that once on a TV cop show. No one likes awkward silence, and the longer they go without talking, the better the chance of you breaking down and saying something you didn't mean to say.

"Right now, we're just trying to get a sense of Thea's life," Henley says finally. "Of her character. It sounds like you knew her better than most."

"She was my best friend," I say, uselessly. They already know that or else they wouldn't be here, and the words burn coming out of my mouth. They feel wrong, after everything.

"You must be devastated," Romero says. "I'm so sorry for your loss." She tilts her head to the side and lowers the pen. She has a pleasant face, round and soft-featured, but there's precision in the way she presents herself. Her hair is swept into a tight bun, her nails clipped short and clean.

"Thank you," I say finally, clasping my hands in my lap.

"You lived with Thea and her mom for a few years, didn't you?" she asks. "You must've almost considered her a sister."

I swallow hard and stare down at the grooved, aging table. Mom's had it since I was five, when she picked it up at some garage sale a week or two after we moved back in. For a long time, it was one of the few pieces of furniture we had. Before we got real chairs, we'd eat our dinner in lawn chairs, staring at each other silently across the expanse of this shitty table. Me, wishing I was at your house again. Wishing Mom had never turned back up at all.

"That was a long time ago," I say. So long ago that I only have hazy memories of it—a vague sense that ages two to five were the best of my life. "I was five when my mom came back. I don't have a lot of memories before then."

"Of course." Romero scribbles something on the notepad and takes another sympathetic look at me. "I didn't mean to assume."

"No, it's okay. I did—consider her a sister, I mean. My mom and her mom have been best friends their entire lives. After my dad died, my mom used most of the money she got from his wrongful death settlement to buy this house and Dahlia's place next door. So it's not like we went far when she came back for me. We just moved back in next door. Nothing really changed."

It's a half-truth. Nothing really changed *between us*, but for me, Mom coming back felt like someone had picked my world up and turned it on its head. I hated every second of those first few years, waiting for her to leave again. All I wanted was to go back—but then your mom met David, and Austen came along, and suddenly those years we spent under the same roof felt like a dream. Something everyone else had forgotten but me.

Henley leans back in his chair, rolling the sleeves of his shirt up to his elbows. I notice a dark red stain near the top, like a splotch of ketchup dripped from a burger, and my stomach turns. "I'm sorry to hear about your father," he says.

"I was only a year old when he died," I shrug. "There was an accident at the plant where he worked—this was before they closed it down. It was hard on my mom, but I never knew him."

There's another long beat of silence, and I wonder if they want me to say more about my father, but I can't see how it's relevant. Mom refuses to talk about him in any real way, so all I have are a few pictures and the bare facts. He dropped out of high school when he found out mom was pregnant and took a job at the chicken plant to support us. They were married at eighteen and Mom was a widow by nineteen. He gave me my red hair and my wiry frame. Sometimes I catch my mother looking at me and I swear it's him she's seeing instead, even now that he's been dead longer than he was alive.

"Why don't you tell us about Thea?" Romero asks, getting us back on track.

I open my mouth, then close it again. How would I even begin to describe you?

"Thea was amazing," I say, my voice breaking on the word *was*. Without missing a beat, Romero pulls a Kleenex from her pocket and passes it across the table to me. I nod in thanks and clutch it tightly in my fist. "She was generous. Selfless. Ambitious. Family-oriented. You know she postponed her plans to move to New York a few years ago when her mom and stepdad David got divorced so she could stay here and help take care of her little brothers until they started school? She put her whole life on hold for them."

"That's pretty incredible of her," she says. "David wasn't in the picture much, then, after the divorce?"

I shrug, tightening my grasp on the tissue. "He moved to Atlanta a few years ago. He drives a truck, so he's on the road a lot, but he takes the boys for a weekend every once in a while. He's hardly pulling his weight in the childcare department, though. It's why Thea had to step in. Dahlia sort of fell apart when the marriage ended. She needed some extra support."

"What about money?" Henley cuts in. "Does David pay child support?"

"Some, not much. Austen and Thea both funnel what they can to Dahlia to help support the boys."

"Austen your ex?"

"Mmm-hmm. He's the boys' half-brother. Thea's stepbrother—ex-stepbrother, I guess."

"Does he ever take his brothers, then?"

I open my mouth, but it takes me a second to answer. "Sure, when he can. We took them for a night once, earlier this year. After we got settled in at our apartment."

Remembering that night now makes me cringe. How stupidly excited Austen and I were to play house. I made cookies with the boys while he assembled some ridiculously expensive toy guns he'd splurged on for the occasion, complete with blinking lights and rapid-fire sound effects. I remember watching the delight on their small faces as they tore across the apartment, constructing an elaborate, imaginary fight scene. For a moment, I'd pretended they were our children, loved and protected and cared for, and I'd wanted it to be true so badly I could've screamed.

"Thanks, Marley. That's helpful context," Romero jumps back in. "Let's get back to Thea. Why don't you tell me more about her?"

I chew on my lip, trying to find my way back from the image of Milo and Finn in our living room, toy guns drawn, heads thrown back in laughter. I don't want to leave it behind. Not when my next thought is of you, half charred. Half melted.

"Thea—um—she had incredible taste," I tell them, forcing myself to continue. "Like, an amazing eye for fashion. A little over a year ago we started this fashion account called Vintage Doll together on Instagram—she styled all the outfits, and I wore them. It was amazing, what she could put together. People really responded to it. She wanted to become a personal stylist in New York. Maybe open her own vintage store one day."

"She was ambitious, then," Romero says, scribbling it down in her notebook.

"She was talented. More than she realized."

Henley speaks now. He leans slightly forward, pressing his elbow into the table. "Tell us about the fight," he says.

"It was stupid," I say immediately. Because I can see that now. How little that fight actually meant in the grand scheme of things. How our friendship was so much bigger and more important.

"It was just . . . I found out Austen was texting another woman. Someone I'd warned him about before. He said they were just friends, but I didn't trust her, and I was upset with him about it."

"And why did finding out that Austen was texting another woman cause a fight with Thea?"

"It's . . . complicated," I say, trying to figure out how exactly to explain it. At the time, it all felt so solid. But now that I'm trying to put it into words, I realize how ridiculous it must sound. "It wasn't a *fight*, exactly. Not with Thea, at least. When I found out about the texting, I was upset. Thea happened to be there and she tried to defend Austen. I lashed out. Said some . . . unkind things. Things I didn't mean. Then it all sort of blew up and I left."

I stay quiet while Romero scribbles on her notepad and Henley takes a sip of his tea. I don't want to tell them the end of the story, so I stop there. After all, what's the point of reliving the rest of that night? The anger that swallowed me whole and turned me into someone I don't even recognize now. I want to declare temporary insanity and undo it all.

"And you had no contact with her after that night?"

"No. The last time I spoke to Thea, I insulted her."

"I wouldn't blame yourself, Marley," Romero says. "Friends fight."

Henley adjusts the collar of his shirt and rests his elbows on the table. "Do you think Thea had the capacity for violence?"

I knew this question was coming, Austen told me as much yesterday, but it still catches me off guard. "No," I say simply. "I don't."

Romero jumps in. A look passes between her and Henley. A flash of something, too quick for me to catch and a nearly imperceptible shift in the air. "I know it can be difficult to think about the ones we love in these scenarios," she says. "But you knew Thea better than anyone. Maybe even better than she knew herself."

"We just want to bring some peace," Henley adds, grudgingly. "And in order to do that, we have to know what happened."

"And I'm telling you—Thea wasn't violent. She'd never hurt anyone. You're asking me if she could've lit the house on fire herself," I say slowly. "You want to know if she's the arsonist."

I have this flash of you in front of a burning house, your eyes filled with high, wild glee. Fingers twitching as the flames lick higher. It feels like looking at a doctored photo. Like uncanny valley. Almost real, but not quite.

"It's a possibility we have to consider," says Henley, setting his pen on the table. "Her car was found at the scene. She seems to have driven herself there, at the very least. Right now, we just want some insight into her state of mind."

"What about self-harm?" Romero asks, tilting her head to the side like a curious puppy. "Thea . . . attempted suicide once, a few years ago. Isn't that right?"

It takes a few seconds to answer that. I can feel the silence settling in around me. Austen's words echoing through my head, "*They've already decided what happened. They're just looking for evidence to confirm it.*"

And maybe he's right. After all, you're exactly the kind of person they'd believe could've done this. Someone who'd worn her anger on the outside. Who kept to herself. A River Rat, dressed perpetually in black leather and combat boots. Still, I can't lie to them—at least, not about a diagnosis I know will be on your medical record.

"Thea was diagnosed with depression a few years ago. In high school. But she's gotten a lot better since then," I say finally. "It's hard to know exactly where her head was at this summer."

"Do you remember the date of your fight with Thea and Austen?" Romero asks, pressing her pen lightly to the notepad.

"What does that have to do with anything?"

"We're just trying to get all the facts. The whole time line of Thea's summer."

I bite down on my lip, so hard I can taste blood. "May third," I say. The words feel heavy leaving my mouth, though, because I know exactly what they're thinking. Can smell the thing they're circling like blood on prey.

The fires started one week later.

"And you didn't see her again after that?"

"After Austen and I ended things, I moved back here with my mom. I didn't have anywhere else to go. Thea lived with her mom and the twins, so we were next door to each other all summer. I saw her. We just didn't speak anymore."

Henley nods thoughtfully. "Thanks, Marley. Really. We appreciate your insight."

"One more question, then we'll see ourselves out," Romero says, leaning forward in her chair. "Was Thea seeing anyone that you knew of?"

I know they must see the shock flitting across my face. "No," I say. "Thea wasn't seeing anyone. Not anyone I knew about, anyway. Not . . . ever, actually."

Henley nods, but Romero doesn't move. I can feel her eyes boring into me for just a second too long.

"Why are you asking me that?" I ask, but it's too late, the professional mask is back up and she offers a dispassionate shake of her head in response.

"We're just gathering all the information we can."

"Thanks again," Henley says. "We'll be in touch if we have any more questions."

I sit back in my chair, lips pressed tightly together, and watch the two of them stand and leave. Once the door shuts, I get up and peer out the window as they walk to their car. There's a strong wind today—a small, dark cloud rolls across the sun, but only for a second. Then it's back, bearing down on their sweat-slicked faces like an angry god.

They look almost vulnerable out there in the street. The only trees in a field, with a lightning storm kicking up in the distance.

They don't know us.

They don't know you.

They don't even know what they're looking for.

6

Thea

THE CHICKEN SHACK has a smell.

Grease and burn. It's always been there, now that I'm thinking of it, but I never noticed it much until today. I swallow hard—feel it settling like a thick lump at the base of my throat. And something else too, a feeling close to dread, but not quite.

I grind my heel into some loose gravel along the edge of the parking lot and eye the building in front of me. Mostly it looks like your average fast-food joint, except for the ten-foot-tall plastic chicken mascot, Hooster the Rooster, protruding from the roof like a funhouse popup. The sight is familiar yet foreign—something I've seen a hundred times driving through town, or idling in the drive-thru lane, but never really noticed before.

It strikes me now, though. How could it not? Hooster's got one wing on his hip and the other contorted into a feathered approximation of a thumbs up. He's wearing a shirt that says *Feather Lickin' Good!!*—a catchphrase I heard the shop was almost sued for a few years ago.

Before I can dwell for too long on the absurdity that my life has become, I head toward the entrance. There's a guy leaning against the glass doors—more of a kid, really, since he can't be older than fifteen. He's got his eyes glued to his phone, and I approach him tentatively.

"Hey," I say. He doesn't look up, so I clear my throat and try again. "I'm Thea. I'm new."

The boy takes his eyes off the screen just long enough to clock me. "Sup," he says, sounding every bit as tired as I feel.

When I realize he isn't going to say more, I give up and cup my hands over my eyes to peer inside the glass. I've gone through the drive-thru at the Chicken Shack a hundred times, but I've never really thought to go inside before. No one does, as far as I know. Still, there are tables set up on either side, Formica tabletops in primary colors, that '80s bowling alley print screened onto each. There's a long counter for ordering at the front, as if whoever designed the place was expecting big crowds and long lines.

I turn back around, resting my back against the hot glass, feeling the pit stains beginning to form against my favorite shirt, an old Ricky Martin concert tee I found at my favorite thrift store out in Macon. At ten AM, it's already boiling, even in the shade, and I regret my decision to wear the three-quarter sleeve lace undershirt with the tee. I'm considering another attempt at conversation with phone kid when a beat-up Honda finally swings into the lot and parks, askew, off to the side.

The door swings open and I squint at the guy getting out. He's a little older, mid-twenties maybe, with wild hair that catches the light like spun sugar sticking up in all directions.

"You're Theresa, right?" he calls to me.

I raise an eyebrow. "Thea," I say. "And you're my boss?" I sound doubtful, but he doesn't exactly look like the managerial type. He's better than phone kid, though.

The guy shoves his hands into his pockets and shrugs. There's a cigarette stub dangling from between his lips, shedding ash onto the toe of his boot. "I guess," he mumbles, drawing a ring of keys from the deep pocket of his oversized jeans.

"What's your name?" I ask, as he shoves one of the keys into the lock and forces a turn.

He takes the cigarette from between his lips and drops it onto the concrete, "James," he says. "Butler."

There's a rush of cool air over my face as James pulls the door open and flips on the lights, which kick on with a gentle hum and bathe the room in a harsh, sputtering white.

"Did you meet Daryl?" he asks as phone kid drifts past us both toward the back of the shop.

"Sure," I say, and James gives a knowing smile.

"Break room is back there," he says, nodding toward the back, behind the counter. "Drive-thru window there." A head nod to the left, also behind the counter. "That's pretty much it."

I nod, slowly, that feeling settling again at the base of my stomach. It's a job, and I'm lucky to have it after the Macy's shuttered its location in Sherman Hill and left me without one. Still, I can't help thinking of Marley heading off to her managerial shift this morning at Southern Moon—the relentlessly, almost satirically preppy boutique where she's worked since high school. She's managing the recently opened Athens storefront now, and I wonder what she's doing at this exact second. Probably making amicable small talk with some undergrad clutching daddy's credit card, complimenting her expensive highlights and offering to pull a different size if need be.

"All the food is premade—shipped over from the kitchen in Dover— so you don't have to worry about cooking shit, but there'll be more than enough customers to keep you busy once we open the window." James walks while he talks, leading me behind the counter toward the break room. There's a small card table and a mess of aprons hung up on the back of the door. Daryl has already slid one over his head and busied himself with what looks like an inventory sheet. "There's usually three people to a shift, but we've been short staffed ever since Eric quit, so it'll be nice to have someone else around. Daryl isn't much of a talker—are you, Daryl?" In response, Daryl only grunts. James raises his eyebrows and hands me an apron, looping his head through the other.

"Anything I can do to help," I say, tying the strings behind my back.

We spend the next hour going over procedures—how to open the store and how to get the cash register's one wonky button to work; by the time we're finished, the lunch crowd is starting to roll through.

"Daryl and I will take the window. You can man the counter since it's your first day," he says, pulling a ratty baseball cap over his eyes and smoothing his features like he's about to walk out onto a stage.

The counter is easy work. Three people wander inside during the lunch rush, each with a kind of far-off look in their eyes. They order chicken sandwiches or wraps and park themselves at the small tables with books or newspapers or nothing at all. When the store closes at eight I have to tell two of them to leave. James and Daryl bounce around like pinballs all day, from window to register to refrigerator to soda fountain. I try to help when I can but end up feeling like I'm in the way most of the time. They're almost scarily efficient.

When I escort the last, lingering customer out and lock the door behind him, James pulls the cap off and tips his head back.

"Is it always that busy at the window?" I ask with something like dread as I flip the sign on the door to "closed."

James throws me a look, but the corner of his lip is turned up in a smile. "You got no idea what you're in for, sunshine. That was a slow day."

"Christ," I mutter, and I think I hear him laugh. James, Daryl, and I work quietly for a few minutes, wiping down the counter and counting out the money in the register. James shows me how to set the alarm and, when we lock up, he bumps his shoulder against my own.

"You did alright, kid. For a first day, I mean."

I shrug, blushing irrationally. "Thanks," I say.

"You want a smoke before we head out?" he asks, fishing the pack of cigarettes from the pocket of his oversized jeans and nodding toward the side of the building not facing the street. I catch the "no" as it bounces onto the tip of my tongue, throwing my eyes out toward my car in the nearly empty parking lot. Marley and I were supposed to meet in Athens for drinks after our shifts tonight, to celebrate her landing the manager position there, but she hasn't told me where to meet her yet and, absurdly, I picture her with the girls at Southern Moon—the ones everyone calls "Moonies"—clinking cocktail glasses together, their nails all painted delicate shades of shell pink, and something rises up inside of me. I nod at him instead.

"Yeah, why not?" I say as Daryl floats toward the door, raising one hand in a goodbye wave without taking his eyes off his phone.

We amble around back and James passes me a cigarette, lighting it with a candy apple red lighter produced from his other pocket. I put it to my lips, sucking the air into my mouth and blowing it back out before I can take the smoke into my lungs.

"So," he says before taking a long, deep drag from his own. "What do you do for fun?"

The question is normal enough, but it still takes me by surprise, somehow. *Fun.* It's ridiculous how foreign the concept feels to me. "Um," I start, taking a moment to think. "Well, I'm into fashion, I guess. My best friend and I have this Instagram account where we style different outfits and she models them. It's actually doing pretty well. We just hit ten thousand followers."

James raises his eyebrows and rubs at his patchy facial hair. "Wow, that's impressive."

"It's not really," I say, looking down at my scuffed Doc Martens. "Ten K isn't actually that many followers these days."

He pinches the cigarette between his thumb and forefinger and lifts it off his lips, a curl of smoke escaping as he speaks. "Well, it's ten thousand more than I have," he says, and I smile. "So, you want to be one of those designers, then? Like on that *Project Runway* show my fiancée always has on?"

I blink, pushing my shoulders back against the warm brick. "Sort of," I say, flicking ash onto the ground. "I want to open my own vintage store one day, in New York. Or become a personal stylist. Or both maybe. I don't really know."

James raises an eyebrow at me. "Big Apple, huh?"

"That's the plan." I feel a bit pathetic admitting it here, in the parking lot of the fast-food restaurant where I now work. New York has always been my sharpest, clearest dream, but somehow, even though I've spent the last few years counting down the days until I can go, it feels further away than ever. I clear my throat. "What about you?"

He pulls the cigarette from between his lips and taps the ash onto the asphalt. "Ah," he says, staring out at the back of the lot, which runs up against a slim bank of trees and, beyond that, the highway. "Who knows, I guess. Just found out I've got a kid on the way, so that changes things. My fiancée likes it around here, so I guess I'm . . . around. For the time being, at least."

"Oh. Congratulations," I say, feeling suddenly awkward. He doesn't seem happy about any of it. He smiles ruefully and takes another drag, smoke drifting around his head like a halo.

"This place ain't shit," he says after a long moment, and there's a beat where I can't tell exactly what he's talking about—Riverside or the

Chicken Shack—maybe both. "Get out of here as soon as you can. Go to New York and stay there, or at least don't come back here."

I keep my eyes fixed on the middle distance to match him. There's something underneath his voice—a grave, private desperation that I feel like a kick to my gut—and it doesn't seem right to look at him now. "I had planned to go after high school," I say, dropping my cigarette and stomping it underneath the heel of my boot. "But then my mom found out she was pregnant with twins, and my ex-stepdad left her. So I felt like I needed to stay and help."

I think about telling him more—about Mom's online poker habit and the bills we always seem to be falling behind on. About the panic I felt when the Macy's closed, and the scramble to find something, anything, to bring in a paycheck. But I hold my tongue.

James looks at me and I can feel it on my skin, like heat from a stove. "That's nice of you," he says. "But don't ruin your life for kids that aren't even yours."

I press my spine uncomfortably against the brick. "They're still my family," I say.

James shrugs and we stay quiet for what feels like ages, but it's not awkward. It's . . . almost nice. Here, with the dull hum of cars passing on the road and smoke growing thicker around us, I feel like I could say anything, and it would be okay. A judgment-free zone. It's something I haven't felt in a long time.

After a few long seconds, my phone vibrates in my pocket. I check it and see a text from Marley.

SO sorry—just clocked out and Austen surprised me with dinner reservations! Could we do tomorrow instead?

I purse my lips and slip the phone back into my pocket.

"What happened?" James asks.

"Nothing," I say tersely. Then, after a beat, "My friend and I had plans tonight, but she canceled."

"Bummer. The Instagram friend?"

I lift one shoulder in a half-hearted shrug. "Yeah. Her name is Marley Henderson. I doubt you know her. She works over at Southern Moon—she's the manager at the new one they just opened in Athens."

James lifts his eyebrows so high they almost disappear beneath his hairline.

"What?" I say, instantly defensive.

"Nothing," he says. "I'm just . . . it's weird. You don't seem like someone who'd be friends with that crowd. You're like, way cool. And they're—you know."

I press my lips together. It's not like I haven't heard it before. Nothing about our friendship makes much sense on the surface—but I'm not usually the one people think is slumming it—and suddenly I feel a swell of pride. For Marley. For the friendship we've built and kept going for so many years, despite our differences. "Well, I am," I say. "Besides, Marley's not like the rest of them."

"What, you mean she's a River Rat too?"

"Don't say that," I snap. I'm not sure why I'm so defensive. I've been called a River Rat my whole life—everyone from Riverside has. The richer, classier Sherman Hill stock use it behind our backs to describe those of us who live on the wrong side of the water separating our two towns, but at some point we adopted it and began to wear it with stubborn pride. Still, the way James says it feels more derogatory than usual, and I don't like what he's implying. Like Marley's position at Southern Moon makes her better than us.

James just shrugs and takes another drag from his cigarette.

"Look, all I'm saying is, there's no point in ignoring the natural order of things. People like us and people like them—there's a reason we don't mix. But maybe you and your friend are different."

"We are," I bristle. The no-judgment zone that existed just a few minutes ago disintegrates around us and suddenly I feel cold. "Besides, what makes you think I'm like you?"

James flashes a smile at me, and I'm surprised by the intensity of it—the thousand-kilowatt energy that burns for less than a second before it's gone. He drops his cigarette on the concrete, smoke still curling at the tip. "I know a kindred spirit when I spot one," he says. As he speaks, his eyes dart quickly to the spot where the sleeve of my lace undershirt has ridden up to reveal my forearm. I look down at the row upon row of thin, white lines scratched across the skin, all of them bisected by a larger, vertical scar, still visible even after all this time.

I yank the sleeve down and grimace. I feel uncomfortable, suddenly, with the thought that James noticed and that he's using the knowledge to try and bond with me. What kind of a sick person does that?

"I should go," I say, digging into the pocket of my shorts for my keys.

James only shrugs, the hem of his threadbare T-shirt lifting against his lean hip. And then, with a smirk, he says, "I'll see you tomorrow, kid."

7

Marley

Yᴏᴜ ᴡᴏᴜʟᴅ'ᴠᴇ ʜᴀᴛᴇᴅ your funeral.

For one thing, it's cliché—chock full of platitudes about how you'll "live forever in our hearts" and how you're "in a better place, smiling down on all of us." When the pastor opens the Bible and starts reading that passage about "the valley of the shadow of death," I can practically hear you rolling over in your coffin, groaning.

I mean, there's no body in the coffin. I know that. But still.

I'm sitting in the pew right behind the one marked *family*, wearing a black dress I picked up yesterday because everything I had was too short or too tight or too colorful. If you were here, you'd smile at all the black and nudge my shoulder. *Hey, Marley, you're stealing my look.*

We're singing now. Some hymn I can barely work out the tune to. I've got my eyes fixed on Austen. On the bead of sweat rolling down the back of his neck, disappearing underneath his suit jacket. The rigid set of his shoulders. Military posture, just like his father, who's seated next to him. I want to reach out and put my hand between his shoulder blades, to cool the tension drawing them together the way I used to, but then I see the way he looked at me the other day when I kissed him—like I'd done something wrong, taken something away—and I know that my days of touching him thoughtlessly are over.

"Please, be seated," the pastor says. Everyone around me goes down, but I can't seem to make my legs bend, and suddenly people are staring.

"I—I need some air," I whisper to Mom, slipping out of the pew and down the side aisle as inconspicuously as possible.

Still, I can feel the eyes on me as I go. Quick looks, burning like cigarette butts against my skin until I'm outside the church.

Austen and I talked about a church wedding for a while. I even made a Pinterest board to visualize it. A wedding dress bathed in the golden hour light of a stained-glass window. Old wooden pews draped in magnolia and baby's breath. I liked the idea because it felt real and solid and traditional in a way our relationship never quite had. Undeniable in the eyes of God and man.

That was three months ago. Twelve weeks. A lifetime, now.

"Marley?" the voice springs up from the church steps. I jump at the sound of it. The sight of her sitting there, tan legs splayed out, blonde hair fallen uncharacteristically flat in the heat, a pink vape clutched between her fingers.

"Sky," I say, forcing myself to unstick from the wall and breathe in the stale air. "I didn't see you."

She rolls her shoulders back and lifts her chin to look at me. I doubt she expected anyone to find her out here. It's improper, after all. Unladylike. Worse, it goes against her brand. Under normal circumstances, she'd have stood up by now and dusted the loose concrete off her skirt. She'd already be in the middle of an excuse. But today she doesn't seem to care. Probably because it's me.

"Do you want a hit?" she says after a long moment. "You look like you could use it."

I bite down on my lip and chew, considering for a long moment before I sit down next to her, tucking my dress up underneath my thighs so the brick doesn't burn them. I want to laugh at how ridiculous this is—me, skipping out on your funeral to vape with Sky—but after a second the irony doesn't seem so funny anymore.

"Why not?" I say grimly, even though I know exactly why not. Sky's never done anything but make my life worse. Take things that used to be good and destroy them with a smile on her face while she pretends to be my friend.

I take the vape and bring it to my lips, inhaling deeply. "I didn't expect to see you here," I say, vapor drifting past my lips. Practically the entire town is, but even so, I didn't figure she'd want to associate the Southern Moon brand, or her own, with this kind of unpleasantness.

Unless she's here for Austen, of course.

"I felt like I should," she says.

I fix my eyes out toward the overgrown patch of weeds spilling over each other in the church lawn—everything growing through, up, and around the rest, trying to find some way to survive.

"You know, for what it's worth, I'm sorry about Thea."

"Yeah, me too."

"Did you and Austen ever make up after—"

"You know we didn't, Sky." My words are sharp. Biting.

She takes a deep breath, her knee shaking up and down as she sits back on her hands. Sky's always had a zippy, compulsively cheery energy about her—it's gone a long way in helping her build the gracious, Southern, #girlboss brand she's so proud of. But I know her well enough to recognize this slide into anxious jitters.

"You didn't deserve all the hate you got," she says, so quiet it's almost a whisper.

I bite down hard on my lip, until I can taste the sharp iron of my blood, and nod. I wonder if this is her admission of guilt—her apology for spearheading it. For destroying my reputation and what was left of my relationship in a targeted, two-pronged attack. But then I think, *of course it's not*. Women like Sky don't dwell for too long on the messes they create. They don't have to.

"You're holding up okay? I mean, with the Thea thing. How she died and everything . . ." She trails off and cuts her eyes to me, just for a second. It occurs to me that maybe she wants me to be the old Marley again—the Marley I was back when we were friends. Work wives. When I practically worshipped the ground she walked on. When I cleaned up all her messes and let her take all the credit. We had some good times then.

But this is a different world. You're gone and I'm not that Marley anymore, so I glare at her instead. I don't even care that she's technically my boss.

Sky clears her throat. "I should go back in," she says, pushing herself off the steps and running her hands down the front of her dress. It's from Southern Moon, of course, and it's been recently pressed, like everything she wears. I want to grab the fabric and shred it.

"You shouldn't have done what you did," I say, swallowing back the bile rising in my throat. The words send a shot of adrenaline through me. I keep my eyes on hers. I want to watch her squirm.

But she doesn't. Instead, she just sighs, the vulnerability from a moment ago gone. I can see the shutters closing up behind her eyes. The cool, dispassionate gleam I know so well flicking on like a light in a window. "I didn't *do* anything, Marley. You did."

I use my thumb to squish a stray ant on concrete, concentrating all of my anger into the movement. "I know you created that Instagram account."

She laughs at that. A layman would mistake it as friendly, but I'm not a layman. I know exactly what Sky is capable of and I know she created @Vintage_Whore—the anonymous Instagram account that launched a vicious attack on me in the wake of my very public mistake and ran our @Vintage_Doll account into the ground inside seventy-two hours.

"Please, spare me the victim impact statement, Marley. Isn't it possible that people turned on you because you did something terrible? Because *you* were the one to cheat on Austen, not the other way around? It's not my fault that you hooked up with someone else in front of the entire town."

I close my eyes for a second. Just long enough to force it all back down again. It was stupid to think I could get her to admit her role in all of it. To take any responsibility at all. But I had to try.

Sky goes back into the church, and I should go back too, but I can't seem to make myself. Can't deal with all of those people in there staring at me. So instead I sit on the steps, cracking my knuckles as a hard knot anchors itself in the pit of my stomach. Knowing, in the same gut way I knew I wanted Austen all those years ago, that this is the new normal. That if hope is the thing with wings, then pain is the thing with roots. The thing that keeps you where you've been. That pulls you to the earth until you can't sustain the weight of being anymore.

Even outside, I can hear the final hymn being sung. The sounds of a hundred voices float out of the church, almost gentle from a distance.

If you were alive, if this were anyone else's send-off, you'd be right here next to me. You would probably have snuck a couple of tiny whiskey bottles into your purse for the occasion. I didn't have the foresight, though, so I walk to my car instead and sit inside with the AC on, watching as people stream out. It's the curious onlookers who leave first—the ones who didn't know you. Who were only here so they could gossip about it later. They shoot out of the church quick as cats before ducking into cars and peeling out of the parking lot with as little ceremony as possible, probably disappointed by the lack of drama.

The second group out are those in the *felt-like-I-should-come* camp. They're more sheepish about leaving, but they do. I watch as Austen's father, David, makes a quick exit, his head bent low, looking almost as tired and sad as the rest of us. Then, behind him, Scott Martin, the badges on his police uniform glinting against the sunlight. He's with a group of other officers who seem to move together as a pack, but he still stands a head taller than any of them. I wonder where his wife is today. If she's on bedrest at home. She must be close to delivering her baby now.

There's a knock on my window. Sharp and insistent.

I jump and refocus my eyes on the passenger's side window, where Austen is bent down, looking at me, his face hovering inches from the glass. I roll it down and stare at him.

"What do you want?" I ask.

He leans inside the car, his broad shoulders barely fitting their way through the space. "You left. I wanted to make sure you were okay."

I press my lips together and consider my answer. "It was just a lot," I say finally. "I couldn't handle it."

He nods and pushes the hair out of his face—he's put some kind of styling mousse in and it looks slick and black as an oil spill. "Look, about the other day—"

"We're good," I say quickly. "I shouldn't have done that."

We're quiet for a moment. There's part of me that wants to unlock the car door, let him in, and sit here listening to him breathe.

"I saw that the police came your way," he says. "What did they want?"

I shrug. "Just to talk, I guess. About her. And they wanted to know about the fight."

"What did you tell them?" There's a catch in his voice, and I recognize the desperation worming its way up.

"The truth," I say. "What else is there to tell?"

"Marley," he says—and there's the crack. The shift. The anger that only ever shows itself in flashes. It's so unfamiliar, his anger. So at odds with the patented Austen Brown persona—volunteer children's soccer coach, favorite personal trainer of wealthy Sherman Hill women over forty—that it always feels a bit like a practical joke when it rears up. It never is, though. When Austen is mad, he's *mad*. Boiling over, no simmer. "You know they'll use that fight to build a case against her. The timing is too coincidental."

I glare at him now. These moods of his scared me once, but not anymore. Now I know them like sailors know ocean tides. We used to be like that, he and I. We used to know each other's rhythms like clockwork. "What was I supposed to do then, lie? I told them she wasn't violent. I can't control what they'll think."

"Don't you see what they're doing, Mar? This is only the beginning. We have to stop them."

"Stop them from what?"

"From framing her!"

"We don't even know what happened that night."

Austen's nostrils are flaring and he slams his hand against the side of the car. It bangs against the metal like a gunshot, and I hate that it makes me jump. "What are you saying?" he asks.

"I'm saying we don't know shit, Austen. Now back up and calm down."

He does, and it's all very *Austen*—this anger that blazes into existence, then out of it just as quickly. I watch his eyes close and his shoulders rise in one, two, three deep breaths. When he looks at me again, he's contrite.

"I'm sorry," he says. "I've been on edge."

"We aren't engaged anymore, so I don't have to deal with your shit. Check yourself before you come to me." I adjust the rearview mirror to check my reflection. There's a faint spray of freckles darkening the bridge of my nose. I frown and push the mirror back into place.

"But it's like you don't even care about her."

I press my lips into a flat line and breathe. "Don't you dare say that," I tell him. The words come out a whisper. "You know I do."

He leans into the window again and meets my eye. "Then listen to me, please. I really need you right now."

"To do what?" I ask. I realize that I've balled my hands together in my lap and I glance down at them—pale and bloodless and grasping at each other. Sometimes I'm still jolted by the sight of my bare ring finger. Still have to fight back a brief moment of panic that I've lost my ring before I remember the night I gave it back. I pull my fingers apart and smooth the fabric of my dress across my lap.

"To help me," Austen says. "Look, I may never know exactly what happened—why she was in that house. But I can't do nothing, especially not with the police looking to pin it on her. Help me find who did this to her. Help me clear her. I know the two of you fought, but she loved you."

"I know," I say, barely a whisper.

"Then help me."

There's something about his tone that hits me. A note I can't quite place. Harsher than I would've expected from him. More urgent.

"What if we find something we don't want to find?" I ask. I can't help it. It's the fear I haven't been able to shake since he brought it up that first day. Obviously, you had secrets. What if I don't want to know what they were?

"Then at least we'll know we tried."

I take a deep breath. He's right, and I know it. What kind of person would I be if I abandoned you now, after everything? How could I live with myself if I let you go down for all of this without a fight?

"Okay," I say quietly. "What did you have in mind?"

"The scene," he says.

"Austen, you can't be serious," I say. "The police will have gone through it with a fine-tooth comb. They'll have taken anything worth finding."

"Look, I know it's a long shot, but it's all we've got, right? That house sat on a lot of property. It's always possible they could've missed something."

"I guess," I admit quietly. The thought of being *there*, though—of standing in the ashes where you died. It feels as impossible as walking through the fire itself. "I just—I don't know if I can."

Austen reaches out and wraps his hand around my wrist. His palm is warm, his fingers callused from gripping weights at the gym. "You're the strongest person I know, Mar. You can."

I frown. I'm a lot of things, but I'm not the strongest person he knows.

"Fine," I say tersely. "Tonight then, around midnight? I can drive."

His grip loosens and he nods. "I'll be ready," he says. Finally, I draw back my wrist and roll it as the hair stands on end.

8

Thea

"KILL. ME." JAMES groans, throwing his head back as soon as I flip the Chicken Shack's sign over to "closed."

I laugh, locking the door eagerly and turning to press my back against the glass. "How often is it that busy?"

He shrugs, already ripping off his apron. Behind him, Daryl does the same. "Every once in a while—usually on a Saturday, people just go chicken crazy. Whole town turns into hungry sum'bitches."

"That was exhausting." I tilt my head back so it rests against the warm glass. I don't feel like I have the right to complain, though. James moved twice as fast as I did all day long.

"Don't know what I would've done if you weren't on shift," he says, and he sounds almost shy. I smile at him and he clears his throat. "You too, Daryl."

Daryl looks over from where he's hanging his apron on the back of the door. "Any chance I can take off early? I got this big . . . uh . . . paper due Monday and I gotta work on it."

"Yeah, man, no worries. Okay with you, Thea?"

"Sure," I say, crossing the room on sore legs and pulling the apron over my head. Underneath, my clothes smell like grease. My skin is sticky with sweat. I let myself dream for a second of the shower I'll let myself have when I get home—the hot water cranked so steam soaks every pore—and then I pick up the broom and start sweeping underneath the tables while James wipes down the counter.

We don't speak again until Daryl shuffles out, his phone already gripped firmly in his hand. "So what do you think the chances are that he's actually working on a paper tonight?" he asks.

I snort a laugh, sweeping up a plastic fork from underneath a chair. "Zero. You just got played for sure."

"Well, damn," he says cheerfully.

"What about you? Big plans tonight?" I ask, just to make conversation. We've been a bit tentative with each other ever since my first day, when he called us kindred spirits and spotted the old scars on my arm. I know he knows it made me uncomfortable, and he's been keeping things reasonably professional ever since.

"Why?" he says, tossing me a goofy smile. "You trying to ask me out?"

"Har har." I roll my eyes and stick my tongue out at him, and he laughs. Now that the restaurant is empty, I can feel him coming back to himself. The stoic, efficient mask disappearing as the real James seeps through. It's a transformation that I watch at the end of every shift, and it still amazes me—how much someone can alter themselves in the space of a few minutes.

James has set the baseball cap at the end of the counter, and his hair sticks up in all directions, catching the fluorescent light like a crown of down feathers. "Nah," he says finally. "No plans, really. Iris can't drink because of the baby, and she's sick of hanging with our friends if she's the only one who's going to be sober, so we're staying in this weekend."

"That'll be nice," I say, looking at him out of the corner of my eye as I scoop up the dust pan and tip the contents into the trash. The corner of his mouth ticks and he sprays the counter with the cleaning solution a few more times than strictly necessary. "I mean—unless it won't?" I say, awkward now. I'm not usually one to pry, but the way he's acting, it's like he wants me to. Like he's dying to talk about it, he just needs someone to ask.

He looks at me from underneath bushy eyebrows. "Don't have kids, Wright," he says grimly. "Mine hasn't even been born yet and my whole fucking life is different."

I snap the broom back onto the plastic dustbin handle and return it to the breakroom. "The pregnancy stage is hard," I say, trying not to grimace as I remember what it was like to live with my mom back when she was pregnant with Milo and Finn. I've heard that pregnancy is like the calm before the storm, but it didn't feel like that in our house—not after David left three months into Mom's pregnancy. Instead, I look back on those months and all I remember is the dread that pervaded everything. The silence of the house without David in it. The way I tiptoed around my grief-stricken, petrified mother and watched her abdomen protrude farther and farther as the rest of her shrunk back, receding into shadows. At least, once the twins were born, there were diapers to change and bottles to make and little, warm bodies to rock. Things to focus on besides the rubble of my mother's marriage and the financial burden of raising two more kids.

"Things will be different when the baby is born," I tell him.

He shrugs. "Different," he says, disdainfully. "A lot harder, probably. Do you have any idea how expensive a kid is?"

"I have an idea," I say, a bit ruefully. David hasn't been remotely consistent in his child support payments, so I've been funneling most of my paycheck toward the twins since they were born. Austen helps too, and Mom's job as an at-home care aide for an elderly man in Sherman Hill brings in decent money. Still, with her . . . habits, it never seems like enough to get us on solid ground, even with the house already paid off.

"Well, then you know. They're expensive," James says. "A lot more than I can fucking afford. That's for sure."

He meets my eyes across the room, and I can feel the animosity for it all rolling off him in waves, but something else too—something more subtle. Something like pleading. I blink, but it's still there, underneath the anger. He's daring me to judge him, and desperate for me not to.

It's a look I recognize, a feeling I know deep in my gut.

I straighten my spine and pull my ponytail tighter against the back of my head. "You don't have to be happy about a baby just because everyone says you should be," I tell him, watching his shoulders fall in relief. "But you can't bail on it either."

"I know that," he says. "Believe me. I know that." He looks at me again, the pleading gone, replaced by something else.

I dart my eyes away and take a deep breath.

"What about you?" he asks—a concerted effort to change the subject. "Plans tonight? An actual date, maybe?"

"No," I say, scoffing at the thought. I grab the mop from the break room and dunk it into a bucket of water.

Mom asked if I could watch the twins while she and June go for a girls' night, and even if she hadn't, it's not like I would have a date lined up.

"You're single?" He sounds surprised, so I lift my eyebrows as if to say *what of it?* He just shrugs.

"Sorry," he amends. Then, "I make you uncomfortable, don't I?" It takes me off guard, the frankness of his statement.

"Yeah," I admit. "Sometimes."

"I'm sorry," he says. "I'm not trying to be creepy. It's just—you remind me a lot of me, is all. I don't meet many people like that. I feel like I can talk to you."

I bite down on my lip hard, considering. The truth is, he makes me feel uncomfortable *because* we're so much alike. Because I know what he's feeling without his having to actually say it. I remember my first day—that judgment-free zone. The way we so easily sank into sharing our dreams and fears. I don't meet many people like that, either.

"It's okay," I say finally. "I'm sorry too. For being standoffish. It's been a long time since I made any new friends."

I catch the corner of his mouth twitching upwards in a small smile. "Me too," he says. "Maybe we can figure it out together."

Something about the way he says it fills me with a warmth I don't care to explore, and there's a gleam in his eyes when they meet mine. Relief, I think. But then I consider for a second longer and I realize it isn't relief at all. It's hope.

9

Marley

AT MIDNIGHT I hear the tap on my window. It's pitch black outside, so I can't see Austen, but I can picture him there, watching me through the thin glass, waiting for me to acknowledge him. I take my time, pulling an old, denim button-down over my camisole and throwing my hair up before I push the window open and meet his eyes.

"You can come through the front," I say dryly. "We're adults now."

"Sorry. Force of habit," he says, his fingers curling into the window-sill. "Are you ready?" I nod and pick up my cell from its place on my comforter.

"Leave it. We don't want the police to be able to track us to the scene, do we?"

I stare down at the phone in my hand and back up at him. "Fine," I mumble, tossing it on the bed.

Austen takes my hand and helps me duck out. I haven't gone out my bedroom window since the night before we moved into our place together. The night he surprised me by setting up a small picnic in the backyard. A celebration of what we thought was our last night apart.

"I can't wait to sleep next to you in *our* bed," he'd said, brushing the hair from my cheek. "To start building *our* lives. Together."

I shut the window behind me, and the night sounds swallow us up. We walk in silence out to my car parked at the curb, listening to the crickets scream. I can't help thinking, though, that it should be you climbing into my car for a late-night drive. That it should've been you waiting outside my window in the first place. Because these things—the adventures that buzzed and sizzled and sparked with adrenaline—that was always us.

Austen was for the times I wanted to feel warm and safe and sure of myself. Hours stolen underneath blankets or wrapped up in his arms. Skin on skin and whispered conversations.

But it's all backwards now, so I might as well get used to it.

I start the car and cut the headlights. There are only a couple of other houses on our street and everyone's light is out, or their curtains are drawn. Still, I can't help the nervous energy coursing through me at what we're about to do. I roll down the window and gulp down a gust of balmy air before rolling it back up again.

"So tell me what we're looking for," I say finally, when I can't take the silence anymore. Austen and I used to talk endlessly. Neither of us ever liked the quiet much, and our apartment was always filled with a steady stream of noise—the two of us chatting, a Spotify playlist, our sound machine, or some combination. The silence between us now feels alien. Dangerous.

I make a left-hand turn onto an even quieter road than ours, careful to drive slowly, but not suspiciously so. Before the fire that killed you, Riverside was crawling with cops—patrolling every corner and crevice, especially at night, while they waited for *the arsonist* to make a move. But now there's practically no one. Riverside is back to being just as empty as it was before. I guess they really do think that you did it.

"Anything," he says, his eyes fixed intently on the road ahead.

I wait for more, but there isn't any. "Gotcha."

"I guess we'll know it when we see it, won't we?"

"Guess so." We're quiet again until I can feel us coming up on it. I knew the house was closer to town than most of the others, but now it hits me just how close. You were less than two miles away.

There's no house on the lot anymore, and the land looks barren without the familiar silhouette. Once, I would've barely noticed it—just another in the dozens of abandoned properties dotting the land out here—but now the empty space looms like a black hole, menacing in its absence.

I park about a quarter mile up the road and we walk back toward the house, yellow crime scene tape catching the faint light of the moon like a reflective banner, beckoning us to cross. The air is suffocatingly hot, even now in the middle of the night. I try to think of the last time we had rain—even one of those quick, violent summer storms—but I can't remember.

"Shit," I mutter as we approach. "Did you bring a flashlight?"

Without a word, Austen produces two from the front pocket of his hoodie and passes one to me.

"Once a Boy Scout," he says. I almost smile before I remember where we are.

"I guess I'll start over there?" I say, pointing my flashlight vaguely in the direction of where the house used to stand. It's just cinders now—a half-crumbled brick fireplace the only thing left standing—and suddenly I feel paralyzed. This place feels haunted, not by you, but by something darker. A force that wants me out.

"Why don't you go around the perimeter, and I'll pick through the inside?" Austen says.

I swallow the lump in my throat and follow him, dead grass scratching at the leg of my jeans and brushing my ankles, the crickets screaming underneath my feet. I have to resist the urge to take off sprinting.

I reach down and pinch hard at the meat of my thigh, trying to force myself back to reality, but it doesn't help much. I still feel as though I'm hovering two feet above the ground.

"You know what I don't understand," Austen says, his face pulled into a furrow of concentration as he picks his way through the debris.

"What?" I ask, pointing the flashlight at the ground and staring at the dry grass and the cinders like they might spring to life and bite me.

"Before Thea, whoever was setting these fires didn't hurt anyone. In fact, they went out of their way to pick abandoned houses far away from the part of town people still live in."

"Mmm-hmm," I manage, doing my best to keep to a straight line where the northern face of the house used to stand.

Why would you ever come here alone?

"That tells me they're not violent. Not by nature, at least. So why Thea? What about her made her a target?"

"Maybe it wasn't even the arsonist who killed her," I say. "Maybe it was someone else who wants everyone to think the arsonist was responsible."

Or, maybe, it really was just you, I add silently.

"Maybe so," Austen says quietly, as though the thought hadn't crossed his mind. "Do you see something?" he asks. I whip my head up and find him staring at me, his head tilted to the side. I realize I've been staring at the same spot.

"No," I say, clearing my throat. "Sorry." I push forward and dart the bolt of light out ahead of me, so it lights up a circle of grass a few feet away.

We search in silence for a few long minutes before his voice breaks the eerie stillness.

"Mar, come look at this," he says. I jog over to the spot where he stands. It would've been the back of the house once, but now it's nothing. A pile of half-burned-out floorboards and debris.

He's holding something in the palm of his hand, cradling it, almost—his flashlight aimed to get a better look. I squint against the flash of metal in the beam of light. A ring—a single strip of silver gleaming like a beacon.

"I don't recognize this," he says. I swallow the brick in my throat.

"It was Thea's," I whisper. "I was with her when she bought it."

A memory bubbles up to the surface of my mind of the day we bought those rings. Us, at that vintage store in Macon, raiding their stock before anyone else could get to it. It was last winter—a lifetime ago now, right after Austen and I got engaged, and I remember the look on your face, like pure elation, when we walked through the doors. I'd been trying to cheer you up, I remember now with a skittering sense of doom. You wouldn't admit to anything being wrong, but I knew your funks almost as well as you did. Could feel them like a swell of bad energy, the same way my mom gets before a bender. I'd worried that this one was my fault—that I'd spent too much time focused on the wedding and managing the brand-new Athens location of Southern Moon, right when you needed me. After your boss at the Chicken Shack, James, died you were different. And I got distracted by my own life—let you drift too far out of orbit while I considered taffeta and silk samples and flipped through the bridal magazines you clearly had no interest in.

We still had the Instagram, of course. But Vintage Doll was growing faster than either of us expected, and suddenly your New York deadline felt like a threat. A looming end point neither of us was quite sure how to handle.

That visit to Macon had been my attempt to remind us both of the way we used to be together, and, for a few hours, it worked. We sifted through heaps of clothing and peeled the best items away for ourselves—a pair of truly phenomenal leather culottes for you and a tea-length floral peasant dress for me. We laughed at the really heinous pieces and tried on the outrageously expensive coats we'd never be able to afford. We even got some content for Vintage Doll that didn't feel forced. And then we spotted them, the two rings laid out beneath the glass case register table, one gold and one silver.

"Let's get them," you'd said, winking at me. "They'll be like our own version of wedding rings."

"You mean like friendship rings, then," I'd corrected.

You shook your head. "No. I mean like our own version of wedding rings."

I got it that time. I felt the permanence beneath your words. The commitment. Friends, yes, but something deeper than that too. Something like sisterhood.

"Why wasn't this with her body?" Austen asks, cutting into my thoughts. He straightens his shoulders and purses his lips—like I've done something wrong.

"I don't know," I say, and I wonder if he can hear the crack in my voice. "Maybe it fell off? It was a little loose."

Austen closes his palm—snaps it shut, clenching his fist.

"It's just a ring, Austen," I say carefully, but really it isn't. I want to pry open his fingers pull the ring back. To wear it on a chain around my neck.

I'm about to say something else when a beam of light catches me, hitting the corner of my eye blunt and harsh.

"Stop!" someone is saying. Another voice joins in. A third. Figures dressed in blue emerge from nowhere, and before I know what's happening, someone is grabbing my arms and twisting them behind my back. Rough, calloused hands and the cold slap of metal against my wrists.

Austen is resisting. Letting his emotions get the best of him like an idiot. I try to catch his eye, but it's no use.

"Hey, let me go!" he insists, twisting out of the policeman's hold. The officer pushes him to the ground and yanks his hands behind his back.

"You're under arrest for trespassing and evidence tampering. Both of you," the officer says, shooting me a dirty look.

"You have the right to remain silent . . ."

10

Thea

THE PARTY IS a big one. I can feel the energy of it from the street, like smoke coming off a bonfire. I haven't actually been to a party before, but this one feels like a cliché. Something from a '90s teen movie. My stomach drops at the sight. "Not too late for a movie night, guys," I say to Austen and Marley as we climb out of the car. There's a late fall chill in the air, and I pull my jacket tighter across my chest, a shiver running over me.

Marley frowns and tucks a piece of pin-straight hair behind her ear. She's wearing a top from that new boutique she started working at a couple of weeks ago, Southern Moon, with a smocked bodice and god-awful puff sleeves that she's pushed down her shoulders, so her collarbone is on full display. She looks like a sorority pledge, and a peal of resentment rolls through me—not so much for Marley as for this outfit. This version of her.

"Thea, c'mon. You promised," she says. "It's one party. No one bites."

The lights from the house hit us here, but only just, and I watch the shadows playing across Marley and Austen's faces for a moment, searching for a crack in their resolve, finding nothing.

"Fine," I say, my shoulders dropping. She's right—I did promise— and the more optimistic version of myself who made that promise really did mean it. A few hours ago, I thought I could do it—come to this party, meet all the Moonies Marley can't stop talking about, and maybe be someone different for a few hours.

It's just . . . now that I'm actually here, that feels impossible. I want to make a run for it.

Marley smiles in relief and I wonder for the hundredth time why she was so insistent on bringing me along to a place where I don't fit, with people who wouldn't want me here anyway, when she could've just come with Austen. But there's no point in dissecting it now that I'm here, so instead I put my game face on as we trudge up the yard and into the front door where a gush of heat and light and sound swoops us up.

"Marley! Austen!" someone calls out from the living room, and I see Skylar Weller charging toward us, a red plastic cup sloshing beer onto her hand. She throws her arms around Marley, fat droplets of her drink splashing onto me. "Oh my God, *love* this on you," she says, pinching the shiny blue fabric of Marley's top between her fingers. "And Austen, I'm glad she was finally able to drag you to one of these things. I was beginning to think I'd never see you off the soccer field." Skylar winks at Austen and touches her hand to his bicep, and I catch a ripple of awkwardness passing over all three of them.

"And Thea too," Marley says as she tilts her head toward me. I think I catch something like a dare in her voice and I don't know whether to feel grateful or angry that she didn't let me disappear. Still, I give my best *happy-to-be-here* smile as Skylar's eyes flick over to me. I can feel her assessing me—the dark jeans and the black T-shirt tied into a knot at my waist—as if she herself doesn't look completely ridiculous, her hair curled and coiffed into a caricature of volume, her tiny frame in a dress covered with monstrous ruffles.

Sky is a year older than us, and her family is richer than the rest of Sherman Hill and Riverside combined. Last year, her parents bought a storefront on the square and opened Southern Moon. There were already clothing boutiques in Sherman Hill, but it has quickly become the most popular. It's where the cool girls work. Where the trends start. And Sky is the queen of it. Her mom's already training her to take over as manager and "Director of Brand Management"—whatever that means—when she graduates in the spring.

I know this, of course, because Marley told me. She can't seem to shut up about Sky these days, and when she looks at her, I can practically see the drool pooling at the corners of her mouth. The envy flashing in her eyes.

"Of course," Skylar says, a little tightly. She recovers quickly, though, her face softening back into a genuine smile. "All of you. Food and drinks are in the kitchen, and there's a fire in the pit out back with s'mores stuff. Marley, grab a drink and meet me on the deck. We're talking about the holiday dresses we just got in."

Something swells inside me at Skylar's tone, so familiar, like she and Marley have been close for years, not weeks, but I swallow it back and follow Marley and Austen to the kitchen. "What do you want to drink?" Austen asks, plucking two cups off the top and setting them on the counter. Marley is already pouring herself a club soda, dropping a wedge of lime into the bubbles. She doesn't drink much, but she doesn't like to call attention to it, just like she doesn't like to call attention to anything that sets her apart from the other Moonies.

I bite my lip, unsure, before my eyes settle on the dark rum bottle, fuller than the rest and sitting back slightly. "Rum and Coke," I tell him, then reach for the cup. "But I got it."

He shrugs, thinks better of the cup he's put out for himself, and grabs a beer from a six-pack in the fridge as I mix Coke with a generous pour of the rum.

"Are you guys gonna come to the deck?" Marley says, sipping from her drink.

"I'd rather stick a needle in my eye, actually," I say, regretting it instantly when I see Marley's shoulders drop. She looked so happy when we walked in, and suddenly I feel like a bitch for the way I've acted. Sullen, a child throwing a temper tantrum. Still, something about the thought of standing in a semicircle with the Moonies, trying to work up passable comments about $100 sweater dresses, makes me want to vomit.

"I'm gonna hang back too," Austen adds quickly, and then, "But you go, babe. Have fun. I'll catch up with you a little later." He kisses her and she plasters the smile back onto her face before slipping away into the crowd. Perfect Marley with her perfect mask.

Sometimes I hate myself for not having a better poker face—for not being able to fake it the way she does. Maybe if I were better at it, I'd belong here with her, instead of being the weird friend she has to drag around kicking and screaming.

"I hate these things," Austen says as soon as she rounds the corner, his eyes still on the spot where she was.

I snort out a laugh and take a swig of my drink. It's strong, but I'm glad for the burn down the back of my throat—the warmth settling like an ember in the pit of my stomach. "Skylar is . . . a lot. And I think she has a thing for you."

He shakes his head, so quick it's almost a wince, and there's a flush spreading quickly up his neck. "I know her from soccer, and she's Marley's boss. I have to be friendly," he says, a little defensively.

"We could've outvoted her, you know," I say, deciding to change the subject. "About this party. We could've stayed in like we always do."

Austen takes a pull from the neck of his bottle and sets it down. "Yeah, but she clearly wanted to come, and we always stay in. I felt like I owed her this."

He's right, we probably both owed her this after all the movie nights we've foisted upon her between the two of us. But there's something at the core of me that chafes against all of this. Everyone all dressed up and putting on a face. Marley's ridiculous puffy sleeve shirt from Southern Moon and the way I'm seeing more of those stupid clothes begin to fill her closet. So different from the all the pieces she's carefully curated through our countless trips to thrift shops and vintage stores.

I open my mouth, then close it again, unsure of exactly how to put it into words—the thing I can feel happening. Marley, disappearing into the role of pretty, popular, conventional girl. Letting people like Skylar Weller swallow up everything special and interesting about her.

Southern Moon has been good for Marley—I can see that, objectively—it's good money, she has new friends, and she's been happier these past few weeks than I've ever seen her before. But it's harder and harder not to be bitter about it. Especially when I can feel her pulling away from me—from all the pieces of our friendship that used to define it in favor of this place and these people.

"Besides . . . ," Austen continues, trailing off. He doesn't have to finish the sentence for me to fill in the blank. Our parents have been fighting lately—more than usual these past few months—and tonight before we left, it was hard *not* to detect the tension rumbling between them. The electric hum of resentment, drawn tight as a live wire ready to snap and electrocute us all. On nights like this, it's best to clear the area entirely.

Suddenly, I think of what might happen if Austen's dad and my mom actually pulled the trigger and got divorced. Would David take Austen back to Atlanta? The thought is enough to send panic coursing through me. Besides Marley, Austen is my oldest and closest friend. What would my life be like without him in it every day, especially with Marley pulling back?

I scratch reflexively at the thin scars along my forearm and shake my head, willing the thoughts away. "At least they have decent food," I offer, plucking a Chips Ahoy! cookie from a half-empty package.

There's a spark in Austen's eyes as he raises his eyebrows. "Go for four," he says, resting both hands flat on the counter.

"Here?" I say.

He pulls one shoulder up in a small shrug and gives me a look like *unless you're scared.*

"Fine," I say, smiling despite myself. "But you're playing too." I take out three more cookies and slide the case toward him. "Five for you."

"Five?" he argues.

"Your mouth is bigger than mine." I give him the same look he just gave me and watch him cave to it. He snatches five cookies out of the pack and we each hold our stacks up to prove we have the right number.

"Ready?" he asks.

"One second," I say, then use my free hand to take a gulp of my drink, feeling the alcohol unroll itself through my limbs. "Okay, now I'm ready."

We each shove the stack of cookies into our mouths, Austen struggling to get his teeth around them as I try not to laugh. My mouth goes dry and I have to resist the urge to cough, spewing chocolate chip cookie crumbs across the kitchen. I close my lips around the mouthful and concentrate on chewing and swallowing, feeling the stares as they aim themselves, slyly and not so slyly, from all directions. When I finish and hold my mouth open to Austen, he's still chewing. He smacks his hand against the counter in frustration, and when he's finally done he washes it all down with a sip of beer, shaking his head in defeat.

"That wasn't fair," he says, but we're both laughing now. The kind I can feel shaking me all the way through, that makes it hard to breathe.

"C'mon," I say, once I've gotten some control over myself. "Let's go outside. We can rematch with the marshmallows if you want. Sore loser."

Austen grabs his drink and follows me, the bottoms of our sneakers sticking to the beer-slick kitchen tile. We bob and weave through the thick knot of people in the living room, and out to the deck, where the night air hits me sharply, so I can feel the goose bumps rising up on my arms, even underneath the faux leather sleeves of my jacket.

I cast an eye toward the stairs that go off the deck and down to the backyard, where I can see the fierce, orange glow of the fire, just offshore of the small lake the house backs up to. But before I can take a step toward it, someone calls Austen's name and we both spin to face the familiar voice.

"Scott," Austen says, his face breaking out into a smile. "I'm so glad to see you, man. I didn't know you were in town."

"Just a couple of days, for fall break," he says. They do that guy greeting thing that's half handshake, half hug, and then Scott spots me hovering behind Austen's shoulder and smiles again.

"Thea," he says, swooping me up into an unexpected hug that nearly takes the breath out of me. It's only been a few months since Scott graduated and moved to South Carolina for school, but I'd almost forgotten how big he is—everything about him broad and sharp and Clark Kent handsome. When he was still in high school, he dwarfed the rest of the soccer team, even Austen, who's six two. "I'm surprised to see you here," he says, setting me back down so my feet touch the ground. "Doesn't seem like your scene."

I shrug. "Trying to branch out a little."

"How's Clemson?" Austen asks, taking a pull from his beer and shoving one hand deep into his pocket.

"It's great," Scott says. "The team is awesome. It's, like, a thousand times more intense, but so worth it. Tell me I'll see you there in a couple years."

Austen pulls his hand through his hair, his Adam's apple bobbing. "Yeah, maybe," he says, and I feel a strange sinking sensation I can't quite make sense of, like Austen's leaving me too, even though my plan is to leave for New York the day after graduation.

"Well," Scott says, sensing the emotional dip and course correcting smoothly. "How are things around here? How's the team?"

"Team's great. Undefeated so far, but we're up against Rollins next week, so who knows."

The guys talk soccer and I find my mind wandering, eyes roving the deck. I catch sight of Marley, Skylar, and a few others hovering by the railing, laughing about something, their faces cast with harsh shadows from the beam of the porch light. A few yards away from them, I spot a tray of tortilla chips and salsa laid out on an expensive-looking outdoor table. Eager for something to do besides stand around and look awkward, I head toward it, my drink clutched tightly in one hand.

"Seriously, Marley—I know you're nice to her, or whatever, but I told you to bring *Austen* tonight. Not his weird sister," Skylar says.

I freeze with my back to their group, my blood going cold.

"Don't be nasty, Sky," someone, not Marley, says. "Who cares if she's here?"

"I do," Sky goes on. "I have a right to enjoy my own party—you do too, Marley—and that girl throws the vibes way off. I mean, the way she looks at you? It's like she wants to wear your skin or something. I'm telling you, it's *creepy*."

There's a soft tinkle of laughter from the group and, finally, Marley speaks. But her voice doesn't sound like it usually does. Instead, it's soft, almost apologetic. "Thea's just quiet," she says. "She keeps to herself. Besides, we go way back. Our moms are tight. Can you please just be nice to her?"

"Fine. Anything for my protégé," Sky says, indulgently. "By the way, I meant to ask, did you see our latest post? You looked *so* hot, and the numbers are crazy."

I step back away from the table, feeling unsteady on my feet. Ahead of me is the sliding glass door that leads inside, the warm light from the living room filling it out, making it glow like a beacon. I focus on it, drowning everything else out. The world feels as if it's coming to me through water.

I need to get off this deck. Out of this house. Now.

When I'm a few feet away, an arm reaches out of nowhere and grabs me, pulling me back.

"Whoa, where do you think you're going?" Scott asks, crushing me to his side. Austen is still there, eyeing me curiously.

"Are you okay?" he asks, his eyebrows scrunching together.

I open my mouth, but nothing comes out. The last few minutes feel like a fever dream.

"I'm fine," I manage after a long moment. "I just . . . need to go home, I think. I don't feel well."

"Been there," Scott says before Austen can respond. "One drink too many, right? You probably just need some food on your stomach. Why don't we go down to the fire and make s'mores?"

I look at Austen, but he's got his gaze fixed across the deck at Marley. She has one arm up, waving in our direction, looking flushed and . . . happy?

"Austen," she says. Then, like it's an afterthought, "Thea. Come over here. I want y'all to meet some of my friends." Next to her, Skylar is eyeing us—eyeing me, really, her mouth open in a small *o*. I blink a few times before I realize what she must see. Scott Martin, with his arm around me.

The world refocuses itself. "Actually, s'mores sound great," I say, looking up toward Scott. He smiles, and I turn back to Austen. "I'll catch up with y'all in a bit."

"Are you sure?" he asks, the corner of his mouth tipped downwards. "I thought you were sick. I could drive you back, if you want."

For a brief second I consider it. I could let Austen drive me home. I could curl up in bed and replay the conversation I just overheard over and over again. Marley reducing our entire friendship to proximity. Skylar calling me creepy.

Or I could do something about it.

I shake my head. "I'm sure," I say, leaning further into Scott's side.

The fire pit isn't as popular as I'd expected, and when we get close, I know why. The air this close to the lake smells like half-rotted fish and stagnant water. Scott doesn't seem to mind, though. He grabs two metal skewers and the bag of marshmallows and passes me one of each. I spear mine and stick it straight into the fire, watching the marshmallow light up, its soft, white skin bubbling black and molten.

"So, you're one of those," Scott says, grinning slyly as he holds his own marshmallow a very safe three inches from the licking edge of the flame.

I take mine out, now charred practically to a crisp, and blow on it harshly, twirling the roasting stick to make sure it's all extinguished. "The burn is the best part," I say, only sounding a little sullen as I dig out two graham crackers from the box and a square of chocolate, smashing it all together in a burned, gooey, delicious mess.

He laughs, dipping his a little closer so it browns lightly and evenly. "How've you been?" he asks, awkward, but there's real interest there. I take a small, crumbling bite of the s'more.

"Alright," I say after a long, considered moment. He doesn't need the gritty details. "Stressed, but I guess most of us are. Junior year, y'know?"

He nods thoughtfully. "I hated being a junior," he says. "Just hold out for next year, though. It's awesome."

I frown slightly at the thought. All the parties and the pranks and the end-of-high-school slideshows that I won't have any place in because I didn't want a place in them. Because I didn't ever try to make friends that weren't Marley and Austen.

"Do you still draw?" Scott asks. I look at him, his face in the half-shadow, unreadable.

"I do," I say as a drop of chocolate plops onto the grass beside my shoe. "I didn't . . . realize you knew that about me."

Scott scratches the back of his neck. "Yeah," he says. "You did that piece for the art show last year. The one with the flowers. It was really good."

"Oh. Thanks." I clear my throat, remembering the piece. A bouquet of wilting flowers in a vase overflowing with water. I'd called it *Water, Water Everywhere*, which seemed clever at the time, but feels trite and overbearing now. "Tell me about college," I say. Suddenly, I feel desperate to know what the *after* is like. What life looks like when it isn't dictated by an eight to three PM class schedule and the overwhelming, suffocating stuckness of this place. These people.

Scott smiles and pulls his own marshmallow back from the fire, checking it for underdone spots before folding it into the middle of his own, much neater, s'more. "It's . . . hard," he says. "Like, all the shit that doesn't seem like it matters here suddenly does. Grades and showing up for practice on time and everything else."

I nod, doing my best imitation of sympathy. People like Scott—handsome, talented guys, even the ones hovering toward the bottom rung of middle-class—they can't fathom a life where those things have always mattered. Where the first chance might be the only one you get. And, for a second, I wonder what it must be like to live a life assuming the world will undress and lay itself bare before you, splayed and ready.

"I need another drink," I tell him, my voice rough. "You want anything?"

Scott pops the whole s'more into his mouth and talks around it. "I think I saw a cooler underneath the deck," he says, and then he's charging forward and I'm following.

Sure enough, there's a spare cooler tucked up underneath the deck, and Scott digs two ciders out from the ice, popping the top off one and handing it to me. I take a swig, cringing at the sweetness of it on my tongue and down my throat, like pure, fizzing sugar.

Scott leans his shoulder against one of the wooden support beams and looks at me. It's dark here, the only light falling from between the small gaps in the deck, but I can still make out the path of his eyes as they sweep up and down the length of my body.

"You're a cool girl, Thea," he says—whispers, really, and I can feel my mouth falling open in shock, which makes him laugh. He reaches out and tucks a loose curl behind my ear and the smoothness of the gesture surprises me, like he's done it before—like he's been waiting to do it for a long time. "I always had kind of a crush on you."

"Shut up," I say reflexively, and he laughs, unfazed.

He takes a step toward me, and it feels like all the air around me is sucked up by the vacuum of his presence. "Okay," he says and then, suddenly, he kisses me. I go stiff, my back pressed into the wooden beam. Paralyzed by the shock of it, even though this is exactly what I wanted to happen.

I swallow hard and force my lips to move. Force my tongue to engage with his. He tastes like chocolate.

I'd like to say that I've always had a thing for Scott—that this kiss is a real fairy tale, full-circle moment for me. But that would be a lie. The truth is a lot simpler, and a lot harsher. Scott Martin is objectively hot, and any one of the Moonies standing in a semicircle directly above me—Skylar included—would kill to be where I am right now.

I kiss Scott underneath the deck for a long time. I let him run his hands underneath the hem of my shirt. Let him cup my ass in full view of the others sitting out by the lake. And when he breaks the kiss and whispers "Let's find somewhere more private" against my mouth, I nod, my heart skipping. He grabs my hand and swivels his head, eyes catching on a door to our right, barely visible in the deep shadows.

I follow Scott as he twists the knob and steps inside. Wherever we are, it's dark, but I can hear the sounds of the party in the next room over. Scott turns on the flashlight on his phone, throwing a harsh beam of light across the space.

"Damn, they really are loaded," he whispers, letting the light rove across all the features of the Wellers' home gym. Rows upon rows of weights and resistance bands. Several workout machines that look vaguely like medieval torture devices.

The floor is laminate laid over with padded workout mats, and Scott shuts off the flashlight and pulls me down onto them. A squeak escapes my lips against my will, which makes him laugh.

"You're cute," he says. He's straddling me, his knees on either side of my hips. I can feel him, but I can't see him here in the dark. I'm glad for the cover, though. Otherwise, there'd be no way to hide how nervous I am.

With shaking fingers, I reach up and tug at the collar of his shirt. Scott follows my lead and yanks it off quickly.

"Straight down to business. I like it," he says, lowering himself over me so his bare chest brushes against my T-shirt.

"I haven't done this before," I tell him, unable to keep the tremble out of my voice.

I feel his hands on my face, his thumb brushing gently across my jawbone. "I'll go slow," he says.

I nod before I realize he can't see me, but he's already pulling the shirt up over my head and tossing it to the side. Then my bra. My jeans. My underwear. I hear him wrestling with his own jeans, and then I feel him on me again.

"Um, do you have a condom?" I manage, my mouth going dry at the word.

My heart is slamming against my ribcage. I want this, but it's happening so fast.

"Yeah." He slides off of me again, and after a few seconds, I hear the crinkling of a foil packet.

Scott repositions himself on top of me and, after a second that feels like a year, he grabs my hand and guides it to his erection. I gulp, unsure of what to do next. Finally, he covers my hand with his own and moves himself between my legs before pushing into me.

I don't know what I was expecting, but not the sharp pain that rips through me. Not the overwhelming sensation of fullness.

"You like that?" he asks, drawing himself out of me, then pushing in again. I squeeze my eyes closed and try to catch my breath. The music on the other side of the door sounds fuzzy and distorted.

"Yes," I manage, through gritted teeth.

"Say my name," he says, gathering a fistful of my hair and pulling hard.

"Scott."

"Say it again."

I say it again. And again. And again. I moan and I try, very hard, to sound like I'm enjoying myself until I feel him tense and shudder above me. Until his weight disappears and the cold air slides into the space where his body was. Scott turns the flashlight back on and pulls on his clothes.

"That was fun," he says, zipping up his jeans. He looks different now than he did at the beginning of the night. The harsh white light casts his cheekbones severely against the rest of his face, and there's a glint in his eyes that wasn't there before. Something smug and self-satisfied.

"Aren't you going to get dressed?"

I nod and reach for my shirt, aware suddenly that he can see my naked body.

"I should probably go back upstairs," he says. "I told some guys from the team I would find them later, and I want to catch them before they leave."

"Go ahead. I'll be up in a bit."

He nods and then, mercifully, he leaves me there. Once he's gone, I finish putting on my clothes and scoot myself back on the floor until my spine meets the cold, concrete wall, pulling my knees up to my chest.

I always assumed sex would make me feel different. Older and more world-wise. More self-assured. But I don't feel that way at all. If anything, I feel stupid.

Eventually, my phone starts to ding, then vibrate, so I shut it off and slide it away from me on the mat. Instead, I listen to the sounds of the party coming from behind the door. There's a little sliver of light at the bottom and I can see the shadow of feet going back and forth. People out there going about their lives. Having fun. Playing drinking games. I wonder if Marley has thought about me at all since I left the deck with Scott. If she thinks about me at all anymore, period. Or if she truly sees us as nothing but childhood friends.

The sound of the door Scott and I came through opening nearly makes me jump out of my skin. Another flashlight beam almost blinds me.

"Thea? There you are. Thank God."

Austen flips on the lights and I squint as the whole room is bathed in harsh fluorescence. His demeanor changes when he sees me.

"What happened?" he asks.

I mean to tell him that I'm fine. To unstick myself from the wall, say my phone died, and plaster on a smile, but the words get stuck in the back of my throat and instead I say, "Can you turn the lights back off, please?"

He does, but then I feel him right beside me in the darkness, sliding down the wall next to me and kicking his legs out in front of him.

"Thea?" He doesn't touch me, but I can still feel the heat coming off his body.

Without thinking, I reach out and grip his forearm. Suddenly, feeling like I need the tether. He inches closer and places his free hand over mine.

"Someone said they saw you come in here with Scott," he says.

"Yeah," I manage, and feel his whole body stiffen.

"Did he—"

"No," I cut him off before he has the chance to say it out loud. "He didn't. It was my choice. I wanted to."

Austen takes a deep breath, but none of the tension goes out of him. And why would it? Why would he understand? His first time with

Marley was probably planned days in advance. He probably lit candles, and scattered rose petals on the bed, and put on a curated playlist.

"I see," he says, a little awkwardly. "Well, I hope you're okay."

"I'm fine," I tell him, sounding stiff.

"Do you want me to call Marley?"

"No." The thought of talking about this with Marley just makes it worse somehow. "I'm okay, really. I just . . . needed a minute. But I'm fine now. I promise."

To prove it, I make myself stand up. I grab my phone from its spot on the mat and push it into the back pocket of my jeans.

Austen follows my lead, and we're just coming out from underneath the deck when I spot Marley over by the firepit with several of the Moonies whose names I've never bothered to learn, and Skylar, of course, whose eyes are fixed intently on the pair of us. When Marley spots me, she breaks into a smile and runs in my direction.

"Oh my God, Thea. Is it true? You and Scott?" She waggles her eyebrows suggestively, and I offer up a tiny nod and a smile. She squeals and wraps her arms around me, lifting me off my feet with surprising strength and spinning us around in a circle, but I don't feel anything at the gesture, or her excitement. Now I just wonder if it's fake.

"*Good* catch," she says, setting me down. "How was it?"

"It was great," I say, doing my best to sound earnest.

Marley squeals again and, behind her shoulder, I meet Austen's gaze. He has his eyebrows raised, his shoulders visibly tensed, but I shake my head. What he just saw stays between us.

Thea pulled Scott Martin. Simple as that.

Let them all choke on it.

CHAPTER

11

Marley

THE INTERROGATION ROOM at the station is freezing. I wonder if they keep it this way on purpose, to throw people off balance. To make them more uncomfortable than they already are. I wonder if the officers and the receptionists even notice it anymore, or if they've resigned themselves to it.

I snap the ponytail holder off my wrist and twist it in my fingers for the fifteenth time since I sat down. There's a one-way mirror across the room, and I try not to look at it, try not to think about who's watching me from behind that wall.

Finally, after what feels like a lifetime, the door opens and Romero steps in. She's remarkably polished for the middle of the night—makeup uncreased, like it's been freshly applied, blazer buttoned and wrinkle-free.

"Marley," she says with surprising warmth. She places her notebook and a water bottle on the table and takes a seat, the metal chair screeching as it's pushed back.

"I thought you might be thirsty," she slides the water across the table toward me. Her fingernails are clean and spare, no polish. The bright green on mine looks garish by comparison.

"Thanks," I say, but don't touch it. I've seen too many episodes of CSI. I know the water trick.

Detective Romero removes the pen from behind her ear and bites the cap off. There's something almost savage in the movement—the relish of it, like she's been aching to sink her teeth into something. "Now," she says, snapping the cap onto the back, "why don't we talk a bit about what happened tonight?"

She regards me gently, but the soft demeanor feels like a flimsy mask now.

"I know we shouldn't have been there," I say, glancing at the dented tabletop.

"I can't imagine how hard these past few days must've been for you. Losing anyone you know is tough—but losing a close friend? No one should have to deal with that."

My instinct is to glare at her, to snap that I don't need her pity or her patronizing tone. But the words don't find their way to me. Instead, all I can manage is a single nod.

"And I would guess that, to lose someone so important in such an unexpected way was even more difficult. You must've wanted answers. Some kind of closure."

I nod again.

"I'm not here to judge you, Marley. It's clear to us that what happened tonight wasn't malicious and we're not pursuing further legal action."

Now I look up and meet her eyes—they're slate gray and unreadable. "Really?" I ask. "You're dropping the charges?"

"We're dropping the charges," she says solemnly. "We just want to know why you were there."

I lean forward in my chair, fighting not to collapse in on myself. "Austen," I say after a few seconds. "He's convinced that you're going to pin the fires on Thea, and he wanted to see if there was anything you could've missed at the scene that would help her case. He asked for my help."

Romero takes a deep breath and scribbles something down in the notebook. "And what about you?"

"What about me?" I ask, bristling at the question, a ripple of fear running through me.

"Do you think we're trying to pin the fires on Thea too?"

"I don't know."

"Do you think she could've done them?"

I freeze, my heels digging into the floor, so I can feel the cement underneath the carpet. "We've already talked about this."

Romero narrows her eyes. "I'd like to talk about it again, if you don't mind. It's just us, this time. I suspect that will make things . . . easier."

I force myself to draw my shoulders up. To imagine that my spine is reinforcing itself with steel. "Why is that?"

She smiles. Just barely, but enough. "My partner Detective Henley is good at what he does. But he's . . . old school in his approach. Very traditional. I have a sneaking suspicion that this case is less cut and dried than he's inclined to believe."

There's a long moment of silence, which Romero spends studying whatever notes she's written in her book.

"Are you saying that you *don't* think Thea did this to herself?" I ask, tilting my head to the side.

"I'm saying I don't have enough information yet. Which is where you come in."

"I'm not sure what you want from me."

"The truth," Romero says. I can see the empathy bearing down on me in her gaze. Can feel the weight of it soaking through even those two words.

"I don't know the truth."

"Maybe not, but you knew Thea. You knew *her* truth."

I bite down on my lip. Hard. "I don't know about that anymore," I say carefully. "We stopped speaking months ago."

"People don't change who they are in a matter of months, Marley. They don't even do that in a matter of years. The Thea who went into that house was still the woman you knew. We might not know exactly how she got there, but we can start trying to untangle why."

There's a long beat of silence. "Tell me what you want to know," I say quietly.

Romero takes a deep breath and looks down at the notebook lying flat between us. Suddenly, I wish I was able to read upside down. To go through every line and see what she's been able to find. Is the truth buried in those scribbled lines?

"I want to know who she was," Romero says. "Really. I want to know the Thea that you did."

I sit back in my chair and push against the floor with the toe of my sneaker, so the two front legs rear back a few inches. "You can't," I say after a moment. "I mean, not without meeting her. I know how she must look to you—all the black clothes and the suicide attempt. I know she didn't have a whole lot of other friends in town. But Thea was . . . kind. She had a tendency to wall herself off, but the people she was close to, she loved hard."

"You mentioned that she'd originally planned to move to New York after high school, before she decided to stay and help with the boys. Did she intend to follow through with that plan once they started school at the end of this summer?"

"As far as I know," I tell her.

She nods thoughtfully. "And why do you think she wanted to leave Riverside so badly? You said that she walled herself off. I gather she didn't fit in so well with the folks around here."

I can see what Romero wants. She wants me to call you a loner. An outcast. A woman with no strong ties binding her to this community—one who wouldn't think twice about burning it down. But instead, I just raise my eyebrows and shrug tersely. "Would you want to stay in a place like this forever?"

She smiles a bit ruefully. "I'm from a small town too, Marley. I know exactly how hard they can be to get out of, especially if your resources are limited. I imagine that must've been extremely difficult for her. She was lucky to have a friend like you."

I press my lips together, willing the familiar guilt not to show on my face. There's a lot that Romero doesn't know about us—about our friendship—but I think she knows as well I do that you weren't lucky to have me.

She takes a slow, deep breath and holds my eyes with her own. "Tell me about the Instagram account."

I swallow hard and twine my fingers together in my lap. "We started it about a year and a half ago. Thea and I always loved thrifting and visiting vintage shops—it was like our thing. It started when we were kids, trying to make do with less spending money than our friends, and then it sort of took on a life of its own. Thea was always a better stylist than me. She just knew what was going to look good together. The Instagram account started on a whim one day when I was complaining about balancing my vintage pieces with the trendier stuff I have to wear at Southern Moon. She went into my closet and put together this outfit using pieces from both that was just perfect, so I took a picture and posted it. It got a ton of likes, and we thought it would be fun to see what else we could create. We didn't expect it to go anywhere at first, but when the account started to pick up a following, we decided to lean into it and see how far we could take it. Thea thought it might open some styling opportunities for her once she moved to New York, and it was good for my career, too. For Southern Moon. It helped us get our name out there."

"But you deactivated the account in May, didn't you? After your fight with Thea?"

"I did," I say, trying and failing not to sound defensive. I knew when I did it that it would upset you—all that work for the whole thing to go belly-up in days—but I didn't realize at the time what I was taking from you. Your whole portfolio. The greatest proof of your skill. The only real résumé you could've taken with you to New York.

It doesn't make a difference now, but I regret it all the same.

"Was the fight the reason you took down the account?"

I shrug. "Sort of," I say, choosing to skirt around the rest of the story. "What does that have to do with anything?"

"This fight between you and Thea—I'm curious, who was more upset with whom?"

"I—I don't know, me at first. Then her, I guess. I said something awful to her. She was mad at me for that, and then afterwards she was mad at me for cheating on Austen. I was upset with her for taking his side. She knew what I was going through, and she never reached out . . . even when things got really bad."

"You thought her loyalties were to you over Austen, then."

"I thought she'd always be there for me. No matter what. I was *always* there for her, through everything."

I'm getting heated now—can feel the anger rising in my voice, my muscles coiling with it. For a second, I'm almost able to convince myself, but it wasn't really like that, was it? I tried to be there for you when things got bad—after what happened with your boss James, and during your bad times—but there were times when I slipped, like when I took the manager job in Athens and again after Austen proposed.

Times when I was too wrapped up in my own world to be the friend you needed me to be.

Still, I would never have abandoned you if you were going through what I did. I would never have let you do that alone, no matter who else it hurt.

Romero studies me for a long moment, and I wonder what she sees.

"Why don't you tell me about her love life," she says.

I blink, trying to absorb the whiplash from the sudden change in subject. "I—what?"

"Her love life," she repeats, as though I might not have heard her. "Romantic relationships, sex. You said before that she never dated anyone. You're sure about that?"

I bite down on my lip hard as I consider the question and cast my mind back as far as I can. Scott Martin is the only person I've ever seen you show interest in. And even then, it was only that one night. You never wanted to talk about him after that. Not even when he dropped out of Clemson two years later and moved back to town to join the police force. Not even last winter at that bar in Sherman Hill, when you said you were going to the bathroom, and I found you ten minutes later sequestered in a dark corner with him.

"She didn't *date* anyone," I say. "At least, not anyone she told me about. She hooked up with Scott Martin once, but that was back in high school. And then, a few months ago, I saw her talking to him at a bar. But nothing else happened that I know of, and there hasn't been anyone else."

Romero raises her eyebrows at me, and I lower my gaze to the floor, a furious blush creeping across my neck and face. "Officer Martin?" she says, and I nod.

"Like I've been telling you, though, we didn't talk toward the end. She could've picked up with someone else I didn't know about."

"Do you think that's likely?"

It stings more than I'd like to admit, the fact that I can't answer this question. It feels like such a glaring omission in our friendship. Why *don't* I know more about your love life?

From the side of the room, a dull buzz picks up. The AC turning itself back on, as if it isn't already cold enough. "Not really," I say after a long moment. "Thea never seemed interested in dating anyone. I guess . . . I always sort of thought that maybe she was gay, and that was the reason she wanted to leave so badly."

"Really?" Romero asks, eyebrows lifting just enough to give away surprise. "And what made you think that?"

I chew on my lip. By now I can almost taste the blood pooling beneath the surface. "Just a hunch," I say quickly. "She never said anything to me, and I never said anything to her. I just . . . I don't know. I thought maybe, you know? Maybe that's why she never seemed interested in anyone here—not even Scott—not really. I figured she'd talk to me about it when she was ready."

Romero leans in an inch. All of her movements have become small and contained. "Tell me something, Marley. Did you and Thea ever—"

"No," I say firmly. "We were friends. Besides, I've been with Austen for eight years. Or I was."

Romero flicks her eyes to the table and back up again, and I know she's thinking about the night of May third. About how Austen and I ended—about what I did. I wonder if she wants to point out that clearly Austen was no obstacle when I didn't want him to be.

"No," I tell Romero again, squaring my shoulders and meeting her eyes.

"Alright," she concedes, backing off. "I believe you."

But I can see it behind her eyes that she doesn't. That she won't let go so easily.

"Tell me what you think," I say, leaning forward. "About Thea. About what happened to her."

"My opinion isn't the valuable one here."

"It is to me."

Romero eyes me, warily this time. All the softness gone. "I think that Thea had her fair share of secrets. I think she was in a great deal of pain that no one saw. I think she was smart and conflicted and that clearly things got away from her in the end."

"So, you *do* think she did this."

"I think she knew that house was going to burn down. Whether she set the fire herself, or intended to die inside, I'm still not sure."

"You think she followed someone in there? A person she was seeing or something?"

"I can't speculate about that," she answers stiffly. But I can tell by the flat tone of her voice that I'm onto something. That something is leading the police here and there's a reason she's asking me what I know about who you were seeing.

"Detective Romero—" I say, but she's already squaring her shoulders and positioning her pen.

"There's something else I'd like to talk to you about," she says and, without waiting for me to respond, she reaches into her pocket and fishes out a small plastic bag, placing it on the table between us.

"The ring," I say, swallowing hard. The metal looks duller here, under the fluorescence.

"Yes," she answers curtly. "Our team must've overlooked it at the scene, but you and Austen picked it up tonight, correct?"

"Austen found it."

"And you're sure it belonged to Thea?"

"I—yes. We bought them together. I have a matching one that's gold. But I stopped wearing it after our fight."

The corner of Romero's lips turns down into a slight frown. "And Thea continued to wear hers?"

I shrug. "Apparently."

She touches a finger to the ring underneath the plastic and traces the small circle contemplatively. "There's just one more thing," she says, her voice careful, like she's wading onto unsteady ground.

I shift my weight in the chair and tug the sleeves of my shirt over my hands. "Okay."

Detective Romero fixes her gaze on me. Her eyes are a soft, rich brown, like the soil after a steady rain. Suddenly, I'm struck by how sad she looks. "Did Thea have access to a gun?"

My blood runs cold. "A gun?" I repeat. Somehow, it's the last thing I expected her to ask. It takes a few seconds for the question to begin to make sense. "I—Austen's dad, David, had a gun when he lived there. But I always assumed he took it with him when he left. Thea hated guns."

Romero nods and writes my answer down in her notebook.

"Why? Was Thea shot?" I ask. My tongue feels dry and rough in my mouth.

"I can't discuss the details of an open investigation."

"If Thea was shot, she didn't do it to herself. She—she wouldn't have done that. Ever."

Romero blinks, glancing down at her notebook, then up at me again. Her face is blank, but I can see surprise in her eyes.

"What makes you say that?" she asks.

"I just know," I say. "I know her. Please, just tell me. Was she shot?"

"Thank you for your time, Marley. You can collect your things on the way out."

"Wait, I—"

Romero walks out and closes the door behind her, and I stay seated for a few seconds, trying to collect myself—to put a label to all the ways life has flipped on its head, then sideways—but there's too much to catalogue. I wonder if there's an identical room somewhere in this building where Austen is doing the same thing.

Why would she ask me about a gun?

Finally, I kick my chair back from the table, collect my things at the front, and push my way out into the night. The air is buzzing like neon with trapped, restless energy.

Austen isn't here, and my car is still parked over by the scene. My phone is sitting on my bed and there's no one I'd call anyway, except you. So I'm walking.

I take a deep breath and start down the road. It's only a couple of miles home, but the thought of going that distance with just my own thoughts feels like torture. I keep playing back the conversation in my head, trying to untangle each moment from the before and the after.

There's a guy, or a woman—the police seem convinced you were dating someone, but who? I rack my brain, trying to remember anything I can, but you never seemed to care about dating at all, even when we were teenagers. I always figured it was because you were on your way out of town and didn't want to form any unnecessary attachments. But I must've been wrong.

Still, who would you start seeing now? Milo and Finn are nearly four. They start pre-K in a week. You could've left and started your new life in New York.

I shove my hands into my pockets and walk faster, sinking into the weight of one more failure on my part. Friends are supposed to know these things about each other, but I always felt like you didn't want me to ask you about it, so I didn't push. Clearly, I should have.

I try to picture it—you with someone. Try to fill in the blank space in my mind with details. It couldn't have been Scott, could it? For a while, I thought that you and James must've had something going— you were completely devastated when he died—but he's been gone for almost a year, so it couldn't be him.

And then—the thing I can hardly stand to think about—the gun. Ever since we were kids you've hated guns. Been squeamish even at the sight of them. I never saw you paler than the time, years ago, when Austen casually asked if you'd like to go hunting with him and David.

Suddenly, there are footsteps behind me, pounding. Getting faster. I don't even spare a glance before I start to run.

"Marley, it's just me!" Austen calls out from behind me. I slow to a stop, breathing hard.

"Well, would it have killed you to say so?"

"Sorry," he mumbles, jogging toward me, looking genuinely ashamed.

Once he catches up, we walk in silence, Austen's hands clenched into fists, his eyes straight ahead while mine dart in every direction. Looking for something, I'm just not sure what.

"So?" I say once I've had enough.

"It was that Detective Henley guy again. He said they were dropping the charges. Just wanted to grill me about why we were there."

"What'd you tell him?"

He shrugs. "The truth," he says. "No reason to lie. What about you?"

I replay the whole conversation with Romero in my head, ending with that question about the gun. I think about telling Austen, but some primal instinct tells me not to. To keep this one close to my chest until I know what the hell is going on.

I breathe in through my nose and, on the wind, I catch the smell of manure. Bullshit, to be exact.

"The same," I tell him.

CHAPTER

12

Thea

I'M SEVENTEEN THE night things break, finally and for the last time, between Mom and David. It's a night in early spring, chilly with a dense fog hanging in the air, two months before Austen and I graduate high school.

They're in the kitchen making dinner, David chopping tomatoes for his homemade pico de gallo, Mom browning ground beef in a pan. They're singing along to a Spotify playlist of hits from ten years ago, making each other giggle, and Austen and I are in the living room with a rerun of *The Office* playing in the background. I've got a book on my lap and I'm struggling to keep my focus on the page, instead of on the screen. On the other side of the couch, Austen plays a game on his phone, the tip of his tongue poking out between his lips as he concentrates.

There's a kind of tenuous peace in the air. Mom and David aren't fighting. In fact, they seem happier than they have in a long time, since they found out about Mom's pregnancy. Happier than they have since I took a razor and sliced a shaky line up my forearm almost a year ago.

Mom's breathy singing voice drifts in over David's laugh. They're about to start loudly singing the chorus when the doorbell rings.

"Thea, could you get that?" Mom asks, and I don't think much of it as I close the book and cross the room to open the door.

The man across the threshold is short and husky. He looks older, mid-forties maybe, with sharp, green eyes that glimmer underneath the porch light, and thinning brown hair that's been slicked carefully away from his face.

"Sorry, can we help you?" I say, my eyes darting around, searching for a clipboard or a rolling suitcase of Cutco knives—something to explain his presence here. But instead, I spot the black leather sheath hooked to the waistband of the man's jeans, the metal handle of a gun sticking out.

"I'm here for Dahlia," he says. "Dahlia Wright."

"I—who are you?" I ask.

"Thea? Who is it?" David calls from the kitchen. The playlist cuts off, leaving only the soft chatter of the TV.

"I'm a friend," he says, placing his hand on the gun, a gesture that makes me shrink back. "I need to talk to her. She owes me some money."

I hear footsteps behind me, then David rounds the corner. I turn toward him and watch as he takes in the scene—my shocked face, and the gun at the man's waist.

"Thea," he says, his voice low and careful, like we've come face-to-face with a wild animal. "Go to your room. Take Austen."

Without another word, I back away until I'm outside the man's view, then I run to the living room and grab Austen's hand, pulling him up off the couch.

"What are you doing?" he asks, but he quiets when he sees the look on my face and follows me to my room. Once we're there, I crack the door and the two of us hover against the doorframe, listening.

"You came to my *house*?" Mom is saying now. She sounds hysterical. "My kids are here."

"You knew the consequences when you bought in, Dahlia. Now it's time to pay."

"I don't have the money right now," she says. "Please, Archie. I get paid in a week, I—"

"Enough, Dahlia. No more excuses. I get the money tonight, or the next time I come back, I won't be so nice. That's a pretty girl you've got. Looks just like you."

Mom shrieks with rage and my blood runs cold. Behind me, Austen places a protective hand on my shoulder and squeezes, as if he's ready to pull me away from the door and barricade it.

"Everyone, calm down," David says, his voice steady. "How much does she owe you, exactly?"

"Four grand."

"Jesus, Dahl," he spits. "Why didn't you tell me?"

"I thought I could handle it. I—"

"Never mind," David cuts in. "It doesn't matter now. Look, Archie—it's Archie, right? I've got some savings—enough to cover this. Why don't you come to the ATM with me?"

There's a grumble of acceptance from Archie. Then the sound of David's keys being taken off the ring. And, finally, the door closing behind them. Austen and I stay still for a long time after that, until I hear the thump of my mom's body hitting the floor, followed by a ragged sob. I close the door and press my back against it, feeling a tremor of fear move through me.

"What the fuck," I whisper, as Austen pulls his hand through his hair. He opens his mouth to speak, but no words come out. Instead, he wraps me into a hug, squeezing me tight enough to stop the shaking.

We stay in my room, not speaking, until we hear the front door opening again. The keys being hung back on the ring.

And then we get the screaming match of the century. David's voice booming all the way to the back of the house, reverberating across every corner. And my mother, sobbing. Groveling.

"I didn't think he would come here, David. I swear. I never thought—"

"We're *done*," he says. "I can't take this anymore. You just put our whole family at risk."

"Please, David. Don't do this," she says.

They carry on arguing, and Austen tugs me back toward the window in my room and opens it. We climb out and press our shoulders to the cool cement, facing each other, neither of us speaking for a while. We can still hear them, but it's fainter now. Familiar accusations resurfacing. Old wounds reopening.

"Do you think it's for real this time?" I ask.

He shrugs. "Maybe," he says. "I don't care, though. My dad can't make me leave. Not now that I'm eighteen. I'm not uprooting my life again."

I feel relieved, knowing he wouldn't leave, but it's not enough to cut the sharp edge of pain blooming in my chest.

"This is my fault," I say.

"No, it isn't."

"Yes, it is. She was better for a while, but she hasn't been the same since I did this." I hold up my arm and Austen looks away, like he always does when I mention my scar.

"She's an addict, Thea. She has been for years. Since way before . . . that."

I bite my tongue to keep from arguing. There's no point, since neither of us will ever concede.

"That man," I say finally. "With the gun."

"He's gone. He won't hurt you."

"He could come back."

"He won't," he says. "But even if he did, graduation is only two months away, and then you'll be in New York. We just have to make it until then."

"Right," I say, something in my chest deflating at the mention of New York. I think of leaving this place behind. Leaving Mom and, soon, the new baby with that man on the loose. Leaving them all and going to what? A city where no one knows me?

The thought sends a cold chill prickling along the back of my neck.

"It's all going to be okay," Austen says, and I almost want to laugh at how stubbornly, stupidly positive he is, but instead I find myself nodding along.

Tonight I'll choose to believe that he's right.

CHAPTER

13

Marley

"FUCK THIS WHOLE night," I mutter as Austen and I shamble onto the street where our childhood homes sit side by side. I've got no idea what time it is, but I can't imagine it's earlier than three AM. My feet are wet from a mud puddle I stepped into a mile back, and I can feel this town's dirt settling into every crack and crevice in my skin.

"Seconded," Austen says, pulling his hand through his hair. He looks every bit as exhausted as I feel.

Finally, we round the corner and the houses come into view, perched next to each other like twins against the curb. Mom bought them both at the same time, using almost all of the money she got from Dad's wrongful death settlement to ensure permanent housing for her and Dahlia. But, despite being roughly the same size and layout, I'm struck by the differences between them. The brightly colored children's toys littering Dahlia's yard; the small light hung up by the front door casting a warm, yellow glow. And, by contrast, Mom's house, with roofing tiles hanging askew and a brick missing from the front step. The way it sinks back into the darkness, like a shadow of itself. Ever since we were kids, Dahlia's house was always the one that felt more like a home.

Austen walks beside me, and I spot his car parked in front of Dahlia's place. I think, longingly, of our old apartment. The one he gets to drive back to tonight.

"Marley," Austen says when I slip the key into the lock. I turn to face him, my hip resting on the door. His eyes are on me, naked with vulnerability I haven't seen in months. "Tell me you don't want to be alone tonight either," he breathes.

I take a deep breath like I'm thinking, but it doesn't take a second to make the decision. I don't even need to say anything. He follows me inside the dark house, and I toss my keys on the table where Mom always throws hers. They aren't there, which means we're alone.

"I'm going to wash up," I tell him, ducking into the bathroom off the den. When the door closes, I hear him walking down the hall toward my room.

Before I can let myself think too much about it—Austen in my room, Austen spending the night—I strip off the dirty clothes and step under the weak stream of the shower, turning the water colder and colder until I'm shivering, my skin ghostly white and pricked all over with goose bumps. I scrub everywhere. Under my arms, the bottoms of my feet, my face, doing my best to erase all the traces of tonight from my body.

When I'm done, I stare at myself in the mirror. Even to myself, I look strange with no makeup. Pale and round and faint, like I could disappear right here right now, and no one would even notice. Maybe I could.

Austen is sitting on the edge of my bed, elbows resting on his knees. He starts at the sound of my door opening. He looks strange in this room, his size dwarfing everything around him. It's the first time I've really noticed how much muscle he's built since high school. How much like a man he looks now.

"Hey," he says, rubbing underneath his eyes. I can tell he's been crying again.

"Hey," I say, sitting next to him. It's been so long since I've been tentative with Austen, but I have no idea how to touch him or what to say. We may as well be strangers. I rest my head in the crook of his shoulder and he snakes his arm around my waist.

"Austen," I say quietly.

"Yes?" I can feel the vibrations of his voice against my cheek.

I almost don't say it—it won't change what's going to happen. I know that. Still, in this moment, I can't bring myself to deny the truth. "I can't lose you too."

He looks at me and I sit back away from him, just an inch or two. Enough to meet his eyes. There's something there I can't quite place. "You won't," he says, and there's one second—one thrilling, all-consuming, death-defying second—when I believe him.

And then he's kissing me, and it all feels so easy. Normal. Here and now, it's what it has always been. I know my way around him again. The pressure of his tongue on mine and the tilt of his hips. I run my fingers through his hair and pull him on top of me. Wrap my legs around him like I'm desperate to hold him to me. To keep him here.

And the thing is, I am.

* * *

Afterwards, I bury my face in his chest, pressing my lips to his skin as his breathing settles. We haven't said anything, and I know that we won't. Austen will leave and go back to the apartment sometime before dawn. Or maybe he'll go to Dahlia's, instead. He'll shower and put the coffee on and dress the twins and head to the gym for another day of training country club moms. We'll pretend like this never happened and go back to being exes. But for now, we're here, and the moment feels so familiar that it hurts.

It isn't, though, and I know that. For the first time since Austen stepped across the threshold, I've come up out of the fog and that thing I've been ignoring is back, right in front of me. The you-less-ness of life now.

I can feel the finality of it spreading through my veins like ice water. Suddenly, there's a sob forcing its way up my throat and out of my mouth. The ferocity of it surprises me—like a case of the hiccups I'm trying to swallow back, but can't. My body convulses, my nails digging into Austen's skin, legs winding their way through his.

Austen grips me, tighter than he ever has. Like he's trying to moor me to port in a storm. "I know," he says, grim and resigned. Then, softer. "I know, Marley."

I don't know how long we stay like this—me, sobbing into Austen's chest. Trying to force my mind around the concept of you not being around—before the door opens. It's my mom, standing at the threshold, looking bewildered.

"Oh," she says quietly, crossing the room. I've never felt more exposed than I do in this moment, but I can't make myself stop crying. Can't even bring myself to cover up. I don't care anymore.

Mom kneels by the bed and brushes the hair from my face as Austen pulls his T-shirt off the floor and deposits it in my lap. I tug it over my head, wiping my face with the hem. "Breathe," Mom tells me sternly, taking my cheeks in her cool hands so I can smell her lavender moisturizer. I do and, to my shock, it works. "Good. Again."

I keep breathing. In, out. In, out. Mom drops her hands and smooths them over her bare legs. I can smell the alcohol on her breath, but it's not as bad as it usually is.

She shoots a look at Austen. Something knowing, like the two share a secret or a burden. "It's late, Austen. You should go."

"Yes, ma'am," he says as his weight dips out of the bed. I watch him out of the corner of my eye, slipping quietly around the room as he pulls on his pants and shoes. "I'll see you later, Mar."

Mom and I are quiet until we hear the front door close, and then there's a collective exhale.

"I'm sorry," I say.

Mom pulls the hair back from her face. She's in her going-out clothes, her face meticulously made up, but there's cheap foundation collecting along the creases in her skin, making her look older than usual. "I was out at The Tavern when someone told me they'd seen you and Austen leaving the police station together."

"Oh."

There's a long beat of silence. "It's your business, and you don't have to tell me anything," she says. "But if there's something I *need* to know to protect you, I'm listening."

The words send a chill along my spine. Something she *needs* to know to protect me. Is she accusing me of being involved in all of this? Is she insinuating that *she* is capable of protecting me when she's never done it before?

"Austen wanted to go to the crime scene," I tell her. "The police think Thea is the arsonist and Austen wanted to go to where it happened and find something to disprove their theory. To clear her name. I said I'd help him."

"Marley . . . ," she says quietly, in disbelief.

"I know how stupid it sounds. But they didn't press charges and I had to see the place for myself. I couldn't stand the idea of not knowing what it was like there. I needed the closure, I think."

"Did you get it?" she asks.

I rankle at the question. "No," I tell her. "I don't know if there is closure for this."

"There isn't," she tells me quietly. "Trust me. Closure is a lie we tell ourselves to justify not moving on."

I bite down on the inside of my cheek until I can taste blood.

"Look, Marley, there's something I have to tell you, okay? Something I think you should know." She grabs my hand and squeezes it hard, then harder, until pain shoots through.

"Ow—"

"Thea was pregnant."

I freeze and stare at her. "What did you say?"

She lets go of my hand, but I feel like now I might need it as a tether. "They found a pregnancy test buried in the trash at her house. Dahlia swears she hasn't taken one in years. It was positive. Obviously, it . . . changes things."

"How—how . . ." I trail off, unable to put together a full thought, let alone a coherent sentence. I feel sick.

"Dahlia told me. She's processing a lot right now."

"I—who was the father?"

"They don't know. No one seems to know."

I pull my hands together and crack the knuckles on each of my fingers, each pop going through me like an electric shock. "Don't they have a DNA test for that?"

"They do, but the—" She swallows hard, and I know she's gearing up to say that word again. "The remains are too damaged, and she wasn't very far along. They can't pull DNA."

I nod as the gulf between you and me widens again. One more thing I didn't know.

"I don't understand," I say, more to myself than to Mom.

"You don't have any idea who the father could be, then?"

I turn back to her, slowly. "Does it *look* like I have any ideas?"

"I know it's a lot to deal with, Mar. I can imagine what you're going through."

"No," I snap. "You can't, actually. I just—I need to be alone right now, okay? Can you please go?"

Mom looks me over, wary, but she leaves, closing the door behind her.

I stare at it for a long time. That door. I'm waiting for the news to hit me, I think. Waiting for the drop. The pit in my stomach that means I've absorbed the information and started processing, but it just sits there, like a sheen of oil on water.

Pregnant. *You*. Pregnant.

Even with everything that happened, why in God's name didn't you tell me?

When I look down at my hands they're shaking. I tuck them underneath my arms and sit on the floor, but the shaking doesn't stop. Instead, it takes me over, leeches any warmth that's left from my bones, racks my brain inside my skull.

I think about what Romero told me—it was just hours ago now, but it feels like days.

People don't change who they are in a matter of months.

The thing is, though, if you were pregnant when you died, it means they were wrong. I didn't know you then.

Or maybe it means I never knew you at all.

14

Thea

"BE HONEST, DO I look like a vampire?" Marley turns to me from the driver's seat, her brow wrinkling in the early morning light. She flips down the mirror and checks her reflection for the third time in as many minutes. She does look pale, actually, and tired. There are bags under her eyes, not fully concealed by the heavy layer of foundation.

"Do you want to?" I ask, squinting at her. She's gone for a darker look than usual today—a black, swingy skirt that hits a few inches above the knee and a cropped maroon camisole on top. Even a swipe of dark lipstick that makes her mouth look dark and morose, like a slash. It's more my color palette than hers. She looks like Transylvania Barbie.

Marley frowns and flips the mirror back up, fixes her eyes on the empty road we're bumping down, tall summer grass on either side bending gently underneath the weight of the dew. Riverside doesn't have much going for it, but there is something about the mornings that makes it all feel *right*. Like the whole world has spun itself around the existence of this place. Cosmos pulling themselves together for the sole purpose of these sun-drenched fields. "I don't know," she says. "I felt like the undead when I woke up this morning. Thought maybe I should lean into it."

I nod, silently. Not awake enough yet to respond.

"Sorry again. I know I'm dragging you to work way early, I just—"

"You have to do inventory. I get it. Besides, I should be thanking you." I cut her off. My car is in the shop for the third time this year, and I'm trying very hard not to think about the cost of more repairs, so instead I watch as the main street of Riverside rises up in front of us. The strip of small, sagging storefronts. A Piggly Wiggly. A diner. Sun-faded decals on all the windows advertising long-gone sales.

The moment of morning glory disappears quickly, and I feel a ripple of resentment, at this place, and at Marley for leaving me here every day for brighter, shinier places like Athens and Sherman Hill, but I push it back. Refuse to let my bad mood get the best of me.

At the far edge of the main drag, the Chicken Shack sits back from the road. "Is your boss already here?" Marley asks, swinging her car into the parking lot and nodding at the gray sedan parked at an angle, toward the back of the lot.

"Uh, I don't know," I say, unbuckling my seat belt. Sure enough, though, it's his car in the lot, and even from here I can make out the slope of his head through the window.

Marley bites her lip. I can tell she's weighing her options. Leave me here in the empty parking lot with the weirdo sleeping in his car, or be late for work? I decide not to let her figure it out.

"You should go," I tell her, opening the door.

She raises an eyebrow, relieved, but trying not to show it. "Are you sure? I can stick around for a bit."

"I'm sure," I tell her. "He's harmless. Don't be late on my account."

"I'll text you when I'm headed your way tonight," she says. I pull my bag over my shoulder and wait until she's back on the road before I approach the car and knock softly on the passenger's side window.

Inside, James shoots bolt upright and lets out a yelp before he sees me and falls back against his seat, muscles slackening with relief.

"What the hell, Thea?" he says, reaching across the passenger's side to roll down the window—one of those old-fashioned crank kinds I didn't know still existed. "You scared the shit out of me. What time is it?"

"Seven ten," I say. "My car's in the shop and my ride had to go into work early. Did you sleep here?"

"Iris kicked me out," he says, reaching into the back seat for his baseball cap and tugging it down over his forehead. "She says I can come back when I get my shit together."

He pulls open the glove compartment and snatches a pack of cigarettes out. A lighter, too. "Smoke?" he asks, holding it out to me.

I wrinkle my nose. "No, thanks," I say. "But I'll sit with you."

James shrugs and nods toward the passenger seat, cranking his own window down with his free hand. "It's so fuckin' stupid," he mutters, sticking a cigarette between his lips so it bobs up and down as he speaks. "We used to never fight. About anything. Now it's all *the dishes have been sittin' there all day* and *when are you gonna get out and mow the grass* and *why don't you get a second job.*"

"I'm sorry," I say, fingers curling into my bag, eyes fixed ahead on the parking lot. "That sucks."

"And the worst part is, she's right. I am a lazy piece of shit."

"No, you're not. I've seen you at work. She doesn't tell you that, does she?"

"She doesn't need to. I can see that it's what she thinks. Besides, once we have the baby, it's just gonna get worse. Everything'll be harder than it already is."

"You don't know that," I say. James shoots me a look and lights his cigarette.

"No offense, but what the hell do you know?"

"I'm just trying to help."

"Okay, well, learn a lesson from someone older and wiser," he says, exhaling smoke. "It doesn't get better. Just messier."

I press my lips together. Keep quiet. I'm afraid to look at him—afraid of what I'll find there if I do. That look in his eyes, like a scream only I can recognize. Brokenness that matches my own. That feels like two puzzle pieces snapping into place.

That's exactly what I'm afraid of, I want to say, but I can't make myself form the words.

James reaches across the space between us and jostles my shoulder. When I venture a glance, he's smiling.

"Fucker," I say, but I'm smiling too.

"Wish I was lying," he says. The tension's gone out of his voice, but not the darkness. I can still feel that lurking somewhere between us. "So, how're things with you? The great escape plan still proceeding at pace?"

It takes me a second to work out what he's talking about. "Oh, New York? Yeah, it's . . . I mean, I still have a while before I go. The twins don't start pre-K until next fall."

"Why do you have to wait for that, again?"

"Um, well . . . at first I was just going to stay until they were a year old. But then things were still so rocky, and the money was really tight, and Mom couldn't afford day care, so I decided to push it to two years. And then it just sort of . . . went on like that for a while. When the twins are able to start school, childcare will be a lot easier, and they won't need me so much anymore."

James takes a drag from his cigarette and tosses it out the window with a flick of his wrist. "Bullshit," he says.

"Huh?"

"That's bullshit. There will always be a reason not to go. Your family isn't holding you back. *You're* holding you back."

"You don't even know my family."

"Has your mom ever told you that you need to wait until the twins start school?"

I open my mouth to speak, but nothing comes out. My gut says yes, of course, but now that I'm actually thinking about it, I realize I can't call one single instance to mind.

Still, it doesn't matter. She never had to say anything. It was clear in the way she looked at me after David left—clear in the defeated hunch of her shoulders. In the liquor bottles I found stashed underneath her bed one night a few weeks after the twins were born. The scratch-offs and lottery tickets that crowd the kitchen table, taking up space beside overdue bills. The debt collectors hovering constantly at the edges of our lives. Mom needs me. Milo and Finn need me.

"You're making my point for me, kid," he says after a few seconds of silence. "Look, you're lucky. You've actually *got* a family, for one thing. And for another, they're not actively trying to undermine you. You should take advantage of it. Actually, like, *go* to New York."

I raise my eyebrow and hunch down in my seat, resting my feet on the dashboard. "You don't know what you're talking about."

"Yeah, well. Whatever you've got, it's better than no family at all."

James pulls another cigarette from the pack and lights it. We sit in silence and I watch the curls of smoke dissipating into nothing in the space between us. Then I feel it again. The mood shifting back. Blackness that had tucked itself into the corners of our space for a few moments unfolding itself across him.

"What's your family like?" I say finally. James sighs, some of the restless energy draining off of him.

"My older sister and I bounced around in foster care for most of our lives," he says. "For a long time—until I met my fiancée Iris, actually—she was all I had."

"Jesus," I say, pointlessly. He keeps going.

"When we were kids, she was very protective of me. But then, as soon as she turned eighteen, she split. She wasn't alright in the head. The stuff we went through—it broke her. Now she comes around once in a blue moon to check in. But for the most part, I never have any idea where she is or what she's doing. If she's even fucking alive, really."

Without thinking, I reach across the space and put my hand on his wrist. He looks down at it, then flicks his eyes up to me.

"Sorry," he says, smiling a wry smile. "I didn't mean to, like, trauma dump or whatever."

"I'm really fucking sorry."

He doesn't say anything, just flips his hand over and twines his fingers through my own.

I take a deep breath. "My mom gambles. And drinks—but mostly, she gambles. That's why I had to stay. Why there's never enough money. A few years ago, she got in too deep. That's when my stepdad left. He bailed her out, but he couldn't take it anymore, and ever since then, I feel like it's on me to keep everything together."

"Christ, Thea."

"My brothers deserve to be protected. And, if I'm honest, I don't trust my mother to do it herself. I never have. My stepbrother—ex-stepbrother, I guess—he helps too. But he's not there like I am. Not every day. He doesn't really understand how bad the gambling is. That we're perpetually in debt. It's mostly manageable, though, as long as we don't take on any loans, which I'm worried my mom will do once I leave."

James squeezes my hand tight and, for a long time, we just sit there. The silence between us thick with understanding. The weight of his hand in mine is like an anchor. The first real one I've had in years.

At some point, I realize how hard we're gripping each other's hands. So tightly that our knuckles have gone white, and there are little crescent moon shapes where my fingernails have dug into his skin. James seems to notice at the same time. He looks at me.

"Thea," he says, "I'm really glad we're friends."

I nod. "Me too."

And, for a few seconds, the darkness shrinks itself back just enough that we can both breathe.

CHAPTER

15

Marley

I CHECK MY REFLECTION one more time in the flip-down mirror in my car. It's bad, but not as bad as it could be, considering. The attempt to cover the dark circles under my eyes didn't do much, but at least I'm having a good hair day.

Reluctantly, I get out of the car and smooth the sundress over my thighs, staring at the sign for Southern Moon like it's a snake that may come to life and bite me.

"Marley?"

I jump at the sound of my name, and a head pops up from the SUV a few spots down. Wide, gray eyes and chestnut brown hair cascading past slim shoulders.

"Britt," I say, dipping my head in acknowledgment as I grab my purse from the back seat and sling it over my shoulder. It's not like I didn't expect her to be on shift—she's my assistant manager, after all— but a little part of me was hoping, anyway.

"God, Mar," she says, scrambling out of her car and slamming the door closed behind her. "How on earth are you doing? I haven't seen you since . . . you know."

I try for a faint smile, but I can't hold it more than a second. Even here in Athens, thirty miles away from Riverside, the news about the arsonist who died in her own fire has spread. Usually, Athens is bustling with its own energy, so big and loud that it swallows everything else, but until the undergrads come back in a few weeks, things are slow and there's nothing much to talk about besides *this*.

"I'm holding up," I tell her. Suddenly, I wish I was a floor worker again, instead of a manager. That way I could spend my shift in the back, stickering merchandise or floating around the store folding sweaters, instead of working the cash register, trying to upsell the new necklaces we just got in.

Britt tilts her head, soft curls bouncing, and eyes me pitifully. "Poor thing," she says, her delicate mouth turning down in a frown. "You look like death. You must be totally wrecked. Sorry I didn't make it to the funeral, by the way. I meant to, I just couldn't deal with it, you know? Too much bad energy."

"I get it, Britt," I say, slamming my car door behind me.

"Honestly, I'm surprised you're even in today." Britt hitches her signature Chanel bag over her shoulder. "If I were you, I'd ask for, like, a month off just to process."

I grit my teeth and nod vacantly. I'm lucky to have my job. Girls like me—River Rats, if you want to be nasty about it—don't usually get jobs at Southern Moon, let alone become managers. In fact, the time you spent serving fried chicken out a drive-thru window was a lot more on brand. But I have the "right look," so Sky's mother hired me on a trial basis when I was sixteen, not long after the flagship store in Sherman Hill opened. Since then, I've fought my way through the ranks tooth and nail. I used my paycheck to buy the clothes, and even nicer brands too, when I could afford them. I studied Sky—one year my senior—and her friends carefully. Learned to talk like them. Act like them. Even think like them. I practiced until I was a near-perfect mimic. Until I could play the role almost better than they could. I started Vintage Doll with you and had more followers than all of the other girls put together, Sky included.

Slowly, painstakingly, I turned myself into Sky's right-hand woman. Worked myself into the Southern Moon operation so thoroughly that, as the brand took off, they had no choice but to bring me along. I became the manager of the Athens location—which brings in more money than the original store. On top of that, the Vintage Doll account brought in media features and collaboration opportunities and influencer attention. Our clothes became a fixture on #bamarush outfit of the day videos.

Sky is technically the brand's face, but we both know it's only because her parents own it. *I* made Southern Moon what it is. I came up with the ideas for our most successful ad campaigns and put out the biggest fires. While Sky played Businesswoman Barbie, I kept things running. Kept them thriving.

I worked my ass off to make myself fit and, for a few years, I did more than that. I excelled. At least, right up until I torpedoed my reputation and tarnished the Southern Moon brand along with it.

I push my way into the store, Britt following at my heels, and the bell above the door lets out a high, delicate *ding*. It always makes me think of those women in the matching coral skirt suits at the Sherman Hill country club—the ones who organize charity luncheons and loop thick strands of pearls around their necks. Pretty much all of Sherman Hill has that vibe—tiny, elegant storefronts dotting the square, all lit up with tea lights. Lovingly restored hardwood floors and exposed brick walls and hand-lettered sandwich boards out front announcing sales and discounts. Go out a few blocks and the houses become classic brick mansions framed by giant magnolias, or white farmhouses with gabled roofs and purple hydrangeas spilling over the front steps where Atlanta-based film crews like to set up shop.

Riverside is only a few miles up the road, across a small, smelly excuse for a river, but it feels like a different world. Ever since the accident that killed my father—the one that drove the production plant employing most of the town into bankruptcy—it's become a broken, distorted reflection of itself. A ghost town dotted with abandoned properties and overgrown farmland, and those of us unlucky enough to have nowhere else to go.

They don't call us River Rats for nothing.

"Sky!" Britt sings, breaking me out of my thoughts. She shakes out her hair and a heavy cloud of perfume nearly suffocates me.

Sky is at the register, ringing up a customer with a long line of others trailing behind.

"Hi, ladies," she says. Sweet, like always, but with that edge of panic that only people who know her can detect. The one that means *the store is swamped, get to work ASAP.*

Britt and I clock in quickly and go to work the floor, where I catch snippets of conversations floating through the air. Two women standing by the shoes, their heads bent together.

"Riverside—you know, that little town just outside Sherman Hill. That's where all those houses got burned."

"Well, thank God she never ventured over here. Can you imagine?"

"We're lucky she got trapped inside one before she ever got the chance."

"Amen to that."

I find Carrie Jones, a freshman at UGA and an Athens local, turning over dressing rooms and looking a little frazzled.

"Carrie," I say, grabbing clothes off the rack labeled *No Thank You!* that we keep just outside.

"Oh, thank God, Marley. I'm so happy to see you. It's been crazy all morning." She leans in conspiratorially. "And the heat's driven everyone insane, I think, so watch your back."

I smile, just a little. My favorite part of being a manager has always been the college students I get to train and manage. I didn't expect it. After all, they're almost always from Sherman Hill or somewhere like it—pretty, rich Georgia peaches like Sky or Britt who never considered the possibility that they *wouldn't* land a gig like this. Girls with an Instagram following large enough to serve as free marketing for the store. I should hate them. But the way they look at me—like they want to be *me*—it's why I've been so meticulous about shaping myself into someone they could respect. The one with the formidable platform of her own. The one who always had their backs. Even now, after everything, I know they still prefer me over Sky. It's one of my few remaining points of pride.

"Thanks for the heads-up," I say, folding the stack of unruly clothes over my forearm and tilting my head toward the break room. "Now you go clock out. I've got this."

I always lied to you about work. I told you that I hated Southern Moon and everyone who worked here. That the only good stores were vintage stores and that I only used the clothes on the Instagram so that I could stay in Sky's good graces and keep my paycheck. The truth is, though, it's the only place where I actually get to be someone important. Where my ideas really mean something. I wouldn't have worked so hard at something I really hated.

When I go to put the clothes back in their correct place, I see why Carrie and Sky are panicked. The store is more packed than it usually is this time of year. Back-to-school shopping for the local high school students, probably. I pinch the bridge of my nose to stave off the headache I can already feel starting to edge in.

"Excuse me, miss. Do you have this in yellow?" a girl says, popping out from behind the nearest clothing rack so fast I almost jump. She's too young for this store—ten, maybe eleven—but she's looking up at me with the giant, sparkling puppy-dog eyes of someone who only sees a pretty woman in a pretty dress and needs no other information to admire her.

"I'm sorry. We only have the pink and the green," I say, nodding to the shirt in her hand. "You should try the green, though. It'll look good with your hair."

The girl nods fervently and skips off, the shirt clutched in her hand like a trophy now. I watch her go, remembering when I was like that. Young and in love with the idea of growing up to be one of *them*—the sparkly, pretty women who I thought owned the world.

"Trina, sweetheart. You can't fit in this." It's the girl's mom. She grabs the shirt out of the girl's hand and holds it up, her nose wrinkling in disapproval. "It's a small. And the style won't flatter you at all. You got your daddy's shoulders. You really shouldn't pull sleeveless things."

The girl, Trina, looks crestfallen. Someone else tries to get my attention, but it's too late, I'm already walking.

"Excuse me," I say, plastering on the *Steel Magnolias* smile I perfected my first week working retail. "Can I help y'all find something?"

"We're fine," Trina's mother says.

"I'd be happy to pull the green one for Trina. I think it would look great on her."

There's a flash of anger in the woman's eyes. Stifled as quickly as it came on. Everything about her screams *money*. The diamonds studding her ears and the tasteful dress tapering across her hips, disguising the thickness of her middle. But most of all it's this—the way she holds her anger in tight control.

When I was a kid, after my mom came back, my anger came out in messy spurts. Screaming fits and tantrums and hours spent punching pillows. Kicking at the bed frame again and again until my feet were bruised. But when I started working here—when I decided that I wanted to pass myself off as one of them—it was the first thing I learned. How to hone the anger. To sharpen it and release it in needle-fine doses, like poison. How to make it work for you, not against you.

I'd almost convinced myself that I'd mastered the skill until this summer. Now, the urge to lash out consumes me.

"We're fine, *really*," she says through a smile before looking down at her daughter.

"Then what about this?" I say, lifting a shirt off the nearest rack. It's giant and shapeless, with some rhinestone detailing along the hem. I'm not even sure why it's in the store, honestly, but Trina is looking at it like it's gold. I know it's only because I'm recommending it.

Trina's mom purses her lips. I've put her in a bad spot, and we both know it. "Fine, she can try it on," she says, biting the end off each word just a little too quickly.

"I'll get Trina set up in a fitting room," I say, and head toward the back of the store with the girl following at my heels. On my way there I slip the green shirt off its hanger and ball it up underneath the big shapeless one, winking at Trina as she ducks into the little, curtained-off section where the words DRESSING AREA are painted on the wall in pink.

I'm back at the front, folding cardigans on the display table, when Britt sidles up next to me. "Watch out," she mutters. "Angry Karen heading this way."

I flick my eyes up and find Trina's mother barreling toward us. She's clutching the green top in her hands, nostrils flaring so wide I can see them from across the store.

"Yes, hello—*ma'am*," she says, catching my eye. I take a deep breath.

"Save yourself," I tell Britt, bumping her in the shoulder. She follows my advice quickly, heels clicking over to the belt rack in record time. I plaster on another smile and cock my head to the side. "What's the matter, ma'am? Would you like me to pull another size?"

"I specifically told you we *wouldn't* like to try this on." She's holding the limp green fabric out to me.

I should apologize—I know that, but I can't bring myself to. Not when I catch sight of Trina hovering in her mother's shadow. "Your daughter clearly wanted to," I say. "I don't see what the harm there is in just trying it on."

"The harm is that I said *no*, and you deliberately ignored me. I'm Trina's mother. I get to decide what she tries on and what she doesn't."

"Shouldn't your daughter have some say in that as well?"

Shock ripples over the woman's features and I get a perverse satisfaction at seeing it there. She's not used to being spoken to like this. "Excuse me? Are you accusing me of being a bad parent?"

I take a small step forward. Realize for the first time that we're starting to draw attention and that I don't actually care. Suddenly a wave of hate comes over me—for this woman and all the women like her. For Southern Moon and everyone here. I tried for a long time, but the thing is, I'm *not* one of them. I never will be. I'll always be a River Rat.

"All I'm saying is that your daughter is beautiful, and I think it's important that a cow like you not keep her from thinking so."

Someone grabs my arm hard and yanks me back as a gasp rolls through the crowd of onlookers. Sky darts out from behind the register and steps between me and the woman who looks like she's about to throw a punch. It's the fastest I've ever seen her move.

"Break room," Britt snaps, looping her arm through mine and pulling me out of the thickening crowd of onlookers and into the break room where Carrie's still gathering her things.

"What happened?" she says as I take a seat at the table. Britt paces back and forth, casting anxious glances at the door.

Britt gives Carrie a quick rundown and Carrie lets out a sharp laugh before covering her mouth with her hand. It makes me smirk, in spite of everything.

"Sounds like she deserved it," she says.

Britt throws her a poisonous look and Carrie bows her head contritely.

"I don't know what came over me," I say, but I do. It was anger, plain and simple. I have too much, and it's coming out sideways. I'm losing my control—or maybe I lost it a long time ago.

Britt stops pacing and rubs her hands nervously down her jeans. "What the hell was that, Marley? You know Sky's been looking for reasons ever since . . ." She trails off, but she doesn't have to finish the sentence. Sky's been looking for reasons to fire me all summer—ever since I became the town pariah and deleted the Instagram account that gave me clout. Ever since it became clear that I am no longer an asset to the Southern Moon brand.

Carrie takes a glass from the cabinet, fills it with tap water, and sets it in front of me. "I have a Xanax, if you want it," she says.

"No, thanks, though," I say. My adrenaline is still pumping, buzzing like a faint electrical current underneath my skin. At first, I wonder why both of them are still here, but then I think maybe it's not kindness, just curiosity. I'm a wild thing in their space, and now that I've bared my teeth, they can't look away. "Carrie, you should go home. And Britt, you should go back out there. I'm sure Sky could use the help tamping down the chaos. I promise, I'll stay here."

Britt eyes me warily and I can see Carrie's eyes bouncing between us, trying to read the situation. Eventually, Britt stalks off without a word. Carrie sits down next to me and puts her hand over mine, squeezing gently.

"Look," she says. "I know we haven't talked so much this past summer, but I'm really sorry about what happened to your friend. If I were you, I'd be a wreck. I'd have clocked that woman."

I let out a short laugh. "Thanks," I say. "I kind of wish I had."

"Stay in touch, okay?" She pushes her way back from the table and pulls her car keys from her purse. I nod, but we both know she doesn't really mean it. Once Carrie walks out this door, she'll go back to the calm, comfortable life she's always had, and I'll go back to mine—the life I was always supposed to have in Riverside, before I started believing it could be different. Without this boutique, I'm nothing to people like her.

Once she's gone, I stare at the door, feeling a bit like a prisoner awaiting execution. I want to regret what I did out there, but I can't seem to make myself feel it. It's the kind of antiestablishment, rage-against-the-machine thing you would've been proud of.

Still, there's dread coursing through me when I think about what my life will look like without this place.

Since May third—since the Vintage Whore Instagram account burst onto the scene—Southern Moon hasn't been the same. Despite Sky's best efforts, she hasn't found cause to fire me, but she's scaled my responsibilities way back and removed any trace of me from social media in a thinly veiled attempt to get me to quit.

I couldn't bring myself to do it, though. Up until today, a little part of me thought I could work my way back.

Eventually, Sky pushes her way in, her face blank. She pulls out the chair across the table and sits down, her small hands clasped together on the tabletop. I know that Sky is technically my boss, but for most of the time I've been here it hasn't felt that way. She has been my friend, my enemy, and everything I ever wanted to be, all wrapped into one, but I've never *really* felt like she had authority over me.

Now, though, she looks deadly serious. Almost managerial underneath the harsh lights.

"Mrs. Winterson is getting $200 in store credit. The money will be taken out of your paycheck."

"Okay, fine."

"You're also fired."

"I know."

Sky releases a breath, and her posture relaxes. I don't think she's ever fired anyone before. In fact, it was me who handled firings on the rare occasions we needed to let someone go.

"I'm sorry it all had to happen this way," she says. "You can go ahead and grab your stuff. I'll clock you out."

"Okay," I say, pushing myself up to standing, the chair grating behind me. For a split second, it's not my career I'm worried about. It's Austen. Now that we aren't together anymore—now that Sky won't have to face me at work—will she go after him, like I've always known she wanted to?

"And, Marley?" she pauses, her lips pressed into a grim line. "Go out the back."

16

Thea

"D O YOU PROMISE?" Finn says—squeaks, really—pulling his comforter up beneath his chin and staring at me with big brown eyes that reflect back the glow of the nightlight. He can't quite say his Rs yet, so *promise* comes out more like *pwomise*.

I smile and reach down to brush the wispy hair from his eyes, fighting the urge wrap my little brother in my arms and snuggle him close. "I promise." I glance up at the top bunk, where Milo is looking at me too, his eyes wide with fear he'd never admit to. "No monsters," I say. Then, just to show them I really mean it, I open the closet one more time and make a show of poking my head inside.

I can feel the held breath in the room. The two sets of eyes watching me carefully, and even though I know the responsible thing to do would be to step back out and shut the closet door behind me—assure them that there's nothing inside—I can't resist the urge to have a bit of fun. So instead, I pretend like I'm being jerked inside by a force larger than myself. Finn yelps in surprise as I disappear into the closet and I make a show of stomping my feet and rustling the clothes around.

"Now listen, Mr. Monster," I say, loud enough that the boys can hear me around the door. "Playtime is over. It's time for *all of us* to get some sleep. I know you want to make new friends, but you can meet them another time, okay? Thanks for understanding." I do a bit more stomping and rustling for good measure before jumping out and shutting the door behind me to the sound of the boys giggling.

"Whew," I say, brushing off my hands and pretending to wipe sweat from my forehead. "Sorry about that. Mr. Monster has politely agreed to come back and visit another time. He's very nice, actually. He just has his days and nights mixed up."

I kiss the boys on the forehead one more time and make sure they're both snuggled in tight before backing out of the bedroom and closing the door.

"Any issues getting them down?" Mom asks from her spot at the kitchen table. She's nursing a cup of coffee, her body hunched over the hodgepodge of bills and monthly statements piled up in front of her. We're nearing the end of the month, which means she's probably taking stock of just how far behind we are.

I could ask her about it, but tonight I don't have the energy, so instead I just shrug. "No," I say, eyeing the red OVERDUE stamp on an envelope to her left.

"Thank you." She stands up, crossing the distance to wrap me in a tight hug. "I don't know what I'd do without your help."

"Of course," I say, because what else can I say, after all this time?

Mom squeezes me to her and, for a moment, I decide to let myself be held. I press my cheek into the soft fabric of her robe and listen to the beat of her heart. Feel the stillness around us. A moment of peace in a life that always seems like it's seconds from flying off the rails.

"Do you want to watch a movie or something?" she asks, pulling back. "I can't do any more math tonight."

"Sure," I say, though what I'd really like to do is crash. We're both too tired to hold a conversation as we pop the popcorn, grab two White Claws from the fridge, and settle on the couch, me with my sketchbook and Mom with her phone.

"There's that new romantic comedy," she says, pointing the remote at the Netflix logo on the screen.

"Fine by me," I manage, suppressing a yawn. It's pathetic, really, how tired I am. It's barely even dark out, but dealing with the twins is draining, and I know I'll go to bed tonight worried about the money, which makes me even more tired.

Mom starts the movie and I squash myself into the corner of the couch, tucking my feet up underneath me. Once we settle in, she takes out her phone and angles the screen away from me even though I know, instinctively, that she's playing poker.

I try not to think about it as I start a new sketch—this one is of the imaginary monster in the boys' closet. I give him broad, hairy shoulders and gigantic, fang-like teeth, then add a pair of thick glasses and a small tie to make him less threatening. He looks like a werewolf with a day job in accounting.

We're only thirty minutes into the movie when my phone vibrates in my back pocket. I take it out and glance at the screen, which is flashing a text from an unknown number. Two words.

It's me.

I glance at Mom, but she's fixated on her game, so I slide my thumb across screen as casually as I can and shoot back *hey*. I've only given my number to one person this summer, but I didn't expect him to use it. Not unless something came up at work.

James's response comes fast—*wanna hang? I can pick you up.*

I bite down on my lip and stare at the words, my thumb hovering over the keyboard.

Sure, I send back, before I can overthink it.

Cool. Send me your address.

I send my address and tell him to park a few houses up. *Give me 15 minutes,* I tell him, sliding my phone back into my pocket.

"Mom?" I say, tapping her foot lightly with my own.

"Mmm?" she says, glancing up at me. I wonder if she can sense it—the cold, nervous energy flooding through me, but she doesn't seem too concerned.

"I'm really tired. I think I'm just gonna crash."

She nods, eyes going back to the screen. "Okay. Sleep well. Thanks again for your help tonight."

"No problem," I say, but she's already back in the game.

I go back to my room, close the door, and wait, pacing back and forth across the carpet. I feel stupid for being so anxious. We're just friends—it's not like it *means* anything. Still, I can't shake the feeling that James and I are strapped into something. Hurtling toward an end point I don't understand and can't stop.

When James texts me that he's up the street I tiptoe toward the front door and slip out as quietly as possible.

"Hey," I say, ducking into his car. I feel sweaty and out of breath.

James looks at me, his skin cast in a soft red tint from the dashboard lights, eyes flat and gray. "Hey," he says, lifting his chin.

"What's up?" I buckle my seat belt as he makes a U-turn out of my neighborhood.

"Ah, nothing. I just . . . had to get out for a bit. Thought you might be good company."

"Did Iris take you back?" I ask, staring out the windshield at the scrubby grass on either side of the road, lit to a muddy blur by the headlights.

James scoffs. "Yeah, but she's making me promise we'll go to couples' therapy before the baby's born."

I nod and don't say anything. I know him well enough by now to hear the edge in his voice.

"It's bullshit," he says. He turns the radio on to a country station that's playing something soft and crooning, filled with a yearning I can feel like a space in my chest.

"Therapy sucks," I say. I know because, after my suicide attempt, I had to go for months. Until I could finally convince them that I was fine. That I wasn't going to try again at the first opportunity.

I was a teenager then, but I can still remember the counselor's grim face and the unrelenting press of his eyes. Hands, dry and wrinkled as used tissue paper, always clutching his pen and paper. And the questions, endless and unanswerable, barreling toward me at warp speed.

"She doesn't get that therapy's not going to fix us. Or fix *me*, I guess, since I'm always the problem. No one does. Except you. And even if it could, we don't have the money for that shit."

I pick underneath my nails and try again not to look at James, afraid of what I'll see there.

"I know," I say finally. And the thing is, I do. I wish I was lying— wish that James and I could just be a normal boss and employee. Or just friends. But he's right—we're not. Instead, we're two sides of the same coin, and there's a strange kind of comfort in it.

The worst part of the depression is the alone-ness. The feeling like you've been cut off, abandoned by the happiness everyone else seems to come by naturally. Left to spend your whole life grasping for something that's always going to slip through your fingers, no matter how tightly you hold it.

Marley's the only person who's ever really come close to seeing it in me, even to matching it in her worst moments, but even she doesn't get it. Not like James. It's nice, at least, not to float alone.

"Do you ever get tired of trying so hard?" he says, and I can feel his eyes on me. Can feel the swell of his hope billowing out. Grasping hard at my own.

"Trying so hard at what?"

"I don't know. Everything."

I stare at my feet, my mind running back on all the bad stretches. The days I could barely get out of bed. The weeks disappeared underneath a thick, rolling fog of anger, then sadness, then nothing at all. "I'm tired all the time."

"Do you ever stop, then?"

I swallow hard and nod my head. "Yes," I say, quieter this time, though, like keeping my voice down will keep the shadow of those days at bay, instead of swooping down over me. "Of course I stop."

"And do you ever wonder if maybe it would be easier to just not start back up again?"

I look at him now. A quick, traitorous dart of my eyes. I feel spotted. Exposed. "Constantly," I say. Almost a whisper now.

"I'm so tired, Thea," he says. And there's that tone again—the pleading that makes my whole body ache with recognition. Pain that ebbs and flows, but is always, *always* there.

Silently, I reach across the cupholders and rest my hand on top of his. He weaves his fingers through my own, then flips them, so my forearm is facing up, the lines of my scars exposed. Usually, when this happens, my instinct is to cover them up, but this time I don't see the point.

James turns the car and slows it to a stop. I realize that he's driven us to the Chicken Shack's parking lot. I stare at the outline of Hooster the Rooster protruding from the roof. "Will you tell me what happened?" he asks, nodding toward my arm.

"It's not a very interesting story," I say. "I was seventeen. I'd been in a pretty bleak headspace for a while. One day, I just got so fed up, I grabbed a razor and did it before I could think twice. I knew right away that it was a mistake, so I called my mom. Obviously, it turned out fine. I got it stitched up. Did the counseling thing and the meds thing, blah blah blah. But it really screwed with my mom. Sent her into kind of a relapse, I guess. That's why she got back into the gambling like she did. Why she and my stepdad divorced, eventually. And it's why I have to stay here and help. We're all in this mess because of me."

"I'm sure it's not that simple," he says. The thing is, though, it *is* that simple. At least in my mind. I have years of practice drawing a straight line from my suicide attempt, to David and Mom's divorce, to where we are now, like a line of dominoes.

I shrug. "It doesn't really matter now," I say.

We sit in silence for a long time before he speaks.

"Do you ever feel the way now that you did then?"

"Once in a while," I say. "But then I remember how I felt after I did it. More scared than I've ever been in my life. Terrified that I wouldn't get help in time. That was worse, I think. Besides, now I have the twins, I have people who need me."

He nods, thoughtfully. "I wish I felt like that," he says. "Like someone needed me."

I chew on my lip and look down at my hands. "What about the baby?" I ask, trying for something. Anything.

"The baby would be better off without me fucking up its life."

"The baby would be better off with a dad. A family. *You* of all people should know that," I say, and he opens one eye just wide enough to glare at me, but he doesn't say anything, and I get it. When you've already decided that something like that is true about yourself—about the world—there's no point in arguing over it.

"I need a cigarette," I say, just to say something. James reaches across and flips open the glove compartment.

"Help yourself, kid," he says, and I do, plucking one out of the pack and lighting it with the little red lighter nestled in next to it.

I roll the window down and we sit quietly for a long time, the country singer rasping about a broken heart, and smoke lifting off my lips into nothing. There's a warmth that settles in between us somewhere in the silence, the kind that doesn't go away after the moment ends.

"Tell me about New York," he says finally, rolling his head toward me.

I open my mouth, but nothing comes out. Truth be told, New York feels a million miles away right now—like a life dreamed up by someone else entirely—but I can tell he needs to hear something good, so I talk about the things I know. About my plan to find myself a tiny, dingy apartment somewhere and fill it with plants and books and posters. To work my way into a job as a stylist's assistant and, eventually, to open my own vintage clothing store in the Village. I tell him about the train lines crisscrossing the city like arteries in a bloody, beating heart and the row of artists and performers in Central Park and the restaurant that has milkshakes topped with a whole slice of cake.

Everything I know, I say it, trying to stuff the empty space with small, beautiful things until James is smiling lazily, his eyes still closed, like maybe he's trying to wish it all real.

"Promise me you'll go," he says.

I laugh dryly and drop the cigarette out the window onto the asphalt.

"I mean it."

"Only if you promise to come visit," I counter, fishing for another. I light it with a shaking hand and bring it to my lips.

"I can't promise that," he says, and there's something quiet in his voice. Something resigned.

I inhale and hold the smoke in my lungs until I can't stand it. Until I feel like I'm about to burst. "Don't say that," I tell him, the smoke rushing from my lips. "There has to be something we can do."

He just shrugs, looking indifferent. "I've tried it all, Thea. Medication, therapy, waiting it out. This feeling, like I shouldn't be here anymore . . . it goes away, but it always comes back. I'm starting to think that maybe it's the only true thing."

I look away, out toward the parking lot.

"Thea," he says.

"What?" I ask, refusing to meet his eyes. A piece of ash falls from the tip of my cigarette onto my bare thigh and I wince.

"I don't need another lecture on treatment options, okay? Not from you. I just need you to be my friend, no matter what. I need you to be there for me. Can you do that?"

I fix my eyes on his. The sheen of them reflecting what little light there is outside back at me. He looks scared.

I reach across the space and take his hand in mine, and I feel it again, a rush that accompanies the heat of his skin on mine. That terrible sense of destiny—of fate—tying us together. Something dark rolling toward us. Unstoppable.

"I can do that."

CHAPTER

17

Marley

I DRIVE HOME FROM Southern Moon in a haze, running the whole inter-action with Trina's mother over again and again in my head. I know, objectively, that I could've done things differently—handled myself better—but somehow, it feels inevitable. Ironic. Of course my true self would bleed through the veneer eventually. It was always going to.

I park in the driveway and shove my key in the lock. Mom is dozing on the couch, the TV on in front of her. I think about waking her and telling her what happened, but decide against it. I'm not quite ready to face the disappointment yet, so instead I sneak back to my room and close the door, pressing my back to it. There's harsh sunlight streaming through the window, and the air feels thick and suffocatingly hot, even with the ceiling fan turning frantic circles above my head.

I barely have time to take a breath before there's a knock at the front door, so sharp it startles me. I consider answering it, but decide against that too. All I want to do now is curl up in bed and sleep, maybe forever.

After a long second, the knock comes again, followed by the sound of the door opening. "June," a voice calls out. Dahlia's, I realize, the tension in my spine relaxing. I've barely seen your mother since the funeral—I haven't been able to bring myself to face her—but I take a kind of comfort in knowing that she has my mom. That she isn't as alone in all of this as I feel.

I hear the springs on the couch as my mother wakes up, her eyes probably still half-closed.

"Dahlia," she says. And then, "What's wrong? Come here."

More couch springs. I picture Dahlia sitting next to my mother, and then I hear her crying. The sobs racking through her. I squeeze my eyes closed and try to drown them out, but it's no use. Finally, she speaks.

"Nothing," she says. "I mean, nothing new. I'm just having a rough morning. Austen came over to watch the twins for a while, and I needed to see you."

"Of course," Mom coos. "Can I get you anything?"

I don't hear a response, just more crying, then some sniffling.

"It's bad, June," she says finally. "I . . . I took a hard look at the finances. The funeral was expensive—I had to take on a loan. And without Thea's income, I don't know how long we'll be able to make it. Austen swears he'll contribute more, but it's just . . . not enough."

I expect to hear my mom comforting Dahlia like she did a moment ago. Offering solutions, maybe. But instead, there's a long beat of silence before she says, "Tell me the truth, Dahl. How much do you owe right now?"

Dahlia bristles. I can hear the prickle in her voice when she speaks again. "That's none of your business," she says.

"Yes, it is," Mom interrupts. "You have two kids to feed. How bad is it?"

"A couple thousand dollars, okay? It's a couple thousand dollars right now."

"Jesus," Mom spits. "You've got to be kidding me. You told me you stopped. You *promised* me."

"It's been a hard summer, okay? Really stressful with the fires and everything. I was taking on all these extra shifts at work, trying to prepare for Thea's move to New York. To save up. I thought I could get us more. Double my savings before Thea left."

"That's always the story, Dahlia. Do you even know how many times you've told me that same fucking story?"

"Don't you dare," Dahlia says, her voice cold and vicious like I've never heard it before. "Don't you dare sit there and judge me, June. Not after everything."

"After what, Dahlia?" Mom says, sounding weary.

"After I took in your daughter. After I raised her for three years because you couldn't stay sober long enough to form a coherent sentence."

Mom lets out a frustrated groan, as though she's heard this a hundred times before. "That was twenty years ago."

"You've always thought you were better than me. Since we were teenagers. Just because your baby had a father and mine didn't. Because you had some money, and you bought my house. Well, guess what? We're in the same place now, aren't we? And you're *not* better than me. You're just a drunk, and you're bitter because I had a family."

On the word *family*, Dahlia's voice breaks, and she's crying again. Ragged, desperate sobs that echo through the still air. The sound splits a fissure down my chest. Sends some part of me careening off into orbit. If I piled all of my losses on top of each other, they still wouldn't come close to hers.

Why would you ever do this to us? I think. *Why would you ever force this kind of grief onto people who loved you?*

"Dahlia," my mom says finally, her voice softer now. "Dahlia, it's okay. Look, we'll figure something out. We always do."

"I'm sorry," she says. Her voice is muffled, and I know my mother has her in a hug. "I didn't mean—"

"I know. I know you didn't. We're in this together, okay? We always have been. Nothing's changed there."

I press my forehead to the door, suppressing my own sob. My own grief, this time over what could have been. The future we've lost. There was a part of me that always imagined us with daughters of our own one day. Better girls than us—kinder and smarter and free from this place.

"You're all I have now," Dahlia says. Her voice has gone so quiet I can barely hear it through the door.

I can almost see the two of them there on the couch. Dahlia's small, round body tucked inside my mother's long arms. My mother's sharp chin resting atop her dark curls, matching worry lines creased between their eyebrows, the two of them so tangled they look like one many-armed beast. A thing with a single heartbeat.

"I'm not going anywhere."

18

Thea

July 19, 2023

    Missed Call (2): 770-352-3511

    New Messages from 770-352-3511—Maybe: James

        Hey

        It's me

        James

        New phone

    Thea Wright

        Hey

        What's up?

    Inbound Call: 770-352-3511

        Call length: 37 minutes

August 2, 2023

    Thea Wright

        Everything okay? You seemed weird at work.

    Maybe: James

        Fine.

        Can you talk?

    Outbound Call: Maybe: James

        Call length: 2 hours, 6 minutes

August 23, 2023

James 🧤🏠

> *Iris is driving me INSANE (more insane than usual, that is)*
>
> *Wanna hang out?*
>
> *Hello?*
>
> *Hellllooooooo?????*
>
> *I'm going to keep texting you until you answer . . .*
>
> *T*
>
> *H*
>
> *E*
>
> *A*

Thea Wright

> *Sorry, I was out.*

James 🧤🏠

> 😮
>
> *I forgive you, kid.*
>
> *What are you doing now?*
>
> *Wanna get waffle house?*
>
> *I can pick you up.*

Thea Wright

> *Yeah, sure*

September 4, 2023

James 🧤🏠

> *Hi I miss you*
>
> *Work sucked without you*
>
> *Just me n my buddy Daryl!*

Thea Wright

> *Sorry.*
>
> *Cramps are killing me today*

Inbound Call: James 🧤🏠

> Call length: 42 minutes

September 10, 2023

Inbound Call: James 🧤🏠

> Call length: 3 hours, 46 minutes

September 13, 2023

Thea Wright

Hey

just checking in

. . .

please answer me

James

You're scaring me

Outbound Call: Thea Wright

Call length: 0 minutes

Outbound Call: Thea Wright

Call length: 0 minutes

Outbound Call: Thea Wright

Call length: 0 minutes

Thea Wright

JAMES

ANSWER THE GODDAMN PHONE OR I WILL CALL THE POLICE

I SWEAR TO GOD

Inbound Call: James 🐿️🏠

Call length: 22 minutes

September 17, 2023

James 🐿️🏠

Heads up, I'm going to text you from my other phone for the rest of today.

I think Iris may have seen me using this one

And it's good for us to text from that number sometimes anyway

You're deleting this thread every day, right?

Thea Wright

Ok

Yes. Every day.

James 🐿️🏠

Good

Hey, I know it's weird, but thank you

For being, like, the only person I can actually talk to

Im gonna miss you, wright

Thea Wright
>   *Don't say that.*

James 🏵🏠
>   *You're the best friend I've ever had*
>   *I mean that, kid*

September 20, 2023
Thea Wright:
>   *James*
>   *Please call me*
>   *Ive been up all night thinking*

Inbound Call: James 🏵🏠
Call length: 31 minutes

September 20, 2023
Outbound Call: Thea Wright
Call length: 1 hours, 54 minutes

September 21, 2023
Missed Call (4): James 🏵🏠

James 🏵🏠
>   *Call me*
>   *Pls*
>   *Thea, I really need you rn*

Outbound Call: Thea Wright
Call length: 13 minutes

* * *

I'm helping Mom get lunch together for the boys when I see the texts come through, so I excuse myself as quickly as I can and shut the door to my room. I touch James's contact with shaking fingers and press the phone to my cheek.

"Thea," he answers. The sound of his voice makes me deflate with relief.

"Jesus, James, I—"

"Listen to me. It's time."

My stomach drops. "No," I say. "Please, James. Not right now, okay? Just please give it a little more time."

I cross the room on wobbly legs and plop down on my bed, fighting a wave of dizziness as the blood drains from my face.

"How long?" he asks. Then, before I can answer, "We've talked it to death, okay? There is no more time. I can't take it anymore. I have to do this now."

"Now?"

"I've got a bottle of pills. Iris is out. She won't be back for a few hours. It has to be now."

"Just take a deep breath, James. Please. Just think about this for a minute."

"I've thought about it, Thea. A lot. I don't need you to do anything, okay? Just stay on the phone with me while I take them. Just talk to me for a while."

I press my hand to my mouth to keep back a sob. I can hear Mom with the twins in the kitchen. Their happy chatter. Mom's favorite playlist floating underneath my door.

"James," I manage.

"You've been such a good friend to me, Thea. You're the only person I've ever been able to really talk to. You're the only one who understands. Please. I need you to do this for me now. I need you to be here. To know that this is what I want."

I open my mouth to plead with him, just like I've been doing for weeks, but nothing comes out. He's right—we've talked it to death. There's nothing else I can say to him, and I know it. No way to convince him that staying is the right choice. That the world is a better place with him in it.

And now he's asking me for this. To be here for him at the end. And maybe it's the only thing I *can* do for him. Make sure he isn't alone in this moment. Make sure he knows how much his life has mattered to me.

On the other end of the line, I hear a click. Pills rattling inside a plastic bottle. "Say something, okay? Tell me about New York again."

I squeeze my eyes closed and choke back a sob. "Okay," I say. I take a deep breath. My voice shakes, but I start talking. I tell him about the subway performers I've seen on YouTube and TikTok. About the list of restaurants, bars, vintage stores, and more I keep in a note on my phone. I barely let myself pause for breath, but when I do, I can hear the pills rattling. Can hear him swallowing handful after handful until, finally, it's achingly silent on the other end.

"James?" I whisper when I can't take it anymore.

"I'm still here," he says. "Keep talking."

"I—I'm really going to miss you."

"I'll miss you too, kid."

There's another beat of silence, this one stretching for what feels like forever.

"Please make sure Iris is okay . . . and the baby. Promise me." His words are getting slower and harder to understand, his breathing labored. I fight back a wave of nausea.

"I promise."

"I have to hide the phone now, Thea. Before I pass out. I have to go."

"Okay," I say, my voice barely a whisper.

I hear a grunt on the other end of the line. Something that sounds like slow, painful movement. "James," I say again, "Please, don't hang up. Just stay on the line with me as long as you can. I don't care if they find the phone."

But the only answer I get is the click of the line, then dead air. I look frantically around my room, tears blurring my vision. I have to cover my mouth with my hand to keep my sobbing quiet.

"James," I whisper one more time, after what feels like hours but, of course, there's nothing. He isn't with me anymore. I imagine him passed out on his bed or his bathroom floor, fingers twitching, mouth gaping like a fish.

"I love you," I tell him. And then I put down the phone.

19

Marley

ONCE MOM AND Dahlia leave to retrieve the twins from Austen and take them for ice cream, I spend the afternoon searching online for everything I can find about *the arsonist*, watching YouTube clips of the increasingly hysterical news coverage I've avoided all summer. Solemn-faced reporters standing in front of still-smoking house frames, their voices grave and monotone.

Unprecedented damage being done to this small but proud community. Destruction on a scale we've never seen before.

Honestly, it all feels a little overblown. Like a lot of handwringing over a few old houses that no one was living in, anyway. After all, no one—besides you—was ever hurt in the fires. They weren't even set near occupied properties.

Once I've watched all the news coverage I can find, I google *arsonist*. I read police profiles and case studies, trying to imagine all the ways they might try to connect you to the fires. In a lot of ways, you seem like the exact opposite of who they should be targeting. Most arsonists are male, and underage. They do it for money, or revenge, or so that they can play the hero.

I keep scrolling, trying to make it fit into a coherent picture with you. I think of what it would've taken for you to go to that house by yourself, with a lighter and rags and intention. You must've had a reason.

Or maybe you didn't. Maybe someone took you there and shot you, like Detective Romero implied.

After a while, I slap the computer shut and force myself to make a sandwich. It tastes like ash in my mouth, so I pour a glass of wine instead and take a long sip, savoring the dryness.

Then, in a flash, it swoops me up again. The silence. The absence, flaring like a virus. The night stretching out in front of me, endless and empty, with nothing to fill the time but my own thoughts.

It's been days, but the shock hasn't worn off. The moments when I expect to turn around and see you there. When I think of calling you and realize I can't. I feel like a rat trapped in some awful maze, running frantically for an exit that doesn't exist, trying to find the off switch on this pain. There's no exit, though. You're gone, and besides, you kept secrets. Baby-sized secrets.

I run the fact through my mind over and over, trying to smooth out the sharpness of it. To fit it into place with the rest of you, but I can't. How could you not have told me?

I never thought of you as maternal, exactly, but it was plain how much you loved the twins. Anyone could see it in the way you cared for them—the intricate bedtime routines that involved books and songs and kisses. The dreams you held close to your chest and pushed back year after year for their sake. I always assumed you'd want kids one day, years from now when you were some big shot in New York, but I hate that I didn't ever ask. Now, all I can do is add it to the growing list of failures.

In my back pocket, my phone dings. The sound sends relief coursing through me like morphine—something else to focus on—but it doesn't last long. It's from Austen.

Hey, can you come to Dahlia's house? I found this thing in Thea's room. Kinda weird. Want to see if you know what it's about.

I'm out the door before I have time to think about it, my flip-flops slapping against the dirt on the path between our houses, waning sunlight on my shoulders. I open the door and take in a strong whiff of lemon verbena, which means Austen has probably spent the last few hours aggressively cleaning the place, like he always does when he's anxious.

"Hey," he says, waving me back to your room. I jog to close the distance.

"What did you find?" I ask, wiping at the fine sheen of sweat along my hairline.

Austen pulls a small slip of paper out of his pocket and hands it to me. I smooth it out on the bedside table, scanning the black ink quickly. It's a receipt for a basket of baby toys from Target, marked for delivery, with an address scribbled at the bottom in your harsh, slashing hand. I study the list of toys. A rattle. A felt book. A small stuffed animal. The twins outgrew things like this years ago.

"I don't get it," I say, looking up at him. He shakes his head. "Thea was buying baby toys for someone else?"

"I was hoping you knew something about it."

"It's dated last winter," I say, stomach clenching. Obviously, you weren't pregnant then, but it feels like an odd coincidence all the same. "Let's go and find out."

"To that address? Right now?"

"No time like the present," I clutch the receipt in my hand tighter. It feels almost like I'm clutching you. One more piece of small, undiscovered territory in a place I once thought I knew by heart, but this one is different. This is a question I have a shot at answering.

Austen scratches the back of his neck, casting his eyes down on the carpet. He's wearing that watch again. The old-looking one he's been wearing recently. "I don't know, Mar."

"So, you'll go to a crime scene in the middle of the night to look for clues, but you won't drive to an address two towns over? You're the one who called me over here to take a look at this."

"I didn't see the date before. I didn't realize it was from so long ago. Why would it have anything to do with what happened?"

"I don't know, but we won't know for sure until we go, will we? For all we know, this could be . . ." I trail off. I realize I haven't spoken to Austen since I found out about the pregnancy. I know he knows—he has to, if Dahlia's already told my mom—but he doesn't know that I know.

"What?" he asks, looking at me. I shake my head.

"What if this has something to do with the person the police think she was seeing?" I ask. "We should at least check it out, Austen. Please."

Reluctantly he nods, pulling his hand through his hair so it stands on end. I cast side glances his way as we leave the house and walk to my car, typing the address into my phone to pull up directions. Austen is a lot of things—friendly, smart, earnest, a relentlessly hard worker—but a man of uncharted depths he isn't, and I can't figure out why he hasn't told me about the baby. Maybe getting arrested threw him off. Or maybe he's scared of what we'll find at this address. In any case, the change in him makes me edgy.

Once I start the car, he turns the radio on and up. I don't say anything, just let the music play as he stares out the window at the fields whipping past us in the waning light. All the grass, dying in the late summer heat wave, lit up like burnished gold. He looks sullen, his lips pressed into a grim line, his brow furrowed. I wonder if he's upset with me about last night. If he regrets what happened between us.

The first song ends and another, louder one begins, the bass line so heavy the seats are vibrating with it. Austen squeezes his eyes closed and bobs his head along with the beat, the way he does at the gym when he's focused on hitting a new personal best. Drowning out the rest of the world.

"Austen," I say, reaching over to turn down the music.

He opens his eyes and looks at me.

"I've been so wrapped up in everything that I haven't really asked how *you're* doing with all of this."

"What do you mean?"

"I just mean that she was your friend too, and you can talk to me if you want to. I hope you know that."

There's a long beat of silence before he answers.

"I know," he says finally. "You've always been there for me, Marley. Even when I was an asshole."

"You were never an asshole," I say.

"Yeah, I was. Especially about Sky."

I chew on the inside of my cheek, eyes fixed firmly on the road ahead. I'm not sure what to say.

"Look," he continues. "I know that night didn't end the way either of us wanted it to, but you were right—about that, at least. I shouldn't have been texting her when we were together."

"Thank you for saying that," I say. And then, before I can stop myself, "Are you two still in touch?" I know how desperate the question makes me look, but I can't help asking it. I need to know.

"Sometimes," he answers with a shrug, and I nod my head, regretting it instantly.

We sit in the silence for a long moment after that as I try to push the thought of Austen and Sky out of my brain.

But there's only one other thought that comes to mind.

Screw keeping things close to the chest. I want to catch him off guard.

"So," I say, tapping on the steering wheel. "Do you have any idea who the father of Thea's baby could be?"

Austen looks at me, his eyes wide, mouth falling open in surprise. "How did *you* know about the pregnancy?"

"Dahlia told my mom," I say, unable to keep the irritated snap out of my voice. "Why didn't *you* tell me? I thought we were in this together."

"God, I'm sorry, Mar." He looks relieved to have it out on the table, like he can finally breathe again. "I guess I didn't know how. I mean, I was so shocked. I didn't—I didn't want to make things harder for you when they didn't need to be. Besides, we already knew she was seeing someone, so it doesn't really change anything."

I look at him sharply, gripping the steering wheel. "Doesn't change anything? Austen, whoever the father was—he could've had motive to hurt her."

He raises his eyebrows, looking horrified. "You think someone killed her because she was pregnant?"

"Maybe, yeah," I say, feeling a jolt of energy shoot through me. "If she told him she was pregnant, and he didn't want to deal. We have no idea. At least it's a lead. It's more than we had before."

"Or it has nothing to do with how or why she died."

I narrow my eyes and bite down on the inside of my cheek until I can feel blood pooling just beneath the surface. "What's gotten into you?" I ask him. "Two days ago *you* were pushing *me* to look into all of this. Now I can barely get you in the car to check out a lead?"

"It's not—" he says, looking exasperated again. "I'm sorry, okay? It's just, I'm still . . . processing, I guess. The pregnancy thing threw me. I hate that I didn't know."

"Why would you know? It's not like she was telling people," I say, the words coming out harsher than I mean for them to.

"Yeah," he says grimly, but his hands are still clasped tight in his lap, knuckles white.

We drive the rest of the way in sullen silence. I don't feel like trying to pry more from Austen, and I doubt there's anything else useful there anyway, so instead I turn my thoughts ahead, to the address where you sent baby toys last summer. *Baby toys*, I think, my heart twisting suddenly, painfully, in my chest. There's something unbearably tender in the gesture. Another side of you I thought that only I knew, flashing like a coin on the street, caught by the sun, out for anyone to see.

CHAPTER

20

Thea

I SHOULDN'T BE IN James's house right now. I feel it as soon as I cross the threshold—a foreboding chill that passes through me like a ghost.

I'm carrying a casserole I made this morning before the funeral. Some recipe I pulled off of the internet with noodles and cheese and lots of heavy cream. Comfort food, I guess, though I doubt it will bring any.

I hold it close to my stomach, the aluminum foil crinkling, as I scan the crowd trickling in for a familiar face. There are plenty of people here, most everyone I recognize from the funeral earlier today, but they're all strangers to me—and why wouldn't they be? I didn't know James's other friends. I wasn't actually a part of his real life, just the stretch of it that existed at work, or in his car late at night. Over the burner phone line he got just for me, so we could speak honestly about his plans without raising anyone's suspicions.

"Thea," I hear someone say. I turn to face James's fiancée, Iris, leaning against the doorway to the kitchen, a dish towel slung over her shoulder, one eyebrow raised quizzically as she studies me.

"Iris," I say, the sight of her filling me with relief and guilt in equal measure, just like it has since the first time I laid eyes on her a week ago, not long after James was found dead. "I brought this." I hold out the casserole dish and she tilts her head toward the kitchen, indicating that I should follow her in.

I do, clutching the dish tightly and weaving through the growing crowd. There's a little part of me that wants to hurl it and bolt out the door, but I force myself forward. After what I did, the very least I can do is be here. Bear witness to the pain I helped create. Right?

Now that we're alone, Iris turns to face me, folding her arms across her chest, over the swell of her stomach with James's baby inside. She looks bloated and fragile and ferocious all at the same time, and I feel the hair standing up on the back of my neck. My own internal alert system going haywire.

Iris is not the way I imagined her when James talked about his fiancée. I had pictured someone tall and broad, with strong features and a pinched brow—someone intimidating—but Iris is small in every sense of the word, with lips perpetually tipped into a slight frown and skinny arms resting protectively on her stomach. Mostly, she seems tired and sad.

"I wasn't sure if I should come," I ramble, desperate to say something that fills the silence. "I'm sorry if I'm intruding on a family event."

"You're not," she says, but somehow her words don't feel reassuring. "James doesn't have much family. Everyone here was a friend. Why don't you help me get things set up? I'll put that in the fridge." It doesn't seem like a suggestion, so I place the casserole dish on the counter, heart racing, and nod.

Right after it happened—after I got the call from the owner of the Chicken Shack informing me of James's death—I sprang into action. I hadn't been expecting to, but I couldn't stop myself. Like something in my body knew I'd spend the rest of my life trying to atone for what I'd done.

I baked cookies and took them to Iris that night, after I found her address online. I'd thought I might just drop them off and leave, but instead she invited me in and I stayed for an hour, telling her funny stories about the Chicken Shack. Things James had done and said. About what a good manager he was and how much he cared and how clear it was that he loved her. Some of it I made up on the spot, but some of it was true.

It felt good to make her smile—to bring some small measure of comfort. She told me she hadn't realized the two of us were such good friends, but she was glad to hear that he was close to someone at the end. She said he'd gotten distant since he'd found out about the baby. She hadn't realized he'd been spiraling so badly. She'd thought he was doing better.

And then, she cried, and I hugged her, cradling her in my arms like I knew her. Like we were equal partners in this grief. Like I hadn't sat there, listening, as he swallowed handful after handful of pills.

After that, I was somehow part of it—the rhythms of mourning. I made copies of the funeral bulletin at the Office Depot and adjusted the greenery around his casket before the service, imagining grimly what he looked like inside.

It feels simultaneously wrong and right, being here—my new, tentative friendship with Iris. Like a punishment or a penance. I know, instinctively, that James would've wanted me to stay away. After all, I was a secret for a reason. But James is gone, and what he wanted doesn't matter anymore.

Iris opens her mouth to say something else, but just as she does, the front door opens with a startling crack of the hinges. It's such a shock to the quiet atmosphere that it makes us both jump.

When I turn to look at the front door, there's a woman standing at the threshold, her posture rigidly straight. She doesn't look like James—her frame is short and rounded. Her skin is darker and her hair is curly—but she has the same deep, dark eyes, and I know instantly that this is the sister he told me about. The one who left when she turned eighteen.

Like me, she surveys the crowd for a moment before her eyes land on us in the kitchen. "Iris," she says, stalking into the room. She comes to a stop in the doorway, her eyes darting to me, then back to Iris. "I need to talk to you. It's important."

Iris rolls her shoulders back and shoots me a look that conveys her annoyance. "Julie," she says. "I'm glad to see you. This is Thea. She was James's good friend from work."

I offer up the barest hint of a smile and a small, awkward wave. *She's not right in the head.* Isn't that what James said about her?

Julie's eyes widen at me, and she steps back, looking as though I've hit her.

"Thea," she says, the words barely a whisper. "It's you."

The words make my heart leap in my chest.

She knows. She has to, I think. But how could she know? James and I were careful. We only talked about his plans in person, or over the burner line. We deleted our texts every day, except a few work-related exchanges.

I won't let you get in any kind of trouble, he told me once, his fists clenched tightly around the steering wheel of his car.

Don't worry about me, I'd told him, but secretly, I was relieved he was thinking it through so thoroughly. It made me wonder—would I have, in his position? If it was me planning to die, would I have the clarity to think about the ones I was leaving behind? To make sure my loose ends were tied up before I went? I hope so.

"What's going on?" Iris asks, her eyes ping-ponging between us.

Julie reaches into her pocket and fishes out a flip phone, then drops it onto the table with a clatter.

"What's that?" Iris asks, the furrow between her brows growing deeper.

"It's James's phone," Julie answers, and Iris instantly shakes her head.

"No, I have James's phone. The police gave it back to me yesterday."

"They gave you his main phone. *This* is his burner."

"His burner?" she says. "What are you talking about, Jules?"

My stomach feels like it's free-falling through the floor and down to the earth below.

"Why don't you ask *her*?" she asks, fixing her eyes on me once again.

"I—I don't have any idea what you're talking about," I say, but I'm too taken aback to be convincing.

"Stop. Lying," Julie growls; her teeth are actually bared.

"Julie, that's enough," Iris says, extending her arm protectively toward me, sending another wave of guilt crashing down, so powerful I think it might crush me.

"Iris, please listen to me. I found this phone tucked into one of his shoes this morning. I was going through them to find a pair to bury him in. The texts are all deleted, but there are a bunch of calls to and from one number. *Hers*. I looked it up. Here, see for yourself. He called her, like, right before he died. Maybe as he died. She's playing all of us."

"What?" Iris says, a mask of anger slamming down over her features. "You talked to him that day?"

"I—it's—" I stammer, uselessly, as the two women turn their eyes on me.

"Why didn't you tell me that day you came over?" she asks, her eyebrows furrowing.

"Were you fucking him?" Julie cuts in, her voice rising to a yell. "Is that why he did it? He thought Iris was going to find out?"

"No!" I manage. "James and I were just friends. I didn't even know he had two phones. He just told me he got a new number." It's a pathetic lie, but it's all I can think of in the moment.

"If you and James were just friends, why did he have a separate phone just for you?" Iris says.

"I don't know."

I can tell that neither of them buys it. And why would they? Even I can see how it must look. James was already depressed and isolated. He didn't want to be a father. He drew back and had an affair with a coworker, and he felt so bad that it pushed him over the edge.

"Did he really call you that day?" Iris asks again. I nod, unable to form words. "What did he say to you?"

I open my mouth, then close it again. "Nothing, really," I say finally, tears gathering in my eyes. "He said he was grateful for my friendship. I didn't realize he was—I didn't know what was happening, until I heard the news."

"Why didn't you tell me before?" she asks.

"I didn't know what to say," I answer truthfully. "And I didn't—I didn't feel like it mattered."

"Slut," Julie cuts in. I can tell she wants to say more, but Iris stops her with a sharp look.

"I'm so sorry," I say, uselessly, backstepping toward the door. "Clearly, I shouldn't be here." My purse is hanging by the front door. I swipe it off the hook quickly, slinging it over my shoulder and grabbing for the car keys inside. I have to resist the urge to walk backwards out of the house and toward my car. To keep my front to them like you would a pack of wolves. I'm just opening the car door when I hear the footsteps behind me.

"Hey!" Julie shouts. She flies down the porch steps and across the yard toward me. I swallow hard and grip the door with white knuckles, watching her long, black dress flutter behind her in the wind. When she gets to me, she skids to a halt inches from my face and leans in. She has the same fine-textured hair as James. The same blazing intensity in her eyes. Bizarrely, I almost want to reach out and hug her.

"Julie, I'm so sorry. I never meant—"

"What you did was really fucked up," she says. "And if you ever come near me, Iris, or her baby again, I'll kill you. Do you understand?"

I nod my head, squeezing my fist so tight that the key's teeth bite into my skin.

"Yes," I say.

"Good."

With that, she wraps her arms tightly across her chest and trudges back toward the house, black boots stamping through the patches of yellowing grass. I watch her go. Watch the door close behind her. Then I catch a flicker of movement from the kitchen window. Iris, staring at me through the glass. Her gaze burning a hole through my center.

I was stupid to come, I realize. Stupid to think I could ever make any part of this right.

The best thing I can do for anyone is to disappear.

21

Marley

I BARELY EVEN NOTICE we've arrived at the address until I pull up to the little house and the GPS stops talking with a curt "You have arrived at your destination."

It's a small bungalow house, tucked up at the end of a patchy road in the middle of nowhere. I shut off the car and stare at it for a moment. There are signs of disrepair—a crumbling front step with a missing brick right in the middle, and a row of weeds cropping up around the path to the door—but there are also window boxes stuffed full of colorful flowers, giving the place life.

Austen is the first to speak. "I've never seen this place before," he says, his eyes running carefully over the house.

"Me neither."

"So . . . what's our plan?"

I shrug, shutting off the engine. "I don't really have one," I say. "Do you?" I always work better on the spur of the moment, but Austen is a meticulous planner. It used to drive me crazy before, when my biggest concern about our relationship was that it was too boring, but now I wonder if it was just a harbinger of our doom—a fundamental incompatibility that we both refused to acknowledge.

He shakes his head and reaches out to take my hand in his own, giving it a quick squeeze before he drops it again. "Before we go in, I just want to say thank you," he says.

I press my lips together tightly, willing myself not to let any emotion bleed through. "For what, Austen?"

"For being here. Taking this seriously. I shouldn't have put you in the position I did last night, going to the scene, but there's no one else I'd trust to help me with this."

I'm not doing this for you, I want to spit, but I swallow the words back instead and unbuckle my seat belt. This kind of charm offensive is a classic Austen move, and he's used it to reel me back from the brink of anger more times than I can count, but right now—after keeping the pregnancy from me and telling me that he and Skylar still talk—it feels hollow. "Let's just go," is all I can muster.

I let him take the lead up the broken step and ring the doorbell, hovering a few inches behind him as we wait. There's a baby crying inside—loud, angry wailing that makes me flinch, like a white-hot poker held inches away from my skin. Close enough to see what you might've seen—a baby you weren't ready for, barreling down the pike.

Is that why you did what you did?

Suddenly, the door opens and there's a woman staring at us. She wears faded black leggings and an old T-shirt, her hair in a silk bonnet. Her skin is a warm brown, her face severe and strikingly beautiful—all sharp angles and high cheekbones and thick eyebrows tipped down in frustration.

"Whatever it is you're selling, I'm not interested," she says, stepping back to close the door.

"We're not selling anything," Austen says smoothly, turning on that charm like other people turn on a faucet.

The woman softens, just a little, but she still looks wary. "What do you want, then?" she says.

"Just to talk," I cut in. "My friend, Thea Wright, she sent some baby toys to this address last winter. We were hoping you could tell us how you knew her."

The woman stiffens, drawing her shoulders back and lifting her chin. "I thought Thea was dead," she says softly.

"She is," I say, and she meets my eyes, her gaze probing, searching for something, though I don't know what.

"Come in," she says, walking inside the house. For a second, Austen and I just stand there. Finally, I put my hand on the back of his arm, and we step over the threshold into the living room, where there are toys scattered across the floor and houseplants covering almost every available surface.

The woman, whose name I still don't know, plops down into a chair in the corner of the room, then seems to think better of it. On the rug, there's a little boy screaming, going red in the face, a toy truck clutched in his hands like a lifeline. She scoops him up, so his chin tucks over her shoulder.

"Let me put James down," she says, running her hand over the boy's hair. He begins to quiet, the screams growing softer until they stop altogether once she rounds the bend out of the room.

James. The name makes me sit up straighter, like a string plucked deep in my chest. An alarm. James. Last winter. Baby toys.

"Oh," I say quietly, twisting the receipt in my fingers and feeling it tear. Austen looks my way, but before he can ask the woman reenters the room.

"Sorry about the mess," she says, sitting back down in the chair and pulling her feet up underneath her. "I wasn't expecting company."

"We're just grateful you let us in," Austen says. We both take a seat on the couch, somewhat awkwardly. "I'm Austen, by the way. And this is Marley."

"I'm Iris," she nods. "Iris Anderson."

"Did you know Thea?" Austen asks, leaning forward to rest his elbows on his knees.

Iris looks briefly away, then back to us before shaking her head. "Not well, no."

"Your fiancé was James, right?" I ask. "Thea's boss at the Chicken Shack?"

After a moment she nods grimly. "Yes. Something like that," she says, but she doesn't offer more.

"I see," Austen says, and I can hear the edge in his voice. The realization that we shouldn't be here. We both remember how you were last fall after James Butler committed suicide. I can still picture the haunted, vacant look on your face when you got back from his wake. How pale and breakable you seemed for days afterwards. Can still feel the heat of Austen's breath on my neck from all those whispered conversations while we watched you, worried and clueless.

He was just her boss. I didn't even realize they were close.

Maybe there was something going on between them?

"We're so sorry for your loss," I say hastily. Iris presses her lips together and dips her head in acknowledgment.

"Thea and James were close," she says. "She came to his wake, but Julie scared her off."

"Julie?" I ask, cocking my head to the side.

"James's sister," she answers. "She's . . . a bit of a loose cannon, and she was devastated when James died—they were each other's only family. She accused Thea of having an affair with James. She thought that was part of the reason why he killed himself. I think she may have threatened her to stay away from us."

"Threatened her?" Austen pipes up.

Iris grimaces and nods. "I just . . . I know how Julie can be, and I saw her follow Thea out to her car when she tried to leave the wake."

"Jesus," I mutter under my breath. "Why would Julie have accused her of having an affair with James?"

Iris shrugs, but she looks stiff. I realize how sensitive a subject this must be. "Julie was going through some of James's things when she found his second phone hidden away. She saw that he called Thea close to the time he . . . you know. I mean, the same afternoon that he . . ."

"We understand," I say, and she nods.

"Julie confronted Thea about it. She said it was nothing, but Julie didn't believe her."

"Why would James have had a second phone?" I say, at the same time Austen says, "Could you give us Julie's phone number or her address? I'd really like to talk to her more."

Iris looks at me, then at Austen. "I don't have a number or an address," she says, clearly opting to ignore my question. "Julie's a drifter. She pops up from time to time to look in on little James—she usually crashes here or somewhere nearby for a few days when she does—but she's never given me a way to contact her, or a place to find her."

"Well, when was the last time you saw her?" I ask. "How often does she come into town?"

"Not very often. I haven't seen her in a few weeks, but that's not unusual. Honestly, it could be months before she shows back up."

"Will you call me the next time you see her?" I ask. "I can give you my number."

Iris nods and gives me her phone. I enter my contact info and pass it back to her. As if on cue, a cry springs up from the other room.

"We should get going," Austen says. "Thank you for your time."

Iris doesn't say anything—just nods tightly and goes for baby James while Austen and I leave.

I dig the keys out of my pocket in the driveway, hands shaking as I start the car and speed down the road. We don't speak for a while. Austen is flushed with adrenaline, jiggling his leg to the beat of whatever song is on the radio, his fingers tapping out the rhythm against his jeans. I can feel him watching me, his eyes sliding over to study my profile. My heart is beating fast. Slamming against my rib cage. I feel like I might pass out.

"Marley, pull over. You're shaking," he says. I do, pulling over to the side of the road near a peanut field. It's quiet out here, almost peaceful. I want to scream.

Before I can stop it, I reach out and hit the steering wheel. Once, twice, then three times. Again and again and again, as hard as I can. Austen grabs my wrists in his hands and holds them there.

"Hey," he says, his voice soft and soothing. "Stop. Talk to me."

I open my mouth, but all that comes out is a choked sob.

"Jesus, Mar." He unbuckles my seat belt and grabs me by the waist, pulling me over the center console into his lap like it's nothing and wrapping his arms tightly around me.

"I'm sorry," I say once I'm able to get myself under control. "It's just—deep down, I thought she did this to herself. I really did. But now—this Julie person—I don't know anymore. Christ, Austen, what if someone actually killed her?"

I think again of the question Detective Romero asked me the other night, about the gun. Could this Julie really have shot you and lit the house on fire to cover her tracks?

"Between this and the pregnancy, I feel like I hardly knew her at all."

Austen reaches up and tucks a strand of hair behind my ear. "I understand," he says. "But she loved you."

"What about—"

"She loved you, Mar. Before the fight, after the fight. That's all there is to it. Trust me."

Without thinking, I place my hands on either side of his face and kiss him. The anger still coursing through my veins becoming something else entirely. Austen wraps his arms around me, crushing me to him.

"Marley," he whispers as I undo the button on his jeans. His hands are drifting underneath my dress, up the length of my thighs. His voice is full of longing, the way it used to be before, and I want to drown myself in it. To never hear another sound again for as long as I live. I fist my hands into his T-shirt, where I notice a few short, brown hairs stuck to the cotton fabric. There's a corner of my brain that flags it, trying to place them, before I give up and kiss him again, deeper, slipping my tongue between his lips as he pulls my underwear aside.

Neither of us speaks again until it's over, when I push myself off him and back into the driver's seat.

"I'm always going to be in love with you," I tell him. I didn't mean to, the words just tumble out, and suddenly I feel naked. I readjust my dress, unable to meet his eyes. "I know that doesn't change anything."

He reaches across and rests his hand on my forearm. "Nothing's the same as it was three months ago," he says. "Let's just take things a day at a time."

I chew on the inside of my cheek, trying to process his words. They could be anything—a gentle rejection or a reopening door—so I just nod and put the car back in drive.

"We need to talk about what happened in there." I say after a few quiet minutes. "We need to find Julie—find out what she thinks happened between her brother and Thea."

Austen bites his lip, still slightly swollen. "We need to tell the police," he says.

I feel my grip tightening on the steering wheel. "Not yet," I say.

"Not yet?"

"I'm not sure I trust them yet. What if you're right, and they're dead set on the theory that Thea's responsible? This might make her look worse."

"How?" he asks.

I lift an eyebrow and glance at him out of the corner of my eye. "You really think they're going to believe that she and James were just friends? He had a second phone he was using to call her. What if they really were seeing each other behind Iris's back and it went wrong? Maybe his sister was right and that *is* why he committed suicide. You think that's going to make Thea look more sympathetic to them?"

"It's not about—" he starts, but I cut him off.

"Yes, it is. Everything is about that. *Everything* comes back to how likable you are. How sympathetic. If they already think she did it, we can't play into their hand. At least not until we know more. Okay? Trust me." I grip the steering wheel harder and press down on the gas, putting as much distance between myself and your secrets as possible. Still, I can feel them bearing down.

"Look," I continue when Austen says nothing. "Regardless of whether Thea was seeing James before he died, he isn't the father of her baby, is he? He's been dead since September. So we need to think about who else it might've been. I've been going over it all in my head, and I think there's a chance it's Scott Martin."

"You've got to be kidding." Austen doesn't move a muscle, but I can feel the tension suddenly radiating off him.

"I wish I was," I say dryly. "But he was the only person I ever saw her show any interest in, and a few months ago, when Thea and I were out together, she snuck off and I found her talking to him in the corner of the bar."

Austen rubs the back of his neck. "Well, did you tell the cops about it?"

"I told them they hooked up in high school, but I haven't spoken to them since I found out she was pregnant. But Scott *is* a cop, and it's not like I'm an unbiased witness when it comes to him. Somehow, I doubt they're going to look at him seriously for this."

"Where is all this skepticism coming from?" he asks.

I bite down hard on my lip. I've shown my hand by bringing up your pregnancy, but Austen still doesn't know what Detective Romero asked me about the gun. He doesn't know the way the idea has been festering underneath my skin.

Suddenly, I feel overwhelmed. By Austen. By you. By the events of tonight. I want to go home and fall into a deep, deep sleep. Forget all of it.

"I'm just trying to handle everything the best way I know how. Just . . . promise me you won't go to the cops with the information we found out today. I need to think."

Austen looks at me for a long moment. I can feel his eyes tracing the lines of my profile, studying me. Looking for something—I'm not sure what.

"Okay," he says. "I promise."

I nod and turn up the radio, but the thing is, I don't believe him. I don't believe anyone anymore.

22

Thea

"Isn't this place so cute?" Marley grabs my hand and pulls me through the crowd toward the bar.

"It's a little loud!" I yell, but I don't think she hears me above the din.

"Could I get a Tito's and soda, please? With two limes?" she says to the bartender whose attention she's immediately managed to grab. He nods and they both look at me expectantly.

"Um, a Jack and Coke. Double."

I stand on my tiptoes, taking in the crowd, before Marley hands me my drink and bumps the rim of her glass against mine.

"Cheers!" she shouts.

"Cheers," I repeat before downing half my drink. I feel like I need it to deal with all the bodies pushing in on us. I'm surprised to see this kind of a packed house here in town. Usually people go to Athens if they want to party, but since this place opened up, it's been all the rage.

"I'm so glad we could do this. Things have been so crazy with the move. I feel like we haven't hung out in forever."

"Me too," I say, resisting the urge to grit my teeth. *The move* is basically all I've heard about since she and Austen moved in together four months ago. Negotiating the lease and signing the paperwork and picking up the keys. Then the unpacking and the decorating. The never-ending gushing—about the apartment's character, the lighting in the kitchen, the neighborhood, the young family living next door.

I've been smiling through it, but it's grating, frankly. I'd like to be happy for Marley and Austen in a way that's straightforward. Uncomplicated. But that doesn't feel possible when every conversation is a point-by-point outline of all the things they have that I don't.

"How've you been?" Marley squeezes both limes into her drink and takes a sip, her nose still crinkling in dissatisfaction at the taste of vodka.

Shitty, I want to tell her. "Fine," I say instead. I can't exactly talk to her about what's bothering me, anyway—about James and the way I've been feeling ever since he died, like being stuck here is some kind of punishment for what I did. Certainly not in a place where I can barely hear myself think.

My answer must not be convincing, though, because Marley's got her head tilted to the side, concern softening her features. "I just feel like I've missed so much these past few months. I've been so distracted with the engagement and the move that we've barely had time to talk about anything besides Vintage Doll. But I want to know what's been going on with *you*. How've you been after what happened to your boss?"

I shrug, stirring my drink. Sometimes it's hard to remember that, to everyone else, James was just my boss. A work friend at best. We did a decent job of keeping *almost* everyone in the dark about us, I think, but what I didn't anticipate was having to keep a lid on my grief publicly once he was gone. There's only so much you're supposed to grieve for a coworker you knew for less than six months. "Um, okay, I guess," I tell her. I know I should work up something else benign to say—maybe about how work has been quiet or how I mostly feel bad for his family, but it feels like too much effort to muster it, so I take another long sip of my drink instead, nearly draining it.

"And . . . what about *your* move?" she says tentatively. "I know the twins are starting school in the fall. Have you started planning yet?"

I take a deep breath and pull my hand through my hair. For some reason, I wasn't expecting this question. My move to New York has become a touchy subject since our Instagram account took off. After all, I'm the one who styles most of the outfits, and the one who shoots and edits the photos we take. That's a lot harder to do if I move halfway across the country. Marley is more than just the model—she brainstorms photo shoots, and writes captions, and responds to every-one's comments and DMs—but we both know it wouldn't exist without me, and in the last few months my time line has started to feel more and more like a lit fuse inching closer to an explosion.

"I haven't started to plan," I answer carefully. "It's only March. Six months is still a long way away."

She nods, pressing her lips together, but doesn't say a word, and I feel the awkward silence overtaking us, settling thickly in the air.

"I'll be right back," I say finally, clearing my throat. "I need to pee."

I turn on my heel and duck away from her before she has a chance to respond or follow me. The truth is, ever since we started Vintage Doll, our friendship has changed. Morphed quietly into something I only half recognize. We *need* each other now in a way we didn't before, and I'm not sure I like it. While it's nice to have the validation—tens of thousands of people who follow for *my* styling, I preferred the days when the vintage stores and the thrift hauls were just for us, no one else.

Sometimes I wonder if our friendship would even survive the move. I picture what would happen if I left. The calls growing fewer and fur-ther between. All of our interactions slowly switching from conversa-tions to life updates. Maybe Vintage Doll will be all that's left of it one day. And once that's gone, who knows?

I weave my way through the press of warm bodies, feeling the pounding of the bass in my skull, trying not to meet anyone's eyes. Once I make it to the single-occupancy bathroom, I lock it and press my back against the wall.

I give myself two minutes to scroll mindlessly through my phone, then one more minute for good measure, before I force myself back out into the main room again. Somehow, it feels even more crowded than before and the thought of finding Marley again seems impossible.

"Thea," someone calls out. I freeze at the sound of my name. It isn't Marley. It's a man's voice, one I haven't heard in years.

"Scott," I say, turning around and lifting my face up toward his. Scott has always been tall, but tonight he feels even bigger than I remembered. At least six foot four, his arms and chest densely packed with muscles he didn't used to have.

"Wow, look at you. You're like the Hulk," I manage.

He smiles, and I can tell how pleased he is by the statement. "Well, I had to replace soccer with something," he says, shoving one hand into the pockets of his jeans so I can see the strain of his biceps against his T-shirt. He takes a sip from a half-full cup of beer and sways lightly, either to the music or because he's drunk.

I nod a bit awkwardly and dip my eyes to the floor. I knew Scott dropped out of Clemson his junior year and came back to join the police academy, and I've seen him in passing once or twice over the years, but the last time we really talked was the night of Skylar's party.

Still, I'm struck by how different he seems. There's something hardened behind his eyes that I only caught flashes of that night. The carefree, friendly piece of him feels like it's been filed down to nothing, leaving only sharp edges behind.

"So you're still in town. I thought you were going to New York after graduation." He says it with a spiteful edge, like he's glad I didn't quite make it, and I wonder if it's because he didn't either.

"Yeah," I say, shifting my weight from one foot to the other, feeling defensive. "I was, but I decided to stick around for a bit. My mom had twins. She needed the extra pair of hands. But I'm leaving once they start school in the fall."

He nods and runs a hand over his hair, now buzzed short against his scalp, before stepping closer to me. "That's cool. I'm a cop now. Not sure if you knew."

"I knew," I say.

"It's so loud," he yells. "Do you want to go somewhere quieter to talk?"

I'm about to say no and excuse myself, but before I can he's grabbed my hand and started pulling me toward the corner of the bar, which is only slightly less packed than the rest. It's so dark back here that I have to squint to see, and there's a couple making out against the wall.

"I'm actually here with Marley," I say, pulling my hand out of his. I lift my hand to my mouth and pull nervously at a hangnail with my teeth. "Girls' night out. I should probably get back to her."

Scott takes another step to fill the space between us so we're practically toe to toe, my nose to his chest. I try to back up, but I only get half a step before I feel the wall at my back. "She won't care," he says. "Is she still with Austen?"

"Yeah. They're engaged now."

"Lucky bastard."

"Uh-huh. Look, Scott, it was good to see you, but I really—"

Scott loops his arm around my waist and pulls me right up against him. "You look good," he says, tipping his head so his nose is almost touching mine. "You know, I still think about that party sometimes. About the way you were screaming my name."

I squirm in the hold, still a bit shocked by the force of it. Of finding myself here, trapped by the bulk of his body once again.

"Aren't you married?" I ask. Austen mentioned it to me with faux casualness a few months ago, as though I would care.

A flash of anger crosses Scott's eyes, but then it's gone, and he smiles.

"Yeah," he says, his hand is slipping from my lower back onto my ass. "It's a pretty open-minded marriage, though. I don't think either one of us believes in sleeping with just one person for the rest of our lives. She's cool like that."

I nod, staring straight ahead at his chest. I'm pretty sure he married the local Baptist minister's daughter, Daisy. Somehow, I doubt she's as open-minded as he says.

"I'm really happy for you, Scott, but I should—"

"I'm so glad I ran into you," he says. "I always felt like we had a cool connection."

"I need to go," I try one more time. When he pushes himself closer to me, I press my palms into his chest and push him off, not quite as hard as I can, but close.

"I said I need to go," I tell him as he steps back. He blinks, looking shell-shocked, like it's the first time he's actually heard the words come out of my mouth.

"Jesus, Thea," he says. "I was just being friendly."

I want to laugh at that, but I resist the urge. All I care about now is getting out of this dark corner and back to Marley, but I don't want to risk setting him off further. I spin on my heel to go, but Scott grabs my wrist and pulls me back.

"I can make trouble for you, you know," he says, squeezing my wrist.

"What are you talking about?" I ask, meeting his eyes in the dim light. He smiles and my stomach drops.

"You know there's a file in the station with your name in it? Some woman calls in every couple of weeks to accuse you of murdering her brother. Ring any bells?"

Everything in me freezes. "What?"

He pulls me closer, and I nearly stumble into him. "The death was ruled a suicide, so no one's really bothered to look into it, but what if that file found its way onto a detective's desk? What do you think they would find?"

I study him closely, searching for some hint of the Scott I thought I knew once, but it's long gone. "What do you want from me?" I ask after a long moment.

Before he can answer, someone jostles him lightly from behind. It's barely a bump, but he lurches forward, tipping what's left of his beer down the front of my shirt.

I gasp as the cold liquid splashes down on me, feeling the cling of the wet fabric against my skin and Scott sets the empty cup down on a nearby table, his face eerily calm when he turns back to me. "Shit, I'm sorry," he says. "That guy came out of nowhere. And now look. You're all wet."

He picks up a single, flimsy cocktail napkin from a nearby stack and holds it out to me. I glare at him and grab it, holding it against my shirt as though it will do any good.

"I was going to say I don't want anything from you," he says, fixing his eyes on the spot where the wet fabric strains against my chest. "I just want us to be friends."

Cold fear trickles through me at his words, but I refuse to let him see it. To let him know how badly he's shaken me with this conversation. So instead, I stand up straight and wait for his gaze to drift back up to my eyes before I speak again. "Over my dead body," I tell him before throwing the napkin down and stalking away.

23

Marley

S OMETIMES, WHEN I'M feeling especially masochistic, I think about how easy it would've been for the night of the fight to have gone differently. I think about the sliding doors version of my life where I never saw the text on Austen's phone.

I choreograph it meticulously, like a play in my mind. Austen in the kitchen of our Sherman Hill apartment, standing stubbornly in front of the microwave as he waits for the last kernel of popcorn to pop. You in the bathroom, washing your hands. And me on the sofa, remote in hand, staring intently at the scrolling movie selection. Austen's phone is face-up on the coffee table. The screen lights up with a text, but my eyes stay focused on the TV. They don't slide to the screen. They don't spot Skylar's name alongside the little, green text notification. They don't read the message.

Instead, I pick a movie. You come out of the bathroom, and Austen emerges from the kitchen, popcorn in hand. We sit down together the way we used to in middle and high school, passing the bowl back and forth between us until the popcorn's gone. When the movie ends, you're asleep, your arm tucked underneath one of our throw pillows, and my feet are in Austen's lap. He's rubbing them absent-mindedly, his thumbs kneading gently at my arches. His phone is in his pocket, the conversation with Sky long over.

That night, after you leave, Austen and I get ready for bed together, standing side by side at the his-and-hers vanities I fell so in love with when we toured the apartment. When we crawl into bed, he cups his hand along my hip and draws me closer, tilting his chin down to kiss me. Just once, though. There's a kind of tacit, comfortable agreement between us that we're too tired for sex tonight.

Once I switch off the light, we're both asleep in minutes.

When I imagine it, this is where I linger the longest, on the two of us asleep in our bed. In our apartment. In our life. The one we shared. The one we were building together.

Instead, I saw the text.

At first, I thought it was my phone. I assumed Sky was reaching out about the week's schedule, or the wonky batch of store-branded shopping bags we'd gotten in the day before. But instead, it was an emoji—just one.

I studied it for a second from my seat on the couch before I realized I was looking at his lock screen, not mine. They were both pictures of us taken on the day of our engagement, clutching each other tightly, Austen lifting me off the ground.

"Why is Sky winking at you?" I asked him, setting down the remote and leaning forward to get a closer look.

"Why is Sky doing what?" he said over the sound of the microwave beeping.

"Winking at you," I repeated. "Over text, I mean."

Austen carried a steaming bowl of popcorn into the room and set it on the coffee table.

"Are you going through my phone?" he asked.

"No. It was sitting right there, face-up. I just happened to see the text come through. Why is she sending you flirty emojis?"

A beat of silence passed between us, Austen's eyes fixed on the phone, almost like he was willing it to disappear, calculating his next move. His stance was relaxed, but I could see the flush going up his neck, spreading across his cheeks. "What are y'all talking about?" I asked, trying hard to keep my voice level.

"I—I don't know. Nothing."

I lifted an eyebrow and Austen crossed his hands over his chest. "Is there a problem?" he asked.

Somewhere, deep down, I felt a piece of myself come unpinned from the rest. A small spring, coiled too tight, now released, and panic coursing through me like blood. We'd already had this discussion—this fight—a dozen times before. On and off since high school, really. I was uncomfortable with Austen and Sky's friendship. I didn't trust Sky completely. I knew she didn't waste time with men she wasn't interested in, and it was clear to me that she'd been keeping one eye on our relationship for years.

Since the engagement, things between Austen and me had been rocky. I was feeling the pressure of planning a wedding, and we were both feeling the pressure of paying for it. I was the first of the Moonies to get engaged, and I wanted the wedding to be an event I was proud of. One of those boho-chic Pinterest board nights. The kind that looks effortlessly elegant and timeless. It was turning out to be a lot more stressful and expensive than I'd bargained for.

"So what if we text occasionally, Marley. Don't you trust me?" Austen went on. "Or Sky, for that matter. Isn't she supposed to be your friend?"

"Why should I trust you, Austen?" I countered. "You know how I feel about this, and you do it anyway. It's disrespectful. I don't flirt with your friends."

"I'm *not* flirting with her, Marley. You're making this a way bigger deal than it is."

"Have you ever seen *that* emoji used in a non-flirty context?"

You walked back into the room then, pretending to dry your hands on your T-shirt. I knew you'd been listening from the bathroom and I resented how we must've sounded to you. Like a couple from some terrible sitcom. Nagging wife and henpecked husband.

"What's going on?" you asked. "Everything okay?"

"Fine," Austen said, at the same time I answered, "Not really."

"How often do you two text?" I asked, turning my attention back on him.

"Jesus—"

"C'mon. You owe me that, at least. How often?"

"God, I don't know," he says. And then adds, "Most days, I guess. But so what? There's nothing going on between us. We just . . . talk. That's all."

"About what?"

"Marley—" You tried to cut in, your tone soft and cajoling, like you were going to try and talk me down, but it was too late for that. I was angry now, not just confused or frustrated. I could feel it pumping through me, thick and hot and venomous as a snake. The kind of anger I hadn't felt in months. In years.

It wasn't just about the text anymore. It was about the fact that he talked to Sky almost *every day* and neither of them cared to mention it to me. It was the fact that the world, which had felt stable until five minutes ago, now seemed unsteady underneath my feet.

"What?" I said, turning on you now. I thought you'd back down at my tone, but instead you stood up straighter, pulling your shoulders back.

"You're overreacting. It's just texting."

"Honestly, Thea, shut the fuck up," I spit the words at you, just to watch you flinch.

"I—"

"Let me get this straight," I continued, standing up so I could pace the length of the living room. "I just found out my fiancé chats with another woman *every day*—and not just any woman, someone I've warned him about multiple times. So. Am I really *overreacting* or am I just reacting appropriately?"

"Jesus, Mar. It isn't like that," Austen jumps in now, looking wide-eyed and a bit frantic, like the whole thing has spun too quickly out of his control. "You're making it sound so sketchy. Sky is my friend, just like she's your friend. I've known her for ten years. We talk—that's all. Nothing is going on."

I tried to take a breath, but what came out instead was a terrible kind of laugh—I remember it now, the sharp, hollow rasp fighting its way up my throat. Forcing itself from my lips. "If there's nothing going on, why didn't you tell me about it?" I ask.

"Because there's nothing to tell!" he said, tipping his head back in frustration. "What do you want, Marley? A list of everyone I talk to each day? I thought we were better than that."

"Why don't you both just take a breath?" you said, arms raised toward me like you were approaching an animal. Something you expected to spring forward and bite at any moment. For some reason, it was that—the raised arms—that snapped the last of my brittle self-control in two.

"Christ, Thea, why are you even still here?"

"I'm just trying to help. You're fighting over an emoji. It's ridiculous."

I wanted to scream. This wasn't about an *emoji*. Or a single text. Or even about Sky. Ever since Austen and I moved in together, things had been steadily sliding downhill. Little passive aggressions working their way into our daily routine. Small arguments turning into big fights. About money, kids, the future.

You didn't know because no one knew. Because I couldn't bring myself to admit the truth out loud. So instead, I glared at you and barked, "I don't need relationship advice from the most pathetic person in Riverside and Sherman Hill combined."

I regretted the words the instant they came out of my mouth. I wanted to pull them back inside myself and burn them. To erase their existence, but then there was another beat of silence and I felt dread curling its fingers around me. Crushing the life out of me. I'd said it and, in truth, we both knew that some part of me had meant it.

"What the hell, Marley?" Austen said, shooting me a poisonous look.

You were staring at me, mouth agape, tears welling in your eyes. You looked like you'd been hit.

"I'm sorry," I said. "I didn't mean that. I'm just—I'm angry and—"

"I think you need to leave," Austen cut in before I could finish.

"What?" I looked at him now, his chest heaving with big, angry breaths. Hands balled into fists by his sides.

"I said, you need to leave."

"And go where?" I said, still in shock.

"I don't care."

"Austen, don't do this. Let's talk about this."

"We're done talking tonight," he said, stepping protectively in front of you.

"Thea," I tried one more time, but you looked away from me, down at the floor.

Without another word, I grabbed my keys off the coffee table and my purse off the hook by the door. Once I got out to the car, I sat there for what felt like hours, waiting for one of you to come get me. To tell me it was alright.

You didn't, though, so eventually I started to drive.

I didn't set out looking for a place to go. I was driving aimlessly, the radio cranked high, trying desperately to outrun my own thoughts, when I drove past the new bar off the square—the one you and I had visited just two months before, back in March.

I swung my car into the lot and strode in, my phone clutched in my hand. I would've taken anything, even a *where are you?* text, but nothing came through. And why should it have? Why should either of you want to talk to me after I'd said the things I'd said?

I sidled up to the bar and ordered a shot of vodka, then another. I downed them quickly and was sucking hard at the lime wedge, eyes squeezed closed, when I heard the voice.

"Marley Henderson?" someone said behind me. I spun around, everything going slightly fuzzy around the edges. The room was packed, but Scott Martin took up space.

"Scott," I said, looking up at him. The last time I'd seen Scott had been at this same bar, talking to you, but I wasn't thinking about that then. Instead, I was struck by how much bigger he'd gotten since he moved back to town and joined the police academy. I could see his chest muscles rising and falling beneath the thin cotton T-shirt.

"Is Austen here?" he asked me, swiveling his neck to look at the crowd surrounding us.

"No," I said, bitterness seeping through even one syllable.

Scott raised his eyebrows—thick and rounded like caterpillars. "Oh?" he said. "Trouble in paradise?"

I examined my empty shot glass before turning it upside down on the bar. "You could say that." And then, before he had a chance to ask more questions, "What about you? I don't see your wife around."

"She's at home," he explained. "I'm here for a bachelor party. One of the guys on the force."

I nodded, pressing my lips together, and checked my phone again.

"Can I get you a drink?" Scott asked. He'd pushed through the thick knot of people piled against the edge of the bar, clearing a space for himself despite the chaos.

"Um . . ." I considered for a moment, eyes scanning the crowded room. The tangle of limbs barely distinguishable as individuals in the low light. "Yeah, why not?"

Scott caught the bartender's attention and ordered us both another shot and a can of beer to wash it down with. When the bartender poured our shots, I clinked the edge of my glass to his and threw it back, wincing at the stale, sour burn.

"So," he said, pushing his glass away and picking up the beer. "Want to talk about it?"

"Not really," I said, taking a swig of my own to clear the taste of vodka. I felt lightheaded and a little dizzy all of a sudden. I couldn't remember the last time I'd done three shots back to back.

"Well, whatever he did, he's an idiot. Letting a girl like you wander in here alone . . ."

I fought back the urge to snarl at him and managed a weak laugh instead. "Who says it's his fault?" I asked. "Maybe it's mine."

Scott smiled at that. Wolfish and hungry. "Honestly, Marley, I don't really care whose fault it is. I'm just glad you're here."

It took two more drinks and ten more minutes of small talk for me to grab his hand and pull him back toward the bathrooms. The sex was quick. Animalistic. Scott slipped the bouncer a twenty to look the other way as we tumbled into the single-occupancy bathroom and, as soon as the lock clicked shut, we were on each other. I jumped up and wrapped my legs around his waist as he pressed me to the door, trailing his lips down my throat. We tore at each other's clothes, taking ragged, desperate breaths.

His lips on mine were so different from Austen's—devoid of tenderness. Of intimacy. There was no softness in them, only need. A moan slipped from between my lips as he pushed himself inside me, and another when he wrapped his large hand around my neck, his gray-blue eyes meeting mine.

I'd like to say I didn't enjoy it—that I felt guilty even while it was happening. But the truth is, it was the best sex I'd had in months. I'd forgotten how good it felt to be fucked. Ravaged. To be *desired*.

When it was over and we were putting our clothes back on in silence—cold air pricking along the tracks of my sweat—that's when it hit me, what I'd done. What I'd broken.

I was engaged. Scott was *married*.

"This was a mistake," I said, examining myself in the mirror. I knew I'd have bruises tomorrow, encircling my neck and along my shoulders. I wondered, idly, if he choked his wife that way in bed, or if that was just for women he fucked in bar bathrooms. Maybe we'd both acted completely out of character tonight.

Scott nodded, buttoning his jeans and straightening his T-shirt. "I know," he said. "I feel awful."

"You go out first," I told him. "Go back to your bachelor party. Pretend you got sick or something. I'll come out in a few minutes."

He met my gaze in the mirror's reflection, one eyebrow raised skeptically. We both knew it was pointless. The chances that no one saw us talking by the bar or coming in here together were slim. Probably the whole town already knew. I had to try, though.

"Okay," he said after a long moment.

Once he was gone, I stood alone in the bathroom, smoothing my hair and tucking in my shirt, as if it would make a difference. As if I could hide what I'd done. I listened to the pounding bass and the buzz of chatter through the door.

I waited to feel human again.

I never did.

CHAPTER

24

Thea

WE'RE FIFTEEN WHEN Marley starts sneaking in. It's usually around midnight when she comes. Long after Mom and David have gone to bed. It starts with quick footsteps outside my window, then past me, to Austen in the next room over. The window there barely makes a sound anymore, after so many comings and goings, but I can still hear it through the thin walls. The slight hitch in the latch and the soft thud of her feet hitting the carpet. The deep tenor of Austen's voice, muffled but unmistakable.

It started the summer after freshman year, and it's happened almost every night since. It used to be me whose room she would sneak into, and I think I'm not supposed to know, but really, I listen for it. Almost need the ritual of it before I can fall asleep.

To know that she's safe. That she's here.

But tonight, it's different. I'm tucked up in bed, the covers pulled to my neck, listening for the footsteps. But when they stop, it's in front of my window, not Austen's. I crane my neck toward the pane of glass where Marley's face is looking in, pale and round as the moon. I get up and open the window, not nearly as quiet as Austen's, and step back as she throws her leg over the sill and climbs in, a sheet of cold air coming in with her.

"Hi," she whispers, smiling at me.

"Hi?"

Marley uses her toe to kick off one sneaker, then the other. She's in old running shorts, despite the cold, and a T-shirt. I close the window and stand there, my back to the sill, eyebrows raised.

"I know you know I'm in Austen's room most nights," she says, pulling her hair back into a ponytail. "And I just . . . I can't be at home tonight, but I need a break from Austen. Is it okay if I crash with you?" There's something in her eyes, like doubt, like she isn't sure I'd say yes, that makes me ache.

In answer, I crawl back in bed and hold the covers up for her. She slides herself in so she's facing me, our knees almost touching underneath the cool sheets.

"Are you okay?" I ask, my voice barely audible.

She nods, the movement precise. Considered. "Yes," she says.

"Are you sure?"

Now she looks at me. Blue eyes catching what little light there is and throwing it back at me, like an accusation. She lifts one shoulder in a small shrug. "Mom's not home. I hate being there alone."

"I know," I say.

It's just one more thing that makes us different. Sometimes I'd kill for a night alone in a quiet house. Away from David's heavy footsteps and the squeaking kitchen cabinets, and the stereo always blasting from Austen's room. For me, being alone is peaceful. But Marley's never been like that. She's always bouncing on the balls of her feet, ready to go somewhere, do something, see someone. She doesn't do *alone*.

"Can I tell you something?" she says.

I press my lips together. *You know that you can*, I want to say, but maybe not. Maybe she doesn't. So instead I say, "Of course."

Marley draws her body in tighter. Her back hunching, knees pulling themselves toward her chest as if slowly shriveling. "Austen and I— we had sex. A few weeks ago."

"Oh," I say. And that's it. I try to drag something else out, but there's nothing there. I should've known, and suddenly it feels so blatantly, brazenly obvious—for God's sake, I've been listening to her climb in his window for six months—but at fifteen, everyone is talking about sex, and almost no one is actually having it. I guess there had been some small part of me that thought she would've told me sooner than this, like a real best friend. I hold my breath and listen to the night sounds instead, waiting for her to go on.

"It's been great," she insists, but there's a hollowness in her tone that betrays her. "But, I—I'm on my period right now and it's just—it's awkward, you know?"

I nod solemnly, even though I don't know at all. Wouldn't the person you're having sex with understand something like that? Shouldn't you feel like you could tell them, at least?

In the dark, I shift my knee up so it touches hers. There are so many questions that run through my head, but none of them feel right.

"What's it like?" I ask finally, and as soon as the words leave my mouth, I feel dirty. It's *Austen*, after all. Austen and Marley.

Marley smiles lazily, unhunching just a bit, the knowledge of it unfolding her like a flower in the sun. "It's . . . different than I thought it would be," she says quietly. "But I feel so much closer to him now."

It's not much of an answer, and I want to press her—I want to *know*. But I can't make the words come out of my mouth.

I think about it, though, even though I don't want to. I can't help it. I picture what it must look like, their bodies twisted together. Breath on skin and fingers grazing, grabbing, holding. To know, just for a few minutes, that you're the only thing that matters to someone.

I think of Austen pulling his shirt over his head. Unhooking Marley's bra. Of what it must be like to be touched the way he's touched her.

I can feel the jealousy festering underneath my skin like a smear of rotten fruit, then just as quickly, the shame. I want to bury myself underneath the covers and never come out again. Never have to look either of them in the eye or figure out how I'll manage pretending to be cool about this.

Marley pokes my calf with her toe. "Hey, did you watch that show I was telling you about yet?" Her voice is tentative—like she's trying to feel me out. To mark my place on the emotional map. I wonder if this is why she didn't tell me right away—because, even though everyone has known that Marley and Austen were endgame for years, the three of us are still a trio. And this? This builds a wall between me and them that can't be torn down. This changes things, even if it shouldn't. Because now they're not just Austen and Marley. They're a couple. A real one. AustenandMarley—the entity. I've always known it was coming, but now that it's here, I feel like I've lost something important—something I didn't realize I'd been hanging onto with my fingernails all this time.

Like I don't belong to either of them anymore, and they don't belong to me.

"Thea?" Marley says again, pulling me out of my thoughts.

"Oh," I say, shaking my head. "No, I—I haven't had a chance."

"Do you want to watch it now?"

"Sure," I agree, happy for the distraction of it. To drift off watching something, instead of measuring the silence between us.

25

Marley

THE CHIME ABOVE the gas station door makes me cringe. It's nothing like the delicate ring of the small, silver bell above the door at Southern Moon. It's louder and longer. An electric wheeze that sets my teeth on edge.

An old man saunters in. "You're not June," he says, running his eyes over my chest and my hair.

"I'm her daughter," I answer, meeting his eyes with as much flint as I can muster. It's a trick I've learned since I started taking on shifts a few days ago to make up for the lost income from Southern Moon. Every job has a costume, I'm realizing. At Southern Moon it's a glassy-eyed smile, here it's the dare-you-to-fuck-with-me stare. After watching Mom for years, it hasn't been hard to pick up. "You need something?"

He nods and throws a twenty-dollar bill on the table. "Pump two," he says, and I ring him up. Once he pushes his way out the door, I grit my teeth again and fix them on the TV mounted in the corner of the room, where a telenovela is playing without sound. I've been following the story vaguely all morning. It's about a woman trying to find out what happened to her husband, who was traveling on a ship when it wrecked. Just when the man has washed ashore on some far-flung beach, the door chimes again. I don't bother looking over until I hear him.

"I heard you were working here now, but I thought it was a joke."

"Scott," I say, trying and failing to hide my surprise. "I didn't see you come in."

He has his police uniform on today, his buckles and badge glinting underneath the fluorescent lights.

"Long time no see," is all he says in response. He studies me for a long moment, almost like he did the night of May third, but his eyes are different. The desire from three months ago is gone, replaced by a chilly dispassion.

"What do you need?"

"I'm trying to get gas, but the pump isn't working. Can you come take a look?"

I swallow hard and nod my head. Coming out from behind the counter makes me feel vulnerable. I hate the thought of Scott of all people seeing me here, in my company polo. So far off from what I used to wear to work that it's laughable.

"What do you mean, not working?" I say, pushing open the door against a wave of hot air. I follow him to the truck idling by pump three and bend down to inspect it, but as soon as my back is to him, I feel his hand wrapping around my elbow and yanking me back up to standing.

"Why did a detective come to my house yesterday to ask me questions about Thea?" He releases his grip on my arm, but he has me all but pinned against his truck, his hulking frame blocking the view from the road.

"I don't know what you're talking about," I tell him, though of course I do.

"I know you sent her my way, Marley. I know you told her you thought Thea and I had something going on. You can't possibly think that's true."

"All I did was mention what happened between you back in high school, Scott. I'm sure Romero's just doing her due diligence."

He takes a breath and runs a hand over his short hair. "Look, my marriage *barely* survived what we did," he says. "And I'm pretty sure the only reason it did is because Daisy is eight months pregnant. I can't afford to get sucked into this right now."

"I'm not trying—"

"*You* pulled *me* into that bathroom, okay?" He angles his head down so it's just inches from mine, his tone steely. "And that stupid fucking Instagram account wasn't my fault either. So I don't get why I'm the one you're trying to punish."

"I'm not trying to punish anyone," I say, crossing my arms tightly over my chest and forcing myself to meet his eyes. "I told Romero the truth. That's all."

"Goddammit, Marley. I didn't kill Thea. I don't give a shit about Thea."

"Then why did I see you talking to her at the bar last spring?"

Scott throws his head back and lets out a bark of laughter. "I don't even know what you're talking about. It's a small town and I talk to a lot of people. We were probably just catching up."

"Somehow I doubt you and Thea had much to catch up on," I goad him before I can stop myself. After all, what's Scott going to do? He can't kill me in the middle of a gas station in his police uniform.

I expect the question to make him mad—in fact, it's what I'm going for. I want him to be so angry that he admits something by mistake. I brace myself for him to hit the side of the truck next to my head, the way Austen might. But instead, he rolls his shoulders back and smiles, an eerie calm settling over him.

"Okay," he says, bending even closer to me, his voice so low I have to strain to hear it over the fierce rattle of cicadas. "You want to play this game? I'll play. Let's say I did kill her. And for good measure, let's say I'm the one who's been setting fires all summer, too. Do you really think I'd go down for any of it? I'm a police officer, and this is a close-knit force that looks out for our own. I could do anything—I could kill you right now—and I'd walk away."

"You don't scare me," I tell him, lifting my chin so my eyes meet his. He brings his hand up, curving his index finger and caressing lightly down my neck.

"I should," he whispers, laying his hand across the base of my throat, right where he took hold that night in the bathroom. He doesn't squeeze, but it would take so little effort to wrap both of his meaty hands around my neck and hold me here until I stopped breathing. I feel the lightest tensing of his muscles, like he's considering it, before he drops his hand.

"Leave me out of your little witch hunt," he says before hopping back into his truck and driving away.

I stand out in the lot for a long time, trying to get my breathing under control, and when I go back inside, the rush of air-conditioning feels like jumping into an ice bath. I take my place behind the counter again and glance at the security camera mounted in the corner. There's a blind spot over by pump three, right next to the pay phone. They won't have caught anything, and suddenly I wonder if Scott knew that somehow, or if he even cared.

The door chimes again, and it makes me jump. This time it's two women who walk in, sandals slapping against the linoleum, silver car keys dangling from Kate Spade wristbands. Alysha Pendleton and Katie Selleck—women from Sherman Hill. The kind who've been frequenting Southern Moon since we were in high school. I shrink back, but they don't notice me.

"Of course she did it. She was always kind of weird. Didn't she used to work at the Chicken Shack with that guy who killed himself?" Alysha is saying, and there's a low, bubbling laughter in her voice, like it's funny.

Katie runs her finger over a row of Nutri-Grain bars, crinkling in their foils. "Maybe," she says. "I just have a hard time believing it's a woman at all. I mean, fires? That's a man's ego at work. I'd bet anything."

"What, you think someone is overcompensating?" Alysha laughs again. She checks her reflection in the mirror affixed to the top of the spinning sunglasses rack.

"What if it was like a secret lover? What if he was at the funeral?"

Alysha pulls a pair of aviator sunglasses off the rack and tries them on, her lips pulled down into a frown. "*Everyone* was at the funeral," she says. "But who knows? Maybe they did it together. Like a weird foreplay thing."

"Gross." Katie says, eyeing a massive bag of Doritos with barely disguised hunger, and then, with a small, almost imperceptible shake of the head, turns her attention toward the diet sodas stocked in the fridge at the back.

I lean forward on the counter, head down, ears pricking.

"You know, my mom is friends with the receptionist at the DA's office and apparently Thea was pregnant when she died."

"Really?" Katie says, looking almost gleeful at the gossip. In the shuffle, she pockets a pack of gum nonchalantly, not even bothering to glance toward the counter. Mentally, I file the information away, though I'm not sure why. My days of wielding any kind of social power are long gone.

"Really. Speaking of which," Alysha continues, "how's it going with you and Kyle?"

Katie sighs. "No luck so far. But we've only been trying for a couple of months. I'm not worried yet."

I shift back on my stool and go back to staring at the telenovela, at the woman sobbing into the curve of a younger man's shoulder. He tries to kiss her and she slaps him, hard. Eventually, the bell dings again, Alysha and Katie and the stolen gum pushing back out into the lot, toward their shiny cars.

The women's presence has sparked something in me. A memory of James's fiancée, Iris. The way she refused to meet my eyes the other day—the way she tried not to look at me. At the time, I assumed she was upset, or ashamed, but what if that wasn't the case at all? What if she was hiding something?

The door chimes again. A woman in denim cutoffs asks for a pack of the Marlboro Lights. I take a deep breath and force myself to get swept up in the rhythm of the shift again. The door chime and the metallic clang of the cash register drawer when it shoots open. All the snippets of conversation that pass through the doors, like buses at a depot, all headed to faraway places.

I don't let myself think about Scott. About Iris. About you. Not until Mom pushes in, tying her hair up in a ponytail and straightening her shirt. "How was the shift?" she says.

"Pretty busy, nothing earth-shattering," I lie, stepping out from around the counter and letting her pass by me to the register. "I'll see you later."

Mom nods, her lips pressed tightly together, eyes zeroing in on me like she can see the nervous energy rolling off my skin.

Once I'm out in the parking lot, I don't hesitate. For the first time in weeks, I know exactly where I need to go. I pull out onto the main road, a strip of asphalt shadowed on either side by towering trees, everything choked in kudzu. Riverside is quiet—always, but especially after so many days of unbroken heat. It rolls off the road in shimmering waves, trees reaching spindly, water-starved fingers out to the sky. For a second, I want to scream at nothing. At everything. At this town that I may never get out of and at you for leaving me in it, but instead I keep my mouth closed until I pull into Iris's driveway once again.

It's early evening now, the sun dropping lower in the sky, so I have to shade my eyes against it with my hand as I stalk toward the front door. I knock first, then ring the bell when there's no answer.

Eventually, Iris answers, a can of hard seltzer in her hand. I see the look of surprise cross her face, then something harder.

"Why did James have a second phone for Thea?" I ask, pressing my hand to the door so she can't close it in my face. "I asked before, but you didn't answer me."

Iris frowns, a small wrinkle appearing between her eyebrows. "How should I know?" she says.

"Do you think Julie was right? About Thea and James having an affair?"

"Again. How should I know?" she repeats, her words razor sharp. She looks like she wants to kick me. "I didn't even know they were close until she showed up at my doorstep the day after he died."

"She came here?" I ask, tilting my head.

Iris takes a deep breath and steps away from the threshold, gesturing me inside. After a half-second of hesitation, I follow her lead to the living room.

"The baby is asleep," she tells me, collapsing into the same chair she did yesterday.

"I'll be quiet," I say sitting stiffly on the couch.

She sips from her can, then leans forward, resting her elbows on her knees. "Thea was in and out quite a bit before the funeral. She helped with some of the admin stuff, actually."

"And you never questioned why she wanted to be so involved?"

"Of course I did," she snaps. "I knew James was unhappy before he died.—Our relationship got rocky once I told him I was pregnant.— And then, as soon as he's gone, this pretty girl he's never told me about shows up at my door with tears in her eyes, talking about how close they were? I'm not an idiot."

"Did you ever confront Thea about it yourself?"

Iris takes another swig, studying me. "What are you getting at?" she says finally. "You think I killed your friend?"

"No," I say quickly. "I'm just . . . I need the truth about her."

The corner of Iris's mouth tips up in a bitter smile. "What makes you think I owe you that?" she says, running her finger slowly around the rim of her drink.

"You don't," I say. "But I know that you know what it's like to lose someone you love, and to feel like you're missing important pieces of who they were. To feel like you can't breathe until you understand why you lost them."

I do my best to meet Iris's unyielding gaze as I speak, but it's unnerving all the same.

She takes another slow sip. "Yes," she says finally. "I know exactly what that's like."

"Then please," I say. "Help me understand."

Iris nods her head. It's such a small movement that I almost convince myself I imagined it before she continues. "After everything came out about the second phone, Thea left and she didn't reach back out—except to send me the baby toys when I had James, apparently. I didn't realize they were from her until you showed up."

"So you never saw her again after that day?"

"No, I did. I tried to leave it alone, but I couldn't stop thinking about it. I needed to know the truth about what happened between them. So I found her, and I confronted her."

"What did she say?"

Iris considers my question for a few long seconds before she answers. "She confirmed my suspicions," she says finally, her voice shaking. "And she apologized. I could tell she was distraught—that she regretted it. We came to a kind of . . . truce after that, I guess. I liked being around someone who knew James so well—I know that sounds strange."

"You were friends, then," I say, and Iris nods.

"We were."

I nod, fighting to keep my face neutral at the information. To keep from revealing the sting I feel at hearing that you were confiding in someone who wasn't me. That this woman in front of me probably knew more about your life than I did, in the end.

"Did she tell you she was pregnant?" I ask.

At the word *pregnant* Iris's eyes go wide. The aluminum can crumples slightly underneath her tightened grip. "She was pregnant?" she asks.

I nod, and let the beat of silence hold.

"No, I had no idea. Jesus. How far along?"

"Not far," I say. "It's not common knowledge. But she knew."

Iris looks dazed, and I'm strangely glad you never told her, even though it makes unraveling all of this harder.

"Did she ever talk to you about someone she was seeing?" I ask.

"No," Iris shakes her head. "She never mentioned anyone by name. But the last time she came here, she was really upset. When I pressed her, she said she was in over her head. That she'd gotten involved with someone she shouldn't have, and now it was too late."

"Too late?"

"She must've been talking about the pregnancy."

"Did she say anything else?" I ask, scooting up to the edge of my seat on the couch. "Anything at all?"

"I'm sorry," Iris says. "I tried to get more out of her, but she shut me down. I wish I could tell you more."

"And you're sure she was scared? She told you that?"

"No, not directly. She seemed more upset than anything, but I could see that she was afraid."

"Why didn't you tell us this before?" I ask. I can't help it.

Iris snaps her mouth open, then closed. There's pain bricking up behind her eyes. "It's complicated," she says finally. "I really thought she did this to herself. Even after what she said that night. Thea was . . . a lot like James. Troubled like him, I mean. I thought . . ."

"I know," I say, cutting her off.

Because I do. I know exactly.

"Also," she continues, "that guy you came here with—there's something off about him. I didn't trust him."

"Off?" I say, surprise making my heartbeat pick up. "What do you mean?"

"I can't really explain it. Sometimes I just get a sense about people—I know it sounds crazy. But the way he looked at me, it was like he was . . . desperate. Like he was the one hiding something, not me."

"You're sure?" I ask, biting down my lip, feeling the blood pump coldly through my veins.

A dark look passes over her face before she answers, her tone deadly serious. "I've learned the hard way never to ignore a gut feeling."

CHAPTER

26

Thea

IT'S THE FIRST real day of spring—still weeks until the calendar says it, but the trees tell me so. Little electric green buds just beginning to open, and the winter brown grass standing up straighter. The whole world greening out, slowly coming to life in the sun.

It's my favorite time of year—this little space before summer, when the heat is just a simmering edge to the air, when everything smells like heavy, white magnolia flowers, and the world is pushing its way out of the dirt.

It's sunny today, and spring break. Perfect for going outside, so I grab Austen by the hand once he's done with breakfast and drag him out of the house and across the lawn to Marley's, where I bang on the door.

"What?" she throws it open, looking angry, like she just kicked her way out of bed in tiny sleep shorts and camisole.

"Wanna play sardines?" I ask, pushing my hands into the pockets of my denim shorts—the ones Mom let me take a paint pen to. I've basically outgrown them, and I can feel the waistband squeezing against my stomach, the hem that used to be a few inches above my knee rubbing now against the middle of my thigh, but they're my favorites, so I'll keep stuffing myself into them until Mom throws them away.

"Thea, it's eight AM. I wanted to sleep in," she says, narrowing her eyes at me.

"Well, you're up now."

"C'mon, Mar. It'll be fun," Austen says from behind me. He's got a hopeful look on his face that makes some little piece of me turn over.

Marley looks up and groans. "Fine. Whatever. Let me just get dressed."

She closes the door on us and I turn to Austen. "Why is she so grumpy?" I ask, but he just shrugs. We each face out toward the driveway and sit down on the brick step, kicking our legs out in front of us. In the sunlight, I can see the coarse, dark hairs starting to push themselves through the skin on my legs—longer than Austen's leg hair—and suddenly, they look grotesque. I pull my knees to my chest and tuck my chin over them, my shorts squeezing me in even harder than before.

Austen's only been my stepbrother for a few months now. In some ways, it's good. I like having him around—like the way he laughs at my jokes and the way he always wants to be doing something together. But when it's the three of us, it's different. When he's here, Marley isn't like she is when we're alone, and I'm not either. Instead, we're more. Bigger versions of ourselves. Every action and reaction played for maximum effect. For an audience.

I'm not sure if I like it, especially since I always feel like I'm losing, somehow.

When Marley finally emerges, she's not dressed to play. She's wearing a skirt, and an even tighter tank top than before. I can see the faint outlines of her training bra underneath. I squint at her in the sun.

"Are you wearing makeup?" I ask, studying the smudged line of black around her eyes.

"Just a little," she says defensively, crossing her arms over her chest. "Why do you care?"

I can feel my face screwing up, confused. "Why are you being so weird?"

"I'm not being weird," she says, but there's a snap in her voice.

"Why don't you be it first, Marley?" Austen cuts in, looking anxious. It's a peace offering, we all know—Marley loves to be *it*.

Her shoulders rise and then fall. Her face unclouds. "Okay. Count to fifty," she says.

Austen and I nod and close our eyes. We count to fifty in unison but break into a fit of giggles in the middle after Austen pitches his voice up high and I pitch mine way down low. When we open our eyes, Marley is gone, disappeared somewhere in the neighborhood.

"What's the bet?" I ask him, scanning all the nothingness for a sign of her. Austen and I always make a bet when Marley's it—something to make the game more interesting.

"Thirty minutes of control over the TV?" he says.

"One hour," I counter. I usually win.

"Fine."

We turn toward each other and nod, once, then set off in opposite directions—Austen toward the mouth of the street, and me toward its end. I know most of her hiding spots by now, but sometimes she squeezes herself into some corner of the street I've never noticed before.

The sun rises slowly as I look, the heat climbing by degrees until I can feel my thighs rubbing together below the too-tight shorts, the skin going redder and patchy with irritation. I tug them down and keep going. Check behind the O'Learys' chicken coop and at the top of the magnolia tree. At some point, I circle back to our own houses and toward the area Austen went to search. I have a bad feeling that he's already found her—that they're together somewhere, without me.

"Marley?" I say, ducking around a wild spicebush and finding nothing. I know she won't call back to me, even if she can hear me, so I go back to the street, which has a better view of everything on either side. But as soon as my feet hit the pavement, I hear something. A sharp intake of breath, a rustling, and a *shhh*.

I step toward the source of the sound. A massive, sprawling oak, with branches and leaves drooping close to the ground, tucked back from the road along the edge of the Watsons' ramshackle property. It doesn't take long to spot them now that I'm looking. I can see their legs, dangling between the branches, their feet touching. They haven't spotted me yet, but Marley knows I'm close. I can tell by the rigidity of her back and the sharp tilt of her head, like she's watching. Waiting. Like she's getting ready to leap from the tree and make a run for it. A piece of prey in a predator's grasp, even though I'm the one who lost the game.

"Hey!" I call out.

Marley's shoulders sink and she hits Austen in the arm, but she's smiling now, and so is he.

"How long have y'all been here?" I ask as they hop off the tree branch, Marley smoothing her skirt down across her long, stick-thin legs in a way that makes me think of my own. Of the burning skin on my thighs and the way they jiggle when I do anything, especially in these shorts.

"I found her, like, twenty minutes ago," Austen says, smiling so hard I think his lips might fall off. "We thought you were never gonna figure out where we were."

"Well, I did," is all I can say.

"Let's go again," Marley claps, doing a little hop. "Thea can be it this time."

"But I won," Austen says, a whining edge to his voice.

"*You're* the reason she got around to finding us at all," she says, and it doesn't really make sense, but it's still enough to shut him up. She turns toward me. "Go hide, Thea. And make it really good. We'll count to a hundred."

I press my lips together, my eyes ping-ponging back and forth between the two of them as they trade a look. Brief, but unmistakable. Suddenly, I don't want to leave them here alone together. Suddenly, I regret asking Marley to play at all. "Fine," I mutter, waiting for them to close their eyes before I dart off, back in the direction I came from, their countdown ringing in my ears as I go.

I feel unreasonably panicked as I run—the skin between my thighs stinging more with each step and sweat dripping down my tailbone underneath the suffocating waistband of these stupid shorts. Finally, I skid to a stop in front of an abandoned lot, hands on my knees. I can still hear Marley and Austen's voices rising up over the faint breeze, but I can't tell what number they're on anymore and I've got no idea where I'm hiding.

The voices stop and I whip my head around, like I expect them both to come barreling toward me at once, but they're around a turn in the road, just out of sight. I scan the area for anything and my eyes settle on a clump of overgrown grass and weeds set back from the road, at the far edge of the empty lot. I don't let myself think before I run toward it and throw myself down, spreading myself as flat as possible in the scratchy grass. It's not much of a hiding spot, but as long as I'm not visible from the road it'll have to do.

I squeeze my eyes shut and try to control my breathing. To will the sticky sweat sliding down my nose back into my pores. Down here in the dirt, I feel like a mole or an opossum. Some dirty, unwanted thing. Somewhere close, there's a mewling, pitiful *squeak*. I lift my head for a second, then force it back down. There are dust gnats buzzing around the frizzy edges of my hair, and an anthill a few feet away. I fix my eyes on the little line of ants marching out of the hill and *center*.

After a while, once my breathing has calmed down and the sweat has stopped, there are footsteps, light and fast down the road. Marley.

"Thea?" she whispers, her voice barely reaching me from the road. I hold myself completely still, but near me there's another barely audible *squeak*. Then the sound of grass bending underfoot in slow, deliberate steps. I can feel her coming up on me, but I can't make myself give it up.

Squeak.

"Ha!" she says, her shadow looming over me, blocking the sun.

I look up at her, squinting. "Could you see me from the road?" I ask.

"No," she says. She's already flattening herself into the grass next to me. "This is a good spot."

"Then how did you know I was here?"

She smiles. "Best friend radar," she says, resting her cheek on the back of her hand, her face turned to me. I think for a second of how strange we must look, nestled down in the tall grass this way—Marley especially, in her nice clothes, her makeup done.

Squeak.

I open my mouth to say something, but nothing comes out, and suddenly I feel like there's nothing to say. Like there never has been. I turn myself over and stare up at the sky, sweat dripping down toward the back of my skull, slithering underneath my curls. I think of Austen and Marley perched in that tree, their legs swinging in unison, like they would've been just as happy to stay hidden forever. The way Marley went rigid when she heard me coming. And then of my shorts, and the way I must look to them both. The stupid, eager girl who dragged them both out to play like a child.

Squeak.

"Are you okay?" Marley asks. I jump and turn my head toward her.

"I just—what *is* that sound?" I ask, rolling back over so my nose practically touches the dirt.

"Could be anything,"

I pull myself forward on my elbows in a kind of makeshift army crawl toward the squeaking, which takes me out of the grass and toward a clump of dead trees along the edge of the lot, their branches covered underneath a thick layer of purple wisteria vine.

"What are you doing?" Marley hisses. "Austen'll see you if he comes up this way."

I don't care, though. I keep crawling. Listening for the occasional chirps until I'm practically on top of them and I see it. A small bird—a baby—splayed out on the dirt. It's so young, it's mostly bald, the white down feathers just beginning to poke up through pale skin.

"What is it?" Marley asks.

"Come and see," I tell her, pushing myself up into a squatting position. I look up, searching for the nest it fell out of, but I can't see anything in the dense, vine-covered branches overhead, and even if I could, they're way too high to reach.

"Oh, God," she mumbles.

We stare at it for a few seconds. It's alive, but just barely. Enough to writhe and chirp, but not much else. Its eyes are still skinned over. I watch it stretch its neck out, like it might be searching for food, or its mother. Watch it grope blindly for something, anything, to hang onto, and suddenly I feel a wave of hate wash over me like nausea. A bird like this isn't built to survive. Maybe it wasn't ever meant to.

"What do we do?" I ask, bumping Marley's shoulder with mine.

I look at her—the mascara making her lashes swoop dark and thick where they used to be invisible. The kiss of sun on her cheeks and the flame of her hair and the small breasts starting to poke out from her chest—and suddenly I hate her too. And Austen. And the world that made a bird like this and would let it starve to death in the dirt. But myself—I hate myself most of all.

"It won't survive out here," she says. "We can't save it."

I nod, something inside me clenching like a fist.

We look at each other for a long second, both of us trying to work up the courage to move. Of course, it's her that goes first. Her leg, lifting and coming down on the little bird. Then mine. Over and over and over again, until the chirping stops, a fine cloud of dust rising up around our feet.

"We should go back to the grass," I say when it's over. My voice sounds different in my own ears. Older.

She nods, still watching me carefully. I press my lips together and walk back to the grass, where I spread myself out, but Marley is still standing there, staring down at the little bird's broken body.

Without a word, she lifts her leg once more and brings it down, grinding her heel into the dirt.

27

Marley

THE CAR HASN'T even had time to get hot again when I climb back in and drive away from Iris's. I chew absent-mindedly on the cap of an old Diet Coke bottle and mull over our conversation as I drive back to town.

There's something off about him. The words play back in my mind over and over again. I try to remember how Austen acted during our visit with Iris—if he seemed strange that day—but I was too distracted for anything much to make an impression. Too caught up in the pregnancy news and my own drive to figure out what happened to you. Still, Iris's impression stays with me. Everyone likes Austen. He's got a kind of effortless charm that puts most people at ease. When we were together, he used to joke about all the gossip he collected from his work as a personal trainer. The secrets women would tell him during their sessions. "I know where *all* the bodies are buried," he used to say, laughing.

After a long moment, I shake my head to clear the hijacking thoughts away and refocus on the more important pieces of what Iris told me.

Involved with the wrong person. Too late.

That's what you told her the last time you saw her, and now I'm desperate to know who you could have been talking about. Could it really have been Scott?

I can still feel the ghost of his hands around my neck at the gas station this afternoon. He'd be capable of it—of shooting you, of setting the house on fire to cover his tracks. I'm sure of that. But after that night in high school, you never mentioned Scott again, even when I tried to pry after seeing the two of you together at the bar.

When I pull into my driveway, something feels off. I shut off the car, jangling my keys in my hands, and go straight to your house. I need to talk to Austen about this, and I'm hoping he's here, not in Sherman Hill at the apartment I still can't bring myself to face. At first, I think about going around the back, but there's some force dragging me toward the front door instead. I haven't had the courage to lay eyes on your mom since it happened, but I can't avoid her forever. Not now.

I climb the steps and stand at your front door, take a deep breath, and knock. For a long time, there's no answer. I knock again, listening closely for the twins' playful, simmering chatter or the TV, anything. But all I hear is the AC shuddering and a deadly kind of quiet. Finally, there are footsteps, quick and sharp across the living room, and the door swings open.

"Marley," your mother says, looking surprised. "I . . . I wasn't expecting you."

I dig my toe into the brick and study her for a moment longer than I should. Her face, lined with wrinkles I've never seen, her hair fallen limp and shiny with grease. She looks like she's been holding the world up.

"I'm sorry to bother you," I say and, for a second, I forget why I've even come, but then she steps over the threshold and sweeps me up into a hug. The move is so sudden that it takes the breath out of me, but I throw my arms around her and hold her tightly.

When I close my eyes, I pretend that she's you—that you're here in the flesh—and I have this violent ache to unspool you like yarn. To pull the skin off your body and count the organs. To unthread your veins and lay each piece of you out like inventory to be counted. Assessed.

Yes, she's really here—all of her.

But you're not really here, and I'm shocked by the way my body feels the loss of you. The way your absence feels like a gaping mouth.

"Come in," your mom says, and there's something almost unbearably hollow in her tone.

I swallow and follow her inside. The house is dim somehow, even with the lights on, and there's a muffled quiet to it all. I glance down the hallway and find all the doors closed, no light coming from underneath them.

Before I can ask if Austen's around, I'm sitting on the couch, Dahlia gripping my hand like a lifeline. "I'm so glad to see you," she says, but I can't help wrinkling my nose. She sounds wrecked, but not the kind of days-off-the-tragedy wrecked that I would expect—would understand. Instead, there's frantic, pulsing urgency underneath her words.

I know your mother's grief well. I've studied the angles of it the way a jeweler studies a diamond. I know the contours of it because I've seen them more times than I can count, whenever my mom relapses. I see it when she helps me clean Mom up and put her to bed—the way she looks at her, like she's watching someone she loves disappear right in front of her. I saw it when David left her.

Your mother's grief and I are old friends, which is why I know she won't tell me what's wrong now. Maybe it's the gambling debt she told my mother about, or maybe it's something else.

"I'm sorry I haven't been over to see you," she says quietly. "I've been meaning to check on you for days. To see how you're doing. But I just . . . I haven't really been able to get myself out of the house." She offers a watery smile.

"Dahlia," I say quietly. "You have nothing to apologize for. I'm—I'm so sorry. About everything."

She reaches out and puts a hand to my cheek. I want to take it with my own. To hold it to me and curl up with it the way a child would.

There were moments growing up, after Mom had come back, when I'd watch Dahlia hug you, or brush the baby hairs off your forehead and press a kiss to your skin, and I'd find myself wanting to rip her from you like a doll, and drag her away for myself.

"Marley," she says now, her voice quiet. Suddenly, I realize Milo and Finn must be asleep already. "She loved you so much."

"I loved her too," I tell her, feeling bereft now. Wrung out.

"Did you know about the baby?" she asks, and then she's crying. I watch her face crumple and pull her to me again, feeling the writhing of her body like it's my own.

This is the thing no one tells you about grief—they don't talk about the strain of it. The constant, never-ending reach. The feeling that there has to be something you can *do*—cry harder or scream louder or kick furiously enough—to make the universe take pity. To make someone un-gone. And then, the most brutal part, the day when you realize that there's no one listening to you scream—that the person who you're grieving will never be un-gone—and you keep straining anyway. You can't stop yourself because *what if?*

"I really didn't," I tell her finally, when the sobs have died down. "I wish I had. I wish we'd never stopped talking. I can't believe—it just doesn't feel real, you know?"

She nods, pressing her lips together. I watch her chest lift and deflate with a long, steady breath. "I do." She dabs at the corner of her eye with her shirt collar. "I'm starting to feel like I didn't know my own daughter at all."

"That's not true," I say reflexively. But then I think, *No, she really didn't know you at all*, and neither did I, when it came down to it. Maybe James did, or Scott, or Iris. Or maybe no one did. Maybe you liked it that way.

You mother smiles at me, just barely, but there's something real in it. A kind of resignation. It's a look I know well—a look we've shared a million times before, taking care of Mom. "We don't ever really know people, I guess," she says. "Even our own children. You grow up. Become adults with minds we can't ever get inside. It's how it's supposed to be. I just wish it wasn't so brutal."

I nod quietly, but there's a pit opening up in my stomach, because she's wrong. I may not have known you the way that I thought, but you knew me to the marrow. You had parts of me that I never showed to anyone else. *Could never* show to anyone else.

"Can I ask you a question, Dahlia?" I ask. I hadn't planned on it, but now that I'm sitting here, I can't help myself. I've been so focused on chasing down who the father of your baby is that I'd almost forgotten about the other question that's been plaguing me.

"Of course."

"I'm sorry to bring this up, but I know that David had a gun. Did he take it with him when he left, or is it still in the house?"

Dahlia stares at me blankly for a moment. "He took it with him," she says. "Why?"

I shake my head quickly. "No reason," I say. "Just . . . this whole thing, it has my head spinning. I want to make sure you and the boys are safe. That you've got some kind of protection. That's all."

Dahlia's shoulders soften. "That's sweet of you," she says. "We're alright, though. I promise."

I nod, feeling jumpy. Uncomfortable. "Has Austen already gone home for the night?" I say after a long silence. "I know he's been helping out since the funeral. I was hoping to catch him, but it looks like I'm too late."

Your mom shakes her head, looking tired again. "He isn't here," she says quietly. "He's down at the station. That detective came and asked for him a few hours ago. Said they had more questions for him."

I can feel my eyebrows furrowing. I shake my head. "What questions?"

She shrugs. "Who knows?" she says, but there's a ragged kind of pain underneath her voice—the same pain that I heard earlier and, just like with Detective Romero that night at the station, I know there's something she isn't telling me. Something she's holding close to the chest.

I swallow hard, racking my brain. Is Austen a suspect? For a moment, I try to picture him setting a house on fire—trapping you inside. The image doesn't fit, though. And besides, what reason would he have?

Then I run my eyes over the mantel above the fireplace—the photos of all four kids, lined up like little soldiers—Milo and Finn clutching each other as infants, and then one of you and Austen. It looks like it might've been taken outside the church the day of Dahlia and David's wedding. You're both around ten. You're wearing a pink dress and Austen's in a little suit, and you're smiling at each other. Beaming, really, both of you half doubled over in laughter.

Involved with the wrong person. Too late.

The way he looked at me, it was like he was . . . desperate. Like he was the one hiding something.

The words hang there, limp and lifeless for a moment before, suddenly, they snap into place. I look at your mom and she meets my eyes straight on. Neither of us speaks, but we don't have to. We're thinking the same thing. The thing neither of us can say out loud.

What if you didn't tell me because you couldn't? Because the father was the one person I'd never forgive you for?

"I need to go," I manage, pushing myself off the couch and out the front door in a kind of half-daze that I stay in all the way home. I barely realize what I'm doing—jamming my key into the lock and forcing the sticking door open with my shoulder.

What I do remember is this—the keel of my stomach and that gaping mouth of your absence opening wider. Swallowing me whole.

28

Thea

"O KAY, I THINK that's everything," Mom says, wrapping a shawl around her shoulders and slipping on her one and only pair of heels. "They're zonked tonight, so you shouldn't have any trouble with them."

June shoots me a knowing look from her spot by the door, but there's a fond smile tugging at the corner of her lips. Even now, after all this time, Mom still gets jittery about leaving the twins at night.

"I know. I helped put them to bed," I say. "Now go have fun. You deserve a night out. Both of you."

"Hell yeah," June agrees. She's squeezed into her usual going-out attire—a sparkly strapless dress that looks like it was plucked off a rack in 2004, and cowboy boots. Mom is a bit more conservative in a soft, swingy skirt and a V-neck T-shirt, her curly hair hanging loose over her shoulders. I'm always struck by how young she looks when she gets ready with June. Like I'm catching a glimpse of the girl she was before me—just seventeen when she found out she was pregnant.

She must've been so scared then. Marley's mom had Lawson, Marley's dad, but mine was completely alone. My grandparents died in a car accident when she was young, and she'd been in foster care since she was seven. She told me that she didn't even know who my father was, though she suspected a drifter who'd come through town to work in the factory for a while.

"I don't remember that time in my life well," she'd said once, with a grimace. "But whoever he was, he must've been beautiful and smart. Because how else could I have gotten you?"

"Okay," she nods now, running her hands nervously down the fabric of her skirt. Now that I'm thinking about it, I can't remember the last time I saw her wearing one.

"You look beautiful," I tell her, and she flushes, dipping her head.

"You look *hot*," June says. She's already a little drunk, swaying lightly in her shoes.

On the rare occasions it's come up, I've always told people I was raised by a single mom, but looking at her and June now, I wonder if, really, I was raised by two. I think of all the nights I've spent at June's over the years. It was June who took me shopping for my first bra, and June who taught me how to drive a car. The men have come and gone, leaving varying degrees of damage in their wake, but Mom and June are the two most constant presences in my life, besides Marley. For better or worse, they're my family.

Mom grabs her purse from the counter and pulls me into a quick hug. "Thank you," she says. "Now leave the porch light on, okay? We don't want the house to look abandoned."

I almost laugh. "The arsonist isn't going to come for us here," I say. But, really, why wouldn't they? At this rate, it's only a matter of time before they make a mistake and pick the wrong place to torch. Before someone gets swallowed by the flames.

Reluctantly, Mom lets herself be shepherded out the door. When she and June are finally gone, I turn to the empty house and take a deep breath. I haven't even had a chance to plop myself on the couch yet before my phone begins to buzz in my back pocket.

Austen the caller ID declares. I sigh and hit answer, pressing the phone to my ear.

"Hey, what's up?" I ask, like I don't already know. Since he and Marley broke up, he's called almost every day. I don't think he knows what to do with himself anymore.

"What are you doing tonight? Want to go to a movie or something?" he asks. I can tell that he's at the gym—I can hear the grunts and the clank of metal in the background. He's been there even more than usual recently. So much it's actually beginning to worry me a little.

"I'm watching the boys while Mom and June are out in Sherman Hill. They even got a hotel room so they could be debaucherous without paying for an Uber."

"Ah," he mutters. "Gotcha."

"You can come over, if you want. The twins are already in bed. We can watch something here."

"Great, I'm on my way. Be there in ten." He hangs up and I go to the kitchen and preheat the oven for the frozen pizza we've got on hand. I'm slipping it out of the box when Austen walks in.

"Marley's car is in her mom's driveway," he says.

I shrug, slicing open the plastic wrapping around the pizza with kitchen scissors and placing it carefully on the oven rack. "It usually is. She lives there now."

"Have you talked to her at all?"

"No," I say flatly. "I haven't."

"Do you think she saw me come in?"

"I don't know, maybe. What's it matter, anyway? You can't hide from her forever. You were engaged, for Christ sakes."

He hangs his head. "I know."

I stand with my back against the counter and take a deep breath. "Hold on," I say, grabbing two mugs from the cupboard and a bottle of wine from the fridge.

I pour us each a generous glass and tilt my head toward the living room, farther from the boys' room than the kitchen. "Let's talk in there," I say, grabbing my mug in one hand and the rest of the bottle in the other.

We settle on the couch, me tucked into the corner where I always sit, and Austen sprawled a bit awkwardly on the other end. I wonder if he feels out of place here now, after living on his own. Like he's outgrown this tiny, dingy house on its dead-end street.

"I just—" he starts, but I hold up a finger to stop him and take a long gulp of wine. He does the same.

"Okay, now let's talk," I say, feeling fortified. Since what happened two weeks ago, we've been mostly tiptoeing around the subject of Marley. Both of us doing our best to pretend she never existed, even though she's been in the house right next door ever since. After all, what do you say when the equilibrium you've known since childhood disappears? What do you do with the vacuum of space and time and emotional energy that it leaves behind?

"I don't know what to say to her," Austen says.

I take a deep breath. "That's understandable," I say, careful to keep my voice even. I never liked being Marley and Austen's relationship middleman. It feels different now that Marley did what she did, though. Before, I could just be a listening ear. Now I have to pick a side.

And how could I pick Marley's after she finally admitted what I've always suspected—that she thinks I'm pathetic? After she deleted our Vintage Doll account without even warning me that it was coming?

"I'm still angry," he says, his voice cracking. "Like, *so* angry."

Me too, I want to say, but I don't. He wouldn't get it, really. Austen gets angry about things that are concrete, not ideas—not the spaces in between. The things you can feel happening, but can't articulate.

The truth is, Marley has been leaving me behind for a long time. She's done it slowly, not all at once, maybe never even completely, but she *was* doing it all the same. More days spent at Southern Moon or with Sky, less time with me. We almost never hung out alone anymore, unless it was to get content for the Instagram. It was always with Austen, or at a crowded bar somewhere with one or two Moonies tagging along, monopolizing the conversation.

And now that those people have all shown her what they really think of her, now that she's told me what she really thinks of *me*, we can't ever be like we were. I'll always wonder if her apologies were because she had nowhere else to turn.

This line of thought doesn't quite erase the guilt I feel for not reaching out to her in the wake of the Vintage Whore Instagram account and the hell I know she's been going through since that night—but it comes close. Close enough that I've continued to keep my distance, at least.

"Do you think you'll forgive her?" I ask Austen, tucking a piece of hair behind my ear.

He glances at me, something in his eyes I've never seen before. "No," he says. "I mean, yes. Probably. With some time. But we won't get back together."

I blink, trying to make sense of the words, and the way he said them, like he's finally decided to tell me a secret that he's been keeping for a long time.

Austen and Marley have been together since we were fourteen. It never occurred to me that they'd ever *not* be, even with what happened. I've been assuming the two of them would smooth it out after a few months.

"We'd been rocky for a while, even before that night," he says. He looks tight, like he has every muscle held under strict control, and I have an irrational desire to reach out and touch him. To run my hands over his skin and unwind him like a coil of rope. "Ever since we moved in together, I guess."

"You had?" I ask, genuinely surprised. To hear Marley tell it, everything was perfect at the new apartment.

"I don't know, it was like . . . she changed. I always knew she wanted to be in Sherman Hill. That she wanted to be like Sky and all the others at the shop, but actually moving there—getting engaged—it was like it sent her into this frenzy. Everything was about what we could and couldn't afford. Sometimes I felt like she had a running list in her head of all the things I couldn't give her and I just started thinking, *is it always going to be like this?*"

"I'm sorry, Austen. I had no idea."

The corner of his lips quirks up grimly and he takes another long gulp of wine, nearly draining his glass. "I never told anyone. We were together for so long, I didn't feel like I could. I figured everyone just expected us to be happy."

I don't say anything, because he's right—we did.

"Anyway, I'm glad I have you. My other friends haven't been much help. They keep trying to drag me to a strip club."

I can't help but laugh at the thought of Austen in a dimly lit club, stuffing ones into some stripper's G-string. Even single, heartbroken Austen. The image feels out of sync with the rest of him. "It might not hurt," I say, unable to keep the smile out of my voice as I sip my wine. I can feel the drink slipping through me like silk, pulling loose the corded muscles in my back and shoulders, slowing my heartbeat and my breathing. For the first time all summer—all year, really—I realize I feel okay. Normal.

Austen cracks a smile at that—a real one. "Yeah, right," he says, pouring himself another mug, his cheeks tinging red. "It feels weird to think about even talking to another woman. Let alone, I don't know, touching one. Marley's the only person I've ever been with. The only person I ever even *thought* I'd be with."

"You talked to Sky," I say, and his smile drops. I defended Austen that night, but the more I've thought about it, the more I understand where Marley was coming from—at least in that regard. Sky can be slippery, and anyone with eyes can see she's been interested in Austen for years.

"I know," he says. "I just . . . things were rough with Marley, and you know how Sky can be—so insistent. And really, nothing was happening between us. We were just texting."

"Did you *want* something to happen?" I ask.

He takes another sip of wine, wincing slightly at the question. "No," he says, but I'm not sure I believe him. "But Sky is, um . . . well, she's made it clear that if I ever did want something to happen, it could."

"So Marley *did* have a reason to be worried."

"I don't know," he admits, looking miserable. "Maybe. But that doesn't mean she had a reason to go at it with Scott Martin in a public bathroom."

"No," I say, emptying my cup and setting it down on the coffee table. "It doesn't."

Austen refills my mug without a word, a heavy pour. "Did it . . . did it hurt you that it was Scott?" he says, his voice tentative, like it's a question he's been building up to.

I press my lips into a flat line and think about that night, years ago, in Sky's basement. The suffocating heat of Scott's body as it pressed into mine and of how I felt afterwards, like someone had taken a wrecking ball to my body. The way I sat in the dark until Austen found me.

"That was a long time ago," I say finally. "I just hope, for her sake, that he's learned some new tricks since then."

I try for a smile, but I can tell by the look on Austen's face that I haven't quite pulled it off.

"What about now?" he asks finally. "I feel like we never talk like this anymore. Are you seeing anyone?"

I raise an eyebrow. "I live with my mom and two four-year-olds who I spend all my free time babysitting. What do you think?"

"I guess I didn't think about that," he says.

Has he ever thought about it? I want to ask in a flash of spite. Has he ever wondered what it was like for me to stay here while he moved out and moved on, or did he assume I'd wanted to do it? That putting my life on hold was something I was enjoying?

It hasn't occurred to me until now just how differently the twins affected our lives. For Austen, they're little brothers he can pop in and visit whenever it suits his schedule. He can spend a few hours chasing them around the house and giving piggyback rides before getting in his car and driving home to a quiet apartment. Sure, he's been siphoning a portion of his paycheck to us ever since his dad walked out to help pay for necessities, but so have I, and on top of that, I spend all my time here, building Legos and reading picture books and cutting grapes in half. No one ever expected Austen to do that. To sacrifice the things that I have for the sake of a family he didn't create.

I clear my throat. "Besides, I'm going to New York anyway. There's no point in dating anyone here."

"Right. When are you planning to go again?"

"Um, in the fall, when the twins start school," I say. It's been my answer for so long that it slips out of my mouth immediately, but as soon as I say the words, I realize how close we are to the deadline. Only a few months away now. I swallow the lump in my throat.

"That's sooner than I realized. You must be excited," he says, nudging my knee with his.

I force a smile and take another sip, then another. "Yeah, I am. Of course."

I can tell that Austen clocks the weirdness, but he doesn't say anything, so we sit in silence for a bit, listening to the faint hum of the AC. I feel my heartbeat picking up as I consider the possibility of leaving Riverside. Of planting myself a thousand miles away from everyone and everything I've ever known. Who will I be then? Without the twins, or Marley, or even the Vintage Doll account to define myself against?

Before Marley deleted the account, I felt like I had a stepping stone into the world I wanted to inhabit there. Proof of relevancy. But it's gone now. All wiped away with the press of a button.

"Do you remember being their age?" Austen cuts into my thoughts, nodding to the picture of the twins on the mantel. "Sometimes I wish I could go back to that. Being so carefree all the time. Assuming that things were going to keep getting better and better. That everyone you loved was always going to be around."

Austen's mom left when he was six, but I only know that because David told me once. Austen doesn't talk about it, like I don't talk about the dad I never knew. It's a common thread that has always bound Marley and Austen and me together even more tightly. We all knew exactly what it felt like to be left behind.

"I remember," I say. Another sip of wine. *I'm drunk*, I realize idly, wrapping my hands around the mug as if it contains something hot. "When I was the twins' age, Marley was living here." Then, after a pause, "Sorry. I know you don't want to talk about her anymore."

"No, it's fine. I'm going to have to get used to it at some point, right? I mean, the two of you will always be friends."

I don't say anything. Just let the silence sweep over us. I wonder if he forgot what Marley said to me that night. Maybe he's been too wrapped up in what she did to him—I wouldn't blame him.

"Okay," he says, leaning in conspiratorially. *He's drunk too*, I notice. More drunk than I've seen him in a long time. The realization makes me fizzy with excitement. I can't remember the last time I got drunk with someone. Can't remember, either, the last time I talked to Austen this way, like a friend—not my ex stepbrother, or Marley's fiancé. Before Austen moved out, before he proposed, before he even asked Marley on a date, we used to be friends. Used to make each other cry with laughter. We'd spend entire weekends together, binge watching movies or teaching each other card games. Somewhere along the way, though, we lost it.

"What?" I ask.

"I'm sorry, I know I should drop it. I just . . . I can't stop thinking about it."

"About what?"

"You can tell me to fuck off."

I shove him in the shoulder, hard enough that a drop of wine splashes on my leg, but I'm smiling. "What?" I ask.

"Is Scott the only person you've ever been with?"

The question takes me aback. I draw in a sharp breath, feel my heartbeat rachet up a notch.

"I'm sorry, ignore me. I'm drunk," he says, setting his mug on the coffee table and pushing it away. "That was a stupid question."

"No, it's okay," I say, gripping the handle tightly. "Embarrassingly, the answer is yes."

"And it was shit?" he says.

I nod.

He studies me for a moment, lips slightly parted, his eyes traveling up and down the length of my body. "Thea," he whispers my name like it's a confession. It changes the air in the room—charges it with pulsing, live-wire electricity. Suddenly, I feel combustible. Like one wrong move will fry me.

"Yes?" I whisper. I can hear the blood rushing in my ears. Can feel my own heart pounding inside my chest. For the first time, I realize how close we've gotten, our noses nearly touching, his knee pressed against the side of my thigh. I've never let myself think of touching Austen for more than a second or two for fear of unlocking exactly this. The longing I've pushed down since I was a child. The want I've trained myself to turn away from.

Because I can't have Austen. Not when I was a girl with a crush, and definitely not now, after ten years spent pretending to be happy with the way things are. After Marley.

Austen reaches out and takes my hand in his, bringing it up to his mouth and brushing the knuckles softly with his lips. There's naked fear in the movement. The kind that comes with doing something you can't take back. Of crossing a line you can never uncross.

He pulls gently on my hand, turning it over to kiss the underside of my wrist, and I wonder if he can feel the frantic hum of my heartbeat just underneath. His lips are soft, and the graze of them against my skin makes my blood feel fizzy and my breathing falter. I hold myself perfectly still as he works his way up my arm, following the line of my scar up to my elbow. When he's done, he draws himself up to look at me again, his face just a few inches from mine.

"I could make you feel good," he says.

"Austen," I breathe his name and he moves even closer, pressing his forehead to mine.

"Hmm?"

"Nothing would ever be the same between us."

"We're already there, Thea."

He's right, I realize. The thought makes goose bumps rise up on my skin. There's no coming back from this moment.

"You really want to?" I ask. I can't help myself.

The corner of his lip ticks up in a smile. His voice is low and smoky. Seductive in a way I've never heard it before. "Don't tell me you've never thought about it," he says.

"That's not an answer to my question," I say.

"Yes, it is," he counters, his lips so close they almost touch mine. He reaches up and brushes a strand of hair away from my face, tucking it behind my ear. "I want this. You. I always have."

"If you're looking for a rebound, anyone else would be a less complicated option. Even Sky."

He arches an eyebrow at me. "You can tell me no. We can pretend this never happened, if that's what you really want."

"It's not," I say, too quickly.

"Then tell me what you do want."

I swallow hard, feeling the heat come off him. His fingers twist lightly into the fabric of my T-shirt, like he wants to grab me and pull me closer. I'm acutely aware of the few inches of space between us and how little it would take to erase them.

"I need you to say it, Thea. Say you want me the way I want you."

"It isn't that simple," I tell him, but my brain is fogging over. Here, with his breath feathering across my neck and his hands tangled in my shirt, I can't think straight.

"Yes, it is."

I reach up and press my hand to his jaw, feeling the rough stubble underneath my palm. I've wanted to do this for so long and, somehow, it's exactly how I pictured it—on the rare occasions that I did let myself picture it. And the way he's looking at me makes me feel like someone other than myself—someone beautiful and sexy and *interesting*. Someone like Marley.

The thought shoots through me with a white-hot intensity that's almost painful. Marley.

For a second, a ripple of doubt goes through me. I know what I'm doing will hurt her, probably more than anything. It will break us forever. But the thing is, we're already broken, and she's the one that broke us. Austen and I are the left behind, not the leaving.

And as much as I'd like for it not to be true, there's something thrilling about it.

"Okay," I say finally.

"Okay, what?" he asks, tightening his grip on my shirt and pulling me closer, so my lips hover just an inch from his.

"Okay, I've thought about it before. Okay, I want you the way you want me."

He smiles at that and, Jesus Christ, it's dazzling. Suddenly, I wonder how I've managed to make it twelve years in his orbit without this.

There's no real beginning to the kiss. No warming up. As soon as I press my lips to his, we're in the thick of it, Austen's hands wrapping around my waist, pulling me to him so that I'm not sure where the lines of my own body begin and end. I can feel his heart beating as fast as mine as we tangle ourselves together, limbs hooking each other frantically, desperately—his hands fisted into my hair, my legs around his hips. A hunger like I've never known scorches through me and suddenly I understand why people burn their whole lives to the ground for this.

Why we are burning our whole lives to the ground for this.

29

Marley

I DRIVE TO SHERMAN Hill in a blind panic, hands shaking on the steering wheel, brain playing a skipping track of memories. The three of us playing hide-and-seek and card games and watching movies. Driving to school together. Trick-or-treating. Attending parties.

You and Austen were stepsiblings. Then, when your parents divorced, you were friends. You weren't anything more than that. You couldn't have been. I would've *known*. I would've sensed the possibility even before it materialized.

I pull into my old apartment complex—just Austen's now—and don't let myself think before grabbing my keys and stalking up the stairs toward the second-floor apartment.

When I moved out, I left my key behind, but I forgot until a few days later that I'd had a copy made and kept at Mom's in case I lost mine. I haven't used it before today, though. In truth, I've been scared to come back here. Scared of what I might find in the apartment we used to share. Evidence of another woman. Of a life I was no longer involved in. But this is so much worse than any scenario I could've imagined.

I unlock the door and stand for a moment in the dark entryway. The place smells like Austen—like Old Spice and lemon verbena and clean laundry. It's so strong it almost bowls me over. My hand finds the light switch and the room is thrown into harsh white light. It's a bit messier than I kept it—there are dishes in the sink and water rings on the coffee table I refinished, but other than that, it looks mostly the same. Somehow, it's more unsettling than a full-scale renovation would've been.

"Austen?" I call out. I know he's at the police station, but I can't help it. I shut and relock the door behind me, pressing my back to it and looking out over the space.

The last time I was here was the night after the Scott Martin incident. The news was already spreading by then. Already taking on a life of its own. People saw us talking by the bar and they took pictures of me pulling him into the bathroom. There was even a video of him reemerging, looking rumpled and smug.

I'd put off coming back for as long as I could, but when I slipped in and closed the door behind me, I found Austen sitting on the couch, staring at nothing, a half-empty beer bottle in his hand and three empties on the coffee table in front of him.

"Austen?" I said softly, taking a step toward him. He didn't seem to hear me. Didn't even acknowledge me until I walked over and placed my hand on his shoulder. Then he flinched.

"How's Scott?" he asked bitterly, leaning forward out of my grasp.

I opened my mouth, but nothing came out. I couldn't exactly deny what had happened—not with so much evidence. So many witnesses.

"Austen," I said again, rounding the couch and sitting down next to him. I had an awful sinking feeling as I looked at him. Any hope I had that we could fix things draining away when I took in the rigid set of his shoulders. The popping muscle in his jaw.

"Want to know how I found out?" he asked, his eyes darting to me, and then away just as quickly. He paused, as if waiting for an answer. When I said nothing, he continued. "Skylar called me. Last night, around midnight. She wanted to see if I was okay. When I said I didn't know what she was talking about, she sent me some of the pictures of the two of you. Said her friends had sent them to her. That it was all over town. Everyone already knew."

"I'm so sorry," I said finally, a tear rolling down my cheek. "I made a mistake."

Austen brought the half-empty beer bottle down on the coffee table with enough force that it shattered. I jumped, as the shards of glass landed on us both, beer pooling on the table and soaking into the carpet. "A mistake," he said, his voice deadly quiet as he flexed and fisted his now empty hand. "Was that what it was?"

"Yes," I whispered. "A terrible mistake. I was just angry and drunk, and I—"

"I don't need to hear it," he said, rolling his neck from side to side, joints cracking with the movement.

"Okay," I said carefully. "What do you need to hear? What do you need me to do? Tell me and I'll do it. I'll do anything."

He looked at me again, his lips pulled back into a cruel imitation of a smile. "Anything?" he said. "What if I told you I wanted to get even? Would you let me pull Sky into that bathroom? Would you be able to look at me the same way afterwards if I did?"

My heart twisted at the thought. "I'm sorry," I said again. "But please—it's been eight years. We can't just throw that away."

"Really? Seemed like you threw it away pretty easily last night."

"I didn't—"

"Be honest with yourself, Marley. We were on rocky ground before this happened. We have been for a while. I think it's time for us to face up to the truth."

I bit down hard on my lip. "And what's that?" Asking the question felt like standing on the edge of a cliff, looking down over the precipice and waiting for a gust of wind to take me over. I knew what he was going to say before he said it, but the words still hit me like a freefall.

"That this is over. That we aren't right for each other. Maybe we never were."

I blinked hard as tears streamed down my cheeks and Austen sat next to me, pressing the heels of his hands into his eyes.

"Please don't do this," I said when I was able to form words again. "I love you."

He stared at me, his eyes dry, his face devoid of expression. "No," he said finally. "You don't."

And then he reached out to grab the empty bottle closest to him, and he smashed it too. Followed by the next, and the next. When he was done, he stood up, brushed the shards of glass from his pants, and left without another word, glass crunching underneath his shoes on the way out the door.

Now I stand blinking at the empty space, reliving it, tears pooling in the corners of my eyes for a few moments before I remember why I came here.

I unstick myself from the door and head back to the bedroom. *This* room Austen has changed. The duvet I bought at Home Goods is gone, replaced with Austen's old navy blue comforter from high school. The bed is unmade, the sheets wrinkled.

I poke through the closet and the chest of drawers, finding nothing out of the ordinary, then set my sights on the bedside table where there's a bottle of water, a remote control, and a book called *The Science of Strength Training*. Inside the table's one drawer, I find a mostly empty box of condoms—something we never used after I got my IUD—and my engagement ring. The sight makes me jump back like I've been bitten by a snake.

Once I've recovered, I press a hand to my mouth and go to the bathroom, surveying Austen's things until my eyes catch on two toothbrushes poking out of the toothbrush holder.

Out in the living room, I hear a sound. The bolt being unlocked. Then footsteps. For a moment, I consider hiding, but that's not why I came here.

I poke my head out of the bathroom and watch him stand in the living room, his back hunched, dark circles shadowing his eyes.

The sight of him like this is so unfamiliar that it makes me ache in some deep, empathy-soaked place I didn't even realize I had, but then, fast as a flash, that feeling is gone, shifted out entirely for the anger pulsing hot and thick underneath my skin.

I slip out of the bathroom and stand in the hallway in front of him. There's fear bulging on Austen's face when he spots me—the whites of his eyes going wide, and the sharp intake of breath, like I'm coming at him with a knife.

I force myself to stay still, but what I really want is to jump on him and *grab*. To tear joints from their sockets and hear the crunch of his bones underneath my foot. I want to burn him the way that he's burned me, but I never could.

For a long second, we just stare at each other, and I feel sunk, the anger rushing out of me like a plug pulled on a bathtub drain and only a kind of longing left in its place as I take in the ruined look in his eyes. *I wanted to marry you once*, I think, but it's a hollow thought. I feel a million miles away from the woman who wanted to marry Austen Brown.

"Marley," he says. "What are you doing here?"

"Tell me it's not true," I say, and I hate how much it sounds like a plea, even though it is one.

"What are you talking about?" he asks, his eyes darting toward the floor, but I can tell he knows exactly what I mean.

"There are condoms in your drawer. There are two toothbrushes in the bathroom. Tell me they're for someone besides her, please. I *need* for you to tell me that."

I expect him to break—to hang his head in defeat. But instead he glares at me, his nostrils flaring. "I don't need to tell you anything," he says. "We broke up. You don't live here anymore. I don't owe you an explanation."

"Yes, you do," I say, my voice cracking with anger. "You're the one who brought me into this. Who insisted that we investigate. I'm here because of you."

"Look, I already told you—the pregnancy had nothing to do with how she died. I didn't even know about it, okay? I swear." He takes a step toward me and, finally, I can see the desperation it only took Iris a few minutes to identify.

How could I have been so oblivious?

"Jesus Christ, Austen. Do you even hear yourself? She was your stepsister. She was my best—" I don't let myself finish the sentence.

"Your best friend?" he prompts, his face now twisted into something close to a sneer. "Was she really? It didn't seem like it when you called her pathetic."

"I was angry. I was angry at *you*. I tried to apologize, but you kicked me out."

"Right. And it didn't even take you an hour to get over it and fuck somebody else, did it?"

I flinch at the words. I've seen Austen wear a thousand faces over the last twelve years, but I've rarely known him to be cruel. "I wasn't over it," I say, the words barely a whisper. "I was the opposite of over it. You have to know that."

He backs off a little at that. "It doesn't matter now," he says. "We can't go back and change what happened. Neither of us."

"When did it start?" I ask, forcing myself to meet his eyes again. To search for the man I used to love inside them, but it's useless. He isn't there anymore. Maybe he never was.

"June," he answers. "A few weeks after we ended things."

"Who initiated it?"

Austen shifts his weight from one foot to the other, and I know he's bracing himself. "I did."

"You did," I repeat numbly. I don't know which answer would've been worse, but for some reason, I was expecting it to be the other way around. You had hidden spaces inside yourself. You were capable of wounding people—even if you didn't like to acknowledge that side of yourself. But Austen? Austen was supposed to be simple and uncomplicated and *mine*.

He was supposed to be mine.

"Did you do this to get back at me?" I ask.

He pinches the bridge of his nose and releases a breath. "No," he says. "It didn't have anything to do with you, actually."

Somehow, the answer hurts more. "I find that hard to believe," I mutter, the words escaping my mouth before I can stop them.

"You shouldn't," he says, angry now. "Thea was the best person I've ever known—a hell of a lot better than you. I loved her."

I take a step back, the word *love* wrapping itself around my neck like a choke hold. It means that I was wrong about the only thing I thought I knew for sure.

"I see," I say, my voice quiet.

There's a long pause now. The kind that stretches time itself—pulls everything so thin that it almost snaps.

Austen pulls his eyebrows together. "Marley," he says; his voice has gone soft and cajoling. He sounds almost like he did last night as he ran his fingers up my thighs and pulled my underwear to the side.

"You've been fucking me for days. You knew about the pregnancy. Knew it must've been yours, and you did it anyway. You told me we could take things one day at a time. What did you think was going to happen?" I ask.

He doesn't answer.

"Austen," I say after a long second, my voice breaking.

"I don't know. I was just—I was in shock and I needed—"

"You *needed*?" I say. The words are just short of a screech. "You used me."

"I screwed up, okay?" he says, throwing his hands up in a kind of surrender. "Is that what you want to hear?"

The question almost makes me laugh. "We are so far past what I want to hear, Austen."

He reaches up and pulls his hand through his hair and there, glinting in the moonlight, is the watch I noticed a few days ago. Dull brass and tarnished around the band.

Suddenly, I realize where I've seen it before.

"I hope you burn," I whisper.

And before he can say anything else, I brush past him and out the door.

30

Thea

Iᴛ's 8:03 ᴡʜᴇɴ I hear the knock on the glass door of the Chicken Shack. The sound makes me jump, and I look up expecting to see a hungry customer, or someone complaining about getting the wrong order, but there, silhouetted in the evening light, is a figure I haven't seen in months.

Iris.

She isn't pregnant anymore, and I'm struck by how small she looks now. How helpless.

"Iris," I say, unlocking the door and cracking it just wide enough to poke my head through. "What are you doing here?"

"I wanted to talk to you—I've been wanting to for a while, actually—and I thought I might find you here. Alone."

"Look, you shouldn't be here," I say, casting my eyes out to the empty parking lot and the road behind it. Daryl only left a few minutes ago.

"I know Julie threatened you," she says. "She told you to stay away from me, but I haven't seen her in months." I haven't seen her either, not since the wake, but I can't help looking for her all the same, remembering what Scott told me back in March about her calling the station.

I stiffen. "I've already done enough damage to you, Iris. To your family."

"Did James ask you to help him commit suicide?"

"What?" I manage, feeling lightheaded. It takes all my strength to keep myself upright—if I had more, I'd close the door and lock it. I'd hide in the back until she drove away.

"Did he ask you for help? Did you give it to him?"

I force air into my lungs, then back out. The black spots hovering toward the edge of my vision start to fade. "Come inside," I tell her, stepping aside and opening the door wide enough for to her to squeeze in.

I lock us in and we each take a seat, facing each other down across the linoleum tabletop.

"Why would you ask me that?" I say, taking one of the sugar packets on the table and shaking it nervously.

Iris clasps her fingers together, resting them in front of her. She still wears her engagement ring, I notice, and I'm struck by a sharp pang of sadness. "Because," she says, "he asked *me* early in our relationship."

I open my mouth to speak, but nothing comes out. It never occurred to me that James could've done this before.

"Obviously, I said no," she continues. "I wanted to fix him back then. I really thought I could. Eventually, I assumed he'd gotten over it, but when Julie brought up the burner phone at the wake, and the fact that he called you right before he died, it got me thinking that maybe he'd finally found someone who was willing to help him."

I rip the sugar packet open and pour it onto the table, using the paper packet to straighten the loose sugar into a zig zag pattern. I can't look Iris in the eye.

"Thea," she says sharply. "Please, just tell me. I need to know that he wasn't alone at the end."

Now I do look at her. There are tears welling in her eyes, and I feel so ashamed, I think it might swallow me whole. "He wasn't alone at the end," I whisper.

Iris looks at me for a long time and I force myself to hold her gaze.

"I'm sorry," I say, finally. "I tried to talk him down. For weeks. I really did."

She nods, slowly, breaking our eye contact. "I know how stubborn James could be," she says. "I don't need you to tell me."

"Nothing else happened between us," I add, because it's all I can think to say. "There wasn't—I mean, we didn't . . . we were just friends, is what I'm trying to say. He loved you. He was just . . ."

"I know," she says.

"He was really sick."

"He was scared of being a father," she says. "I knew it. I just didn't realize it had gotten so bad. I underestimated the help he needed. If I'd been more present—more attentive, I could've—"

"You did nothing wrong, Iris. I did. I should've come to you right away. As soon as he said something to me."

Iris shrugs, like she's already had this discussion with me a hundred times over inside her head. "What's done is done."

I could have saved him, I find myself thinking. I could've hung up the phone and called 911. I could've told Iris what James was planning weeks before it happened.

But all I can do now is nod. "I guess so," I say.

"I'm sorry to bring all of it back up," she says, pushing herself up to standing. "I just needed to know for sure."

I feel an unexpected pang of urgency, watching her prepare to leave.

"How are you so calm?" I ask, rising from my chair so quickly that it nearly topples over behind me. "James is dead because of *me*."

"James is dead because of *James*," she says, looking at me sharply. "He dragged you into something you should never have been a part of, and now you have to find a way to live with it. We both do."

She tucks a loose strand of dark hair behind her ear and unlocks the front door, pulling it open against a rush of warm air.

"Thea?" she says, turning to face me once more.

"Yes?"

"I don't want this to come off the wrong way, but James . . . he had a knack for finding people that were . . . like him, I guess. People with a kind of darkness to them. He gravitated toward it."

I don't say anything, but I can feel her words bristling along my spine, making the hair on the back of my neck stand up straight. Once again, I have the strange sensation of being seen all the way through. Of being recognized in the dark. Iris knows the worst thing I have ever done, and she's still here, looking at me with something like tenderness.

"What I'm saying is, if *you* ever need to talk, I'm here. Like I said, we both have to live with this. Maybe it would be easier if we could share it."

"You want us to be friends?" I ask. Iris shrugs.

"I don't know," she says. "You might be the only person that knew James almost as well as I did. I'm not ready to lose that."

"What about Julie?"

"Julie is gone," she says sternly. "I haven't seen her in months. And now that James is dead, I'm not sure she'll ever come back."

"And if she does?"

Iris frowns, her thick eyebrows knitting together. "Then we'll handle it."

31

Marley

AFTER THE CONFRONTATION with Austen, I drive home in silence. I don't know what happened to you, but maybe that's for the best. Maybe I don't need to know anything else about your life.

The house is empty when I get home—Mom's out, God knows where—and I throw my keys on the table where she usually throws hers. Before I know what I'm doing, I've grabbed a bottle of bourbon from the cabinet, poured myself a shot, and gulped it back.

I stand at the kitchen counter, waiting for the drink to settle in my empty stomach, and try to think of anything in the world besides you and Austen. It doesn't work. My mind is spinning out imagined scenes faster than I can keep track.

You and Austen, in our bed. In our shower. On our couch. You and Austen spoiling every inch of the space *I* created. Spoiling every memory I have of either of you.

I wonder, uselessly, if the two of you ever talked about me, or if you avoided the topic. Or maybe you didn't have to. Maybe I was already irrelevant.

I pour another shot and swallow it, wincing at the white-hot slither of the alcohol going down my throat. I consider walking next door and telling Dahlia, but I decide to let her stay in denial a little longer. I'm sure someone—the cops, or maybe Austen himself, will tell her tomorrow.

The cops.

An image of Detective Romero comes to mind, her white teeth bared in a cold imitation of a smile. What does she think now that she knows about the two of you? Does she suspect that Austen is responsible, or does she believe him when he says he had nothing to do with it?

Do I?

Austen's reputation in town is impeccable, but every bit of extra goodwill he worked up when I cheated on him would've been ruined in an instant if people found out about the two of you. Especially if that news involved a baby.

Could Austen really snap like that? Could he have shot you and burned your body inside that house?

I would've said no once—even twenty-four hours ago—but now I'm not so sure. Now I don't know who he is.

I put my shot glass down on the kitchen counter and slide it away from me. My head is swimming, and suddenly I know that I can't let this go.

I take my phone out of my pocket and hit call on a number I haven't touched in years.

"Marley?" the man on the other end answers. He sounds groggy, like maybe he was sleeping, and I realize that I have no idea what time it is.

"David," I say. "I'm sorry to bother you. I won't keep you long."

I can't tell how drunk I sound, but somehow I doubt David cares either way.

You are a clone of your mother, he told me once, a few years after he and Dahlia married. He said it with a smile on his face, but I felt the acidity underneath his words. My mom has a long history of animosity toward the men in Dahlia's life, and David was no exception. The two of them moved like polarized magnets around her, one never getting too close to the other.

"Okay," he says. Then, "I'm sorry, by the way, about Thea. And about you and Austen breaking things off. I didn't get a chance to talk to you at the funeral, but I hope you're alright."

"Thanks," I say dismissively. Then, "David, when you moved out, did you take your gun with you?"

There's a beat of silence on the other end, like he's deciding how to answer me.

"What's this about, Marley?"

"Nothing," I lie. "Just, please—answer the question."

"I left the gun behind," he says. "I didn't feel right leaving Dahlia there with no protection. Not while she was pregnant. She knew the combination to the gun safe."

"Did anyone else have the combination?"

"Sure. Austen's always had it. It's his birthday. Why, is he in some kind of trouble?"

"No," I say numbly. "No, not at all. Thanks, David, I'll let you go now."

I don't wait for him to respond before I set the phone back on the table and pour another shot.

* * *

When Mom comes home, she finds me on the couch, head between my knees as the world spins around me.

"Marley?" she says, clomping toward me until I see the toes of her cowboy boots.

"Hmm?" I answer, unwilling to lift my head.

"Have you been drinking?"

It's more of a rhetorical question, since I know there's a half-empty bourbon bottle somewhere on the living room floor.

The couch dips with her weight and I feel her hands on my arm.

"What's wrong?" she asks.

"Austen and Thea were sleeping together. He was the father of her baby."

She actually laughs at that. "Come on," she says. "That's a sick joke. What's really going on?"

I don't say anything else, just lift my head to look her in the eye and wait for it to sink in.

When she speaks again, her voice is quiet. Barely audible. "Oh my God," she says. "Are—are you sure?"

I shrug. "He told me himself after the police took him in for more questioning a few hours ago."

Mom chews on her lip. I can tell she's trying to process—to figure out what to say to me—but I just shake my head.

"Want a drink?" I say. Just the thought of more makes my stomach lurch, but I don't care. I want to drink myself into oblivion. Into a stupor so intense I can't think of anything but breathing.

She nods, looking relieved, and I grab the bottle off the floor, untwist the cap, and pass it to her for a swig.

"You don't think he did this to her, do you?" She fiddles with the pendant necklace hanging into her cleavage.

I shrug petulantly. "I really don't know," I tell her. I thought once that finding out who you'd slept with would make the rest of the pieces fall into place, but it's done the opposite. Now nothing makes sense, including our whole friendship. It's like spending your entire life looking at a picture, memorizing the shape of each figure and the contours of each face, only to realize later that it was upside down the whole time.

"He told me that he loved her," I say, not quite sure why. I just need someone else to bear witness to the night's carnage.

Mom looks shattered at that. I know she thought of Austen like a son.

"He loved you, too," she says.

I nod, but the idea doesn't hold a lot of comfort because I'm not sure that Austen's the kind of person I want to have been loved by. Not anymore. The truth is, Austen's love meant something to me because of his goodness. If Austen loved me, I figured, there had to be something good at my core, even if I couldn't see it.

Mom rests her hand drunkenly on my knee and tilts forward, almost falling off the couch. "Do you want to know my greatest regret?" she asks.

I turn to face her, my stomach churning sourly with the movement. "Okay."

"My greatest regret was leaving you behind those two years. When I came back, it was like you didn't know me anymore. Like you were happy having Dahlia as your mom and Thea as your sister. Sometimes I wonder if I should've stayed away forever. If you'd be happier now."

"Why are you telling me this?" I ask. I can't help it.

Mom squeezes my leg, her nails digging into my skin. "I didn't protect you then," she says. "I couldn't—I wasn't capable of it. But I can now, and I want you to know that."

"I don't understand," I say, narrowing my eyes at her, trying to make sense of the words. The meaning she so clearly wants me to grasp.

Mom shakes her head, and I see now just how drunk she is. "What I'm trying . . . what I want to tell you is that if you had something to do with any of this—with the fires. With Thea and how she died.—I would do whatever I could to protect you. I hope you know that."

I take the bourbon bottle and swallow down another sip, hands shaking as I lift it to my lips. "You would?" I ask.

"Yes," she says, and in this moment, she's the only person on earth I believe is telling me the truth. Maybe I haven't given Mom enough credit all these years. Maybe she's always been able to see exactly who I am.

I place my hand over hers and squeeze it hard. "Then there's something I need to tell you."

32

Thea

WHEN THE FIRES start, I don't think about them much. I'm too preoccupied trying to balance the pieces of my fucked-up life to spend much time thinking about who's burning down the town, even though it's all most people can talk about.

I develop a routine. Days are spent at work or with the twins, trying hard not to think about how messy my life has become in the last year. At night, I'm either hanging out with Iris or at Austen's, drowning out the thoughts with other distractions. Sometimes it works, and I feel okay for a while, but it doesn't stop the guilt from coming out sideways. Slicing down like a guillotine's blade whenever I get too tired to divert myself from it.

I tell myself it's all okay. Good, even. For the first time, I've got a whole life that doesn't have anything to do with Marley. What she doesn't know about Austen can't hurt her, and besides, it's just a fling. Just something to get us both through this hellscape of a summer. It's not like it can go anywhere real.

And James wanted to die. I *didn't* kill him. He asked for my help, and Iris has forgiven me.

I haven't done anything wrong.

I haven't done anything wrong.

I haven't done anything wrong.

I keep the words playing on repeat for weeks—until one night, I get back from Austen's late, and I notice that Marley's car isn't in her driveway. And then it happens again, and again, and again. All on nights when fires go up.

One night, I sit at the front window of my house for hours, watching the curve at the top of our street, waiting for her car to pull in. It's nearly dawn when it does, and a few hours later I hear the news.

The arsonists didn't strike once that night. They struck three times. Three different crime scenes, scattered across Riverside and the surrounding territory. Whoever did it was technical. Precise. Ruthless and ballsy. Someone with nothing left to lose.

Someone like Marley.

It isn't even hard to catch her at it. I wait one night until everyone is asleep, climb into the back seat of her car, and I hide. It takes less than an hour for her to get in, stealthy as a cat, placing something in the passenger's seat that she removed from the trunk. She drives smoothly, like she knows exactly where she's going, and I wonder if she plans which houses she's going to hit ahead of time. The radio is on, volume low, and I squeeze my eyes shut and listen to the quiet, thumping bass. The music and the soft rumble of the motor. It's all so familiar. Almost relaxing enough to make me fall asleep, but then Marley stops and cuts the motor. I can hear the crickets instead. She sits back and breathes out.

I should tell her I'm here now. I should stop her, but I can't seem to make myself. I haven't been this close to Marley in weeks, and honestly I'd forgotten the sheer force of her will. The glare of it like the sun itself brought inches from my face. It's a wonder she hasn't been burning the houses down just by looking at them.

"Okay," she whispers to herself. She grabs whatever she put in the passenger's seat and pops open the car door. I wait until she's shut the car door, then look up through the windshield. Watch her run the short distance to the abandoned house and stuff something that looks like old rags underneath the doorjamb. She pours gasoline from an old gas can, lights a match, and throws it onto the pile. I watch the fire spring to life, lighting up the gasoline and rags, then the front door. Leaping, climbing, consuming everything in its path.

I once heard a firefighter say that there's a moment in every house fire when the fire stops being the thing in the house and instead becomes the house. When it consumes everything else about the house that was important. When there is nothing left to save, only damage to control.

Marley stands back and watches, and I watch her. All my life, I've thought of Marley one way: All precision and fine-boned delicacy and self-containment.

But she's not that at all.

I can see it now, with the hot light pressing down on her. Can see her chest rising and falling rapidly. The subtle twitch of her jaw that makes me think, *How could I have missed it for so long?*

My best friend is—always has been—a storm tide of fury balanced on the head of a pin. A house on fire.

And now she has come undone. I can see it in the set of her shoulders—the break, somewhere deep in her bones, sudden and impossible to ignore. She is like an animal who's fought too long to conceal an injury, gone frantic and feral from the pain.

In my head, I see her cracking, spilling open, bleeding out beyond the edges of her body. I can hear the scream that's been going up for years from her marrow. That howling, bottomless rage that you can't unfeel. Can't unknow. Can't unrecognize.

And then it hits me—*I'm* the one who's responsible for this. I abandoned her when she needed me most. I could've helped, and instead I stood by and watched as it got worse and worse. As everyone else in town turned their back on her.

I'm not the arsonist, but I may as well be.

I don't have time to duck into the back seat of the car when she turns her back on the flames and begins to run. I'm lost in it all. The sight of the flames licking higher and higher. Smoke billowing up like gray velvet against the black. The smell of burn in my nostrils. It's almost beautiful.

Marley throws open the car door and yelps, jerking back when she sees me.

"Marley," I manage. I reach for her, but she pulls herself back. I can make out the sirens now, wailing that throws itself out toward us, then pulls back. Distant, but racing closer. "C'mon," I say. "We can still get away if we hurry."

She looks at me for a few seconds longer, like she's trying to decide whether or not she can trust me. I guess I can't fault her for it. Finally, without another word, she climbs back in, guns the ignition, and cuts the lights.

I force myself to sit in the back seat and buckle in as Marley swings out of the lot and onto the road, the pavement hitting our tires like hot butter before she floors the gas and sends me reeling back against the seat backing.

"Are you okay?" she asks, glancing at me in the rearview mirror. Her eyes are bloodshot. Frenzied. I've never seen her like this before, and there's something wild about it. She looks somehow nothing like herself, and more herself than she's ever been.

"Yes," I say. She nods, squaring her shoulders and fixing her eyes on the road ahead, her fingers gripping the steering wheel so tightly I can see the small cuts and burns on the skin. The sirens are gaining on us. But Marley's stealthy, not just quick. After a minute that feels like an eternity, she cuts off onto a side street and parks the car up toward the cul-de-sac.

"What are we—"

"Shhh," she snaps, curling herself into a ball so that she's not visible from the street. "Just hide like you were doing before."

Now doesn't feel like the time to ask questions, so I undo my seat belt and crouch down again against the floor mats.

"What the hell are you doing here?" she says harshly from up front. I know I deserve the hostility in her voice, but it still pains me to hear it. I rest my chin against my knee and look up through the opposing window, at the sliver of trees and sky I can see from my viewpoint. At the stars burning through the black.

"I—I thought it might be you. I wanted to see for myself."

"Well congratu-fucking-lations then. You figured it out."

Behind us, the sirens wail louder, louder, louder, until they start to fade. I hear Marley breathe a shaky sigh of relief and sit back up. I follow suit and catch her looking at me again in the rearview.

"Marley, I'm sorry."

"For what?" she says, raising an eyebrow. "You're sorry for what?"

I bite down on my lip and sit back, feeling the cast-off wave of her anger ripple over me. "Everything."

She smiles bitterly. "Right."

"Really, I—"

"You ignored me for *weeks*. You knew the shit I was going through— you saw that stupid account tearing into me, the things people were saying—and you didn't even text. I was right next door."

I look down at my lap. My skin feels hot at the thought of these past few weeks. The thought of Austen and me and what we're doing. "I'm sorry," I say again, a wave of revulsion at myself running through me. "It's . . . hard to explain. Austen's not really ready to deal with it yet."

Marley doesn't say anything for what feels like a very long time. Then she turns around. I can't meet her eyes, so I look out the window at the street where we're parked. Not so different from our own.

"Since when are you two a package deal?" she says. The words sting and I fight not to let it show.

"We're not," I say, too quickly.

"I know what I did was wrong. And it was stupid. I wanted Austen to be hurt—that's why I did it—but I didn't expect *you* to drop out like you did. I'm sorry for what I said to you. You *know* I didn't mean it. I was just angry."

"Jesus, Marley. That's not why I was so upset. I mean, it was at first, but—"

"Then why—"

"You *deleted* our account. You didn't even tell me you were going to do it. That was my whole portfolio. It was everything I had to show for myself as a stylist, and you wiped it out. I don't even have screenshots."

"I—I'm sorry," she says quietly. For the first time, she looks like she's at a loss for words.

"It's not like I had other professional stuff to fall back on, like you. That account was my one shot at getting my foot in somewhere in New York, and you took it away."

"I didn't think about it that way." Her voice is barely a whisper.

"Of course you didn't. You don't think about anyone but yourself."

"That's not true," she says. "Thea, please—"

But now that I've started, I can't stop. I cut her off again. "It *is* true. Once the account started to take off, you never wanted me to go to New York. You didn't care about our friendship, or what I wanted. Just about what you could get out of it."

"I *did* care about our friendship. I've always cared," she fires back. "*You're* the one that shut me out. After Austen and I moved in together, you totally changed. The account was the only way I could get you to talk to me. I reached out every day for weeks after that guy you worked with died. I could barely get a response."

I open my mouth, but nothing comes out. About this, at least, she's right. I barely talked to anyone for months after James died, and when Austen and Marley moved in together, it was like an unbridgeable gap opened up between us. The account was the only thing we had in common anymore. The only thread that held us together, before she severed it.

"Thea," she says. She looks desperate, like maybe she wants me to tell her that everything will be okay. "You're my best friend, okay? You're the only real friend I've ever had. I need you in my life. I'm always going to need you."

I hold her gaze across the dark space. Feel the pieces of the girls we used to be snapping back together like magnets. It was stupid, I realize, to think I could ever be done with her—that she could ever be done with me. There's more holding us together than I knew.

We hurt each other, we hurt ourselves, and we move on.

That's what friends do.

And maybe, here in the dark, we can build back what's been broken. Can take what we have and make it something better than it was before. Maybe she never even has to know about Austen.

For a second—one fleeting, suspended second—it feels almost possible.

33

Marley

I CALL IN SICK for work at the gas station the next morning. It isn't a lie, exactly—the massive hangover makes it a lot easier to fake a convincing stomach flu over the phone, and Mom is sympathetic enough to fill in for me, after what I told her about the fires this summer. Once she's gone, I set up a perch by my bedroom window, with a view of your house, and wait for Dahlia to leave with the boys.

For a while, I'm scared that she won't—that she'll keep them in all day, and I'll never get my chance—but after a couple of hours, I see her wrangling them into the car. Fussing with Finn's car seat, adjusting Milo's socks and shoes for what feels like an eternity before driving away.

Once they've turned the corner, I don't waste any time jogging around back and slipping through the boys' bedroom window. It used to be Austen's, so I know it doesn't lock properly. The room feels dark, even though the sun is blinding outside. I take in the sight of the bunk beds—galaxy printed bedding, and Buzz Lightyear pillows—before creeping into the hallway and, finally, to Dahlia's bedroom.

I haven't been in this room in years, and I'm struck by how similar it looks to the picture frozen in my head, like Dahlia's touched nothing since I was a kid.

Before I can stop myself, I open the closet and drop to my knees, remembering the time Austen and I snuck in here. He'd told me about the gun his father had, and I hadn't believed him. I couldn't picture sweet, mild Dahlia letting any weapon in the house, let alone a gun, but he took me to the safe and showed me himself.

"Please be here," I mutter now, pushing aside a few long dresses. Sure enough, Dahlia hasn't moved the gun safe.

I take a deep breath and enter the digits of Austen's birthday, breathing a sigh of relief as the buttons flash green and the lock mechanism hums quietly, the bolts sliding back.

But when I open the door, a pit forms in my stomach. The velvet mold where the gun should be sits empty.

I feel like kicking something. Like screaming. But I force deep breaths instead. I make myself go through the scenario logically.

I don't *know* that this is the gun that killed you. I don't even know that you were killed by a gun. It could be missing for any number of reasons.

But if that's the case, why did Dahlia lie and say David took it with him? She wouldn't cover for Austen if he killed you, and she'd never have anything to do with your death herself. In fact, Dahlia wouldn't cover for anyone but you.

But *you* hated guns. I doubt you'd even touch one, unless you were desperate, or terrified.

I take a deep breath and sit back on my heels, studying the empty safe for a long moment as my resolve sets.

I will never *know* you, not really. Not now. But I have to know why you died. I owe our friendship that, if nothing else.

In an effort to keep moving, I close the safe and stand up, trying to keep a level head as I evaluate my next move. The police have already been here. They've already searched the house for anything that could be relevant to the case. But that doesn't mean they got everything. After all, they missed the ring at the crime scene, didn't they?

I leave Dahlia's bedroom and head down the hall toward yours. The door is closed, and I can see the sunlight spilling out from underneath the crack. I push it open and step across the threshold, bracing myself, though I'm not sure what for. I was in here a few days ago with Austen, examining the receipt he found in your drawer. But I was distracted then. I still thought you'd done it to yourself. I wasn't looking for signs of foul play.

Your room is exactly like I remember it with the dark green bedspread, and the desk pushed up against the wall. The curtains are drawn, and there's light streaming in, so bright it makes me squint.

I don't know exactly what I'm looking for, but I go through your things all the same. On the desk there are loose-leaf sketch pages in a stack. I flip through them, tracing my finger over the lines your pencil touched. There's a soft quality to your art—something that betrayed the prickly image you projected in public. Your drawings have always made me feel a little lighter, a little happier, than I was before I saw them.

Today, though, even they can't crack through my anxiety. I go to set them back on the desk, but I lose hold of one—a cartoonish drawing of a creature you've named Mr. Monster—and it flutters softly to the floor. I'm bending to pick it up when something catches my eye. A small, red speck splattered on the wooden leg of your desk. I study it for a long moment, heart pounding. It's barely visible against the dark wood, but it's there. At first, I think it must be paint, but you never painted. You only drew.

I crouch down and study the wood until I find another on the side. The droplets are so small, it's a wonder I caught the first one, but now that I'm looking, I notice a few more, all on the front left leg of the desk. I check the floor, the windowsill, the baseboards, but they're all clean. Suspiciously so, in fact. Like someone's gone over them recently with a sponge. I think of the other day—the chemical citrus scent of Austen's favorite cleaning product permeating the house.

How would he have even found that receipt unless he was in here himself, looking for something, or wiping away evidence?

I squeeze my eyes closed and shake my head, willing the thought away, but the spatters are still there when I open my eyes. When I stand up, my legs feel shaky. My stomach churns, sour and sick, and I have to convince myself that I can't actually smell the blood. That it's just my imagination.

I wrestle my phone out of my back pocket and take pictures of the splatters, then scramble out the boys' window and back into the bright sunlight, breathing hard.

And somehow, I know in my gut—you didn't die in that burned out house. You weren't burned alive. You were already dead.

You were shot with David's gun right here, by someone who knew you. You died in your own room.

34

Thea

AFTER THE FIRST fire, I watch for Marley out my window at night. I can just make out the edge of her yard if I angle myself perfectly, so if she's going out her window to get to the car, like I think she is, I should be able to catch her.

I sit for hours, waiting, my neck going stiff with the angle, the muscles in my back tensing with each sign of movement—each breath of wind winding through the uncut grass. While I wait, I practice what I'll say to her. I write and rewrite the conversation in my head, but nothing feels right.

Out of the corner of my eye, I catch a flash of movement, there, and then gone so quickly I almost miss it, but I'm drawn tight as a live wire, so instead I spring into action, throwing my window open and hoisting myself out. Marley hears me hit the ground and stops dead in her tracks, turning on her heel to face me.

We stand there silently for a moment, facing each other from opposite sides of the yard, each a mirror image of the other. I roll my shoulders back and square them, like I'm readying myself for a fight, but Marley just stands there, frozen.

Slowly, she raises her free hand, and with one definitive flick of her wrist, she waves me over. My feet move before I tell them to, drawn to her by the same magnetic pull as always.

"Thea," she whispers when I'm close enough, so quiet I can barely hear her. "I'm so glad you're here. Let's go."

She reaches out and grabs my arm. Pulls me toward the car in the driveway, like this was always the plan. Like we're in it together.

"Marley," I say, digging my heels in and skidding us both to a stop. "I can't—I mean, *you* can't. This has to stop."

She turns to look at me again, confusion on her features melting into something sharp and naked. Fear. I swallow hard—I've never seen her afraid before. Not like this. Not of me.

"So you're turning me in, then?"

"What? *No.*" I'd be lying if I said I hadn't thought of it, but I'd dismissed it almost as quickly. Turning Marley in was a nonstarter. After all, didn't I do this to her? Didn't I abandon her when she needed me? Didn't I betray her in ways she doesn't even understand yet?

And besides, it isn't like she's hurting anyone. It's just old houses. Just a bit of excitement for a town that hasn't had any since the plant closed.

I open my mouth, then close it again, suddenly feeling a lot less solid in my convictions.

"Just come with me, Thea. We don't have to light anyplace up. Just take a drive with me."

I feel myself nodding, then walking. Despite myself, I feel electric. We're Thea and Marley again, in this small, dark space. Two people who understand each other almost perfectly.

We drive for a long time in silence. Marley handles the car smoothly, eyes sharp, like a hunter out for blood as she scans each street looking the perfect house, as if it's a habit she can't break.

"I only do abandoned houses," she explains as we bump down the road, Marley's headlights throwing a harsh, yellow glow onto the road in front of us. "I need you to know, I'm not trying to hurt anyone. I just . . . like to watch them burn."

I study her profile in the dim light. For a moment, I want to drink in this new version of her—brittle and savage and bursting with restless, defiant energy. Want to coil myself around her like a vine around a tree and sap her of it. Take it for myself.

"You probably think I'm crazy."

"I don't," I say, and it's the truth. For all the things I've thought since I found out, *crazy* has never been one of them. "Sometimes you just need something to happen, or you feel like you'll explode."

James's face pops into my head again. I've clung to the idea that I did what I did because I cared for him. Because I wanted to help him, even if the logic was twisted. But sometimes, in dark moments, I wonder if maybe I just wanted to. If I fed off the thrill of it. If I liked having that kind of power—of holding someone's fate in my hands.

"Yes," Marley says, cutting into my thoughts. "Exactly."

I swallow hard and fix my concentration on the street. There's only a sliver of a moon tonight, and everything is set in such complete darkness that I think we may be the only two people who exist anymore. Just us and a thousand houses ready to burn.

"Would you burn a house like this one?" I ask, tapping the window to point out the house we're cruising past. It's clearly abandoned—no lights in the windows, no cars in the driveway. Molded shutters hang off the windows like broken teeth. It's set back in a dense clump of trees, far enough from the rest of the neighborhood that we could get in and out without being spotted.

Marley slows the car down and takes a look. She shakes her head. "It's too close," she says. "Those trees—they could catch too easily and spread it to other houses. It's been ages since we've had rain. It wouldn't take much to set the whole town on fire, so I try to be careful."

I nod, surprised. There's more strategy to it than I'd realized.

"I usually like to go farther out of town if I can. Or at least along the edges where it's sparse. It also takes the fire department longer to get out there."

We drive for a while longer, until the neighborhoods start to fade out, the houses thinning with the trees the farther we go.

"When did you know it was me?" she says.

"I've suspected for a while," I tell her. "I started to notice your car was never around on nights when fires were going up. Besides . . . it felt like something you might do."

The shadow of a smile creeps onto her lips, then disappears. "Does Austen know?"

I shake my head. "He has no idea," I say. She breathes out, her shoulders lowering an inch.

"Good. That's good. Austen . . ." She trails off.

"He wouldn't understand," I finish.

"He wouldn't understand," she repeats.

I think of him now. Of the way he sleeps—one arm thrown over his face, mouth open. A position of total abandon. Austen doesn't know what it's like to have a black hole at the center of you, always raging and ready to eat you from the inside out. He doesn't know what it's like not to be able to relax, ever. To be afraid of yourself. For a long time, I didn't think Marley did either, but now that I can see her, really see her, I know that she does. That we may look different, but on the inside we're more alike than we ever realized.

The feeling of kinship is so strong that I almost want to tell her what I did to James. What I'm doing with Austen. I want to share all my secrets with her, but the balance of this space is too delicate. If Marley knew the things I'd done—the weight of my karmic darkness— it would flip us like a table. She wouldn't forgive it.

"Do you think what you're doing is wrong?" I ask her instead.

"No," she says, quickly enough that it's clear she's given it thought. "I'm not hurting anyone, and people don't care about these old houses, anyway. They're a reminder that it used to be better here. No one needs that."

I press the pad of my finger against the cool glass of the window and fog it with my breath. I have the crazy urge to smoke, like I haven't since James died. "Are you scared of getting caught?"

Marley licks her lips, her body tensing. "Yeah," she says. "Terrified, actually."

"Then why are you still doing it?" I ask.

There's a long second where she doesn't say anything, and I think maybe I've offended her. Upset the balance without even trying. But then she takes a breath and curls her fingers even tighter around the steering wheel. "Because it's the only thing that makes me feel okay," she says.

I have to resist the urge to reach out and touch her. To tell her I know exactly what she means. That her—this moment—it's the first time in a long time that I've felt okay, too.

"What about you?" she says, flipping her hair away from her face, eyes still fixed ahead. "Are you scared of getting caught here with me? There's rags and gasoline in the trunk."

I want to say *yes, of course*, but the words don't come out, and after a second I realize it's because they aren't true.

"No," I answer. I can feel it again—the darkness moving down on me. I feel dizzy with it suddenly, like it's been waiting for the right moment to knock me over the head. It's always there these days, but there are moments when it's worse.

The truth is, right now I'm not even sure what I have left to lose.

"Now, this place," Marley points ahead of her, at a small ranch house with a sagging roof just ahead. She rolls the car quietly through the grass until we're in front of it. "It's perfect."

We glance at each other. The air between us sparking with something I can't quite place.

I told myself I'd come along to talk her out of it, but I hadn't expected this—this excitement. This adrenaline. This feeling like I'm *alive*. Like maybe I can fight the darkness just by lighting it on fire.

Suddenly I wonder how many lines I would cross for her. How many I've crossed already.

"Let's go," I say, and then we're both springing into action, my heart beating so fast I think it's going to leap right out of my chest.

Marley unbuckles herself and grabs the supplies from the back, her eyes suddenly alight, fixed on the target house with blazing intensity, and I realize, with a stab, that I was wrong before. I didn't break Marley. I didn't *make* her the arsonist. I love her *because* of it. Because whatever it is that makes her capable of this—of darkness that most people wouldn't even consider—I have it too.

I love her because we share something unburnable at the core—a rot that's chewed us both through.

35

Marley

THE DEATH IS in full swing today—that laziness you only find in late summer, when the heat crushes anyone who dares to venture outside. Usually during this time of year people don't leave the radius of their front porch if they can help it, but as I stand on the edge of the parking lot looking up at the police station, I'm surprised by the buzz and energy coming off the building. Outside the front doors, two men in suits are staring at something inside a file folder. From the open window I can hear the low, electric hum of people inside. The phone rings and rings again. I can make out words but not phrases as people walk through the building.

One last deep breath and I force myself inside, the AC climbing over me, throwing goose bumps up over my arms and down my back. It makes me think of the game we used to play when we were kids—your hands running up and down my spine and the warm breath against the back of my neck. *Spiders crawling up your back. ATTACK ATTACK ATTACK.*

"Can I help you?" the man at the front desk says.

"Yes, I'm here to speak to Detective Romero."

"Your name?" he asks, picking up the phone, his finger hovering over the call button.

"Marley Henderson." I take a step back and grip my purse strap tightly between my fingers as he mutters into the receiver, then pops his head back up. "She'll be with you in a moment. You can take a seat by the window."

I nod and plant myself, standing, in the waiting area, eyes skipping across the barren station lobby. Three chairs and a reception desk, naked sunlight spilling across the floor with maddening intensity. I want to grab at it. To hold the light in my hands and rip the heat off of it. To have one split second of relief.

"Marley?"

I swivel toward Detective Romero and press my lips into an imitation of a smile. "Hi," I say tightly, taking in the sight of her. Sensible loafers and black work pants. A camel blazer without a wrinkle in sight. The only sign that she's human, not a mannequin in an Ann Taylor window, is the ballpoint pen sticking out from behind her ear. She's regarding me with equal curiosity, I notice, her head tilting just barely to the side.

"Why don't we talk in my office?"

I follow her back, through a maze of hallways that smell like cigarettes and spilled drugstore cologne, before we come to a small room tucked into the back corner of the station. The blinds are drawn, the sunlight coming through in angry, blade-sharp slats. The walls are empty—the room devoid of any attempt at a personal touch. I suppose there's no point in decorating your office when you're someone like Detective Romero, moving from town to town and case to case.

"I'm glad to see you," she says, taking a seat behind the large desk dominating the room and motioning toward the opposite chair. I perch myself on the edge of it and force myself to be still, hands in my lap.

"I wish I could say the same," I say, raising an eyebrow.

She shrugs. "Occupational hazard."

I grip my hands tighter in my lap as silence falls over us. I know it's a tactic, but I can feel myself cracking under it all the same. "I know about Austen. About him being the father of her baby," I say, eyes on my lap, unable to meet hers.

"I see." She doesn't sound surprised. "Did he tell you that?"

I nod, unable to pull the words out of my mouth.

"That must've been quite a shock. How are you holding up?"

I look up at her now. At her brown eyes open wide, mouth turned down into a small frown. There's genuine sympathy there, but something else too. Something I can't quite pick out.

"I don't know," I answer honestly. "I'm still processing, I guess."

"That's understandable. I was surprised too, when he admitted it. But Henley had a hunch. Said the way he talked about her isn't the way a man talks about his sister or his friend."

"Do you think he did this to her?"

Romero sits back in her chair and considers for a long moment. "We're keeping several lines of investigation open," she says finally. "Do you?"

I shrug. "Actually, that's why I came."

"Oh?" says Romero, reaching toward the phone on her desk. "In that case, do you mind if I record this? It's just a precautionary measure."

"Okay," I say, waiting for her to set up the recording. When she nods, I clear my throat. There's something different about the way you speak when you know you're being taped. Suddenly all the words that seemed right before aren't anymore.

"I want to know if Thea was shot."

Romero raises her eyebrows. "Why are you asking?"

"Because, like I told you last time I was here, she would never have shot herself. If she died from a gunshot, it means she was murdered."

"And is there someone that you think would've shot her?" she asks.

"Possibly," I say.

"Who is that?"

I lick my suddenly dry lips and sit back. "Scott Martin attacked me," I tell her. It isn't *quite* the truth, but it's close enough. And if Scott ever does do something to me, I want it on the record that I was afraid of him. "He came to the gas station where I work—there's a blind spot on the security cameras by one of the pumps. He took me there and grabbed me by the throat. Told me that you'd come by to ask him questions about Thea. He said he could've murdered her and gotten away with it, if he wanted to."

"That's a very serious accusation," she says.

I swallow hard and continue. "Scott has his own service weapon, so I know that he has access to at least one gun. He could have a personal weapon, too. There was also a woman named Julie Butler who hated

Thea—who threatened her. She thought Thea had something to do with her brother's death. I don't know if she had a gun, but it isn't hard to get one, if she didn't. And . . ." I pause, hesitating for a beat before I press on. "Austen. For obvious reasons."

Romero takes a deep breath, her small chest rising. "Does he have a gun?" she asks.

"His father has one that he left with Dahlia when he moved out. The code to the safe where it's kept is Austen's birthday." I don't tell her that the gun is no longer there, or about the blood I found on your desk. There's no way to explain away how I'd know about either piece of evidence, and I'm still not sure how much to trust her with.

Romero nods. "Anyone else?" she asks after a long moment.

I shake my head.

"That's quite a list," she says finally, leaning forward on her elbows, studying me across the small space.

"I'm just trying to do what I can."

She nods. There's a long moment of silence. I think about leaving, but I can't seem to make myself.

"I understand how desperate you must feel," she says, finally. "Learning that someone you loved betrayed you, it's painful. And learning that *two* people you loved were keeping such a big secret from you—it would make anyone want to lash out."

I blink, feeling like someone's reeled back and hit me. "I'm not *lashing out*," I say. "I'm trying to tell you that there were people—several people—who had a motive to hurt Thea. I'm trying to tell you she didn't do this to herself."

"It's interesting that you bring up motive," she says. "It's a common misconception about the justice system, but actually, we don't *have* to have motive to prove a murder case. Don't get me wrong, it helps, but all you really *need* to bring a case to trial is enough circumstantial or physical evidence to tie a suspect to a crime beyond a reasonable doubt.

"In fact, motive can be a shaky foundation on which to build a case. If there's one thing I've learned since taking this job, it's that real life isn't like the movies. More often than not, people who commit crimes don't have well-thought-out reasons for what they've done. They're just people who've been caught up in ways they never intended to be. They take things further than they thought they would. They get angry or scared and they react. Even good people."

"What are you saying?" I ask.

"I'm saying that it's easy to delude ourselves into thinking we understand people, but that's a dangerous assumption. My job is to follow *evidence*. That is what solves cases. Not half-baked theories. Not threats or grudges or feelings."

Now it's my turn to study Romero. Despite her size, she looks fierce behind the desk, her shoulders rolled back, eyes fixed on me with striking intensity. And I realize, all at once, that I've underestimated her. Gravely.

"And where does your evidence point?" I ask, refusing to drop her gaze.

"When was the last time you spoke to Thea?"

"I've already told you, May third."

"Yes, I thought I remembered that. And why was it that the two of you stopped speaking, exactly?"

"You already know why."

She sits back now and tips her head in a poor imitation of informality. "I'd like to hear it again, if you don't mind. The whole thing, in your own words."

I narrow my eyes and do the same. Feeling the electric buzz of adrenaline running through my system. "I got into a fight with Austen," I say. "Thea was there, and I lashed out at both of them. After that, I stormed off to a bar and hooked up with Scott. Austen ended our engagement and Thea stopped talking to me. I couldn't figure out why she was being so standoffish. At the time, I thought she was just hurt by what I'd said to her that night. Or maybe that she was upset I'd slept with Scott. Obviously, now I know what was really going on."

Romero quirks her head to the side. "What was that?"

"She was sleeping with Austen," I say. "He told me it started a few weeks after the fight. I'm sure, once it started, she felt like she needed to keep her distance from me."

A cloud rolls by outside and cuts the harsh shadows around the blinds, fading everything to soft gray. I pick at a loose thread along the seam of my jeans. They're my favorites, snagged years ago at a thrift store in Braselton—vintage light wash with a seam straight down the middle of the thigh and a flare on the ankle—and they make me think of you. All those days spent digging through sales racks and donation piles for that thing that was *just* right. The one that pulled all those disparate pieces of the outfit together and made it something—made it *wow*. I haven't felt that thrill in a long time. Not since we started Vintage Doll, come to think of it.

"That must've been a difficult time for you," she says. "If it was me, I would've felt alone. Abandoned."

"I did," I say. "But what does it matter now?"

"Actually, I think it matters very much."

I cock my head to the side. "Why's that?" I say—daring her to continue. I'm not sure exactly what she's driving at with this line of questioning, but I'm eager to get to the point.

"From what I understand, you faced some pretty severe backlash in town after what happened with Scott."

"You could say that," I mutter, trying to keep the bitterness out of my voice.

"I hope I'm not overstepping, but I did some digging. The most vicious online attacker you had, publicly at least, was an anonymous Instagram account called Vintage Whore. Several people posted about who they suspected was running the account, and I noticed that you liked a comment accusing Skylar Weller. She was your friend at the time, wasn't she?"

I swallow hard and roll my shoulders back, lifting my chin. "I don't see what this has to do with Thea."

"Ah, good point. Here's where it all comes together. According to your statement, the last time you had any contact with Thea was on the night of your fight—on May third—is that correct?"

"That's right."

"Were you aware that Skylar Weller's tires were slashed in her driveway a few weeks ago?"

I can feel the blood draining out of my face. The air being sucked right out of my lungs. "I heard about it," I manage, my voice barely above a whisper.

Romero nods, like she was expecting the answer, and opens a drawer to her left, pulling out a thin manila file and placing it on the desk between us. "Skylar reported the incident the night it happened.

There were two suspects—women, judging by what Ms. Weller could see, but they escaped into the woods around the subdivision and were never caught. They did drop this, though, when they ran for it."

She reaches into her drawer again, this time pulling out a plastic evidence bag. Inside is the knife from your kitchen. I don't have to look at it to know, but still, I do. "What's your point?" I ask, willing myself to stay calm, my eyes fixed on her.

"That," she points to the knife, and there's a hint of glee in the movement. Just a flash, and then it's gone, sifted underneath a layer of professional aloofness, but it's enough. I can see it now—the pieces of her snapping into place like the pieces of a puzzle. I know exactly where she thinks her evidence is leading.

"That knife," she continues. "It looks an awful lot like the set in Thea's kitchen. In fact, there's one knife missing from the block there. Dahlia Wright described the size and shape to me, and it matches this one perfectly. She said it went missing a few weeks ago, around the same time that the tires were slashed."

"I—"

"Now, this seemed strange to me at first—why would Thea slash Skylar Weller's tire? But then I started thinking about the two suspects seen fleeing the scene. The one who dropped the knife, the slower one, was short with a medium build, but the one who took off running first was described as tall and thin, and I thought, *Now who does that sound like to me? Who matches that description and has a reason to hate Skylar Weller?*"

"I came here to try to help," I say, laying my palms flat on the desk and pushing myself to standing. "Not to be accused of a crime I didn't commit."

"You came here to help me solve this case, didn't you? So do it," she says—that veneer slipping again. The flash of fury in her eyes and the core of her split open right there in front of me. And then the mask goes back up. The fire dampened as quickly as it flared. "If you're innocent, let me clear you."

I glare at her. The memory of that night playing back in my head. There was a time once when I wondered what you would do for me, even after we started setting the fires together—but that was the night I stopped wondering—the night I knew you loved me the exact same way I loved you. The first time I really tasted it, like copper, or blood on my tongue.

The first time I realized we were dangerous.

"I already told you, Marley—people lie all the time. They get angry and they react. It's human nature. I know you lied about the last time you spoke to Thea. The two of you were together weeks after her affair with Austen began, and if she told you about the two of them—about the pregnancy—I would understand if you reacted in kind. If you did something you wish you could take back."

I feel shaky now. Unsteady as I push myself to standing and stare her down. She regards me softly, like she really does feel bad, and I have to resist the urge to lunge across the table and throttle her on the spot.

"I won't speak to you again without a lawyer present," I tell her, turning on my heel to leave.

36

Thea

SOMETIMES I WONDER if Marley remembers the day we ran away.

Probably not. We don't ever talk about it now, and there are times when I think I must've made it up—dreamed it, or built it from pieces of other memories, the way a bird builds a nest.

But then, something about that night is too clear to dismiss. When I close my eyes, I can put myself right there. The first bite of fall in the air and red tinging her cheeks as we walked along the roadside. The fine cloud of dust we kicked up around ourselves and the sound of my own blood rushing in my ears as the sun sank lower, lower, lower in the sky. The panic and the thrill.

I thought that we might die together that night, two thirteen-year-olds clinging together in a clump of trees off a deserted roadway. I couldn't admit it to myself at the time, but actually, I felt okay with it. Almost relieved.

It started after school, in my room. Marley perched on the edge of my desk chair, her legs kicked up and resting on the desk; me cross-legged on the bed. I don't remember what we'd been talking about, but I remember being struck, not for the first time, by the long, graceful line of her body in the chair. Everything about her lean and spare, like a dancer. Nothing like my squat, curvy frame.

"What's wrong?" she'd asked, her sharp eyes boring into me.

"I—nothing," I said with a shrug. It was nothing I could tell her about, anyway.

I knew that Marley knew she was pretty. We both saw how the boys at school looked at her—how *Austen* looked at her. When we went out together, even grown men let their gaze linger on her for a flicker too long, and I could see her absorbing the energy—the attention—like a flower in the sun. Standing up a little straighter, pushing her small chest out a little further.

She wouldn't understand what it meant to crave that sort of attention at the same time you were being taught to fear it. To be simultaneously repulsed and obsessed with the development of your own body. The already full breasts. The softly flaring hips. Watching it all grow bigger and wider and further out of your control, all while you stood next to her every day.

"Okay." Marley raised her eyebrows, like I'd snapped—which maybe I had.

"I'm just tired," I muttered.

"You're always tired."

"That's not true." This time I did snap.

Marley rolled her eyes, but said nothing.

"Do you ever think about running away?" I asked her. I wasn't exactly sure where the words came from, but it felt good to say them.

"All the time," she answered. I almost reeled back in surprise.

"Really?"

"Of course. Don't you?"

"Yes," I said, a bit wistfully. "If you ran away, where would you go?"

She shrugged. "California, maybe. Or Seattle. Somewhere that's the exact opposite of here."

I nodded. "I'd go to New York City." I could be someone different there—someone better. Smarter. More driven. Just *more*.

Marley broke into a smile, so bright it almost blinded me. "I like it," she said.

"Really?"

"Yeah, really." And then she jumped up from the chair, her whole body suddenly alight with energy. "Thea, we should go," she said, reaching for my hand and squeezing it tightly with hers. I became suddenly aware of her—of how close we were.

I'd taken to wearing long sleeves since I started cutting a few months before. I kept the extra fabric pulled down over my knuckles so no one could see, but I couldn't shake the impulse to pull them down further now. To hide the evidence of my pain from Marley.

I opened my mouth to respond, but no words came out for a few seconds. "Right now?"

"Yes," she said. Then again. "Yes, right now. Why not? We could do it together. We could go there and find jobs and a place to live. People tell me that I look eighteen all the time. I could get us fake IDs."

My head was spinning as she spoke. I was shocked by how quickly the picture materialized. How easy it was to visualize it. Us, there. Together.

"I—I mean, how will we get there?"

"Hitchhiking," she answered, like it was obvious.

Marley was already up and moving, pushing my school backpack into my arms and telling me to start packing, and before I knew exactly what I was doing, I felt myself get up and pull the schoolbooks out. I felt myself smile, my whole body coming to life. A flush of pure, unadulterated joy running through me.

"Okay," I said, my throat dry. It felt fragile, this moment. Gossamer as a spider's web. And suddenly, I realized I wanted it more than anything. "Let's do it."

We packed quickly, stuffing our school backpacks to the brim with supplies. A change of clothes, extra socks and underwear, a can of Pringles, two bottles of water, a box of Band-Aids, matches. My favorite sketchbook for me and a faded *Cosmo* for her. We hardly let ourselves breathe until we were out the door and far enough down the road that our houses had disappeared behind a bend in the street.

"I can't believe we're doing this," she said, hitching her thumbs into the straps of her backpack. A nervous laugh bubbling up from her throat.

"New York City," I answered. The words felt magical on my tongue.

For the first time in months, I felt right again. We played "I Spy" as we walked away from town and dreamed up elaborate, imagined futures for ourselves in New York, passing the Pringles can back and forth. I did a cartwheel when we made it past the town sign. I felt a hundred pounds lighter.

It didn't occur to me to panic until it was too late. Until the sun had already begun to set, and the shadows of the trees grew so long that they touched our legs, casting them in cool half-shadow.

"We're headed toward the highway, right?" Marley asked, slowing to a stop, pulling the backpack over her shoulder.

"I think so," I nodded. We'd been avoiding the main roads, so people in town wouldn't see us leaving and call our moms. We were relying on an instinctual knowledge of dirt-paved back roads to get us there.

I spun in a circle, eyes peeled for anything familiar, but it was just trees and the road stretching out in front of us like a thin, unending ribbon. Everything looked the same.

"I just feel like we should've hit it by now," she said, snapping the ponytail holder on her wrist. I closed my eyes for a moment, listening to the small, anxious *thwap* of the elastic hitting her skin.

"I think it's just ahead." I dipped my head forward. Forcing my feet to keep moving. I wouldn't let myself think of stopping. Not then. Not after the adrenaline rush I'd felt as we walked away from town. I couldn't go back there, even if it was the only direction left to go. Couldn't sink myself back into the darkness I'd been feeling recently. The hopelessness.

I kept walking, and Marley followed me. It was impossible to know how long we went on like that before either of us spoke. It felt like eons—the darkness swallowing up any light. Any warmth—and a stubborn silence settling between us.

"Thea," she said, finally. Desperate in a way that made me stop in my tracks. "We're lost."

I spun on my heel to face her, arms crossed, folding in on myself in the chill. "I know."

"We need to go back."

"No," I said, gritting my teeth. "We can't. We'll just stop here for the night and figure out where we are tomorrow."

"It's too cold. We don't even have a blanket."

"We have extra clothes. We'll just put them on. And matches. We can start a fire."

Marley chewed on her lip and nodded tentatively. "Fine," she said, dropping her pack and unzipping it, pulling out the sweatshirt she'd stuffed into the top and the pack of matches.

"See if you can find some sticks or something. I'll look for rocks," she said. "We'll make a fire pit."

I pulled the extra shirt over my head and got on my hands and knees in the dark, feeling for kindling. When I came back to her with my arms full, she already had the rocks arranged in a rough circle.

We worked together on arranging the twigs in the center, leaning them up against each other the way we'd seen in movies and throwing dry leaves around the base, both of us shivering, shoulders hunched against the cold.

When Marley lit the match, I caught the first real glimpse of her in hours. Her nose had gone red and runny, cheeks ruddy, lips chapped. Despite it all, she looked excited as she lowered the match onto the dry leaves at the base. She blew at the small flame once it caught, a thick stream of smoke already clouding the air between us. The leaves burned quickly, and we threw more on the pile, trying to get the sticks to catch, but they wouldn't. I huddled as close to the meager heat as possible, watching the leaves burn.

"It's not working," Marley said after a few minutes of scrambling to collect more handfuls of leaves before the others burned off.

"It will," I said. "We have to keep trying."

"No, Thea. We don't." Marley stared at me. She was barely visible in the dying light, but I still caught the flash of fear in her eyes. "We need to go home. We did this too fast. We can try again in a few days when we have a better plan."

I opened my mouth to speak, but the words stuck in the back of my throat, so instead I just nodded, sucking in a breath. I knew, even then, that if we turned around, we wouldn't try again. That this fleeting, fizzing moment of hope would be gone.

She used the last of her water to kill the fire and, in the dark, she reached back for my hand. "Walk with me," she whispered, gripping my fingers in hers and pulling me close.

We walked shoulder to shoulder, the heat of our skin soaking through the fabric of our clothes. I wondered if our moms were looking for us. If Austen was out there somewhere calling Marley's name.

A sharp pain went through me at the thought. Ever since my mom married Austen's dad, the three of us had been inseparable, but I could feel us changing in ways I didn't really want to acknowledge. The string between Marley and Austen drawing tighter and tighter—and me, helpless to do anything but watch.

The wind whistled through the dry leaves overhead, knocking them down around us. Her fingers curled into my arm, tighter and tighter as we went. I could see the small clouds of our breath blooming in front of us. Could feel the rhythm of our steps all the way down to my bones until nothing else existed. Just us.

For a moment, I felt almost okay. Solid and real, like I'd snatched some piece of myself back from the void. I was sure, whatever she and Austen had, it wouldn't be *this*. It wouldn't be what we had. Nothing could touch that.

By the time we spotted headlights in the distance, we were leaning against each other, moving forward at a slow shuffle, our arms tangled together, heads bent close. It was David who found us. He said we almost scared him off the road. That we looked like zombies huddled together like that.

That, for a second, he could hardly see where one of us ended and the other began.

CHAPTER

37

Marley

IT'S NEARLY DARK out by the time I get back from the police station, and I feel exhausted all the way down to my bones. The kind of tired I haven't felt in months, even with all the sleep I've lost this summer. All the nights spent cruising the back roads of Riverside with my headlights off, or tearing away from crime scenes trying to outrun the sirens at my back.

Still, I can't bring myself to sleep. My conversation with Romero has left me restless. Anxious. Now that she suspects me, it's only a matter of time before she finds something that connects me to the fires, and then it's over. I'll go down for your murder, and people will believe it.

I shake out my hands and roll my neck from side to side, feeling claustrophobic, penned in by the small house. I have to resist the familiar itch to get in my car and find another house to burn. I'm so used to giving in to the impulse that it takes more effort to resist than I anticipated, but I *can't* just sit here and wait for Romero to come for me. I can't wait, like a caged animal, for her to connect the dots. But I also can't burn another house. As much as I hate it—as much as I wish it wasn't the case—your death gave me the perfect out on the fires.

For a flash of a second, I wonder if that's why you did it, but I brush it aside just as quickly. The more I learn, the more I'm sure you *didn't*, and even if you did—even if Romero only brought up the gun to throw me off balance, and you really did burn in that house—I wouldn't have been the reason. It could've been the pregnancy that drove you to the edge. Or whatever happened with James. Maybe you had other secrets that I'll never know.

When I can't take it anymore, I force myself out the door, leaving my keys on the kitchen table. If I bring them, I know I'll start driving, and if I start driving, I know I'll start scouting.

Once I'm out the door I clench and unclench my hand by my sides, looking from one side to the other before I begin to walk. Just like earlier, no one's out. It's too hot to do anything but wallow, even now.

Still, I put one foot in front of the other, making my way up toward the far end of the street. I can't remember the last time I went this way, come to think of it—the rest of Riverside and Sherman Hill are in the other direction, but it feels good to move, to put distance between myself and everyone else.

After a few minutes, I find myself walking by the clearing where you and I used to hide from Austen, my eyes lingering on the patch of tall grass, then on the tree where the baby bird fell. Where we ended its fragile life in a fit of something between rage and mercy.

It's strange to think that we came back here after that day. That once we'd found it, the patch of grass by the tree became our secret place. Of all places, this is where we felt the safest, the most real and solid and wild. We spent hours lingering in the possibility of the place. You sketching contentedly, me braiding strands of grass into friendship bracelets and flower crowns. This was *our* place. The only one Austen never made it into.

Without thinking, I wade toward it and take a seat, listening to the dry rasp of rain-starved grass in the gentle breeze. I can't help but feel like I'm waiting for you. Like you're following just a few steps behind.

I can't take back the ways I left you behind or the things I said. You can't take back what happened with Austen. We'll never get a chance to mend everything that's been broken, so this moment—whatever closure I can get from it—will have to be enough.

I remember, with a wince, the bleating chirp of the little bird. Its body lying broken in the dirt.

"*Wait*," I'd said, grabbing at your hand once you'd turned away. "*We should at least bury it, shouldn't we?*"

You looked at the bird, then at me, something softening in your eyes. "*Okay*," you said, turning your gaze back to the road where Austen was still searching for us. "*Tonight.*"

We'd done just that, marking the small grave with a rock, a cross painted across the top in red nail polish.

Idly, I search the spot to see if it's still there. I haven't thought about it in years, but suddenly it feels important that it is, and, sure enough, my eyes catch on the stone, bigger than the others around it. The nail polish has long since faded, but there are still remnants. And something else, too. I squint and scoot closer.

There's an edge of something poking out from underneath the base of the large rock. A folded sheet of notebook paper, smudged reddish brown with dirt.

With shaking hands, I lift the rock and grab the page. Unfold its weather-torn edges to reveal a full sheet of paper covered in your harsh, shaky handwriting.

Marley,

I know you may not find this note—in fact, you probably won't. That, or the rain will get to it before you do. (I never thought I'd be hoping for this drought to hold out a little longer.) But I needed to write it down anyway, and this felt like the right place for it, somehow.

By the time you read this, if you read it at all, everything will already be over and, assuming everything goes according to plan, I'll be dead and everyone in town will know that I was responsible for the fires this summer. Just me.

I have been a worse friend to you than I can say—and there are things I can't tell even you about who I am and what I've done. Things I can't face anymore.

This isn't how I hoped it would all play out, but I need you to believe that it's what's best. Trust me. And please, please (God, please) forgive me.

I love you. I mean it.

Thea

38

Thea

"**A**RE YOU OKAY? You look pale." Austen says, his bushy eyebrows knitting together in concern from his spot next to me on the couch.

I nod, the small movement making my stomach flutter, unsettling the food I picked up on the way to his place.

"I'm fine," I say. But it's a lie. The rolling waves of nausea have been coming on for about a week in fits and starts, like a stomach bug I can't shake. And something darker, too. A sharp, pervading sense of dread—of being watched—digging its way underneath my skin.

I try to tell myself that it's nothing. That I'm only being paranoid. With all the secrets I've kept this summer, how could I not feel anxious? But I can't seem to shake the feeling of a presence at my back. A figure around every corner, waiting for me.

Austen reaches out a hand and tucks a strand of hair behind my ear, then rests the back of his hand on my forehead to check my temperature. "Are you sure?" he says. "Could you be coming down with a fever or something?"

I shrug, feeling the effort of the small movement in my whole body. "I don't think so," I say, swallowing back a wave of bile that's risen in my throat, trying to pretend I don't feel the weight of his eyes on me.

"I'm fine, really. But maybe we can just watch a movie or something tonight?"

"Of course," he says, grabbing the remote and opening Netflix. "Let me know if you need anything."

I press my lips together and fix my eyes on the screen, eager to think about anything besides the roiling in my stomach.

"Did you see the article in the paper about the arsonist?" he asks, flipping through options on the screen.

I look down at my hands, sitting limply on my lap, and study them, hoping Austen's too focused on the TV to notice all the remaining color that drains from my skin at the mention of the arsonist. "You're the only one who reads the paper," I tease, doing my best to sound lighthearted. "What did it say?"

"Sounds like they may be closing in on someone. Whoever he is, they say he's escalating. Aiming for bigger houses, closer to town. Either because he's running out of options farther away or because he's getting cocky. Apparently, they found tire tracks at one of the scenes."

"Really?"

"Honestly, I don't understand how they don't already have someone pinned for it." Austen says. "There's a new fire practically every night, and all they have are some tire tracks? I saw a news crew over by the station this afternoon. The van said CNN."

"CNN?" I say, a little too loudly. Austen looks at me, so I sit back against the couch cushions and raise my chin. "Riverside's a national story, then."

The thought makes me nauseous again. So nauseous I can't hold it down anymore. I push myself off the couch and run to the bathroom. There's a sharp tug in my throat and then my dinner staring back at me. I frown at the white chunks of chicken, floating undigested in the toilet bowl, and flush.

"Thea?" Austen's leaning in the doorway.

I wipe my mouth with the back of my hand and pull my hair up into a bun with the elastic around my wrist. "Sorry," I say. "Could I get some water, actually?"

He disappears and comes back a moment later, the glass of water in his hands still settling from the tap. I take it and force down a sip, but it doesn't do much to ease the burning at the back of my tongue and down my throat.

"I'm fine," I say again, setting the glass on the bathroom floor and pressing my palm to the cool tile.

"Clearly, you're not," he says, eyeing me cautiously. For a second, I let myself imagine what he must see. The sunken hollows around my eyes and the pallor of my skin. The transformation has been slow but unmistakable. Really, it's been happening since James died. Every day I look a little less like myself and a little more like someone else. *Something* else.

"I must've been wrong before. I have a stomach bug or something."

"You want me to call Dahlia and have her come get you?"

"No," I say quickly. "I told her I was going to a friend's tonight."

He nods, his cheeks flushing slightly, like he'd forgotten why we've been sneaking around. What we've been doing almost every night this summer.

"I can drive myself back. I just need a couple of minutes to make sure all the food's out of my system," I say, hoping it's a suggestive enough image for Austen to leave me alone. He does, and once he's gone, I brush my teeth with my finger and take some deep breaths.

Tire tracks. Could they trace those to Marley's car? If they got to her, would she tell them about me?

There's a soft knock on the door that makes me jump, and then Austen is there again, looking sheepish this time.

"Is there anything else I can get you? I have some Tylenol somewhere, I think," he says, his hands folded together in front of him, looking grim.

"Thanks. I'll be alright. Probably just need a good night's sleep. I'm heading out soon."

"You can stay here, if you want to."

I almost smile at the thought. "You know I can't," I say.

I could probably pass it off with Mom—tell her I decided to crash at my friend's and keep the details vague—but I don't like taking those kinds of chances, especially not as the feeling of being watched grows more and more pronounced. I find myself checking for the presence constantly these days. Glancing in the rearview mirror of my car every few seconds to make sure no one is following me. Staring out my bedroom window for minutes at a time, hoping to catch a flicker of movement in the trees behind the house.

Austen rolls his shoulders back, pulling me out of the paranoia, and I'm struck, once again, by the sheer size of him. The way he blocks the entire doorway with his frame and the impossibility of slipping past him if I needed to. Austen is a good man. He would never force me to do something I don't want to do, but right now, I feel trapped.

"God, I'm tired of sneaking around like this," he says, and there's an urgency in his voice that sparks something in me. A memory of that first night. Of his lips pressing against the underside of my wrist and the way it made me feel—like a weight going off my back for the first time in years. An understanding spreading through me warm and slow and thick, like honey. How eager I was to lose myself in the fantasy of it—of Austen having wanted me this whole time.

But now I look at him in the harsh, blue sheen of the fluorescence, and I feel anxiety more than anything, over all the ways this very delicate relationship could derail.

"What other choice do we have, Austen?"

"We could make it official. Go public," he says.

I freeze, my whole body going stiff. "What did you say?"

"Look, I know it's complicated, and I know it wouldn't be easy, but it's not like it's illegal, us being together. We're both adults, and our parents have been divorced for years. We're not actually related, for God's sake."

We're not together, I want to say, but instead I stand stock still, gaping at him. The time we've spent together this summer has been lovely. Warm and intoxicating and intimate. But never once did I think it was building to anything. That we were going to be *together* in the real world.

"Can—can we not talk about this right now?" I ask finally.

"We do have to talk about it at some point," he says, lowering his voice.

Do we? I want to ask because, suddenly, what I'd really like is to take it back. To turn back time to the night of that fight and smooth things over and make it all normal again. But I can't do that, and instead every day I feel more cornered—Austen and Marley and Scott, and now the police and the national media circling like wolves on the hunt, drawing closer. I feel like I'm watching my escape window, the one that's been shrinking since James died, throw out its last glimmer before disappearing entirely.

"I know we need to talk about it," I say. "I just don't have the energy tonight."

"I love you, Thea."

My stomach flips again. "What?" I ask, willing myself not to have heard it.

Austen's eyes go wide, like he's surprised himself by saying it, but that only lasts a second before I see the resolve settling over his face. Hardening there like a glaze. "I said I love you," he whispers again, taking another step toward me. "I needed to say it out loud. To get it off my chest."

"That is a lot to put out there."

"I'm not asking for anything," he says.

"Yes, you are," I snap. "I have plans, Austen. The twins start school in a month. I'm—I'm supposed to move to New York. And now you're asking me to upend my whole life for whatever *this* is?"

"Thea," he says, the corner of his mouth turning up into a disbelieving smile. "Be realistic. You're not moving in a month. You've been dodging the subject all summer. I haven't even seen you look at apartments. Besides, I just told you what *this* is."

"You told me what it is for *you*."

I watch the words hit him. "Oh," he says, stepping back now, his voice the smallest I've ever heard it.

"I shouldn't have said that," I say quickly. "This is all a lot, and I don't feel well. I just need time to think."

"Got it." He shoves his hands into his pockets, his tone clipped. "Take all the time you need." He spins on his heel out of the bathroom and down the hall to his bedroom. I listen to the heavy tread of his footsteps and then to the slam of his door, and press the bathroom door closed again.

My stomach churns and I grip the countertop, taking in my reflection in the toothpaste-spattered mirror. The frizzing halo of curls catching the light around my head makes me think of James.

If he could see me now, what would he say?

Should've gotten out when I did, kid.

I swallow hard and make myself breathe in through my nose and out through my mouth, feeling the words linger there, and then, just one word. Just *kid* sitting there like a stone.

Kid.

Oh shit.

I go to the kitchen and rip open my purse, staring at the tampon I always keep with me and trying to remember the last time I used one. My period has always been unpredictable, but I've never missed one entirely and it's been weeks now, hasn't it? Five at least, maybe six.

"Oh my God," I mumble, looking at Austen's closed door. I shake my head, like I can dismiss the idea that easily. Like I can make it all just disappear. I gather my things and leave, slamming the front door hard enough that he'll hear it from the back of the apartment.

Once I'm out, I get in the car and drive, mind racing.

Austen and I have been careful—every time except the first, that is. And if that's the case, it doesn't take much mental math to tighten the knot in my stomach. I'm already past the point of legal abortion in Georgia.

I feel like screaming. This can't actually be happening.

It isn't until I park that I realize I've been unconsciously driving to Iris's. I stare at the dark house for a moment, then get out of the car and knock softly on the front door. Baby James will be asleep by now, which is good, because I try to avoid seeing him if I can. I can never quite bring myself to look at him.

Iris answers the door in sweatpants and an old T-shirt, blinking blearily at me. "Thea?" she says.

"Can I come in?" I ask, shifting my weight from one foot to the other. Iris nods and steps aside. And I feel it again. The prickle at the back of my neck. A warning that someone has me in their sights. I turn around, but no one is there. The street is empty, almost pitch black.

"Of course. I wasn't expecting you tonight. Is everything alright?" she asks, as I step across the threshold and close the door, shaking off the feeling.

"Not exactly," I tell her, taking in the sight of the living room. Iris's plants have always been the most noticeable thing about the house— they stretch luxuriantly out from their pots on side tables and the mantel, reaching hardy green leaves up and out to fill the empty spaces. I've spent several afternoons this summer asking Iris to tell me about each one—what they all need to thrive and grow. I've always found the space cathartic.

Tonight, though, all I see are baby toys littering the floor, and spit-up rags and baby blankets draped over the couch and the lounge chair. I've never really noticed them before—in fact, I even sent Iris a basket of them last winter in a haze of alcohol-driven guilt—but tonight they send a chill up my spine. The inevitable trail that a baby leaves in its wake.

"Thea, tell me what's going on," she mumbles, flipping on the light. "You look like you've seen a ghost."

Reluctantly, I perch on the edge of the sofa and study her. She still looks groggy, but her big eyes are fixed on me with concern and real attention. This is the way she's always looked at me—the way I see her look at everyone—and for the first time, I can see why she unnerved James so much toward the end. Because she's too good for any of it. My bullshit or his.

"I'm so sorry," I say. "I feel terrible for barging in like this. I didn't know where else to go."

"Thea, it's okay," she says, reaching across the space between us to grip my hand with hers, not unlike James used to do. "What's wrong?"

I shrug, surprised by the weak smile that turns up the corners of my lips. "Have you ever made a huge mistake? One you couldn't take back?"

"I didn't see how badly James was hurting," she answers without hesitation. "I got so wrapped up in the baby, I didn't see the signs. I'll never be able to take that back."

I nod, feeling even more miserable at the mention of James, but Iris just shakes her head, like she's hearing it through my ears.

"Everyone makes mistakes," she says. "It's human."

"Not like this," I manage. I can feel the tears collecting in my eyes and I wipe at them before they can fall.

"Can you tell me what happened?" she asks.

"Not really," I say. "I got . . . involved with someone—someone I shouldn't have, and now it's too late." I know it's cryptic, but it's all I can manage. I don't think Iris would tell anyone if I confided in her, but it feels impossible to form the words. To admit, out loud, what I'm thinking.

"Too late?" she asks, squeezing my hand.

"I'm in over my head," I admit.

"Did something happen to you? Do I need to take you to the police?"

"No," I say, shaking my head quickly. "Nothing like that. Honestly. I just—I have a bad habit of taking things too far, and I think it's finally catching up with me. That's all."

"What can I do to help?" she asks.

For a second, I think about asking her what life is like with a baby, but instead I shake my head and push myself off the couch. I shouldn't have come here. Despite what Iris says, she has enough going on already. I don't need to add to it. "You've done more than enough already, Iris. More than I deserve. Thank you for letting me in."

"Of course. You're my friend. You can come to me with anything," she says, following me to the door. "And Thea?"

"Yes?" I ask, turning to face her, one hand on the doorknob.

"Please, *please* don't do anything rash tonight. Whatever's wrong, I promise things will look better tomorrow."

I look at her for a few seconds longer than I should. Studying the lines of concern that have permanently etched themselves into the skin around her eyes.

She was right when she said that James and I were alike—even more right than I realized at the time. But it's not the depression that made us the same. It's the way we both *take* from people. People like Iris, who deserve better.

I've already ruined her life once. And whatever faults I have, I'm not selfish enough to drag her down again.

Without another word, I leave and I don't look back.

39

Marley

THE MEDIA WAS wrong about the first fire.

It wasn't the house on Brighton Lane—the little, abandoned bungalow three miles outside of Riverside. The one I stayed to watch burn for nearly twenty minutes before I heard the sirens approaching.

The first fire was three days earlier.

I'd moved back into Mom's house, having cleaned out the last of my things from the Sherman Hill apartment. I didn't have much, since I left the artwork and the throw pillows and the coffee machine behind for Austen to decide what to do with. Everything I'd bought since we moved in together—the things that were *ours*, not just mine, felt tainted.

There was a large part of me that still felt sixteen, back in my childhood bedroom. Like the time I'd spent in Sherman Hill had been some sort of elaborate game. A life I'd been play-acting with my apartment, my job, and my fiancé, at least until I'd managed to lose hold of it all in record time.

Mom was at work—she was almost always gone since I'd moved back in. And though I'd given her the basics of what happened, I assumed she was hearing the other, more sensationalized, versions through the grapevine. I probably should've made an effort to set the record straight, but somehow, by that point, I couldn't bring myself to care.

In one version I'd done this before—dozens of times. I'd slept with nearly every man in Sherman Hill *and* Riverside. In another, I'd jumped Scott right there on the dance floor for everyone to see. A third person swore they saw me slip something into Scott's beer while we were chatting.

I knew these versions of the story because they'd all been reposted by the Vintage Whore Instagram account—an anonymous account that popped up the day after it happened.

The profile photo on Vintage Whore's account was a picture of me taken at the lake the summer before. I didn't post pictures in my swimsuit often, but you'd found a retro bikini that went perfectly with my aesthetic, and the picture caught me at just the right angle so I looked long and lean and even a little tan.

Vintage Whore took the picture and added two black bars over my chest and pelvis, covering the suit, so I looked naked. They took other pictures off my Instagram and added more black bars, this time over my eyes or mouth, the words CHEATER and LIAR plastered across the images in sharp red letters. They posted stories with polls asking people to pick the number of men I'd cheated with since Austen and I got engaged.

I spent hours scrolling through it—combing the list of followers. Most were people I didn't know well, but the account was public, so there was no telling how many of the people I counted as friends interacted with it. How many voted on the stories or submitted rumors of their own to be reposted.

One photo of me with the word HOMEWRECKER pasted over it had been liked by four of the Moonies.

The Vintage Doll account wasn't much safer. People flooded the comments. One woman I didn't even know took it upon herself to comment SLUT on every picture we'd ever posted. Men DMed me to detail the ways they'd like to rape and kill me. To make me pay for what I'd done.

Vintage Whore killed Vintage Doll inside forty-eight hours. Months of work—learning photography and SEO, responding to comments and answering questions and filming content. Writing captions as you pieced together unique outfits that incorporated just enough Southern Moon merch to keep the brand on my side while staying "authentic."

Earning brand partnerships and an engaged and active follower base of 68.4K. All of it gone. All of it for nothing.

Strangely, it wasn't a rape threat, or a new post on Vintage Whore that set me off that first night. It was a comment. Just one—six words. No caps, no exclamation marks.

this girl is so fucking useless.

I almost missed it, actually. I was sitting on the floor of my childhood bedroom—my only bedroom, now—scrolling for the hundredth time through the Vintage Doll account, thinking about deactivating it completely, when I spotted it underneath one of my older pictures. The picture was from the previous Christmas, but the comment was recent—added post-scandal—like the person had found the account, taken the time to go through it, and considered their decision carefully before posting.

this girl is so fucking useless. It was just that word, really. Just *useless* that played back over and over again in my head. I felt it sinking into me. Overcoming me. I wanted to push back, but with what? What had I ever done, really? What did I have to show for my life but a defunct Instagram account, a broken engagement, a career in flames, and a best friend who didn't want to speak to me?

The anger came on quickly after that, seeping through me like run-off from a crack I'd never even seen starting to form. I looked wildly around my room. Practically empty, except for my closet, which nearly burst at the seams. I could see fabric slipping out between the cracks in the accordion door. Something long with a sequined hemline pooling at the bottom.

These clothes I'd spent my life in—the wardrobe I'd painstakingly collected, piece by piece—the whole point of it had been to show the world who I was. *Dress to be the best version of yourself!* I'd chirped cheerfully on a video just a few weeks ago.

But I had no idea who I was. Not really. I'd been lying to myself all along. These clothes belonged to a stranger.

Before I could think about it more, I deleted Vintage Doll. Wiped the page from the face of the internet. Then I threw open the closet doors and grabbed an armful, yanking them sharply off their hangers and carrying them to the backyard where I tossed them haphazardly in a pile. The moon hung low in the sky, shining a dull red like copper. The crickets screamed.

I went back inside and found the matches in Mom's bedside table where I knew she kept them, moving on autopilot as I opened the little book, struck one, and threw it on the pile. I stood by and watched as the small blue head of flame caught against a cotton shirt and burned brighter. I felt unlocked. Untethered. The anger rising up out of me like a vicious roar. Something I didn't have to push down anymore.

The smoke billowed out, forcing its way to my eyes and nose, choking me until I had to step back and pull my shirt up to cover my face.

A part of me knew it was irresponsible. That the fire could catch—spread to my house, or even yours, before it burned itself out. I thought of a spark traveling on the breeze to the pile of brush a few yards away. The flames leaping out, becoming uncontrollable. Tackling the house. The neighborhood. The whole town.

I thought about what it would feel like to burn it all.

It felt good.

CHAPTER

40

Thea

"WE'RE GOING TO have to make a quick getaway with this one," Marley says, swinging the car off the road and parking it underneath a clump of trees. It's already dark out, but something about the canopy of leaves overhead makes me feel trapped.

I didn't mean to find myself here again—especially not since the feeling of being watched has rooted itself underneath my skin—but Marley's right. Somehow, the fires are the only thing that make me feel okay for any length of time. Besides, I'm sure I'm just imagining things.

"Why?" I ask, unbuckling my seat belt and grabbing a fistful of rags from the pile by my feet as Marley reaches for the can of gasoline. The lighter will be in her pocket—she likes to keep it close.

"I saw a cop a few miles back."

"You what?" I ask, panic shooting through me like a bolt of adrenaline.

"Relax," she says. "He didn't see us. He was ambling in his cruiser, though. Probably waiting for the first sign of smoke. I'd bet they have officers stashed all over town on the lookout, and they know we don't have as many options on the outskirts of town anymore. So let's light this fucker and go."

"Can't we find another house?"

"Nah," she says, almost scary in her nonchalance as she pops open the car door and ducks out. She straightens up, then tilts her head down to look at me in the passenger's seat. "We're already here." My stomach flips, but the look in her eye—the absolute confidence in herself—it's surprisingly persuasive and, to be fair, we probably threw caution to the wind when we started burning down houses, anyway.

I take a deep breath and roll my eyes. "Fine. Quick, though," I grumble, my feet hitting the soft dirt.

Marley pulls the hood over her head and jogs across the open lot toward the little, slouching ranch at the center, the half-empty gas can sloshing in her hands. I set my eyes on the silhouette and plod along behind her. Not for the first time it strikes me how many abandoned houses there are here in Riverside, dotting the countryside like dead bugs on a windshield. I wonder what it must've been like once, before the plant closed, when there were still jobs. Before the rug pulled itself out from underneath us and left us here to shrivel under the harsh sun.

"You get the back door, I'll get the front," Marley says. I hold out the rags in my hands and let her drip gasoline onto them, the harsh smell burning its way down my nostrils and settling in a cloud around our heads. I smell it all the time now—the gasoline. Catch whiffs of it no matter where I am, like a phantom pain.

Marley digs a cigarette lighter out of her back pocket and sticks it between my teeth, smiling wickedly at me. "Quick walk through and light them in five minutes, okay? I'll keep watch on the road."

I nod my head and spin on my heel, toward the back of the house where the door is already ajar, the hinges groaning in the slight breeze. I drop the rags at the threshold and step through as lightly as I can manage.

At the front of the house, I can hear Marley's tread on the creaking porch, probably pacing, her eyes fixed with laser precision on the street as she waits for my *all clear inside* signal.

I slip the phone out of my pocket and turn the flashlight on. There's no reason to tiptoe when I do this, but I can't help it. I feel like a thief walking through these old houses. Like I'm catching a glimpse of a world never meant for my eyes.

This house looks like it was abandoned decades ago—the near-rotting floorboards groaning with every step and the cloud of unsettled dust kicking up around me—but it isn't empty like some of the others. There are still pictures on the walls, barely visible underneath a layer of grime, and a sad, sagging couch pushed up against the far wall.

Who cared about this place enough to hang pictures, then leave them behind? I wonder. The thought fills me with a dread I can't explain, so I force myself to turn down the hall, toward the west side of the house where there's a very dated bathroom and two bedrooms. The first is small and empty, but the second looks like someone walked out wearing nothing but the clothes on their back and never came back.

I step in cautiously, my flashlight throwing a harsh beam of white light across the room, illuminating the dust motes suspended in midair. To my right there's a bureau with costume jewelry laid across the top. I run my fingers over a string of fat, fake pearls and catch the glint of the flashlight beam on a watch's face. It looks almost like it was tossed down. Flung carelessly at the end of a long day, and I pick it up and shove it in my pocket before I can let myself think about it too much.

From the front of the house, I hear a sharp rapping on the wall. Marley, asking for the all clear. I jog back to the front and sweep my flashlight beam across the room once more, even though it's obvious no one's been here in years. Then I knock back. Two knocks means all good and I have thirty seconds to get out, start the fire at the back door, and meet Marley by the car. I get to it, feeling the weight of the watch in my pocket the whole time. I shouldn't have taken it, I know, but something about the look of it—the glint of the flashlight beam across the smooth glass face and the dust that had worked its way into every crevice of the intricate gold band—I couldn't burn it. And besides, who's going to miss it?

I can smell the smoke wafting from the front of the house as I flick the light on and dip the small flame toward the rags shoved underneath the doorjamb. They light, but not quickly. I fan the flames and peer around the side of the house to see Marley running at full speed back toward the car. She turns around, and even from this distance I can see her eyes boring into me. Can feel the shout she's refusing to let escape her lips.

Hands shaking, I try again, lighting the rags on the other end of the door. I can hear the fire popping up front. The wood snapping and groaning. The front of the house beginning to come down on itself, and I know I have to go, that I have to move quickly, but my legs feel like sand. I watch the small flames lick against the base of the door and climb slowly. Watch the edges of the rags go black and disappear. It's strangely mesmerizing. It makes me think of the first house I watched Marley light—the way she watched the fire climb over the house and swallow it whole. The look in her eye, like pure need.

I didn't understand it then, but I do now. The release it provides. The feeling of transferring your pain onto something real and tangible and solid. I think of the scars on my forearm. The hot liquid of my blood slipping over the soft, white skin. The thin, red lines cracking open and the satisfaction that comes with matching the outside to the inside. Of leaving a mark.

The sound of a motor snaps me out of my trance. I look to my right and find Marley's car roaring out from between the dense clump of trees, tires kicking up a trail of dirt as it races toward me.

And then, sirens.

Finally, I feel myself moving. I throw the car door open and jump in, the car already skidding away as Marley floors the gas pedal.

"What the hell?" she's screaming. "What were you doing?"

"I—I'm sorry," is all I can say. She doesn't have time to say anything more, though. She just fixes her eyes on the road and slams on the gas. I turn back and look at the house. The front is burning, but without the fire coming from the back, it hasn't really taken yet. The structure is all still intact as the sirens fly closer.

It's a few tense minutes as Marley cuts down side street after side street, winding us closer and closer to the center of town, the AC vents blowing cool air across my sweaty neck, making goose bumps raise up on my arms.

Finally, we're back in Marley's driveway. The car off. Everything around us eerily silent.

"You keep fucking things up, Thea," she whispers furiously. "Dropping the knife at Sky's and now this? I can't—" She breaks her sentence and turns to face me. "*We* can't get caught. If we do, it could ruin everything. Our whole lives."

"I know," I say, a little defensively. The truth is, though, the more we do this, the more it feels like the only part of my life that isn't already ruined. The only part that actually makes me feel alive.

"Do you?" she raises an eyebrow, and I feel myself tense underneath the glare. "You really think that dirty watch you're clutching was worth the risk you just took?"

"Don't look at me like that," I spit back and grip the watch in my hand. "*You're* the one who started with the fires. And the one who wanted to slash the tires on Sky's car. We're on your rage tour, not mine."

"Exactly, and I don't remember asking you to come along."

I sit back, biting down on my lip. My skin suddenly itchy with the realization that she's right. I just showed up. Made myself part of something that may never have been about me in the first place.

"I see," I say bitterly, placing my hand on the car door handle to let myself out. "Well, sorry that I've gotten so in the way."

"Wait," she says quickly, reaching out a hand and stopping it inches from my shoulder. Suddenly, her face goes white. I stop, my fingers still half-curled around the handle as she stares at her hand, eyes wide like she's just seen a ghost.

"My ring," she says. For a second, I think she must be referring to her engagement ring, but she gave that back to Austen. I saw it there once. Caught the flash of it when I opened the drawer in his bedside table looking for a condom, then snapped the drawer shut, like it had bitten me.

"What ring?"

"My ring," she says again. "The ring we bought together—the silver one. I had it on when we left."

I blink at her, trying to process. First, that she's kept wearing hers, and second that it's gone.

"You were wearing it?"

"I'm always wearing it," she says. "Shit. Shit. Shit."

"Marley, relax," I say sternly, turning my body back in her direction. She looks . . . small, her shoulders hunched, her face pinched. For a flash of a second, I see the pain I know she's been trying to cloak underneath a layer of anger and bravado. "It's just a ring. That house was full of jewelry. They probably won't even notice it, and if they do, they'll write it off as nothing."

"They're closing in," she whispers. "They're going to catch us. I can feel it."

"No, they won't. You're spiraling."

"Yeah. We've committed, like, a billion felonies. Why aren't *you*?"

Because I live in a spiral, I almost say, but I manage to hold my tongue. "We can't both spiral," I tell her instead. "This is just like the knife. They never pinned that on us, did they? And that time they had way stronger evidence. This is just a silver band. Millions of people wear them. Besides, they think a man is behind this.

She nods slowly, forcing a long, deep breath in through her nose and out through her mouth. "Okay. You're right. It's nothing. It's not a big deal."

"Right," I repeat. "Not a big deal."

Truthfully, I don't know if it is or not, but what difference does it make? Marley's right—the police are closing in. If we keep this up, it's only a matter of time before they catch us. The thought should fill me with dread, but instead I feel a strange kind of relief.

If we got caught, it would all be over.

"Thea," she says. "I'm getting tired of this."

"Of what?"

"*This*," she says, gesturing to the empty gas can at my feet. "I started doing it because I felt like I was alone. But now that things are okay with us, I can find a better way to deal with the Austen stuff. I can go to therapy or get a Lexapro prescription or something."

I feel a drop in my gut. "What are you saying?"

"I'm saying let's quit while we're ahead. Let's just go back to the way we were before Austen. We don't need him. We never have."

The breath hitches inside my chest. *We don't need him. We never have.*

I didn't realize until now just how long I've been waiting to hear those words from her. How I've longed for them, in some deep, unchangeable part of myself. A slow-burning fire I've never quite managed to stomp out.

"Marley." Before I can stop myself, I reach out and grab her hand, pulling it toward me. Holding it against me.

She looks at me, her eyes sharp. Pleading. She doesn't draw her hand away. She doesn't move at all. "Please," she says finally, leaning closer. Nearly closing the gap between us. "Thea, please. Say yes."

Instead, I kiss her.

She goes stiff for a second, like she wasn't expecting it, but then she melts, her body softening, lips parting. I pull her to me. Slip my hand into her hair. My tongue into her mouth. The fire inside of me rages, no longer containable.

It's too late, I realize. It has always been too late. *I* am the house on fire, and there's nothing left to do now but mitigate the damage.

After what feels like hours—days, years, millennia—Marley pulls back, drawing her hand up to her kiss-swollen lips.

"Oh," she says. "Thea, I—"

"Please, don't say anything." I cut her off. Because I know, some-how, exactly what she will say, and I can't bear to hear it.

She loves me, but not the way that I love her. Not with the same ache. The same desperation. She never has.

And even if, by some miracle, she did, it's already too late. I think of the pregnancy test I took earlier tonight. The little pink plus sign—confirmation I hardly needed. I'd give anything to go back, but we can't. I've already ruined any chance we might've had.

"I can't be your friend anymore," I tell her, and watch her whole body stiffen at the words, her spine going ramrod straight. The pain roaring back to life inside her eyes. "I can't be your anything anymore."

"Okay," she says, her voice barely a whisper. I swallow hard. Feel myself cracking under the weight of that single word. For a second, I think we're done, but she fixes her eyes on me again, the steel of her gaze pressing into me hot and unyielding as the sun. "I wish everything was different."

"Me too," I say, reaching out, once more, to touch her hand. To feel the smoothness of it against my fingertips.

And then I do the hardest thing I have ever done.

I get out of the car, and I leave her behind.

CHAPTER

41

Marley

I KNOW WHERE I am by the sound.

The angry, skittering *crack* of flames eating through wooden planks. The groan of the house's frame, like a death cry, and the rush of air as the fire climbs higher, higher, higher.

And then the scream. It's desperate. Animal. I try to run toward it, but it's coming from everywhere all at once, and I can't see anything but the flames.

My ringtone jolts me awake. There's that one split second, before my own life comes crashing down on top of me, when I can't remember how I got here, asleep on my bedroom floor, but then I spot the note lying unfolded next to me, and I remember. I remember all of it.

The phone rings again and I stare at the screen, where Skylar's picture is flashing. It's the one that's up on the billboard out by the highway for Southern Moon—the one that has her draped in a white, faux fur vest and vacuumed into crimson leather pants. Atrocious, and oh so Skylar, I couldn't resist setting it as her photo.

I pick up the phone and press it to my ear, feeling the dull throb of a hangover building behind my eyes. "Skylar?" I say, squinting at the bright light streaming through the window. How long have I been asleep?

"Marley," she says. "I'm so glad I caught you. Is this a good time?"

"Is everything okay?" I ask, pulling my hand through my hair, my arm tingling from the way I fell asleep on it. The last time I talked to Sky, she was firing me, and I can't imagine why she'd be calling now.

"Yes, everything's great," she says quickly. "I wanted to see if maybe you had some time to come by my place today. I . . . have something I wanted to discuss with you."

"What?" I ask. I can't help myself. There's something in Sky's tone that I can't quite place. It makes me anxious.

"I want to talk about your future with Southern Moon," she says.

"My future at Southern Moon," I repeat blankly.

I fall back against the frame of my bed and squeeze my eyes closed, willing the headache away.

"Look, I wanted to give everyone a cooling off period before I said anything, but I want you to come back to work, and I think I can get everyone on board. The last few weeks have made it so clear how invaluable you are. The drama will blow over—it always does—and I see big things for you here."

I realize, after a beat of silence falls across the line, that my mouth is hanging open. "What?"

"Just come over, okay? We can talk more once you're here."

"Um. Okay, I'll head over," I manage, too shell-shocked to drum up anything more eloquent.

"Perfect. Come by as soon as you can. I'm excited to discuss it with you," she says before hanging up.

I toss the phone on the bed and stretch my legs out in front of me. The invitation and the offer feel, somehow, like a trick, but I can't figure out what she's playing at. After all, what else could she possibly want from me? What else do I have to lose?

My eyes catch again at your note laid out by my side. The last words you ever had for me. The note that makes it clear that I've been chasing a phantom since your funeral.

You did this to yourself. You meant to go down for the fires. You wanted to protect me. It's as simple as that. It has to be.

So, why can't I stop thinking about the missing gun? About the blood spatters I found in your room?

Please, please forgive me. The sight of those four words scribbled on the notebook page pass through my head for the millionth time today.

I could drive myself insane trying to make sense of it. I nearly did, last night, but who would that help? It seems like you got exactly what you wanted.

No, I think. *Not exactly what you wanted.*

The memory of the last time I saw you roars to life in my head. The last things you ever said to me that night in the car. *I can't be your friend anymore. I can't be your anything anymore.* The desperation on your face. The awful regret that crept over me as I watched you walk away.

I refold the note and stuff it underneath a pile of old sweatshirts in my chest of drawers. There's no point in fixating on it now.

Instead, I force myself to refocus on the day ahead. The idea of working at Southern Moon again sends an unexpected jolt of electricity through me. It's not what I want anymore, but maybe I could use it as a stepping stone into something else. Something better.

I pop two ibuprofens, chug a Gatorade from the fridge, and apply a meticulous layer of makeup. When I'm done with that, I stand in front of my closet, eyes skimming over what's left. Suddenly, I miss the clothes I burned so badly it's almost painful. I miss the version of myself who took joy in them. Who treasured them like heirlooms. I miss the me who thought the past was worth preserving, instead of burning to the ground. Eventually, I pull on a pair of jean shorts and an artfully ripped T-shirt from three seasons ago and decide it's good enough.

I'm still in a bit of a daze when I get to Skylar's. Still riding the buzz of my dream. Of your note.

When I get to the door, I knock, sparing a glance at the driveway behind me. At the spot where you plunged the knife into the tire of Sky's polished pearl VW Bug. The knife that's now in Romero's drawer with your fingerprints on it.

"Marley," Skylar says, ushering me inside. "Thanks for coming by. Can I get you something to drink? You look like you could use a coffee."

I ignore the jab and follow her across the threshold into the living room. She's wearing silk pajama shorts and an oversized sweatshirt, like she may have just rolled out of bed, but her hair is styled in loose, tousled waves that are too perfect to be natural, and she's got on a subtle face of makeup.

"No, thanks," I say, forcing a smile and trying not to stare. Sky typically goes for over-the-top glam, not subtlety. It adds to the feeling that there's something going on here I don't understand.

She smiles placidly at that, shrugging her shoulders. "Suit yourself," she says, taking a seat on the big, white couch in the open-plan living room. There's midmorning sunlight streaming in from every window, and a dog's bed in the corner, occupied by her sleeping golden retriever, Minnie—the one who almost got us caught that night. I feel sweat pooling along my hairline and my headache coming back full force. *God, it's hot in here.*

I take a seat on the edge of a plush armchair facing her and breathe.

"How's the store?" I say, feeling suddenly awkward. Sky and I haven't been together intentionally in ages, and certainly not since things started to sour. When I first started at Southern Moon, I used to relish any time I could get with her. I wanted to drink her in. To absorb all the shiny, pretty things she represented until they were a part of me, too. But that feeling's long gone now and all that's left is the vague edge of bitterness, like a hangover.

I wonder, if someone had told me back then how hard it would be—everything I'd give up only to learn the lesson that people like Sky are born, not made—would I have listened, or would I have forged ahead anyway?

She wraps her hands around a steaming mug sitting on the coffee table and lifts it to her lips. "My mom was on the warpath for a few days, but she's calmed down," she says, holding the mug just underneath her chin. "She hired this new manager to pick up the slack in Athens, and I swear to God, I've spent the last three days training and retraining her on the most basic things. Plus, the girls hate her. They all want you back."

"I do miss them," I say. I wish I could just ask her straight up what she meant over the phone, but it isn't like that with Sky. Every conversation with her is like a battle, a dance. She wouldn't have brought me here unless she wanted something from me.

"*Oh,* I haven't had a chance to tell you," she says, tucking her feet up underneath her, like she's settling in for a good story. "Three days ago, I walked into the storeroom in Athens and Carrie was in there *eating* packing peanuts."

"Shit," I say. I know how I'm supposed to react—shocked and perversely gleeful, like I always do when Sky gossips with me—but instead I just think of the way Carrie squeezed my hand that day in the break room. How she made me laugh when I really needed to.

"What, you knew?" Sky asks, raising one feathered eyebrow, her smile fading.

"She has pica," I tell her, smoothing my hands down my legs. "It's a medical condition. She can't help it. I should call her parents and let them know."

"No, I'll do it. I'm her employer," she snaps, clearly annoyed. I'd have to be deaf not to clock the emphasis on *employer*. The power she wants to remind me that she has, even now, after everything.

"She told me in confidence. I wouldn't want her to think I betrayed that."

"Well," Sky snaps, "Then she shouldn't be doing it at work. Any other employee could've walked in and seen it. We have a reputation to uphold and *weird girl who eats Styrofoam* isn't part of it."

I press my lips together and will myself not to speak. For Carrie's sake and for mine. Anything I say will just make it worse.

Sky sighs heavily when she senses the shift, her shoulders dropping. "I'm sorry," she says, even though we both know she's not. "I've just been so stressed. Things at the store are chaos and I've spent all summer totally paranoid that my house was going to get burned down. I know all the fires were in Riverside, but did you know someone tagged my car a few weeks ago and tried to slash my tires? It's like I have a stalker or something. I thought it was probably whoever was setting the fires because it's like the same kind of twisted, but then *that* was obviously . . . well, you know."

The words hang in the air between us, bait I refuse to take.

"God, it's warm in here," she says, setting her mug back on the coffee table and reaching to pull the sweatshirt off. She tosses it on the couch beside her, and tucks the loose strands of hair behind one ear. "That's better."

Underneath the sweatshirt, she's wearing an oversized tee. It's bright blue, with the logo of Austen's gym screen-printed across the front. There's a small rip in the seam at the shoulder. I recognize it instantly, because I've worn it myself.

"Hey, how are you doing, by the way?" she asks. "I know things have been weird between us, but we've barely talked since the funeral."

I can't say anything. I'm too shell-shocked by the sight of the shirt—*Austen's* shirt—on Sky's body. It's one of his favorites. I'd know it anywhere.

Suddenly, I feel sweat blooming underneath my arms and above my top lip. I feel like I'm going to throw up.

"Where did you get that?" I ask after a long stretch of silence.

"Get what?" Sky asks, following my eyes down, as if noticing the shirt for the first time. "Oh, God. This? Who knows. Why?"

"Did Austen give it to you? Is he here?"

Skylar smiles at that, a light flush creeping up into her cheeks. "Wh—Marley, babe—what are you talking about? You sound a little crazy right now."

And then I realize it, all at once—*this* is why she invited me over. There's no job for me at Southern Moon. No redemption for me here. She just wanted me to know that she had won. That, finally, she'd managed to pluck up the one thing in my life that was better than hers.

Except that thing wasn't better—not really. And Sky doesn't know.

After a moment, the nausea fades. I take a deep breath, looking from her face, down to the shirt, then back up again, before I shake my head. "Sorry," I say. "I'm tired. It's been a tough couple of weeks."

"I can imagine," she says with mock concern.

I sit forward, resting my elbows on my knees, and focus on the rug underneath my feet. It's patterned with brightly colored flowers, but now that I'm looking, I can see a few strands of Minnie's golden hair stuck inside the weave.

The same hair I noticed stuck to Austen's shirt in the car a few days ago.

The sight overwhelms me with spite, and something else too. Something bubbling up from underneath the black well of grief.

I feel *gleeful*.

"It's just . . . it's hard to learn that your best friend isn't who you thought she was," I say. Sky nods, but doesn't respond, so I go on. "There's so much coming out about her—so much that's *going* to come out about her. It doesn't even feel real."

"What do you mean? What's going to come out about her?" she asks.

I bury my face in my hands and rub hard at my eyes. "I don't know if I should say anything."

Sky scoots forward on the couch. "You can trust me," she insists, picking up her mug and holding it against her lips. "Besides, I can tell it's bothering you. Let me be here for you, Marley."

It takes all my willpower not to glare at her. To instead force an appreciative smile and a nod. And then, to tell her. "Thea was pregnant when she died."

"Oh my God, seriously?" Sky says. "Who was the father? Do they know?"

I take another breath. Long and slow, as Sky fidgets in her seat. I am so going to enjoy this.

"It was Austen."

Sky fumbles her coffee cup, dropping it to the floor. It rolls, dark liquid splattering across the white upholstery like dried blood. The noise makes Minnie lift her head from her spot by the window, but Sky barely seems to notice.

"You're joking," she says, a hand drawn up to her heart as if she's expecting it to give out at any moment.

"I wish," I tell her, and that, at least, is true. Then I tell her the story, leaving out only the detail about Austen being in love with you. When I finish, there's a tear pooling at the corner of my eye. I rub it out and steel myself.

Sky is staring at the puddle of coffee on the floor, her mouth agape. She's gone pale in the last few minutes. "Oh . . . my God," she says finally.

She sounds weak, and I wonder, idly, if she might pass out right here in her living room. What would I do if she did? Would I care for her—lay her on the couch and press a cool, wet rag to her forehead until she came to—or would I leave her where she lay? Probably the latter.

"It's fucked up," I say. The thing is, though, that's not really what gets me when I tell it. It's true that the story is lurid. Dirty. But mostly, it's sad. A mud-thick kind of sadness, that blocks that brief ray of light I felt a moment ago and seeps down into my bones. To my marrow. A thing that never quite washes away. The only two relationships I really gave a damn about, both obliterated in one fell swoop and—somehow this is the worst part—neither of you was ever going to tell me.

Sky keeps glancing down at the shirt, then back up at me, as if she wants to rip it off her body and burn it. I know the feeling.

"I'm guessing he didn't tell you any of this when you slept with him," I say, raising an eyebrow.

"No," she whispers. "He left all that out."

"He does that," I say. And then, after a long stretch of silence, I ask her. "How long?"

Sky shakes her head. "It started not long after Thea died," she says. "But—um—God, I hate telling you this, but it wasn't exactly the first time. We hooked up a couple of times back in high school, too. Mostly after away games when we were both drunk. And then one more time, a couple of months before the two of you broke up. He said you'd been fighting."

I nod slowly, surprised by the shot of anger that courses through me—a white-hot flash of schoolgirl jealousy—there and then gone as quickly as it came on, leaving a kind of perverse thrill in its place. Because I *knew* it. All those years I spent haunted by the specter of Sky. All the fights we had, Austen begging me to trust him, *please*. The times I beat myself up over my own trust issues. Over being *the problem*.

"Marley?" Sky's voice pierces the cloud of my own thoughts. She's looking at me like I've cracked, and I realize it's because I've been laughing. Hard enough that my cheeks hurt. That there are more tears collecting in the corners of my eyes.

"Sorry," I say, though I can still feel the laughter ready to roll through me again as soon as I give it permission. And something darker underneath that. Something primal, like a howl. For a second, I have no idea what to do next. "I—I'm gonna go," I say after a moment.

"Mar, please. Let's talk about this."

"Talk about what, Sky?" I say, cocking my head to the side. "About the fact that you've been lying to me for the better part of a decade? About the fact that you slept with someone in a relationship and then ran a smear campaign against me for doing the exact same thing?"

"It was *not* a smear campaign—"

"I know you were behind the Vintage Whore account. I know it was you who turned everyone against me," I say, the dam on my anger bursting, a tidal wave surging forward, so powerful it takes all of my self-control not to wrap my hands around her neck and squeeze.

I think about it for a second. How good it would feel to wrestle the life out of her. To watch the light leave her eyes. My hands flex and I pin them to my sides.

Sky sets her jaw, and I know I've done it. I've goaded her enough. *This*, at least, is a version of her I recognize. "No, Marley. *You* turned them against you," she says, her eyes flashing. "I barely had to do anything with that stupid account. The submissions just kept pouring in once I put it up. You think everyone in Sherman Hill can't see how pathetic you are? You've spent the last ten years trying to be just like me, so don't blame Austen for what he did. And don't blame me for pointing out how screwed up you really—"

I slam the door closed behind me and stalk all the way out to my car without breaking stride. I know she's watching. Know she'll keep watching until I've driven out of sight, so I start the car and hit the gas a little too hard, throwing myself back against the seat.

While I drive, I think about Austen—about the way he fucked me in the car with Sky's dog's hair still on his shirt. I think of him kissing you. Of him and Sky together as teenagers in some cheap hotel room, and again after we moved in together. It makes me want to scream, the ways he's made us all hurt each other. And for what? For *him*?

We were never the real monsters, I realize, a burst of adrenaline tearing through me.

After all the time I've spent blaming myself, or you, or this god-damn town, it has *always* been him.

CHAPTER

42

Thea

AFTER THE LAST fire—the kiss—time begins to unravel in front of me. Hours of the day sinking back into nothing like a tide melting into the sand, nothing to mark them out but bouts of nausea and a roiling sense of dread. Of collapse. A sense that I'm living in the ashes of a life I burned down myself.

I haven't spoken to Marley, or Austen, or Iris. After all, what would I say to each of them? How could I even begin to fix the messes I've made?

I decide that it's better to do nothing—say nothing—until I can figure out what to do about the pregnancy. But it's already too late to terminate here in Georgia, or South Carolina, or Alabama. I'd need to go to Florida, which means I'd also need a place to stay, and a decent excuse for dipping across state lines for at least two days.

I'm contemplating my options on the drive home from work one night when I feel it again, that sensation of being watched. The rush of energy that makes my blood run cold. It's a near constant presence now. A phantom that's always at my back. I've almost convinced myself that I'm imagining it. After all, Mom did the same thing when she was pregnant with the twins, imagining the man with the gun around every corner. Staying up late into the night to pace and watch out the window for his car.

But when I check the rearview mirror, I see that there actually is a car behind me—a police cruiser. The lights flip on and the siren blares. I check my speed and mutter a curse, easing off the gas, then put my hazards on and slow to a stop on the strip of grass at the roadside. I force myself to breathe in, then out, as the cruiser sidles up behind me and an officer gets out. We're hemmed in on either side by banks of trees so dense they block out the light of the moon, and even though another car could drive by at any time, I can't help but feel utterly isolated out here.

After a long second there's a sharp rapping on my window, and I take in the figure of the officer standing just outside, black clad and broad. Reluctantly, I press the button and roll the window down.

"How can I help you?" I say, my voice shaky. And then, to my horror, the officer stoops his towering frame to meet my eyes, and he smiles.

"I can think of a few ways," Scott says, taking me in as though he can't believe his good luck.

I cross my arms tightly over my chest and scowl, trying my best to hide the fear racing through me. The desperate urge to floor the gas pedal and peel away, like Marley did when she was driving us away from a fire. Somehow, Scott feels more dangerous than that. "What do you want?"

"Let's not get testy," he says, resting his elbows against the window frame and leaning in toward me. "You're the one speeding. I'm just doing my job."

"I'll slow down," I say.

Scott narrows his eyes at me. "Why so jumpy?" he asks.

"No reason," I answer, too quickly. "I need to get home is all. It's almost the twins' bedtime."

He smiles again, his eyes traveling down the length of my body. "Step out of the car, please," he says.

"Scott—"

"Don't make this difficult, Thea," he says, holding up his hand in protest. "Just get out of the car and go stand over there. Don't call anyone, either."

With shaking hands, I unbuckle my seat belt and step out of the car, taking a few steps toward the bank of trees he pointed to. My mind is racing, running through the inventory of my perpetually messy car. Is there anything inside that could point to me and Marley for the fires? I don't think so—we always used Marley's car—but what if there's something I've forgotten?

I watch as Scott pokes through the cupholders and opens the glove compartment, then pops the trunk and leans inside until half his body has disappeared.

After a few minutes that feel like hours he heaves the trunk shut and motions me back over. But when I go for the driver's seat, he shakes his head and opens the door to the back seat.

"Sit with me for a second," he says, the tone of his voice making it clear that it isn't a choice.

I squeeze my hands into fists and climb into the back seat, pressing myself all way against the opposite car door as Scott climbs in after me and closes us in, his body swallowing most of the small space.

"Can you tell me what this is?" he asks, producing a small, red lighter between his fingers. "It was in your glove compartment."

My blood runs cold. "It's just a lighter," I say. "For cigarettes."

"I don't see any cigarettes," he says, and I shrug.

"I quit."

Scott flicks the lighter with his thumb, and a small flame dances to life between us. "Funny," he says. "We think this is exactly the kind of lighter the arsonist is using."

"Probably because it's available at every gas station in the world," I say, doing my best to sound unfazed.

Scott releases his thumb, and the flame disappears, plunging us into a thick darkness. "Maybe," he says. "Or maybe it's because of how unassuming it is. The kind of thing you can carry around anywhere without drawing any attention. You know, there's been a lot of speculation this summer about what kind of person could do this. Lots of guys on the force have their money on some hardened criminal. But me? I don't see that. I think it's probably someone normal. Someone with a hidden dark side."

I swallow hard, but I don't speak, so Scott goes on.

"Or maybe I'm wrong and it is someone crazy—someone like Julie Butler. You know who I'm talking about, don't you? You should—she still leaves messages at the station sometimes about you killing her brother. She goes on and on about a secret phone. Obviously, everyone pretty much writes her off, but if she is right and you did have something to do with it, that would mean you have one hell of a dark side. Wouldn't it?"

I shift in the seat, heart pounding, as the still air presses in on me from all sides. I haven't heard Julie's name in weeks. So long I'd started to hope she'd forgotten about me. Clearly, though, I was wrong. Does she know I still see Iris? "Are you accusing me of something, Scott?" I say finally.

He flicks the lighter on again so I can see his smile, and I'm struck, in the half light, by how utterly sure of himself he looks. How comfortable. Like he would happily sit here all night, making me squirm. "Just working out a hunch," he says, as the flame disappears again.

We sit in the dark for so long I lose track of the seconds—feel them stretching on into minutes. Hours. Days. I feel claustrophobic in the small space, paralyzed by the fear coursing through me. After a while, I hear Scott move. I feel his hand coming to rest on my leg, the heat of his skin seeping through the thin fabric of my pants.

"Please don't," I say, drawing myself back as best I can. The words come out as more of a whisper, but his hand comes again, more insistent as he slides it up and down the length of my thigh.

"Why not?" he asks. "Are you mad because I fucked Marley? You know, she begged me for it."

"Scott—"

His fingers curl against my skin. The pressure is a warning, but he doesn't need to warn me. It's clear who has the power here. "I told you last spring that I wanted us to be friends," he says. "Do you remember what you said to that? Because I do. You said, *over my dead body.*" He pauses, smiling faintly, as if it's a fond memory. "But I think you actually need a friend like me. Don't you? I think one day you're going to regret saying that to me when you find yourself in some kind of trouble. Luckily, I'm willing to forgive and forget. You have to do something for me in return, though."

I squeeze my eyes closed and press my lips together, imagining myself somewhere else entirely. Anywhere but here.

For a second, I wonder what my life would've been like if Marley and I had made it to the highway that time we tried to run away. If we'd somehow managed the impossible journey to New York. Marley would have some big shot job in marketing by now, and I'd be a designer's assistant. We'd live together in an apartment somewhere in the East Village or Soho or Brooklyn. Down the street, we'd have a home bar where we'd meet every day after work for happy hour, swapping stories about the day, like they do in the TV shows. Suddenly, I want that life more than I've ever wanted anything, and I feel bowled over by the cruelty of its nonexistence. Of what we have instead.

Scott lifts his hand off my lap and takes a breath. He hasn't done anything to me—not really—my pants are still on, buttoned and zipped. But he's made his point clear. He doesn't want to rape me tonight—he doesn't need to. He just wants me to know that he could if he felt like it. That maybe, one day, he'll decide to come for me, and on that day I won't be able to do anything to stop it.

"I'm going to let you off with a warning this time," he says, popping open the car door and stepping out. "Just be more careful next time."

I stay curled in the back seat until he's gone—until his taillights disappear around the next bend in the road—and then I unfold myself and return to the driver's seat.

I don't go anywhere. I just sit, staring blankly at the darkness ahead. No one has driven by since I was pulled over, and I feel sure that no one else is coming. That I'm the only person left in this whole town besides Scott.

At some point, I become aware that I'm shaking. That I've lost control of my body in the same way I've lost control of my life.

Do you ever feel tired?

James's words come to me, unbidden, and all at once I understand them. I've never felt this tired before. An exhaustion that's burrowed its way through my skin. That's carved itself into the thick, sinuous muscle. That has made itself a part of me, so heavy I can no longer lift my head to look up. To see the sky.

Maybe there is no sky anymore.

Once I stop shaking, I begin to drive. Not home—not yet. Instead, I go back to the Chicken Shack. I pull into the parking lot where James and I had our first real conversations, cigarette smoke blowing from the corners of our mouths.

I turn on the radio and stare at the empty passenger's seat, wishing more than anything that he was here, just for now. That I had someone to take my hand and squeeze it across the center console.

Someone who wouldn't try to talk me out of what I've just decided to do.

43

Marley

THE LAST PLACE I want to go after I leave Skylar's is home, but somehow I find myself there all the same, my car idling in the driveway as I stare at the little house where I've spent most of my life.

Somewhere, there's a therapist who would tell me that this house is the one I've really been trying to burn all summer, and they'd be right. If I thought I could get away with it, I'd have done it years ago. I'd have let the fire burn itself down to ashes until everything—everything—was gone, and then I'd have turned away from the life I razed to the ground, and I'd never look back.

Inside, Mom is on the couch, sleeping, an empty wine bottle resting on the side table. I know it's how I must've looked a few days ago, and the thought sends a prickling chill over me, despite the heat.

"Mom," I say, but she doesn't wake up. Or at least, she pretends not to. We haven't spoken much since I found out about you and Austen—the night I told her about the fires. I get the sense that she's not quite sure what to say, and neither am I.

I swore to her that I didn't know what had happened to you—that I hadn't known about you and Austen when you were alive. But why would she believe me?

Besides, if I had known, I can't say for sure what I would've done. Would I still have gone back for you on the night of the last fire, or would I have left you there to burn or to get caught?

"Mom," I try again, this time tapping her lightly on the shoulder. She stirs, then cracks open hazy, wine-drunk eyes.

"Marley," she says, sitting up and patting the spot next to her on the couch. I look at it reluctantly for a moment, then sit down. The couch dips in the middle, and my shoulder bumps against hers. I can smell her sour breath and the cheap perfume she always wears, and I'm run over by an unexpected rush of comfort at the scent.

I have spent the last ten years trying to crawl out of this life with every weapon in my arsenal, but all I've managed to do is dig myself deeper inside of it, and maybe that's because it's who I am—who I have always been.

"What's going on?" she asks. I wince at the question. There's no point in telling her about Sky and Austen, or the gun, or the blood spatter I found in your room. Your note makes it all irrelevant. The only thing that matters now is the knife in Romero's drawer. The proof that you and I were a team. That we were together after the fight—committing crimes in the middle of the night. It's a small leap to get from there to the fires, and Romero is already on the scent.

"Can I ask you a question?" I say finally.

"Of course."

"What do you want out of your life?"

There's a long beat of silence as Mom considers. "That's a hard question," she says. "What does anyone want? To be happy, I guess."

"And are you happy?"

Now there's an even longer pause. "Sometimes," she answers. "But mostly not. Not since your father died, at least."

I turn to face her now, and I can tell she's surprised by my intensity. "Why did you stay here, once you got the settlement money from Dad's death? You didn't have family. You could've taken us anywhere with that money. Made a fresh start somewhere totally new."

Mom smiles sadly at this. "I had Dahlia to think about," she says. "She was a single mother too, by then. I couldn't leave her behind. Buying the houses felt like the best way to keep us together—to keep us both safe and not dependent on anyone."

"You wanted to protect her," I say, and she nods.

"Dahlia and I have been protecting each other since the day we met. Neither of us had a real family, so we became each other's."

"Like Dahlia taking me in," I say.

"Yes," she answers. "Just like that."

She looks at me like she's waiting for me to contradict her, but I don't. She was never quite cut out for motherhood, but sitting next to her now, I can see that she tried. Once she came back, she stayed. Held down a job. Worked, sometimes unsuccessfully, to keep her most self-destructive impulses at bay. And she loved me, however imperfectly.

I'll take it to my grave, she told me after I'd confided in her about the fires. *And I'll give you an alibi, if it comes to that.*

"Thea and I did a bad job protecting each other. Especially from ourselves," I say.

Mom presses her lips together and tucks a loose strand of hair behind her ear. "You and Thea pushed each other in ways Dahlia and I never did. You were both . . . intense. Ambitious. In a lot of ways, you made each other better."

"And in others, we made each other worse."

"Friendship isn't a self-improvement course, Marley. It's about loyalty. Trust. Having a safe place to land."

"A safe place to land," I repeat.

I think about all the moments we spent together in my car this summer, looking for houses, or just talking. About the patch of tall grass by the bird's grave. About the night we ran away together, and the early days of the Instagram account. About the rings we purchased— our own kind of commitment to each other.

Maybe that's exactly what we were to each other. Not always, but in our best moments. A safe place to land. A place to show the best and the worst of ourselves.

"Marley," Mom cuts in. "Can I ask? What is it *you* want from your life?"

I chew on the inside of my cheek, considering. "I want to leave," I tell her.

"Then do it," she says. "There's nothing keeping you here anymore. Not Thea, not Austen, not your job. You could go anywhere. Be anything."

"What about you?" I ask.

Mom gives me a look. "Don't you dare stay here for me," she says sternly.

"Are you sure?"

She nods, wearily, sliding her hand through greasy hair. "Dahlia needs me right now, more than she's ever needed me before. For the first time in a long time, I can't afford to be a fuck-up."

"Mom," I say quietly. "There's something you should know."

I feel her go stiff beside me.

"I didn't kill Thea," I say.

"I know that," she answers, but I feel her relax, all the same.

"But Romero thinks I did."

"Why?" she asks, and I tell her about Skylar's house, and you, and the knife that Romero now has. I recount my visit to the police station the day before.

"She knows we were together," I say. "She knows I lied about the last time we spoke. She thinks that I knew about Thea and Austen—that Thea told me, and I snapped."

Mom takes my hand in both of hers and squeezes it hard, so my skin goes white underneath the pressure. "Jesus, Marley," she says. "Why didn't you tell me this before?"

I shake my head, a short, jerky movement. "I didn't think it mattered then," I say. But the truth is, I'm ashamed. Embarrassed by so many of the things I've done.

"What do we do?" she asks, looking over to me, her blue eyes welling with concern. And just like that, I'm the adult again. I take a deep breath and squeeze her hand back.

"Nothing," I say. "We don't do anything. But if the cops come for me, I need you to tell them that I was home that night. That you looked in on me in the middle of the night and I was asleep in my bed. Can you do that?"

She nods vigorously, strands of greasy hair falling across her face.

Before I can let myself think about it, I wrap my arms around my mom and hug her tightly.

"I'm sorry," she whispers into my hair. "For everything. I'll do anything I can to protect you."

"I'm sorry too," I say. But it's not for the reasons she thinks. I'm sorry because, once again, I've only told her half of the truth.

I do want to leave. But first, I want to burn what's left of this life to the ground.

I push myself off the couch and roll my shoulders back, then go to my room and close the door. In the drawer of my dresser, I remove your letter, unfolding it and smoothing the creases gently. I read it one more time. Run my finger across a line of your handwriting, tracing the words you wrote.

When I'm done, I kick out the metal trash can from underneath my desk and grab the lighter from its place on the nightstand. I hold the page over the trash can and thumb the lighter quickly, hovering the small flame against the corner of the page until it catches.

Then, when I can feel the heat creeping toward my skin, I drop it in the trash, and I watch it burn to ashes.

44

Thea

AUSTEN ISN'T EXPECTING me. We haven't seen each other since he told me he loved me, and when he answers his door, the color drains from his face.

"Thea," he says, raising his eyebrows.

"I think we need to talk," I say, shifting my weight from one foot to the other.

Austen steps back and gestures for me to come in, and I do, tentatively. I take a seat on the couch and rest my hands in my lap. Austen follows my lead, his expression carefully neutral.

"I have something for you," I say, lifting my arm to show him the watch strapped to my wrist. The band is big, so it's almost slipping off.

He wrinkles his brow and, hesitantly, he reaches out to touch the watch's face.

"I saw this a few days ago—at a thrift store," I add carefully. "And it made me think of you."

"Why?" he asks, flicking his eyes up to mine for a second before returning them to the watch. He runs his thumb across woven gold band, gone dull and tarnished in the dusty, abandoned house.

"Because it's timeless," I say. "And when I look at it, I feel calm. I feel like everything's going to be okay, somehow."

Austen presses his lips together, and I can tell he's trying not to smile. "Thea . . . ," he says, trailing off. He doesn't need to finish the sentence.

"I know," I tell him, shifting my weight a bit uncomfortably. "There's a lot more to say."

Austen shifts, angling his head toward mine, his eyes boring into me. "I don't expect you to feel the same way about me as I do about you, but I need us to pick a lane," he whispers. "I can't . . . I can't keep wondering where your head is at. This—us—it's complicated, and it wouldn't be easy. I know that. So I need you to be all in or all out."

I take a beat to breathe. It probably looks like I'm thinking, but I'm not. I already know what I have to do. What I have to do about all of it. Once I let myself acknowledge it, it seemed so clear. There's only one answer. Only one way to mitigate the damage I've done. To take back the control I've lost.

I reach across the distance between us and put my hand on his cheek. Feel the warmth of his skin and drink in the way he's looking at me, like I'm the only thing in the world that matters.

"I'm not going to let you ruin your life for me."

"Thea—" he starts, but I cut him off, placing my thumb on his lips.

"I know what I'm doing," I say. "You have to trust me. I'm giving us both our best shot."

"You're my best shot," he whispers. "I love you."

I smile at him then. Let my hand linger for a few extra seconds along his jaw. "I love you too," I say, and I'm surprised by how much I mean it. How much pain I feel, knowing this is the last time I'll be able to touch him like this. To touch him at all. I love Austen more than I'd care to admit—just not in the way he wants me to. "But that's not enough—not this time. It's too complicated."

Austen brings his hand up to my wrist and holds it, his skin warm. "Are you sure about this?" he says.

I nod and so does Austen, a deep kind of melancholy settling over his face.

Then, before I can stop myself, I kiss him, and he kisses me back.

We make love slowly, his fingers twined through mine—the gold watchband warm against my wrist. For the first time, I can admit to myself that I wish it was her, instead. I can face the fact that I didn't sleep with Austen only to take something from Marley. It was also to take something *of* her. To access some part of her that has always been out of my grasp.

When it's over, he holds me to his chest, and I listen to the sound of his heart. Its steady beat lulling me closer and closer to sleep.

"Do you know what the worst part of this is?" he asks quietly, running the back of his finger down the bare length of my arm.

"Mmm?"

"I'm going to have to spend the rest of my life pretending I don't love you. I'm going to have to watch you fall in love with someone else, eventually. Marry them. Have kids with them. And I'm going to have to pretend to be happy about it. No one but you is ever going to know how I really feel."

"Austen," I say, tilting my chin up to meet his eyes. For a split second, I think about telling him what I'm going to do. But, of course, I don't. Marley was right that first night in the car—Austen would never understand any of this. "It isn't going to be like that," I tell him. "You're going to fall in love with someone too. And you'll love them so much that this—what we have—it won't even compare."

"That's hard to believe," he says, and I know it shouldn't, but it almost makes me laugh. Here, in this moment, I finally see us for what we really are.

Austen might love me, but he isn't *in love* with me—not really. He just needs to justify what he's done to Marley. He needs to believe he isn't capable of betrayal on this scale for anything less than true love. He needs to be the good guy, not only to everyone else, but to himself. It's a character he excels at playing, but it's a character all the same.

And he'll be fine—better than fine—once all of this has blown over. Sooner or later, he'll find someone new, and he'll make a home with her and one day, he won't think about me at all. The thought is strangely comforting, like a wound healing. Fresh grass growing over a grave.

"But you have to, okay? I need you to believe it. For me," I say. When he doesn't respond I take the watch from my wrist and thread it onto his. "*We* don't have to forget this happened, but no one else can know. You need to promise me that. No matter what, this stays between us."

A shadow passes over Austen's face. I know it's the "no matter what" that's snagging for him, like a fine thread on a splinter of wood. I wish there was a way to protect him from what's coming. A way to warn him about the scrutiny everyone I love is going to face because of me, but there isn't.

"I promise," he says finally, the shadow clearing away.

45

Marley

ONCE I'VE BURNED the note, I sit on my bed and create an Instagram account for @REALSkyWeller, follow everyone in Sherman Hill that I can think of, and post the audio I secretly recorded of her admitting to everything.

I hit the record button on my phone before I even went into the house, acting on a hunch, and I'm fiercely glad I did. The confession ought to do wonders for her personal branding. People will know it's me she's speaking to—me who made and posted the recording—but I can't find it in myself to care. Not now, after everything. I have no reputation left to ruin.

Once it's posted, I turn off my phone, jump into my car, and drive up and down back roads to clear my head, music blasting at the highest volume my shitty sound system will allow. I feel dirty, somehow. Tainted by the events of the day. It's worse, even, than the days after I cheated on Austen. At least I knew that was my fault. I understood the fallout as a consequence of my own actions. But this? This makes me feel pathetic. Powerless. The Austen I thought I knew—the one I was about to commit my life to—was a fiction all along.

After a few hours, on my way back to Riverside, I pass by the apartment complex on the outskirts of Sherman Hill. In the parking lot, the blue and red flash of police lights catches my eye. I put my foot on the brake and roll toward it slowly, counting the cars clustered there. *A fire,* I think for a moment, but that's just a reflex. I never came anywhere near Sherman Hill when I was setting fires. Not because I didn't want to, but because it was too risky.

I spot Austen standing next to a police officer in the parking lot, his fists clenched, eyes downcast, so I pull into the lot and get out of the car. There are police coming and going from the apartment like ants—carrying plastic evidence bags full of everyday items and snapping on latex gloves outside the door.

"What's going on?" I say, jogging over to them. Austen looks up at me, his gaze frantic.

"They came a few minutes ago with a search warrant."

"Jesus," I mutter, throwing up my hand to shade my eyes against the harsh sun. "Well, there's nothing to find, is there?"

"No, of course not," he says quickly, stepping away from the officer to take hold of my arm, like a desperate man reaching for bread or water. He pulls me a few feet away, out of everyone's earshot, and bends his head toward mine. There's something in the familiarity of the movement—how, once, I would've thought nothing of it—that makes me want to gag. I pull my arm back from his and smooth my hands uselessly over my shirt.

"Marley," he says, meeting my eyes. "Did you call them?"

I watch him closely for a moment, as if, by staring hard enough, I can unpick the version of him that I loved from all the rest. I wonder if he's already heard about the recording I posted. If he's aware that everyone in town knows about his relationships with Thea and Skylar. In any case, dealing with the fallout is probably low on his priority list at the moment.

"Of course not," I say, doing my best to look offended.

A bit of tension falls out of his shoulders. "Okay," he says. "Sorry. I just . . . I wasn't sure where we stood after our fight."

Our fight. The words feel so small, like we had a disagreement over football or what to have for dinner. Like I'm a petulant child with a grudge.

I clear my throat and turn back to the apartment, gesturing vaguely to the swarm of uniformed officers. "Is Detective Romero here?"

He scratches the back of his neck. "Inside," he says.

I bump my shoulder to his arm, just for a second. The only gesture of comfort I can manage. "Hey," I say. "They have to clear you before they can look at anyone else, okay? This is procedural 101. You had the motive."

"I didn't know about the baby," he says again, pleading. I shrug. At this point it doesn't really matter, whether he knew or whether he didn't. Not to me, at least.

"You didn't have to. Men kill their partners all the time," I say ruefully, watching officers come and go. It hurts to say it—to refer to you as Austen's partner—but what's the point in denying the truth?

Austen doesn't have an answer for that. Instead, we stand silently, side by side, watching the officers pick through the apartment, as if deconstructing it from the inside out—emerging from the door with items of clothing and paperweights and lighters, all wrapped up in thick plastic evidence bags. There's a small crowd beginning to form in the parking lot and up by the street. People slowing their cars or pulling on their dog's leash to stop and watch the commotion, neighbors emerging shyly from their units to survey the controlled chaos.

The sun sinks lower, the heat growing harsher. At some point, Austen sits on a curb, and I join him, plucking a piece of grass and tearing it carefully in half. For a second, I think about telling him the truth. All of it. There's a small part of me that wants to see the look on his face when he realizes that you weren't just sneaking around with him this summer. That we had our own secrets to keep.

But I stop myself. I still don't know *exactly* why you did what you did. I probably never will, and I'll have to accept that. But I do know one thing, and it's that you protected me. You wanted me to have the opportunity to walk away from the fires and start over somewhere with a clean slate.

For all the damage we've inflicted on each other, all the blood we've drawn, you gave me this chance, and I don't intend to waste it.

"Marley?" Austen says, leaning back on his hands and tilting his face up to the sky.

"Yeah?"

"She broke up with me."

"What?"

"The night before she died, Thea ended things. And when they found her, I was so angry. I didn't want to think that what we'd done had anything to do with it, especially once I found out about the pregnancy. I couldn't let myself be responsible, so I dragged you into it. I'm sorry for that."

"You think she did this to herself, then?" I ask and, slowly, he nods.

"I do," he says, his voice barely a whisper.

I swallow back the wave of nausea that goes through me. Force myself to draw in a long, breath of the thick, hot air.

"I see."

Then something happens. There's a shift in the air. In the way the officers move. The din of their voices grows louder, then softer, their movements slowing to a stop as Detective Romero emerges from the door to the apartment. She's wearing a pantsuit, despite the heat. Khaki with a sky-blue button-up and I get a weird kick of delight from seeing the sweat stains underneath her arms—evidence of the human condition. In her hand she's carrying an evidence bag and her face is deadly serious, set into a mask of grim indifference as she marches toward Austen and me.

"Austen Brown," she says, holding up two evidence bags, one in each hand. Inside the first is a bundle of rags like the ones I used to start the fires, and inside the second is a watch, old-looking, with tarnished gold plating.

Romero hands both to the officers flanking her. "You're under arrest for arson and the murder of Thea Wright."

46

Thea

I LEAVE MARLEY'S NOTE underneath the rock we used as a makeshift headstone once, in the clearing not far from our houses. Somehow, I know she'll find it. I like to think it will give her some peace.

My death will leave questions, there's no avoiding it. But I can't do to Marley what James did to me—let her wonder forever if she's responsible for it. If she could've stopped it.

Even after everything, I don't pretend to know what Marley's capable of. There's something wild about her. If the police closed in, if they backed her into a corner about the fires, I don't know how she'd react. But if she sits tight long enough to let the police investigation run the course that I know it will, she'll be free.

"And they went down alright?" Mom mumbles into the phone. "Okay. Call me if anything comes up. I mean it."

Mom tucks the phone back into her pocket and smiles weakly at me, coming to join me on the couch.

"The boys are enjoying their father's," she says. "I suspect he's letting them run wild. They always come back so keyed up. It's a miracle Austen turned out as disciplined as he did."

"At least it's only once every few months," I remind her, doing my best to keep the furrow from my brows. Everything tonight feels imbued with a sense of doom, so instead of picturing the boys stuffing themselves with chocolate and staying up late, all I can think is that I won't see them again. That they may not even remember me after a few years.

"Thea," she says, sensing my mood. "Are you alright? You've seemed . . . off recently."

"Everything is fine," I lie, and I'm grateful that after tonight I won't have to navigate any of this anymore. That I won't have to tell a lie ever again.

She frowns, the line between her eyes growing deeper. "Okay," she says. "Do you want to watch a movie?

"Sure," I say, because I can't quite stomach the idea of excusing myself yet. Of telling Mom good night, knowing I won't see her again.

She presses play on a movie, and about halfway through she snuggles in closer to me and lays her head on my shoulder.

"I love you," she whispers as I rest my head on top of hers.

"I love you too," I tell her.

She will never understand what I'm about to do. But hopefully, it will keep her from finding out the other mistakes I've made. She'll never have to know about me and Austen, or the fires. She'll never have to confront the ugliest sides of me, the way I've had to confront the ugliest sides of her, and isn't that for the best?

When the movie ends, I make a show of stretching and yawning.

"Go to bed, Thea," she says, resting her hand gently underneath my chin and tilting my head up to meet hers. "I can tell you're tired. You need sleep."

"I know," I tell her. And then I stand and hug her. Too tightly and for too long, but she doesn't seem to mind.

"My sweet girl," she coos. "Whatever it is, it will pass. I promise."

In my closet, I have a bag stuffed with rags and a lighter. In my car is the nearly full gas jug I stole from Marley last night. All I need to do is wait until I'm sure Mom's asleep to sneak out.

I've decided I'll go back to the house Marley and I managed to half burn. It won't take long to finish the job there, and the fact that it's already been targeted means the police won't be watching it. I know they've started posting hidden patrols near other abandoned properties in the area.

"Good night," I say to her. And then I brace myself and watch her pad down the hallway back to her room.

When she's gone, I turn to the big window that faces out toward the street. There isn't much to see—houses on our street are few and far between, and ours faces nothing but a plot of overgrown trees. Still, I study it. There's no movement, but I feel it again—the sense of being watched. I half expect to see someone skirting the tree line.

Eventually, I turn off the light and head for my room. The slight downward grade of the floor has swung my door closed, and when I push it open, I notice that the bedside lamp has been switched on.

Before I can make sense of it, before I can even register what's happening, there's a knife at my throat and a voice in my ear, so soft it's barely there.

"Don't scream or I'll slit your throat."

I swallow hard, clenching my hands into fists at my sides. The voice is familiar, but it still takes me a second to place it. Once I do, though, I feel a sick sense of fate locking into place.

Did I really believe things were going to end any other way?

"Julie," I whisper. "Please. Not here."

"I told you to stay away from them. Did you think I was kidding? Did you think I wouldn't keep watch?"

Julie grabs my arms and pins them behind my back, pressing the knife's blade harder against my throat, so I feel the sharp edge against my skin. She's surprisingly strong for someone so small, but I'm not putting up much of a fight.

"I'm sorry," I tell her, because what else is there to say? After all, Julie hasn't accused me of something I didn't do. I *was* involved in James's death. And I did seek out Iris after she warned me away.

Maybe this is fair—my life in exchange for the one I took from her.

"Sit down," she orders, her voice unsteady. "Sit down at the desk and write out a suicide note. Make it convincing."

"Julie, I—"

"I said *sit down*," she hisses, her voice growing louder.

I do as she says, sitting gingerly at the desk chair, feeling it creak underneath my weight. With shaking hands, I take the pen and press it against the pad already in front of me—the pad I used to write the note for Marley just a few hours earlier.

Suddenly, I'm at a loss.

"Keep it short," Julie says, pressing the point of the knife into my skin, hard enough to make me wince.

It's ironic, I think. If she'd just waited one more night, there wouldn't be a need for any of this. I could've saved her the trouble.

Just as I begin to write, there's another sound. The screech of the door opening behind me, and a scream. My mother's.

"Hey!" Julie says. I feel the knife coming off my throat, and then there's a bang so loud it makes my whole body convulse with shock. Another scream rips through the air, then silence.

It feels like I'm moving through molasses, ears ringing, pulse pounding, as I turn and survey the scene. My mother braced against the doorframe, a gun clutched in her hand, eyes wide in shock. And Julie on the floor, blood spilling from the wound in her head, eyes open, staring blankly at the ceiling.

Marley

I REMEMBER THE DAY I met Austen better than any other day of
my life. It was February, two days before Valentine's Day—cloudy
and unusually cold, with the wind coming in thick gusts that blus-
tered against meager Georgia layers. I knew he would be there at your
house—his house, soon. You'd told me about the new soon-to-be new
stepbrother, and I hadn't been sure how to react.

The evening was planned by both of our mothers, and there was
a strange formality to it. A kind of forced joining between Mom and
me and your new family. We came over for dinner and I felt itchy and
uncomfortable in the sweater Mom forced me to wear.

When Dahlia threw the door open and let us in, the house felt different. There was something heavier in the air, something male and foreign.

I felt like a deer caught in someone's backyard floodlight. Paralyzed
with a fear I couldn't quite make sense of at the time. Men were a force
to be wrestled against—held at bay. They shuffled into my life wearing
T-shirts and boxers and two days' worth of unshaven scruff, asking for
coffee or giving loud opinions about what was in the paper, then disappearing just as quickly, snuffed out like the flame in a candle before
it has a chance to grow into something more sinister. And here your
mother had made permanent space in her life for two of them, and we
had to do the same. Celebrate it, even.

It was David who met us right inside the front door, wiping his hands on a dish towel. He smiled and shook my mother's hand, then mine, like there was no difference between us, and I felt a tiny bit of my animosity fade.

"Marley, I've heard so much about you," he said. "Sounds like you and Thea are as close as your mothers."

I nodded, shyly, fighting the ridiculous urge to slip behind my mother's legs like a three-year-old and peer out at him.

He cleared his throat. "Well, I know Austen is excited to meet you too. In fact"—he craned his neck back toward the kitchen and the back hall—"Austen, why don't you come in here to meet Marley and Ms. June?"

There were footsteps, light and even. Sock feet shuffling against the scuffed hardwood. And then he appeared, bright as a copper coin turned to the sun, already smiling. He was wearing jeans too, and a sweater that looked as itchy as my shirt—hunter green set against tan skin. I couldn't look away. Didn't want to.

"Hi, Marley," he said, waving at me from beside his father.

I felt it then—the want skittering through my system, bristling along my veins like electricity along a wire. It was a child's want, back then. Not lust, but greed. I wanted to possess him. To tuck him away like a gem in a velvet-lined box, safe from everyone but myself.

And God, did I try. I tried to make him love me. Make him want me. I tried to keep him, even if it meant holding parts of myself back. Putting up with his mood swings and his temper and his guilt trips and his lies. Telling myself that he was perfect. That he was more than I deserved.

I made myself smaller for him. I can see that now.

And through it all, there you were. The only person who ever saw all the fucked-up pieces and loved me anyway.

The one I should've been trying to keep for myself.

CHAPTER

48

Thea

"Mom," I say, my eyes darting frantically between her and Julie's dead body sprawled between us. My heart is threatening to beat out of my chest.

"Oh my God," she says, dropping the gun, her hands shaking furiously. "Oh my God, oh my God. I just—"

"It's alright," I cut her off, crossing the distance between us. Without thinking, I grab hold of her and pull her into a hug.

"I thought I heard voices," she's saying as she wraps her arms around me. "I had a terrible feeling, so I just grabbed the gun out of the safe on instinct. I didn't—"

"You saved me," I tell her. "You saved my life."

"Who is she?"

I explain, though I'm not sure how much of the information she actually absorbs. "She was going to kill me," I tell her. "She came here tonight to kill me."

Mom nods. She's gone pale in the last few minutes. "I—I didn't mean to," she says. "I saw the knife. I panicked."

"I know. It's alright. It's going to be alright."

"She's dead."

"I know."

Mom breaks down in heaving sobs, and I hold her, my eyes still lingering on Julie's body, on her bloody face, her lips parted slightly, eyes wide as if opened in surprise.

"We need to call the police," she says. "Jesus. I'll just have to tell them—tell them what happened. That it was self-defense. That she broke in."

"No," I say, almost on instinct. "You can't do that."

"Thea, what else am I going to do?" she asks.

My mind is racing, my senses feel heightened. Everything is clearer, brighter, sharper.

If she calls the police, there will be an investigation. A hundred eyes turned keenly in our direction. Police digging into every facet of our lives. There's no telling what they'll uncover. The fires. My relationship with Austen. My involvement in James's final moments.

I look at Julie—the blood spilling from the wound in her head—and the old fear rises up in me. Of death. Of dying. Of what I came so close to doing tonight.

Suddenly, an idea comes to mind, fully formed, as though it had been waiting for me.

"We need to keep this quiet," I say, grabbing her hand and squeezing it. "If the police start poking around, they're going to find out about your gambling, okay? They might take the boys away."

"They wouldn't," she says, but I can hear the doubt creeping into her words.

"Besides," I say, taking her face in my hands so I can meet her eyes. "There's something else I need to tell you."

And that's when I tell her about the fires. I leave Marley out of it. I don't mention Austen, or the baby. Instead, I keep the story tight. I tell her it was me all along—that's why I've been off all summer. She sobs again as she listens, asking no questions. Eventually, she tilts her head to the ceiling, as if searching for God.

"I have a plan," I tell her. "One that can get us both out of this. But I need you to do everything I say, and trust me, okay? Can you do that?"

She doesn't say anything, but she doesn't protest as I take her to the living room, away from Julie's body, pour her a shot of whiskey, and walk her through the plan. Explain everything step by step. What she's going to do, what I'm going to do. I make her swear that she'll stick to it, no matter what. That she'll never tell anyone what really happened tonight.

When I'm done, we sit in silence for a long moment, Mom studying the bottom of her empty glass before pouring herself another drink and swigging it back.

"How could you keep this from me?" she says finally.

I stare at her across the table. There's a spatter of blood across her cheek, and more streaked across her clothes. Her hair is loose, a frizzing halo of curls framing her face. My mother has always done an excellent job of presenting herself as functional—especially in comparison to June. On weekends, she dons an apron and makes pancakes. She wraps presents at Christmas and does the laundry and sews patches into worn clothing. She taught me to look both ways before crossing the street. To say "please" and "thank you" and to never show up empty-handed as a guest to someone's house. When I was a child, she tucked me in at night and kissed my forehead. In a lot of ways, she is the best kind of mother. And yet I have spent so much life filling in the gaps. The spaces where she couldn't be the best kind of mother. I think of the times I took extra shifts to pay gambling debts *she* racked up playing online poker. The afternoons I spent on the phone with collection companies, begging for another month. Another week, even. The way we hardly even talk anymore—just collapse on the couch with a movie after the twins are asleep. Somewhere along the way, everything got filed down to survival, and I became her partner in it all. Fighting her battles, covering for her inadequacies. How could I tell her, when there was barely room in our lives for anything but getting by?

But explaining this wouldn't do any good tonight. Not after she's killed for me.

"You need to help me get her into the trunk of my car and we need to make sure blood doesn't get everywhere," I tell her, ignoring the question. She looks at me again, her eyes surveying me coldly, as though she doesn't recognize me anymore. But she nods.

We use rags to soak up the blood around her head—stopping several times each to throw up in the bathroom—and pull a trash bag over her torso when we move her.

Julie is heavier than I expected, and moving her is nearly impossible, but the adrenaline keeps me going. Once Julie's in the car, I make Mom go through the checklist with me one more time.

Clean the blood from my room and wash your clothes.

Go to bed and pretend everything's normal.

When they contact you tomorrow because they found my car parked at a fire scene and a burned corpse with my license, identify Julie's burned remains as mine.

Don't say anything to anyone, no matter what.

"Please," I tell her, shutting the trunk. "Be careful. The twins will need you more than ever now."

"I know," she answers, her eyes still fixed on the trunk. She hasn't looked at me directly since we got up from the kitchen table. Instead, she fixes her eyes behind my shoulder and presses the gun into my hands. I take it, turning it over. I've spent most of my life avoiding guns, but I'm shocked by how powerful I feel with the heavy object in my grasp.

"I need to go," I tell her, and she dips her head in acknowledgment. She presses her lips together and bobs her head.

"I'll see you again," she says. "Someday. I won't say goodbye."

"Okay," I say, choosing not to argue. After all, maybe she's right. Pulling this off is a long shot and we both know it. I could be caught and hauled into the Sherman Hill County Police Department before I even have a chance to get out of town, then we'd be in ten times more trouble than we are now.

But if I do make it out, I'm not reaching back out, ever. It would be too dangerous.

I reach out and grip my mother's pale arm. She flinches at the touch.

"Thank you for what you did," I tell her. "I love you."

The corner of her lip turns down, her eyes darting momentarily to my face before they jump away again. "I love you too," she says.

I get in the car and start the engine, making sure the lights are off, and, for the last time, I drive away.

49

Marley

I T'S A DAY before Romero asks me to come in. When I show up, she doesn't lead me back to her office. Instead, she takes me to an interrogation room. The same one I sat in after Austen and I got caught at the scene.

On my way there, I linger a few steps behind, peeking into the windows of the other rooms until I find Austen, staring at a stainless-steel tabletop, his shoulders hunched and palms laid flat against the metal. I stay where I am, just for a second—he must be able to sense me there, because he looks up and meets my gaze through the slit of a window, his eyes red and bloodshot and desperate.

For a second, maybe less, it's just us. Austen and Marley.

I flash him a smile.

When I get settled in my own room, I cross my legs and press my back against the chair. I'm convinced my heart is beating loudly enough that they can hear it through the building, but I take a few deep breaths to steady myself, and by the time Romero comes in I'm as composed as I'm going to be.

"How are you?" she asks, taking a seat opposite me. She smiles, but there's a tightness in her tone. A coldness that wasn't there before.

I shrug. "Glad it's over, I guess," I say. I can't quite meet her eyes, so I shoot for the space between them instead.

"Right. Of course." Detective Romero clears her throat and adjusts herself, setting her shoulders rigidly straight, like someone has pulled a string taut along her spine. "What do you think you'll do now that Austen's in custody?"

I clasp my hands together and hide them underneath the table. My hands always give me away. "I think I'll go to New York," I say. "What about you?"

She shrugs. And then, on the table between us, she places a small recording device and clicks it on. "Back to Atlanta," she says. "I have some paperwork to finish up. Then it's on to the next case."

I nod, not saying anything. I wonder what her life must be like—chasing one monster after the next. Every day coming face to face with the terrible things people do to each other.

"You wanted to speak to me about the case?" I prompt after a long beat of silence.

She nods, a bit warily, and I wonder if she's slept at all in the last twenty-four hours. Probably not. "Yes, thanks for coming in. In light of Mr. Brown's arrest, I wanted to take your statement. I have a few more questions. I'm hoping you'll be able to shed some light."

"I'll do what I can to help."

Romero places her notebook on the table and flips it to a new page. "We were informed about Austen's watch by an anonymous tipper," she says. "They assured us that we'd find stolen items from the crime scene in Austen's possession. We've managed to trace the call back to a pay phone outside the gas station where you work, so I thought you might know something about it." I can feel her watching me closely as she says the words. Scanning me for a reaction.

I hold myself totally still, my eyes on the table between us. "I don't know anything about a watch, Detective Romero. And the pay phone outside the gas station is the only one in town. Anyone could've called in that tip."

"But they didn't, did they?"

I blink at her, forcing my face to remain neutral.

She sits back in her chair now, studying me even more closely than before. With one sharp movement, she reaches a hand out and clicks off the tape recorder, but it's just for show. There's a camera in the corner, aimed down at us, recording every word. "Can I tell you what I really think, Marley? Just between us?"

I press my lips together and, after a second, give a tight nod. "By all means," I say.

"I think you called in the tip about Austen."

"You have no proof of that," I say.

"You're right," she fires back. "What I do have is a lot of evidence to suggest that you and Thea were in contact after the fight where you said you spoke last. I also have evidence that the two of you were committing crimes during that time. At one scene we even found two sets of shoe prints. Two women, judging by the size."

"You're going to have to spell it out for me," I say. "What exactly are you accusing me of?"

"You've pulled off something pretty elaborate here, Marley. Dozens of arsons. A murder. A successful frame job. I'd say playing dumb is beneath you at this point."

"Did you know that Thea broke up with Austen the night before she died?" I say, before I can help it. "Ask Austen, he'll confirm it. And I'll testify to it in court. That, plus the pregnancy? Plus the fact that he had access to the gun found at the scene? It sounds like motive and opportunity to me."

Romero looks me over again, more carefully this time than before. "How did you know the gun we found at the scene belonged to Austen's father?"

I shrug, swallowing hard. "I told you he had access to it days ago—back when you were accusing me of this crime the first time."

Romero takes a long, deep breath and sits back in her chair, but her frame is still rigid, the fight not quite drained out of her.

"One more thing," she says, reaching into her desk drawer and pulling out another evidence bag. "Do you recognize this?"

She slides the bag toward me and I reach out and touch the plastic.

A slim, silver band.

"Yes," I say. It's barely a whisper.

"Would you mind telling me where you recognize it from?"

"I—it was Thea's. Austen and I found it at the scene."

"You're sure it was Thea's?"

"Yes," I say. "Who else would it belong to?"

Romero smiles at that. "I'm glad you asked," she says. From underneath her notebook, she pulls out a photo. It's glossy and large—printed on real photo paper, like she went to the local office supply store and had it made.

It's a picture of us. You and me—taken last fall, during a rare girls' night that had us both tipsy and cheerful. I study it for a moment. We're standing hip to hip, laughing about something I don't remember anymore, my right arm slung over your shoulder, your hand reaching up to hook around my forearm, both of our hands clearly visible.

My stomach drops.

I remember this photo. I remember deleting it too, along with the rest of my social media.

"How did you get this?" I say, and I know I've done a poor job of keeping the worry out of my voice.

"Marley, you know—probably better than I do—that things live forever on the internet, even after they've been deleted."

I press my lips together and drag my eyes away from the photo and up to Romero. "I don't understand what you're getting at," I say, even though I do. Of course I do.

"You didn't spot the rings?" she says. "I'm surprised. It was the first thing I noticed when I saw this picture. You're both wearing them here—but in this picture, you're wearing the silver—the one Austen found at the scene—and Thea's wearing the gold."

I keep my eyes on Romero and off the picture. "So?" I ask. "We switched for a night. My dress looked better with silver accents."

"I don't think that's true, Marley. I went through your other photos too. Any I could find, that is, and you're wearing silver jewelry in all of them. Your own engagement ring was silver. You're telling me that someone who cares about fashion as much as you do—someone who curated a whole Instagram around their personal style—went against the grain and decided to switch their preferred jewelry color for this one piece?"

"You're saying I did all of this, and your only evidence is that I like silver jewelry?" I ask, channeling every bit of resolve I have into sounding confident. She stares at me, her eyes hard. Unyielding. For a second, I feel sure that she knows exactly what I did—sneaking into Austen's apartment with my spare key, hiding the rags and the lighter in the back of his closet. Calling in the tip.

"I'm asking you to tell me the truth," she says. And that's when I know—*really* know, deep in my gut—that she won't let this go. Not

ever. Wherever I go, Romero will always be behind my shoulder, waiting for me to misstep. And one day, maybe, she'll succeed. But the least
I can do is make it difficult for her.

"Am I under arrest, Detective?" I ask.

Romero flinches—just barely, but it's there. "No," she says after a
long, miserable moment. "You're not under arrest." There's a ferocious
undercurrent of anger behind her words, barely disguised, and I recognize myself in it. Recognize you, too. The anger we're so often forced to
hide from the world in order to appear reasonable. It doesn't matter if
we're right—Romero is right about me, after all. And I was right about
Austen, in the end.

Still, when a woman is angry, she's branded by it. So we channel
it. Behind screens or smiles, or both. We play the roles we're allowed to
play, and we find other ways to unleash that part of ourselves.

Romero, you, me, even Sky. We do what we need to survive, until
the moment we can't anymore.

I push myself up to standing and look at Romero one more time. I
can see the desperation there. The frustration.

You protect me, I protect you. That includes your reputation. Your
legacy.

And Austen? He betrayed us both. He doesn't deserve to get away
with that. He needed to pay, one way or another.

"Well," I say, hand gripped on the doorknob, ready to leave this
place and never come back. "If you're ever in New York."

EPILOGUE

Thea

I SAW MARLEY TODAY. In a shop on West 4th Street.

At first I assumed I was imagining it, like usual. I see Marley all the time since I left Georgia. Every time I catch sight of a woman with red hair and a pronounced hippie-chic aesthetic—which is a lot of people in New York—I stop for a second, heart racing. I'm constantly doing double takes or scanning crowded sidewalks, half paranoid, half hopeful that she'll be there, looking back at me.

When I see the woman in the shop, I expect the resemblance to dissolve after a closer look, just like it always does. But instead, all of her features snap right into place. She's flipping through a rack of button-down shirts, her bottom lip caught between her teeth as she concentrates. Her hair is shorter now, with long, feathered bangs that swoop along either side of her face. She's wearing dark-wash bell-bottoms and platform boots, a suede coat cinched tightly around her waist. I study her face, though I'm not sure what I expect to see there. She looks inscrutable, as always. Mask up, armor on.

Once the shock of recognition subsides, I have to fight the urge to cross the distance between us and pull her into a hug. To apologize. Ask her about what happened after the fire—everything I've been too afraid to search online. I can almost picture the shock rippling over her features, followed closely by the anger. The hurt. If she even recognized me at all, that is. I went out of my way to change up my look after I left. Partially because I didn't want to risk being identified, and partially because the symbolism of it seemed important.

New name, new life, new look. New me.

I hold myself back from approaching her. There's a reason I left, after all, and there's no clean way to come back. Not with Julie's body lying somewhere in a grave marked with my name.

"Find anything, babe?" Briar sidles up next to me and bumps my shoulder with their own.

"Huh?" I ask, knocked out of my trance.

The corner of their lip quirks into a smile and they fix their eyes on Marley too. "Thinking of stepping out on me?"

"Sorry," I say, shaking my head. "I wasn't—it's not—she looks like someone I used to know, is all. An old friend."

Briar twines their fingers through mine protectively. I don't really talk about my life before New York with them. They know the basics— that I'm from a small town in the South. That I'm not in touch with anyone from back home. I've let them assume the rest. It's better that way. Easier than concocting an elaborate fake backstory I could accidently contradict later. After all, everyone in New York is trying to be someone new. Why not me too?

"Do you want to see if it's her? Go say hi?" Briar asks, meeting my eyes. I drink in the softness there. The compassion. Briar is *good* all the way to the core. It's what drew me to them the first night we met at a bar in Park Slope. They were huddled up in the back corner with a group of friends, laughing loudly, bright orange hair flashing under the dim lamplight like a flame against a dark sky, radiating good energy, and I knew. I knew I wanted them to be part of my life.

It was Briar who took me in when I had nowhere else to turn. Briar who held me—no questions asked—when I miscarried. Who wiped away my tears of relief, mistaking them for grief. It was Briar who showed me how to navigate the subway and where the city's best-kept secrets live.

Marley only ever brought out the worst in me, but Briar brings out the best. They make me believe I can be someone like them.

Someone gentle. Someone kind. Someone who makes other people's lives better.

"No," I say, squeezing their hand and resting my cheek briefly against their arm, feeling the warmth and the solidness of what I've built here. The weight of who I'm trying to become. It feels good. "Actually, I think it would be better if she didn't see me at all."

RESOURCE GUIDE

Suicide and Crisis Lifeline
Helpline: 988
988lifeline.org

National Alliance on Mental Illness (NAMI)
Helpline: 1-800-950-NAMI (6264)
nami.org

Crisis Text Line
Text HOME to 741741
crisistextline.org

Substance Abuse and Mental Health Services Administration
Helpline: 1-800-662-HELP (4357)
samhsa.gov

ACKNOWLEDGMENTS

Writing is often a solitary pursuit, but storytelling is most definitely *not*. This book would not exist without the talent, creativity, hard work, dedication, and support of so many wonderful people who I feel incredibly grateful to know.

Thank you to my agent, Jess Regel, who has offered boundless support, shrewd editorial direction, and relentless savvy—I cannot overstate how grateful I am to you for everything you've done to champion this book. I feel lucky every day to have landed my dream agent. Thank you to my editor, Holly Ingraham, for being that life-altering "yes," for your deft editorial hand, and for being a tireless cheerleader for this book. Thank you, also, to the rest of the team at Crooked Lane, including but not limited to Thaisheemarie Fantauzzi Pérez, Heather Ven-Huizen, Stephanie Manova, Rebecca Nelson, Mikaela Bender, and Dulce Botello. Thank you to Aashna Avachat for providing feedback on an early draft, and to my beta reader Maddie Woodard, not only for your invaluable and astute feedback, but also for the excellent homemade memes (which were equally appreciated).

Thank you to the friends and colleagues who have supported and encouraged me through the trenches of drafting, revision, submission, and publication, and who have seen me through the many (many) highs and lows: Katie Schmid, Casey Dowd, Jess Fix, Steph Heesemann, Alysha Amerson, Kimberly Simpson, Tyler Key, Caroline Bauerband,

Ginnie Highsmith, Anna Gilbert, Grace Kim, and Ciera Horton McElroy, to name just a few. And to Amanda Wilbanks, who gave me my first real writing job, and the rest of the crew at Southern Baked Pie.

Thank you to my parents, Brad and Cathy Auffarth, and my sisters, Ali Auffarth and Ava Bergeron. You are my greatest blessings in a life filled with blessings. Thank you also to Grandma and Mom Mom and to the rest of the Auffarths and the Capps—everything I know about weaving a good story, I learned from you.

To the teachers and mentors in my life, without whose support and guidance I never would've dreamed of doing something like this—Gay Coleman, the first person to say, "have you ever thought about being a writer?" and Nicole Mazzarella, who fostered a passion for the novel writing form and provided vital encouragement and feedback. Thank you to Erin Niumata and Rachel Ekstrom Courage for going above and beyond to offer support during the years of drafting, and for stepping in with valuable advice along the way.

Thank you to Courtney and Ben Martin, for letting me use your cabin as my own personal writing retreat. I'm so grateful for your hospitality and generosity. To Detective Sunjay Verma for taking time to answer my questions about police interrogation and evidence gathering. Any mistakes are entirely my own. And to Andrea Huige, for guiding me gently and with so much grace through the challenges and milestones of the last several years.

Finally, thank you to you, the reader. You are the only reason any of this exists, and I can't thank you enough for seeing Marley and Thea through to the very end.